MILLE UMBRA

Michael P. Williams

Gotham Books
30 N Gould St.
Ste. 20820, Sheridan, WY 82801
https://gothambooksinc.com/

Phone: 1 (307) 464-7800

Published by Gotham Books (July 20, 2022)

ISBN: 978-1-956349-86-3 (sc)
ISBN: 978-1-956349-87-0 (e)

TABLE OF CONTENTS

Part 1: The downward spiral

CHAPTER ONE

The Storm

(I)

Lisa Spencer sits in the soft white sand on a beach vaguely familiar to her from some distant point in time. A memory perhaps, of a childhood filled with pain and suffering, tragedy and loss. A shout in the distance draws Lisa's attention to a woman standing at the edge of the water letting the waves cascade over her feet. The woman calls out to a small group of children playing waist deep in the surf but Lisa cannot make out her words. The children answer with the sound of splashing, followed by screams, and then laughter. Lisa stands up and looks around, spying a long wooden pier reaching out over the ocean. A memory creeps into her conscious mind, a memory of trips to the coast of North Carolina with her father and her uncle. The winds pick up. Lisa's long hair covers her eyes, stinging her cheeks as the frigid breeze drives each jet-black strand into her face. She brushes her hair aside and the splashing and laughter stops. Lisa scans left and right with her Carolina blue eyes, looking for a sign of the children and the woman who were there moments ago, but the beach is empty. The air around Lisa grows silent, and suddenly, there is no sound at all.

Lisa looks out over the ocean, mesmerized by the fantastic display of light dancing throughout the thick black clouds rolling in. The onslaught of wind and sand makes it hard to see. Lisa closes her eyes and places her hand to her ear, straining to hear something... *anything…*

Wait, Lisa thinks, there is something!

Thud… Thud… Thud…

What is that? Lisa tries to remember the layout of the beach but for some reason all she can remember is the long wooden pier.

Thud… Thud… Thud…

I know that sound! Lisa thinks, but before she can place it a *new* sound fills her ears. She hears a light flapping, like a flag blowing in the wind, slowly growing louder. Lisa suddenly realizes the first sound she heard was her bunk hitting the wall of the boat as it rocked, and with this thought the dam is broken and the memories come flooding back into Lisa's conscious mind. The boat… the waves… the storm!

Lisa can no longer stand against the force of the wind. She lies down on the beach and covers her head as sound returns with a crash of thunder and the sky fills with light. The echo of thunder rumbles into the distance, mixing with the sound of the howling wind, making it almost impossible for Lisa to think. Somehow the thought filters through the chaos around her and she identifies the second sound. It's the sound of a helicopter flying overhead. "Come on you idiot, wake up!" she cries out. The thunder and wind slowly subside and Lisa's world is filled with new sounds.

(II)

Lisa heard shouting, cursing, someone rushing around in panic. She sat up in her cot just as her uncle Bruce rushed by and raced up the stairs with a flare gun in his hand. Lisa stood and followed her uncle out of the cabin. The last time she had been on deck all hell was breaking loose. Lisa had stayed up top through the worst of it. She had watched as her sixteen-year-old cousin, Ashley, was swept overboard, still clutching her pet Schnauzer in her arms. It had all happened so fast, as if the sea had reached up and took poor Ashley, Bruce's only daughter, and carried her off into its murky depths. Bruce's best friend, Doug, who had joined them on the voyage, was almost swept away as he tried to save the child. In the mayhem, Lisa's eyes focused on Bruce, who had just stood there and watched the raging swells, knowing that he could do nothing to save his baby girl, certain that if he left the wheel to even try to help his only child, they would *all* be dead. Lisa Spencer, who had turned twenty eight four days ago, had stumbled down into the cabin, found her bunk, and cried for two hours, falling asleep to the sound of the metal framework of her cot thud-thud-thudding against the wooden wall.

The waves were much calmer that next morning. Small breaks in the clouds let the sun shine through lighting up the water all around the boat. Lisa looked up and watched as the helicopter flew through the remains of the flare her uncle had deployed, causing the remnants to scatter through the air around the spinning blades before raining down upon the ocean. "Why isn't it stopping?" Lisa shouted, her question answered as she looked off into the distance. The helicopter was heading for a small island.

(III)

"Do you think they're all right?" the woman in back asked as she shifted nervously in her seat. Harry didn't like to be around women when they were nervous. "I don't know," he answered. "That boat was a mess. I'll call it in as soon as I drop you off, then I'll head back out there to get a better look." Harry brought the helicopter in for a gentle landing in the small compound on the island. His passenger was Dr. Gillian Black, Assistant Director of Operations for the NeuroTech offshore testing facility. Harry watched Dr. Black collect the few belongings she'd brought with her and step out onto the hot tarmac.

The steam rose up from the helipad distorting the image of the compound. Greenhouses were bent and twisted, the trees and vegetation seeming to pulse with life. Dr. Black saw none of this as she backed away from the helicopter. Harry, on the other hand, noticed a few *more* things that weren't quite right. First there didn't appear to be anyone around. Normally, there were at least a *few* people in the gardens, but on this day the compound was strangely empty. Harry decided what went on with the island was none of his business, and it was time to go check on that boat, when he heard the helicopter door slam shut. It took poor Harry too long to realize that, as the door closed, Dr. Black was standing much too far away to have shut it. When Harry lifted off, he briefly caught a glimpse of the terror on Dr. Black's face. The rotating blades drowned out the sound of the doctor's screams, as they would Harry's.

A sudden sharp pain ripped through Harry's chest. He'd had a heart attack once before but it had felt nothing like this. He let go of the controls and reached for his chest, realizing at that very moment that this was no heart attack. Harry looked down and saw another hand now gripping the controls, only this hand was *not* human! Its skin was dark brown with large razor sharp claws protruding from each fingertip. Through his blinding pain, Harry managed to find the mirror near his head, but he saw nothing behind him. He looked back down at the arm coming *out* of his chest covered in *his* blood. Harry had seen a lot of strange things in his life, but in those last moments, he saw things that made him question what lay beyond the impending darkness that slowly consumed him. The very last thing Harry saw before he died was the helipad of the NeuroTech compound coming at him *way* too fast.

(IV)

The sound of the explosion echoed across the waves and into the boat. No one spoke as a dark cloud of smoke rose from the small island off in the distance. Lisa sat down on the deck and put her head in her hands. "Gather up anything we might be able to use and bring it up on deck," Bruce called out to Doug as he knelt down next to Lisa. Doug nodded and opened the door to the cabin.

"Lisa," Bruce said softly, "I need you here with me." Lisa looked into her uncle's eyes. He looked so sad and yet so determined at the same time. How could this man, who'd lost his wife to cancer four years ago and his only daughter to the waves just the night before, how could he have *this* much strength? *Why can't I be that strong?* "Lisa!" Bruce's voice cut into her thoughts sharply.

"Yeah, Unc," she answered. "I'm moving."

Lisa rose to her feet and descended the narrow staircase leading to the boat's cabin. She sat down on her bunk and pulled down two photographs taped to the wall. One was a picture of her parents. Her mother Claudia had died during childbirth leaving Lisa's father to raise her on his own. She missed her mother, as much as someone can miss a person they never met, but at least she *knew* her. Lisa's father Andrew had made it a point to tell his daughter one story about her mother every night. Lisa still called her father every evening to listen to the continuing adventures of Claudia Spencer even after she grew up and moved out on her own. Lisa pulled out the second photo and placed it in front of the first. It was a picture of her father and her, taken four days after her twenty-sixth birthday, two years ago today. That was the last time she had seen her father alive. Lisa closed her eyes as the memory of that night came rushing back. She'd been in bed asleep, one of those deep kinds where your brain is still kind of functioning normally, when you know you're asleep, but still have rational thoughts. Lisa had had visions like this as a child, visions of things to come before they materialized, but that was before the visions had taken over her life.

The night Lisa's father died, she'd watched as he was torn to shreds by some vile creature and left for dead in a pool of his own blood. Lisa had awoken from the nightmare vision to the sound of the telephone drilling into her ears. It had been her Uncle Bruce; he was crying. He'd told Lisa that her father was dead, murdered by a patient, and that he had asked Andrew to fly down to Raleigh, North Carolina because he'd had a patient he thought his brother might be interested in. The patient's name had been Marcus Quincy. He'd been hospitalized, assessed, determined to be a paranoid schizophrenic, and a murderer. Marcus and his wife Anna had also been her uncle's friends, at least until Bruce's wife, Lori, had died. Uncle Bruce didn't want much to do with *anyone* but immediate family after that, which was why he'd felt so responsible for the death of Lisa's father.

Reality gradually seeped back into Lisa's thoughts as she grabbed the rest of her belongings and made her way up the stairs. Both rafts were already in the water with the back of one tied to the front of the other. Bruce and Doug climbed into the front raft while the back one was filled with various items from the boat including a tool box and first aid kit. "So, how far do you think it is?" Doug asked and pointed towards the island. Bruce stared off into the distance, trying to judge how far away it was.

"I'd say no more than two miles." "Well then," Doug said. "ya'll hop on in; it's time to abandon ship." Lisa looked at Bruce and smiled. "What are you doing in there Unc? I thought the captain was supposed to go *down* with the ship." Bruce stared out over the ocean and began to weep. Lisa knew what her uncle was thinking, who he was thinking of. Lisa put her hand on her uncle's shoulder and brought him into her arms. "I'm *so* sorry Uncle Bruce."

"It's ok." He pushed her back gently and faked a smile. "It's time to go." Bruce clenched the oar tightly and quickly caught Doug's rhythm. Lisa glanced over her shoulder and watched as the abandoned boat slowly drifted away into the distance.

(V)

What the hell was *that thing?* Dr. Black had seen something moving through the compound, though it was no more than a swift shadow between the trees. It had been hard to make out its shape through the rising mist of the helipad, and it was harder still to believe she could see right *through* it!

The only thing Gillian knew for sure was that *something* had raced by her and climbed aboard the helicopter. Whether it had been that *thing,* or the pilot that had brought the 'copter crashing back down, she'd never know. Gillian walked around the compound looking for signs of life but found none. She entered the canopy of trees, a living hallway leading to the greenhouses, where she discovered all of the sprinklers running and the diagnostic equipment was functioning properly. It was hard for Gillian to think clearly after what she had seen, but slowly it came to her, *there must be a storm coming.* Gillian locked the greenhouse door and followed the path back to a one-story brick structure at the center of the compound.

(VI)

Lisa was the first to see it and she thought her eyes were playing tricks on her. She could barely see the boat now through the early morning haze rising up from the water, but there was something further back, far beyond the boat on the horizon. Lisa saw lights flashing in the distance as the sky became darker and the object grew in size. Massive dark clouds rose from the ocean, and lightning struck ferociously throughout the storm, but this was no ordinary storm. The large dark clouds teeming with electricity were the same ones from Lisa's dream. "Um, guys. I think we need to hurry it up a little!" "What are you talking about?" Bruce turned and looked over Lisa's shoulder. "Oh-My-God!" The two men rowed frantically toward the island that was now only a few hundred yards away.

However, the storm moved swiftly, with the abandoned boat now nearly engulfed by the raging sea.

Man, Lisa thought, that thing is moving fast!

"Should we lose the second raft?" Doug called out as he paddled.

5

"No," Bruce shouted back. "We're almost there. We'll make it."

"Not much time to spare," Lisa pointed out.

"We'll make it," Bruce yelled. There was no more talking as they frantically rowed. The ocean around them churned violently and the salty wind made it hard to see. They rowed as strongly as they could through the deluge of water and wind until, reluctantly, the waves spat them out onto the shore of the small island.

CHAPTER TWO

The Island

(I)

Gillian swiped her key card and opened the door. The place was empty. She made her way down the hall to a large steel fire door. The stenciled sign read *Authorized Personnel Only*. She gained entry with her card and the door opened with a hiss. "Hello?" Gillian called out. The lights flickered and died as she descended the unlit stairwell. *"Hello,"* she called again. "Dr. Carlton? Anyone? It's Gillian. Hello?" Every little sound was intensified and it really started to freak her out.

Pit. Pit. Pit. Gillian stopped cold. She fumbled through her purse and pulled out a small flashlight, switched it on, and cautiously made her way down the hall.

Pit. Pit. Pit. Was the sound getting louder?

Gillian stopped and pointed the beam of light into a darkened room to her left and, once satisfied it was empty, searched the room to her right. "Where *is* everyone?" she mumbled. Gillian took a cautious step and lost her footing when her heel slipped, nearly sending her crashing to the floor. As Gillian regained her balance, three consecutive droplets fell upon her cheek. She wiped her face and held her hand up to the light. It was blood! Her first reaction was to look up at the ceiling, so Gillian shined the light above her head and found nothing. She felt moisture again, this time on her chin. Gillian aimed the beam of light in the direction the drops had come from and froze. The blood was dripping *out* of the wall! Gillian watched as three new beads formed on the wall. The blood passed vertically in front of the doctor's face, splashing into a small crimson puddle on the opposite wall, where it then trickled down and pooled on the floor beneath her feet. Gillian was desperately trying to comprehend how this was possible when her heart jumped at a sudden sound. Footsteps!

Gillian switched off her flashlight and darted into the nearest open doorway. Racks of equipment that would normally be running tests stood silent while the refrigerators quietly hummed. She hid behind one of the lab tables, which gave her a good view of the open doorway and excellent cover. Gillian waited. For a brief moment she contemplated calling out. *Maybe its one of the staff,* Gillian thought.

This thought was fleeting as the memory of what she had seen on the helipad came rushing back into her mind, not to mention the blood in the hallway that seemed to defy gravity as well as several *other* laws of physics. *No,* she thought, *I'm staying right here and keeping my mouth shut.* Her mind made up, the footsteps stopped. They were close, maybe even right outside the door.

(II)

It took all three castaways to haul the life raft containing the remnants from the boat on shore. The first raft, the raft that had carried them to the safety of the island, was claimed by the howling wind as soon as Bruce cut the rope with his knife. It didn't take long to realize communication with one another was useless. Rainwater soaked their clothes as they frantically tried to avoid the debris being thrown all around them. Even without the luxury of conversation they all shared one common goal: get into one of the buildings on the island. Thankfully, the closest structure seemed to be the most secure. It was a small brick building that offered much more in the way of safety than the glass-walled greenhouses. As they made their way around the wreckage of the helicopter and approached the building, it became apparent that gaining access would not be easy. The structure's single door was locked with a very expensive looking electronic mechanism.

Lisa pressed herself against the brick wall and slumped down, still clutching the raft that contained all that they had left in the world. She watched as Doug wandered off in the direction of the greenhouses, most likely to find a place to hide. Bruce, on the other hand, was examining the lock on the brick building. Lisa relinquished the raft as her uncle pulled on it. He fumbled through the tools in his toolbox, settling on what he thought he might need to open the door. A couple of screwdrivers, some wire cutters, strippers, and a large hammer. He used the latter first, striking the card reader several times until it shattered and joined the rest of the debris strewn throughout the compound. Next, he pulled out several wires, cut them, and striped off the ends. Bruce jumped and pulled his hand away as a jolt of electricity coursed through his fingers. He shook the pain from his hand and returned to the lock. Bruce worked with his eyes half closed to avoid the sparks as he quickly moved from one wire to the next.

Doug came stumbling back down the path, shrugging his shoulders as if to signify that no shelter could be found elsewhere. Bruce let out a howl of success. Lisa pushed open the door and the three rushed inside, hauling the raft in behind them before falling to the floor from sheer exhaustion.

(III)

One more minute, Gillian thought, and she would have enough courage to investigate the hallway once more. Until then, she would stay right there, curled up beneath a desk like a child hiding from the boogeyman. *You're a grown woman,* Gillian scolded herself, *and a doctor no less! Now get out there and do what you do best. Find out what the hell is going on!* Sure, Gillian was afraid, and if asked would freely admit it, but her curiosity *was* getting the best of her. The doctor pressed her face to the floor and peeked out from underneath the desk at the open doorway. *See,* Gillian's mind taunted her, *no one there. Now get off your ass and get out of here!* A loud **click** echoed throughout the hallway and Gillian almost came out of her skin. She screamed as her body jolted from the sudden noise and her head thumped hard against the bottom of the desk drawer. A soft hum filled the hallway and the lights flickered on. "Nothing to be afraid of," she reassured herself out loud, feeling just a little bit foolish for being startled so easily. Gillian crawled from beneath the table on her hands and knees until she was beside the open doorway. The light from the hallway was bright compared to the room, still dark but for the flashing lights on the test equipment that now beeped and hummed as the PC's rebooted. The sound of the hard drives spinning filled her ears as the monitors lit up to run diagnostic tests.

Gillian carefully extended her head out into the hall, just enough to peek around the corner. She looked right, toward the stairwell that she had used to gain access to this part of the lab, then left, down the hall in the direction she was heading. A pool of blood on the floor caught her attention. The only footprints on the floor were her own. *Shit,* Gillian thought, *lead them right to you, why don't you?* Satisfied that she was alone, Gillian stood. As she reached her full height of five feet, six and a half inches, she realized her error. Gillian stood face to face, or what is left of it, with her stalker.

The bottom half of the man's face had been torn off, exposing his teeth and jawbones. His wet tongue danced around the outside of his open mouth, licking where he once had lips. Most of the man's nose was gone with what remained being a bloody lump of cartilage that moved in and out as he breathed. The only part of the man's face having skin was from the eyes up. The eyes…they were eyes Gillian had seen many times before, though never like this. Bloodshot and hemorrhaged, Dr. Alan Carlton's eyes bulged from his head, pressed tightly against the lenses of the glasses that were somehow fused to his skull. What remained of the doctor's skin seemed to be *growing* over the frames! The horror of the sight made Gillian miss one *very* important observation, though not for long. Dr. Carlton's face was upside down! Gillian suddenly realized why there was no second set of footprints on the floor…

Dr. Carlton had been walking on the ceiling!

(IV)

Doug was the first to get to his feet. He wandered around the building taking in the layout. The entrance opened into a room with a hallway leading to another electronically locked door on the back wall of the building. To the left of the entrance was a small room filled with radio equipment. Bruce observed these things, as well. Lisa decided to let the men check out the electronics while she did some snooping of her own. She found four small rooms with two on either side of the hallway. The two on the left appeared to be labs containing large racks of test equipment and various samples of fruits and vegetables in small glass jars that were tagged and dated. On the right was a large storage room, half of which was filled with cleaning supplies, garden tools, and chemicals, while the other half was brimming with filing cabinets filled with sheets of test printouts and CD ROMs.

Lisa saw two names stenciled on the final door: Dr. Alan Carlton and Dr. Gillian Black. Lisa turned the handle and entered the office. The walls were covered with a few pieces of art and several framed degrees. Dr. Alan Carlton: Yale University, MIT, Nobel Prize nominee. Dr. Gillian Black: Duke University and another Nobel Prize nomination. On the desk were several files and framed pictures depicting family and friends, some were taken outside in gardens, while others were taken elsewhere.

One picture depicted a group of friends in some sort of recreation room, another, in sleeping quarters. Lisa suddenly remembered the door at the end of the hall, the door that required another card. *There must be a basement or sub floor*, Lisa thought to herself. *This is a small island in the middle of nowhere, so they must sleep somewhere.* The wind outside began tearing at the roof of the building. Lisa looked up at the ceiling nervously, expecting it to come crashing down at any moment. To have survived the night on the boat was one thing, but to be trapped on an abandon island in a hurricane? Well, *that* was something entirely different, and that was *not* how Lisa Spencer planned on spending the final moments of her life. Lisa's mind raced with a thousand thoughts at the same time, a thousand memories, some good and some bad. For whatever reason, Lisa's mind chose to obsess over her love life, or lack thereof. She had spent most of her life in a haze, watching time dwindle away from what seemed to be the outside, as if she were watching her life from someone else's perspective. For the most part, Lisa's lack of a love life was self-induced. She had seen so much death in her life, so much heartache. Most of the time she kept people out of her life for fear they would fall victim to her curse, for that's what it felt like sometimes, as if she were doomed to live her life alone. Other times, when Lisa was able to convince herself that the "curse" was just a silly figment of her imagination, she kept people out for other reasons. Not wanting the hassle of a "significant other" or the eventual pain of yet another heartache. Lisa knew that this was not the time or place to be slipping into another depression, and thankfully, there was a distraction.

The computer sitting on the desk in front of Lisa caught her attention. A file was open but all she had time to read was the title before a gust of wind so strong it threatened to pull the roof off in one fell swoop knocked out the power. The title read <u>Project Lucidity</u>.

"Lisa?" Bruce called from the front room. "First door on the right," she answered. A sudden gust of wind was followed by a loud crash. The whole building shook as pieces of the ceiling came crashing to the floor. Water poured in, cascading through the gaping hole in the roof. The wind outside had reached well over two hundred miles an hour and the building was falling to pieces around them. The walls came apart, flung from one side of the room to the other with such force one would be assured a timely death if one were to be in its path. As the roof came down, large chunks continued to fall as Lisa, Bruce, and Doug stood by helplessly. Lisa's mind flashed a picture. A door. Lisa grabbed her uncle's arm and pulled him down the hall dragging the raft behind them. Bruce pushed his niece aside and began to work on the card reader on the far door. "I hope they were smart enough to hook this door up to the back up system," he said. "And what if they didn't?" Lisa asked. Bruce looked up from his work and smiled, "Then we're screwed!"

(V)

Gillian sat on the floor in the far corner of the room with her arms around her legs and her chin on her knees. She watched Dr. Carlton, or whatever that *thing* was, stand there in the hallway, as it watched back. Gillian's first reaction was to scream and fall to the floor and then she quickly crawled into a corner. She thought what a stupid move it was to limit her options like that, but he… *it*… just stood there… on the ceiling! "What the hell happened here?" As soon as the words left Gillian's lips she wondered if it was such a good idea to speak. Maybe it was because, for some reason, the *"Carlton Thing"* turned and walked away. Gillian listened to its footsteps as they proceeded down the hall and slowly faded away. A new sound caught Gillian's attention coming from upstairs. She weighed her options in her head. *Should I go down and try to find somebody or go up and face what's up there?* Up was closer to out, so Gillian rose to her feet and ran as fast as she could to the stairs. She pulled herself forward gripping the rail with all her strength. "There's a lot of noise coming from up there," Gillian spoke out loud. *Just open it,* she thought to herself, *open it and run. You'll be outside in no time.* Gillian reached for the handle. The door swung open and something hit her hard, sending Gillian tumbling back down the stairs, causing her to lose consciousness.

(VI)

Doug stood up too quickly, causing his vision to blur and his head to spin. His arm hurt like hell from cradling the woman's head on the way down the stairs but it was well worth it. The broad had a spectacular set of rib melons that Doug all too willingly placed his face between while tumbling to the bottom of the stairs. He looked down at the woman he still cradled in his arms. "Is she all right?" he asked, placing her on the floor. Lisa crawled to the woman's side. "She's breathing at least." A sound from above brought their eyes to the stairwell; what was left of the building was coming down. "Lets get her out of here!" Doug exclaimed as he struggled to pick up the woman he'd just saved. Bruce rushed to his side and placed one of the woman's arms over his shoulder. They barely had enough time to move out of the way as the building above came crashing down right where they'd been standing. A deafening roar echoed throughout the large hallway, and a cloud of dust expanded outward like an earthen fireball, consuming

11

the light and air around them as they ran. Blind and gasping, they fell to the floor and covered their heads, waiting for the walls to stop shaking and the dust to settle.

Bruce tended to the woman's wounds while Doug and Lisa investigated the nearby rooms. There were six in all, five filled with lab equipment and large refrigerators, but the sixth and final room was locked. At the end of the hallway was another door marked "stairs" that had a simple deadbolt and it, too, was locked. Lisa crossed the threshold of a room at the far end of the hall; another lab from the looks of things. One wall was lined with several large industrial refrigerators, all of them seeming to be filled with the same fruits and vegetables that occupied each unit, just like upstairs. "What do you think they do here?" Lisa asked Doug as he entered. Doug looked around the room at the row of coolers and racks of computers, both gently humming in the quiet darkness of the lab. "I don't know," Doug answered as the woman in the hall awoke with a scream, "but I bet *she* does."

Bruce held the woman's wrists as she thrashed and kicked at him, her screams becoming demands. "What have you done? No, No, No. I need to get *out* of here!" Bruce relinquished his grip and backed away, allowing the woman to pull herself to her feet. "Listen, lady," he said, "unless there's another way out, you ain't going nowhere." Lisa and Doug had now joined the audience and the woman's gaze fixed on the three of them.

"Who the hell *are* you?" She tossed her head frantically, looking in all directions, like a frightened horse in a barn fire. "We need to get out of here!" Her voice trembled as she spoke and tears filled her eyes. She fell to her knees sobbing, repeating her last words. "We need to get out of here…" The last syllable trailed off into her sobs. Bruce knelt down next to the woman and put his hand on her shoulder, trying to console her. "Don't *touch* me!" she screamed and backed up against the wall. Her eyes darted from Bruce to Lisa to Doug. "Who are you? Why are you here?"

Bruce began to tell their story, starting with the previous day's events. He paused once, sobbing as he recounted the death of his daughter; only after several agonizing minutes was he able to pull himself together enough to finish. Gillian had witnessed the next part of the story, the helicopter, the island, the explosion, and the storm. "That was no ordinary storm," Bruce explained, "It was like…like nothing I'd ever seen!"

"This morning…" Lisa cut in. "I had a dream. I was on a beach. There were some kids, and…. and no sound. Then that… that storm, it came so fast, and before I knew it, it was all around me." Lisa wasn't the only one to notice the doctor's odd reaction as she described the dream. How the woman's eyes darted away as if to hide some hint of knowledge that she might possibly understand the events of the day. The woman might even have realized this, as she was the next to speak, saying, "I had a pretty strange arrival here myself." Gillian offered up her own story. "After passing over your boat, Harry and I, he was the pilot, set down outside." She paused as if trying to figure out how to word the next series of events. "I saw it as soon as I got out."

"*It?*" Bruce asked. "What kind of *it?*"

"I don't know; it's hard to describe. I saw something move out of the trees. I backed away and watched it climb on board the helicopter."

"Well, what was it?" Bruce asked again.

"*I don't know!*" Gillian screamed. "I don't know *what* it was! I'm a doctor, for Christ's sake, and *I don't know*, okay? Whatever it was, it was weird." Her voice was much calmer now. "I could see right *through* it, kind of like there was something there that the air just moved around. It had a shape, more animal than human, but it moved like a man."

"C'mon," Doug cut in, "I don't believe any of this crap. Do you guys buy any of this?" He looked around the room but there were no replies. Doug sat back down on a chair he had retrieved from one of the labs and threw his hands in the air. "Fine, go on."

Gillian told the rest of her story. How she'd watched as the helicopter took off, only to see it come crashing back down seconds later. How she'd run for her life as it did so. "I came into the building to find someone. There was no one upstairs, so I came down here." Gillian's head and legs turned down the hall, in the direction of the stairwell, she stopped and pointed to the floor. "Right there, there was blood, *right there*! Where did it go?" By then the three castaways had reached where the good doctor was standing. "It came out of the wall." Gillian moved to the opposite side of the hallway. "It landed over here, then pooled on the floor."

"Jesus," Doug said, his voice full of doubt and rage.

"Then I heard footsteps; it was Dr. Carlton." Gillian cringed, as if remembering a childhood trauma. Tears welled up in her eyes. "He was walking on the ceiling!" She was crying now. On her knees with her head in her hands, she was sobbing her heart out. Doug was about to say something sarcastic no doubt, but Bruce cut him off. "So, who are you, and what *is* this place?"

"Who am *I*?" Gillian screamed. "Who are *you*?"

"Listen," Bruce exploded. "I *told* you how we got here. *My* name's Bruce, this is my niece Lisa, and this... this is Doug, who's really starting to piss me off!" Bruce's voice rose considerably and then softened as he continued. "So please, where are we?"

"Fine!" the woman huffed. "You want to know where you are? Aside from being in the middle of the Goddamned ocean…" she paused and took a deep breath. "This island was built by a corporation by the name of NeuroTech. We're funded by several environmental agencies, not to mention the Department Of Agriculture, and other government agencies I can't disclose. You see, we've altered the DNA of certain fruits and vegetables to withstand climates they would otherwise perish in; out behind the greenhouses, you wouldn't have seen it, but there's a simulated desert. We've actually got apple trees growing in it; can you believe it?" Before she could start again, Doug cut in.

"So why would NeuroTech have anything to do with this? I thought they were just into software development, video games, and crap like that." "Ooh, someone's heard of us?" Gillian's snide side began to resurface. "Hey, I love my video games," Doug retorted.

"What's Project Lucidity?" Lisa cut in. "Doesn't sound like it has much to do with fruits and veggies." For a moment the other woman faltered, leading Lisa to believe she had been right. This woman knew something and she was scared. After a brief pause, the woman began screaming again, this time her anger aimed solely at Lisa. "So what, were you snooping around upstairs? How the hell did you get in anyway?"

"Listen," Bruce said forcefully. "*I* was the one who got us inside and we'd be dead if I hadn't. You saw what happened to the building upstairs, right?" Bruce pointed down the hall at the pile of rubble protruding from the stairwell. His voice was raised and Lisa could tell he was getting agitated. "So whether you like it or not, miss… do you even *have* a name?" "Gillian," she peeped. "So whether you like it or not, Gillian," Bruce speaking more softly, "we're all stuck here unless you know another way out."

Gillian sat down on the floor and retrieved a pack of cigarettes from her coat pocket. She plucked one out, along with a lighter, lit it, and inhaled deeply. "It's always so much better when you're not supposed to be doing it," she looked up at the "no smoking" sign above her head and smiled. "So here it is," Gillian said, "The whole truth and nothing but the truth. A big chunk of our funding comes from the military…" "I *knew* it!" Doug shouted. "Why must the government cover up *everything* it does?" Gillian shook her head and continued, "The Navy, to be precise. This island's far enough offshore that we can do pretty much anything we want out here." Gillian paused to take a deep breath. "About three years ago we finished mapping the human mind. We have software that can interpret every firing neuron, every chemical change, every process in the brain. Of course, everyone's brain is different, but once we have you scanned, we can hook you up to the program."

"So what, this thing can read your mind?" Bruce asked.

"It's much more than that," Gillian answered. "It's a two way street. The program can *extract* information, but it can also *implant* information."

"So what, like mind control?" Doug queried.

Gillian grunted, obviously frustrated. "You're not seeing the big picture. We can dictate what you see when you close your eyes, when you dream, how your dream progresses... Its virtual reality at it's finest."

"Sweet!" Doug grinned widely.

"Of course, the gaming aspects are obvious. As well as training simulations, accident reconstructions, you name it!"

A sly smile crossed Doug's face and he was about to say something when Lisa punched him in the arm.

"Why are you such a pig?" she asked.

"Why don't we ask the Doc here; is there a gene that makes a guy a pig? You know, I try to be good, I really try." Doug leaned back in his chair and chuckled. He received no response.

"So, about a way out of here?" Bruce took it upon himself to redirect the conversation.

Gillian knocked three times on the steel floor. "There are two floors below this one, one in which Project Lucidity takes place. Both of the levels are completely submerged, but there *is* an emergency hatch on the bottom floor." Gillian stood and smiled with a satisfied look on her face, but it only lasted a moment. "So what are we waiting for?" Bruce asked.

"Well…" Gillian stumbled over the word. "What about Carlton? I wasn't just making that up. I'm not so sure I want to go down there."

"Listen, lady… sorry… *Gillian*, I don't think we have much of a choice. How many people work here? I doubt it's just you and Dr. Carlton." *My God*, Gillian thought. As the day's events had unfolded, she had forgotten about the rest of the team. There were two medical doctors, two nurses, seven patients and four programmers on site. Not to mention the gardeners, the chemists, the cooks, and the maintenance people. "Fine," she said, "This way."

Gillian got up from the floor and ground the remains of her cigarette beneath her heel. She sighed once, looking at the faces before her, then walked to the door at the end of the hall marked stairs. Reaching into her pocket, Gillian pushed her pack of smokes aside and found her keys. She held them up in front of her face to get a better look, decided on one, and slid it into the handle. The lock gave way and the door opened. One by one they descended the stairs.

CHAPTER THREE

The Descent

(I)

Lisa could not push aside the fear that something was wrong. The stairs mysteriously narrowed and she had to press her body up against the wall as she descended. Lisa's vision receded slowly at first, as if with each downward step the light dimmed just a little bit more. By the time she was half way down the stairs it was pitch black. Lisa fumbled as she took her next step. "Bruce?" she called out. He had been right in front of her until the stairs darkened. And the woman, Dr. Black, right behind Lisa, mumbling something to the effect of "this is not right, what's going on here?"

Click. A light flickered on at the far end of a long dark hallway and Lisa saw a door. *Click. Click. Click.* One by one the large fluorescent tubes above buzzed to life. *Click. Click.* **Crash!** The bulb directly above Lisa's head shattered and shards of glass along with a fine, white powder exploded in all directions. Lisa fell to her knees and covered her head with her arms. When the last of the shards of glass had crashed to the floor, Lisa stood up and brushed herself off. Her eyes traced the long tubes of light towards the door at the end of the hall and then back along the floor to where she stood. She was alone. "That's weird," she mumbled. Although Lisa was no more than five feet away from the nearest light fixture, she stood in total darkness. She held her hands up to her face but saw nothing, as if her physical body did not exist in this bizarre place. Lisa took five steps and stopped. Three steps and she should have been out of the shadows but she was still no closer to the light. She inhaled long and slow, her muscles tightening and she sprang forward, sprinting down the hall toward the door. Lisa stopped cold. "What the *hell*?" She was still no closer to the door. Lisa exhaled long and slow as she leaned back against the wall. "No *way!*" Did the door just get a little bit closer? Lisa took a step back, and then two, and three. It *was* getting closer. She continued walking backwards with her eyes fixed on the door. *Click. Click. Click.* With each step back she'd taken, a light went out until, finally, Lisa stood below the final fixture and directly in front of the door.

Lisa reached for the knob and saw something odd out of the corner of her eye, something shining on the wall. Just a tiny spec, but when she touched the spot, the paint crumbled away. An area no larger than the palm of her hand was exposed. Was it a picture? No, things were moving. Beneath the dull gray paint on the walls of the hallway was another world, a desert to be precise, and in the middle of that desert stood a lone apple tree. Now, this was *not* the simulated desert that Dr. Black had spoken of on the island above, because *this* desert stretched for miles in all directions. Lisa was convinced that what was in front of her eyes was real. She could smell the heat of the desert and, faintly, the apples. There was another odor in the air as well that was carried with the breeze she felt blowing on her face through the small opening between worlds. The aroma wasn't strong, but it was foul, like garbage and feces stewing in curdled milk. There was an underlying chemical smell too, like bleach, only stronger. They were the kind of smells you'd find at a one-hour photo lab, only these were all mixed up and baking in the hot sun. Lisa took a step back to orient herself with her surroundings. The simultaneous realities collided in front of her and Lisa's vision momentarily went black. Lisa shook her head from side to side until the hallway came back into focus. She knelt down and began to wipe away the peeling, crumbling paint from the wall, making large circles with the palms of her hands until the hall began to fill with sunlight from the world behind the paint. Lisa was temporarily blinded and, when her vision returned, she saw that she was kneeling in the middle of the desert, the hallway now gone.

Lisa stood to examine her surroundings but saw nothing but sand and the lone tree. She saw *something* fall to the ground beneath the branches, something that piled up rather quickly in a dark ring around the trunk. Lisa moved forward to investigate. As she did so, the foul stench from the tree grew increasingly stronger. "My God!" Lisa uttered as she moved closer. Every apple on the tree was riddled with holes, and from these holes, thousands of long, thin black worms poured out. Lisa watched with astonishment and disgust, failing to notice that the thick pool of black worms at the base of the tree had come to life. A form swiftly rose into the air like a twisting, writhing snake, and lunged at Lisa. It captured her legs before she could move. The worms, now all one entity, slithered up Lisa's body and wrapped around her waist, drawing her into their mass. Lisa's screams went unheard as she was pulled into its murky depths.

(II)

"How did I let them talk me into this? I don't even know who the hell they *are*." Gillian had a lot of questions, most of which were bred from shock, and were unimportant. When Gillian reached the bottom of the stairs she was alone and had no idea what had happened to her new companions. At first she thought that maybe the lower levels had decompressed, but there was no water leaking in anywhere, at least that she could see, but sight was hard to come by in the tight stairwell. At last there was the hallway with the lights… the load program. Gillian opened the door at the end of the hall and stepped into the darkness, calling out for the three she'd met upstairs. It was useless; she was alone, but where? A light flickered to life above Gillian's head, a single bare bulb dangling on a cord hanging from the ceiling.

Gillian stood in a small room with three concrete walls covered in dirt and what looked a little too much like blood, the door she had used to enter, gone. Where a fourth wall should be, Gillian saw nothing but emptiness, as if the room just dropped off, abruptly ending in nothingness. With nowhere else to go,

Gillian decided to sit on the only object in the room, a large wooden bench that rested against the back wall. The doctor compiled a list of questions that needed to be answered when the room began to shake and a steady thumping grew increasingly closer and louder. Gillian knew what the sound was, but how could it be? *A subway?* Brakes squealed and hydraulics hissed as the train began to slow. The windows were dark and Gillian saw nothing inside as the train came to a stop and the door opened in front of her. She paused for a moment contemplating her next move. Gillian reached into her purse to retrieve her flashlight and then entered the open door of the train.

The car was empty, and the seats were torn and wet with more blood. She saw various leaflets and papers scattered across the floor, some stuck together in damp, red bundles. The door slid shut and the train lurched forward. Gillian searched the car thoroughly and, finding both doors locked, took a seat untouched by crud, blood and *yuck, was that shit*? As soon as Gillian sat down her flashlight went dead.

She smacked it several times in the palm of her hand. "Damn it!" Gillian sat in the darkness, paralyzed by fear when she heard the familiar sound of a hydraulic door opening, one of the doors that had been locked just moments ago. A shiver ran down Gillian's spine when she heard footsteps coming down the walkway that stopped right beside her. Without warning, the flashlight came back on and, standing in the isle next to Gillian, illuminated in the beam of light, was the *Carlton Thing*!

"Mind if I sit?" It asked in a gravelly voice.

Gillian screamed in terror at the same time that the train brakes squealed. The door hissed open and she sprinted through the opening as fast as her frightened limbs would carry her. Gillian felt strong arms wrap around her shoulders, pulling her down, with her assailant falling on top of her as she struggled to break free. Her vision was blurry; she saw a light swinging from side to side but little else. Any other movement *must* be her attacker, she reasoned. Gillian clenched her small metal flashlight in her fist and swung, connecting solidly with whatever had landed on top of her. "Damn lady, watch it with that thing!"

Gillian's vision returned as quickly as it had left. The train rumbled away into the distance and

Gillian saw that the man standing before her was *not* Carlton. "What's your problem, lady?" Bruce Spencer gingerly placed his hand to his head and then held it up to the light. "No blood anyway, you crazy broad."

"*Stop* calling me lady! My name's Gillian but *you* can call me Dr. Black."

"Am I supposed to be impressed by a few letters in front of your name?" Bruce asked coldly. "I've got a few of my own, you know, so cut the bullshit and tell me what you were screaming about."

"I saw him again, on the train. Dr. Carlton. What the hell is going on around here?"

"I know what you mean," Bruce said. "I've been riding that thing for hours and I just keep comin' back here. How did *you* get on the train?" he asked.

"I was in a room like this one." Gillian looked around the room. "You know, it could have even *been* this room."

"Look down." Bruce pointed out over the black edge where moments ago he had pulled her from the train. "Do you see any tracks?" Gillian did as Bruce had asked. She saw nothing but blackness. Bruce leaned over the edge and spit. "That is sooo attractive," Gillian moaned. "Shhh..." Bruce held up his hand to silence her. *Splat.* "See, it's not that deep. I'm going down." Bruce climbed over the ledge and lowered his body down. Gillian watched him hang for a moment, until his fingers slipped away, and he was gone. "Bruce?" she yelled. "Bruce, are you all right." There was no reply.

(III)

Lisa's body jolted and she gasped for air as she sat up and looked around. She was in a field and the tall grass was flattened from where her body had lain. To her right she saw a dark forest and to her left only blackness. Lisa looked down at the ground that vanished just inches from her fingertips. She expected to see a great wall of exposed rock and earth leading into the depths of a cavern as she looked down, but there was nothing; the grass simply ended in blackness. Lisa turned and focused on the forest, a stark contrast to the void behind her. She stood and walked through the field until she stumbled upon a small path leading into the woods. Thick underbrush clutched each side of the narrow trail and everything around her seemed to pulse with a light that grew dim and brightened repeatedly. The only sound she could hear was a soft humming that seemed to keep time with the pulsing image of the forest. Lisa heard a scream. It was faint, coming from deep within the forest, but another soon followed, closer to her that time. The forest suddenly filled with the sound of horrific screams. Some sounds could have been made by adults, but most sounded like children, and it was starting to get to her. Lisa had to stop and close her eyes. She covered her ears with her hands, pressing hard to block out the noise of the terrible wailing children. After taking a moment to compose herself, what Lisa saw made her take off into a dead run deeper into the forest.

The screams had stopped and Lisa began to hear the distinct sound of footfalls crashing through the underbrush behind her. Lisa ran harder, with the door getting closer, the door that somehow stood in the middle of the path, the door that had a *room* on the other side. Lisa could see pipes and conduit running down the walls into control panels, metal shelving filled with boxes, and the corner of a desk.

Her pursuers were gaining on her. Lisa thought about turning around to face them but knew that there were far too many. She felt their hot breath on the back of her neck and could almost feel their hands on her. Lisa lunged for the open doorway and pushed the large oak door closed. She desperately fumbled with the deadbolt until the door was securely locked and fell to the floor. Her body ached and she wanted nothing more than to close her eyes and sleep.

(IV)

Bruce called out to Gillian, but got no answer, so he began to examine the room around him. The walls and ceiling were carved from dark stone, but, in the center of one wall, a perfect circle had been cut. Bruce grabbed the ledge of the circle and pulled himself up. The hole appeared to be a tunnel of sorts, barely tall enough for Bruce to crawl on his hands and knees. His eyes adjusted to the darkness quickly and, before long, he saw a light flickering off the walls. A sweet aroma drifted from a room in the distance; something was cooking on a fire. Bruce heard a noise and stopped. Was that singing?

"She told me that she loved me, what's a man to do?

She told me that she loved me, then she cut me in two."

The singer stopped and began to laugh hysterically. Bruce climbed out of the hole and dropped down into yet another large stone room. A man in a gray jumpsuit sat on the floor by a fire with his back against the wall. His head was shaved bald. His wrists and ankles were bound with cuffs attached to thick chains that were anchored to the wall behind him. Bruce glanced at the meat cooking on the fire and saw a leg. Not a human leg, it looked more like a goat, but it *did* have a human-like foot. It was impossible to tell what color the skin on the leg had been, as the limb had been placed in the fire some time ago. The man in the jumpsuit looked up at Bruce and continued singing.

"She promised me everything, she said she'd give it all.

Now she only teases me, and chains me to a wall."

The man burst into laughter again. "Did you like that one, mister?" The man looked up at Bruce, flaring his nostrils as he inhaled deeply. "Fresh meat! You wouldn't happen to have a key, would ya'?" The man held out his chained arms to Bruce.

"No, sorry, can't help ya pal." Bruce walked past the man towards a door on the far wall.

"I wouldn't go in there," said the chained man in a sing-song voice. Bruce just ignored him and kept on walking. "Don't say I didn't warn ya! Hey…" the man tried urgently to get Bruce's attention, rattling his chains as he spoke. "Hey… whatever you do, don't kiss the girl!" Bruce turned to face the man.

"Why not?" he asked. The man went back to singing.

"She told me that she loved me, she said she would be true

"She told me that she loved me, and then she cut me in two."

When the man finished the final verse, he lifted himself up on his arms and laughed as his upper body separated just above his abdomen. He rocked his severed torso back and forth over his legs, spraying blood all the while. Bruce stepped through the door and closed it behind him.

(V)

Lisa forced her muscles to move and pushed up with her arms. She looked over her shoulder at the large oak door; the creatures outside pounding and screaming on the other side. Lisa's eyes darted around; she saw large breaker boxes and metal shelving lining two of the walls. In one corner was a massive network of pipes branching off in all directions and, side-by-side on the wall, she saw soda and snack machines. In the center of the room sat a large desk covered in papers, empty soda cans, and candy wrappers. A laptop was hidden beneath the mess and the glow of the monitor softly illuminated the room. Lisa stood and walked behind the desk, stopping in her tracks at the sight of a rather large man cowering underneath. "They can't come in, they can't come in," he whispered as the pounding on the door began to subside. The man was well above six feet tall and it must have taken quite a bit of work to get himself jammed under the desk so tightly. His head had been shaved bald and he wore a dark gray one-piece jumpsuit. He looked up at Lisa with fear in his eyes.

"Are you all right?" she asked. The man stared at her for a long time saying nothing. "My name's Lisa, Lisa Spencer." The girl offered her hand to the man and he looked at it hard. Finally, he arched his back and worked his way out from under the desk. "Derek Philips," he said in a thick Scottish brogue as he reached for Lisa's hand. "Where did you come from?" he asked suspiciously.

"We got caught in a storm overnight; we had to leave our boat."

"How many of you?"

"Just me, my Uncle Bruce and a friend of his. Oh! And we ran into a Dr. Black on our way in here. We seem to have gotten separated though."

"Yes," Derek sighed. "This place seems to have a way of doing that." "What exactly *is* this place?" Lisa asked. "What's going on around here?"

"I take it you didn't get any answers from Miss Black?" Derek chuckled.

"She seemed pretty freaked out when we ran into her. I don't think she knows what's going on and all she would tell us was something about dreams."

Derek leaned against the wall and slid down, seating himself on the floor. He wiped sweat from his brow and began talking. "There were seven of us, test subjects. I've seen the rest of them, and let me tell you, it's not pretty." Derek suddenly jumped up, went to the door, and opened it. Whatever had been chasing Lisa had apparently lost interest. "I've been out there a few times," he said, shuddering. "Never again though. There's *things* in the woods, things that ain't natural. They look like demons; maybe they are…" Derek's words trailed off as if he were lost in thought. When he began speaking again he was more focused. "I've been out beyond the woods. The field goes on for a go' bit, then it's just black. A man can spend hours walking in that black and there's nothing, not a thing, just darkness." Derek closed the door and turned facing the back wall. "Back here." He pointed between the shelves at a vent that gaped open. "You can climb through the ductwork to get to other places, so I don' go inta' the woods no more."

"What *are* those things out there, those demons?" Lisa asked.

"Like I said, they may be."

"What do you mean by *that*?" Lisa looked at the man in confusion.

"They opened a door." Derek once again had fear in his eyes as he spoke in a whisper. "Maybe they're not from Hell, but they be definitely not from here! Who knows, maybe every time you dream, you create a new reality. It's taken over mosta the island. I made it to the surface once but I was better off here." Derek turned his body in a circle while staring up at the walls of the room. "There's somethin' about this room; it's got to be the electricity." Lisa had no doubt that what the man was saying was true. His sanity had taken a beating from what had gone on around him. Lisa listened as he mumbled to himself while he rummaged through the desk, looking in every drawer, shuffling every paper. She walked over to the open vent and looked inside. "I need to find my friends," she said as she ducked inside. "Are you coming with me?"

(VI)

There were three doors, all of them locked. Doug, concerned about finding Bruce and Lisa, walked along the walls slowly, inspecting every inch of the room. Pipes ran along the walls entering and exiting in various places. Here and there, steam forced its way through cracks in the pipes, periodically filling the room with a thick fog. **Click.** Doug turned his head in the direction of the noise and something caught his eye. He saw a key hanging from one of the pipes. Doug pulled it down and inspected it, turning it over and over in his hand. It was just an old skeleton key. He slipped it into his pocket and found one of the doors unlocked and open. Doug peered down the open passageway and counted six bare light bulbs dangling from cords overhead. He watched each bulb swing slowly in a tight circle. He noticed that the even numbered bulbs turned clockwise and the odd numbered bulbs turned counterclockwise. The moving lights suddenly stopped, now limp and hanging motionlessly. A woman began to sing.

Doug picked up his pace as the beautiful voice sang her enchanting song, each note vibrating within him in such an unbelievably good way. The hall ended at a single door with a large keyhole. A thin beam of light streamed from behind the door. Doug fell to his knees and placed his eye to the keyhole. Inside the next room was the woman who sang so beautifully, her song drawing Doug like a moth to a flame. She sat in front of a large mirror singing a lullaby, her reflection all that he could see.

Doug had to close his eyes for a moment, hoping to capture the memory of this woman's perfection within his mind forever, as her flesh was as beautiful as her voice. Flawless skin and scarlet lips, and her body, *oh Lord*, what her body did to him. It was the body of a dancer with muscles and curves that just begged to be touched and kissed. She had long, dark hair that she slowly coiled as she sang, until her jetblack locks were sufficiently piled on top of her head. She reached down to retrieve two large needles that she inserted into her hair to keep it in place. She wore a stunning red strapless dress that draped loosely over large, perfect breasts, the likes of which Doug had only dreamed about. He reached into his pocket and fumbled for the key. Her voice was driving him crazy and he could wait no longer to be in the presence of womanly perfection. He quickly slid the old skeleton key into the lock and pushed the door open. The room was empty.

Doug looked in the mirror, and to his surprise, the woman was still there! She stopped singing and jumped out of her chair as Doug came into view. "I'm sorry Ma'am," Doug panted, "I didn't mean to startle you." He put his hands in the air as a peace offering.

"Oh," the woman gasped. "How did you get in there?"

"In where?" Doug asked.

24

"In my mirror!"

"I..." Doug put his hand on the smooth hard glass. "Who are you?" he asked.

"You mean to say you've never heard of me?" the woman replied seductively. "Men have traveled thousands of miles just to spend an insignificant moment of their lives in my company. *I* should be the one asking *you* the questions." The woman put her hand to the mirror, trailing her fingertips along the glass as she spoke. "What is *your* name?"

"My... my name is Doug." The woman leaned into the glass, staring him in the eyes.

"Would you like to kiss me, Doug?" she moaned. "Go ahead, darling, kiss me." She put her lips to the glass and slowly licked her upper lip, leaving a trail of saliva and lipstick on the mirror. "Kiss me," she moaned once more and Doug put his lips to the glass. As his lips made contact with the mirror the entire room he was in shrank to the size of a three foot cube. Doug was pushed to the floor, his shoulders about to break from the weight of the walls and ceiling, his knees screaming in pain. The woman stood over Doug looking down on him through the small glass box. "Would you like to see more?" she asked. Doug tried to say no, but no sound could escape his lips. The woman stepped back and reached up, pulling the needles from her hair. "Are you ready?" she asked with a devious smile.

Doug watched as the woman's long, jet-black hair come to rest below her shoulder blades, seeming to grow longer before his eyes with each passing second. It took him a moment to notice that the woman's hair was coming apart at the center of her skull, pulling down evenly on all sides. He noticed something else. It wasn't just her hair, but the skin on her face was *also* sliding down her skull. The woman in the red dress stood frozen. Her exposed cranial plates opened and four fingers reached up out of her head. The fingers curled around her skull and a second hand shot up. The hands slowly rose up out of the woman's head and, when the wrists appeared, Doug saw they were tightly bound together with razor wire. A single cable coiled down the emerging limbs to the elbows, where another large tangle of wire and flesh emerged, with the red-dressed goddess's hair and face now hanging down around her shoulders like a turtleneck. ***Craaaack!*** The woman's skull split in two, falling to the sides, allowing the loose hair and skin to stretch and accommodate what was emerging. Arms developed into shoulders, and then a large lump that could only be another head was forced out, causing the red dress to tear and fall to the floor. The flesh of the singing woman blistered and pulsed before Doug's eyes as another body rose up and out of the now headless corpse of the siren woman. Doug saw the remnants of dark makeup smeared around the eyes of the new head, making it difficult to see them clearly at first, but then he fearfully realized that the eyes of this new woman were *sewn shut*! She wore a collar of wire around her neck that trailed down and wrapped around each breast before coiling down to her waist and hips. There was more razor wire sewn into the new woman's knees that pulled taut, binding her to something large wedged within the singing woman's throat. The blockage was that of another arm and the head of a man bound tightly together and merged with the new woman's knees. He, too, was wrapped with the same wire as the freakish woman. The blistered skin of the singing woman then dropped to the floor around the man's feet, exposing the rest of his body. His free arm was behind his back, held in place by razor wire that wrapped down around his naked body to bind his ankles together. The twisted jigsaw puzzle of tortured people suddenly bent over like a horseshoe, forcing the bound woman to stand on her hands. The tangle of razor wire that had combined the two bodies together then opened up and two additional heads with eyes sewn shut emerged within the knot of wire holding the two bodies together. Doug watched as two male bodies, sewn back to back, rose up into the air. Each had one arm bound to their combined torso, and in the other arm of each man was cradled yet another human head, one male and one female. These new bodies, which now totaled four, further expanded as the cradled heads in the men's arms burst out and two more bodies grew to form the arms of the creature that towered over Doug's small glass cage. He tried to move but there was nowhere to go. His heart was racing as he reacted to his fear. *Slow down,* he told it and, miraculously, his heart listened. As the beast outside reached for the box, Doug's heart stopped racing. In fact, it stopped beating completely.

CHAPTER FOUR

The Program

(I)

Gillian, still on the platform where she'd been with Bruce, decided to follow him. She let go of the ledge and slipped into the darkness below. She landed hard on her ass, and it hurt like hell, but she bit her lip and kept the scream inside. Gillian stood and observed her surroundings. She saw a row of sinks along one wall, three stalls along another, a third wall held a row of urinals and the fourth, a large wooden door. Gillian realized she was in a men's restroom. She approached the door and pushed down on the handle only to find it locked. One of the toilets in the stalls flushed. Gillian turned, walked to the center stall, and pushed the door open. "What the…?" Gillian mumbled. There was no wall, no toilet, only a dimly lit passageway. Gillian stepped inside.

The light fixtures hanging from the ceiling were spread apart making the hallway pitch black for several yards in between. As Gillian began to walk, she thought she heard noises in the darkness that sounded like someone breathing. She pulled out her flashlight and aimed the beam into the darkness but saw nothing. She placed her hand into the beam to make sure the lamp was working properly and placed her hand against the wall. Gillian felt cool wall beneath her fingers along with the coarseness of the wallpaper. However, when she flashed the light against the wall that she *knew* was there, she saw nothing. Realizing the torch was useless, she slipped it into her pocket and continued down the hall, feeling her way along when there was no light to guide her. Gillian stopped cold when she reached a passageway that took a ninety-degree turn that shouldn't have existed in that part of the facility. What she saw down the corridor made her stare in disbelief. Were the walls *moving?* Gillian put her hand to the wall and her fingers came back wet. With all that she had experienced in the last few hours she had no doubt what color they would be as she held her hand up into the dim light. The blood on Gillian's fingertips was a deep red, almost black. She wiped her hand on her pants and slowly approached the single door that stood at the end of the hall. Gillian touched the door and felt only smooth dry wood on her fingertips. Whatever had corrupted the walls had not touched the door.

Gillian pushed the door open and was temporarily blinded by a sudden burst of light. When her eyes adjusted she stepped through the doorway and entered a small empty room. The floor was tiled black and white like a chessboard, which matched the ceiling above the doctor's head. The walls were made of brick, some old and crumbling and some brand new, some being held in place with fresh mortar. The door slammed shut behind Gillian, the room jerked, and the lights went out. The room began to move downward and gained speed as it dropped. Gillian lunged for the nearest corner and slid down the wall until she was in a sitting position, her heart pounding rapidly within her chest. Suddenly, without warning, and with no jolt from the g-force of the abrupt stop, the door opened. Gillian took a deep breath and looked out the open doorway. She saw a cave with lit torches mounted to the stone, and in the distance, she heard the sound of dim voices.

Gillian could not make out was being said at first, but as she moved further into the cave, the words became loud and clear. *Gillian. Gillian.* Hundreds of voices spoke her name, the sound echoed off the walls of the cave. She looked around frantically in all directions. *Gillian. Gillian. Gillian.* She tried to block out the sound but it was no use. The hum of the voices only became louder, as if they were *inside* her head. She put her hands to her ears. *"Stop!"* Gillian screamed and the voices quieted, now only whispers and murmurs in the shadows.

The cave widened into a cavern as Gillian entered a vast chamber carved into the stone. Adorning the walls and ceiling were elaborate carvings, some as simple as hieroglyphs, while others appeared to be vast landscapes. In the center of the room was a huge, thick stoned, baptismal-like structure. Gillian cautiously approached the stone ring and looked inside. Tubes were hanging from various places in the ceiling pumping fluid into and out of a man who floated on the surface of a pool of blood. Without warning, the tubes began to pull on the man's skin and slowly lifted him to his feet until he appeared to be standing on the surface of the liquid. *That's* when Gillian got her first good look at the man's bloody face. His head had been shaved bald like the rest of the test subjects at the facility, but through the blood and tubes she could make out a tattoo on his chest. The man spoke. "What's the matter, Dr. Black, don't you recognize me?" The blood in the man's throat made a gurgling sound as he spoke. "Thomas Rothery Hunter," Gillian answered in a doctor-like tone. "Severe head trauma due to a bullet wound received in a shootout with law enforcement, non-responsive to stimuli, comatose for six months prior to being transferred into our facility."

"Very good, Dr. Black, it's nice to be remembered." Thomas Hunter stepped forward slowly, walking across the surface of the pool and stepping up onto the stone wall. "I'm glad you decided to join us." Hunter smiled through the blood running down his face. "Isn't it good to be..." he paused, extending his arms in welcome. "...home!" As the echo of the word faded, the voices in Gillian's head returned. *Gillian. Gillian. Welcome home.* She now realized that the voices had not been in her head at all. All around the room Gillian saw *things* moving in the shadows cast by the torchlight. She could not make out what they were, but their shapes looked vaguely familiar. Had she seen one of *these* creatures up on the helipad? Gillian took several steps backwards chancing a few glances over her shoulder to make sure the exit was not blocked. "There's no escaping here, Dr. Black," Hunter gurgled as Gillian turned and ran.

The vent shaft seemed to change from square to round in an instant. A little further along and Lisa had to straddle the sides to keep from getting her knees wet from a steady stream of water that ran between her legs as she crawled. "Did you find what you were looking for?" Lisa called out, her voice echoing throughout the drainpipe.

"Yep," Derek grunted as he crawled along behind her. "Where does this come out?" Lisa asked.

"The drain runs into a small stream near the cemetery."

"Oh great," Lisa replied sarcastically as she crawled on. She saw a light ahead of her. It was faint but it was there, like the last remnants of day before night creeps in. She listened to the soft cascade of water pouring from the drainpipe and continued crawling until the tunnel ended and Lisa crawled out onto the grass. Lisa brushed the muck from her knees as she sat down to rest while she waited for Derek.

"So, tell me what you know." Lisa leaned back on her elbows and smiled. "How does this work; are we actually inside someone's dream?"

Derek struggled for a moment to free himself from the end of the pipe before plopping out onto the grass. He reached into his shirt and pulled out a pack of cigarettes. "At least you fellow's are still dry," he mumbled and then yelled, "*Shit!* Last one!" Derek retrieved a lighter and lit up. "In answer to your question, yes," he said as he exhaled a lungful of smoke.

"Then who's is it?" Lisa asked as she laid her head back into the soft grass. "Whose dream are we in?" Derek ignored her question. "One by one they started disappearing…" He paused for a moment, as if he had forgotten what he had been talking about.

"Where to now?" Lisa asked as she sat up and looked around.

"Hope you feel like digging," Derek replied as he got to his feet and walked in the direction of a large iron gate. Lisa followed him, his comment spurring her to move.

"What did you mean about digging?" she asked.

"No matter how many times you dig it out, it always comes back. That in itself is proof we're in a nightmare. I'm too damned old for this shit!" Derek pushed the gate open and entered the cemetery. Lisa saw two shovels on the wall to the left. "It was blind luck I found it," Derek said as he retrieved the shovels and continued to walk.

"Found it? *What* it?" Lisa asked.

"This." Derek pointed to a simple granite gravestone. Lisa read the name on the stone aloud. "Mess Hall?"

(III)

"This place keeps getting stranger by the minute," Bruce thought as he walked cautiously down the long dark hallway. Every turn seemed to bring forth a new nightmare. Blood moving on the walls, the walls themselves moving… Some walls seemed to breathe while others simply appeared or disappeared into thin air. And that guy chained to the wall back there, how could he still be alive in the condition he was in? Bruce was now seriously considering that they had all died on the boat last night and were trapped somewhere in the depths of Hell. What other explanation could there be? Bruce Spencer was not a man who believed in the superstitious or the paranormal, he was a *doctor* for Christ's sake! Bruce had *always* been a rational man, but this… this was something else entirely.

The hallway came to an end and Bruce stood before a door that seemed to breath in and out. He took hold of the knob and turned. The door expanded outward as it opened with a crack and a bang. The concussion knocked Bruce back several feet and ripped the door from its hinges. Bruce stood and looked through the open doorway that led to a vast cemetery. Row upon row of headstones stretched out into the darkness in all directions. Here and there a scattered mausoleum broke up the uniformity of the markers. Bruce stepped out of one such structure into the cool night air. He looked up to the sky but saw nothing, no stars, no clouds, only blackness.

(IV)

"Did you hear that noise?" Lisa asked nervously as she hoisted a bucket of dirt out of the hole and dumped it into a large pile. Derek ignored her question for a moment, concentrating on the task at hand. "It's probably nothing," he finally answered, "but it wouldn't hurt to keep your eyes peeled just in case." Derek packed another load of dirt firmly into the bucket and passed it up to Lisa, who was still looking around the graveyard nervously.

"So what happened to the rest of the patients, and the staff?" she asked.

"Mostly dead," Derek grunted. "I think."

Lisa saw movement out of the corner of her eye and almost screamed out loud when she saw the silhouette of a man approaching between the gravestones. Her heart thumped fiercely as the figure's pace increased and the man changed direction. He'd seen her and was heading her way. "We're not alone,"

30

Lisa whispered. "There's someone… Wait!" Lisa recognized the man's gate and his profile; it cold only be… "*Bruce!*" Lisa called out excitedly, dropping the empty bucket into the hole and on top of Derek's head.

"Watch it with that thing!" Derek pushed the shovel into the earth and poked his head up out of the hole.

"Who ya talking to now, Lass?" he asked.

"My uncle. Hey unc, this is Derek; he was a patient here."

"Are you sure he's really your uncle?" Derek asked suspiciously before returning to the task of digging. "Yeah, it's really me," Bruce said as he reached the edge of the hole. He motioned toward Derek. "Is this guy all right?"

"Yeah, Bruce, he's fine. Looks like you're just in time."

"Time for what?" Bruce asked.

"The Mess Hall," Derek called out from the hole.

"If it's anything like the hallway I just came out of, I'm not sure I want any part of it." Bruce knelt down next to the hole to help haul out the last bucket.

"You might want to stay here then," Derek mumbled. "The Mess Hall is rather appropriately named."

Derek handed Lisa his flashlight. "Here, shine it down here."

Lisa aimed the beam down into the hole and saw another vent like the one she had climbed through to get to the cemetery. Derek removed the vent cover and tossed it out of the hole. He looked up at Lisa and Bruce, saying, "Well, come on, let's go." Derek sat down in the dirt, pushed off, and dropped into the hole.

(V)

Lisa sat on the edge of the vent and jumped in, with Bruce reluctantly following. As soon as Lisa's feet hit the floor, she slipped. Derek grabbed her arm and held on until Lisa caught her balance and stood up straight. She looked around. The floor was covered in blood, at points measuring several inches deep. There were bodies everywhere, parts of them at least, scattered about the tables and on the floor of the cafeteria. Lisa could not see a single body still intact, as some were missing one or two limbs, while others were hacked up into pieces small enough to not even be recognizable as human. There looked to be at least twenty-five, maybe thirty, bodies. Innards were strewn everywhere and even hung from the ceiling fans and light fixtures. The floor was not the only place the blood had found because the walls were covered just as thickly. Even on the ceiling pools of blood defied gravity.

Chunks of flesh, brain matter, and shards of bone were scattered throughout the room on the walls, ceiling, and floor. "Who *were* all these people?" Lisa asked, as she looked around both disgusted and awed at the same time. The amount of carnage there was simply… inconceivable!

"Mostly gardeners and scientists," Derek explained. "Chemists, botanists, that sort of thing." Derek let go of Lisa's arm and cautiously made his way back towards the kitchen.

"What *did* this?" Lisa asked.

"Not what," said Derek, "who."

"Well *who* then?" Bruce demanded.

"I don't think she ever had a name, they just called her 'The Madam'. She was part of a game program, somehow given life in this reality." Derek motioned around him.

"So a *woman* did all this?" Bruce asked.

"Well, sort of, it's more like something she made. Let's just hope we don't run into it."

Bruce grabbed Derek by the arms and shook him. "Will you make some damn sense, man?" Bruce shouted. Derek pushed at Bruce's arms, which caused him to lose his balance and land hard on the blood-soaked floor. "Get your fuckin' hands off me!" Derek screamed. He paused and took a deep breath, then spoke calmly. "They were experimenting with our dreams. I was a test subject. Somehow things went… *wrong*. Programs started coming to life, things around us started to change. At first we, and by *we* I mean us patients, thought it was just another program the doctors were running. It was hard to tell dreams from reality at times. *You'd* think so too if you were strapped into that thing."

"So how is the dream program crossing with *our* reality?" Lisa asked.

"It's just one of those things you may never really know," Derek said.

"So how *do* we get out of here?" Bruce cut in.

"Where would we go?" Derek asked, "We're in the middle of the fuckin' ocean."

"Someone's bound to come looking sooner or later," Lisa chimed in.

"You two are the first living people I've seen in..." Derek stopped and cocked his head. "How long *has* it been? The next crew's not scheduled to arrive for at least another month."

"Well find a way out of here," Bruce said, almost convincingly. "I'd rather take my chances out on the ocean."

"What about the storm?" Lisa questioned.

"*Screw* the storm, I've already survived one!" Bruce shouted, and then he closed his eyes and hung his head. "Screw the storm…"

"I suggest we get moving," said Derek. "You don't want to stay in one place for too long. *I* for one would like to live through this ordeal."

"Lead the way," Lisa said.

The trio found more bodies in the kitchen, with numerous pots and pans filled to the brim with severed heads and various other body parts. Derek made his way back to a large stove and started knocking pots onto the floor, their contents adding to the mess. "It's up here." Derek pointed up at the large vent above the stove that was apparently the exit shaft. Everyone jumped when the air suddenly filled with an ear-piercing shriek. "We need to go, *now!*" Derek screamed, tugging on Lisa's collar, pulling her onto the stove with him. Lisa ducked her head down low enough to look under the dangling pots, pans, intestines and limbs to investigate the source of the sound. She watched as the woman Derek had called 'The Madam' began to disintegrate and the creature inside took shape, each limb growing out of the last… and the gleaming razor wire binding it all together. As the last portion completed its metamorphosis, Lisa screamed. There, in the center of the beast, sewn in above the torso of the creature, was Doug. His arms reached out through the air like the antenna of some bizarre insect, his mouth spitting and biting at the air. Doug's eyes were the only set on the beast not sewn shut; they darted back and forth, from Lisa to Derek, from Derek to Bruce. Lisa stood for a moment and watched as the creature lunged in their direction.

"We need to get out of here!" Derek screamed from within the vent. Lisa turned and scrambled up into the vent. "Didn't I tell you that? I told you that!" Derek screeched as he reached down for Lisa's hand and hauled her further up into the shaft.

"What is it?" Bruce asked, turning to see what had frightened Lisa so much.

"You don't want to know," Lisa called out from within the vent. Bruce saw the creature running at them full tilt from across the mess hall.

"What the hell *is* that thing? Is that *Doug* in there?" Bruce quickly jumped up onto the stove and into the shaft. The creature seemed to appear out of nowhere. Its limbs crawled up into the shaft and grabbed Bruce by the legs. He kicked the thing as hard as he could to make it release him, the creature emitting the same ear-piercing scream as before, its prey getting away. Bruce made short work of catching up with Lisa and Derek who were waiting for him at an intersection in the tunnel. Derek had a flashlight and shined it towards Bruce as he made his way to them. "This way," Derek called out from the passage on the left. "Where are we now?" Bruce panted.

"Somewhere near the labs," Derek answered.

"The labs?" Lisa questioned.

"The labs," Derek explained, "where they were doing the experiments."

"Quiet…" Lisa cut in. "I thought I heard something." There it was again! It was a woman sobbing, the sound echoing throughout the cave around them, making it hard to tell which direction it was coming from. "Should we go check it out?" Lisa asked.

"I don't know," Derek said cautiously, "I don't think I've heard that voice before."

"Then we go!" Bruce grabbed the flashlight from Derek's hand and tried to set out in the direction of the sobs. Bruce stopped several times to listen; he seemed to be heading in the right direction. Lisa followed closely behind.

"You don't know what you're getting yourself into," Derek yelled, "though it *is* better than being alone… *Hey!* Give me back my flashlight." Derek ran up behind Bruce and tried to take the flashlight. Bruce jerked the lamp out of Derek's hands and raised it ready to strike. Derek hung his head like a shamed puppy. "It's mine," Derek said sadly.

"You're right." Bruce lowered the flashlight and handed it over. Derek pulled it to his chest shining the light up into his face. "Mine!"

"Well?" Bruce motioned for Derek to lead the way.

Lisa walked closely behind him, inspecting every alcove and turn. "This place is like a maze," she said. Derek stopped and turned. "It *is* a maze," he said. "Now keep quiet and follow me." Lisa noticed the ceiling begin to rise until it was so high that she could no longer see the rocks above her in the darkened space. Derek stopped at an intersection and mumbled, "This way, definitely this way." He chose the passageway to his right. The hall spiraled around in increasingly tighter circles until it ended with a wall and a single ladder.

"It's coming from up there." Derek pointed up into the darkness. Lisa had heard it too. "Where does this go?" Lisa asked as she grabbed hold of the ladder and began to climb.

"The courtyard," Derek answered. "This is a service ladder leading to the surface. It comes out in a small courtyard in the middle of the greenhouses." As Lisa climbed, she began to hear the wind and smell the sea. She looked up and saw a light. Lisa continued on, her head skyward, until she reached the top of the ladder and pulled herself up out of the hole. Lisa stood and looked around at what she could only describe as a canyon. She saw a fire burning off in the distance.

"I thought you said *small* courtyard," Lisa yelled at Derek as he hauled himself up out of the tunnel.

Bruce pulled himself to the surface and surveyed his surroundings. He, too, saw the fire burning, and he noticed Dr. Black sitting on a rock, her head in her hands. "Gillian!" Bruce called out. "Who's there?" she called back. "Quiet, they'll hear you!" Gillian sat on the ground, close to the fire, and watched as Bruce approached but did not move from the relative safety of the gently burning campfire. Gillian nervously looked into the shadows around her. When she decided that Bruce was close enough to chance talking she said, "Tell your friends to keep quiet if they want to stay alive."

"What's out there?" Bruce asked.

"*His* creatures," she answered. Lisa and Derek had now joined them by the fire.

"Where's your obnoxious friend?" Gillian asked Bruce.

"Doug? Doug's dead. He's part of this… *thing*." Bruce paused.

"Ah… the Madam." Gillian stated.

"Have you seen it?" Bruce asked her.

"Thank God, no! Well, I've seen the program, but… *this…*" Gillian looked at the walls of the canyon around her. "*This* is part of *another* program. That's why I came here. The fire's always burning here. It seems to keep them away." Gillian spoke as though she only half believed what she was saying to be true. Bruce placed his hand on Gillian's shoulder and spoke softly. "So how are we here if this is supposed to be some sort of computer program?" he asked.

"That's what *I'm* trying to figure out," Gillian said in a frustrated tone. She looked at Derek. "What about you? You've been here longer than any of us."

"Sorry, doc, don't have a clue." Derek sat down next to Dr. Black and the fire. Gillian looked Derek in the eyes. "So what happened here?" she asked.

CHAPTER FIVE

The Admiral

(I)

Admiral Robert Forsythe awoke from his dream to the sound of someone knocking on his office door. "Come in," he called out, as he straightened himself up in his large overstuffed leather chair.

"Admiral Forsythe?" the young Lieutenant inquired as she entered the office.

The Admiral motioned to an empty chair in front of his large oak desk. "Have a seat," he said. "Thank you, Sir, I'd prefer to stand if you don't mind, Sir." The lieutenant brushed her curly blonde bangs aside with her fingertips.

"Have it your way," the Admiral said leaning forward, placing his elbows on the desk and intertwining his fingers. "What can I do for you?" he asked.

Lieutenant Amanda Briggs stepped up to the desk and dropped a file on top of a copy of the San Diego Union-Tribune the Admiral had been reading before his unscheduled nap.

The file read: "Project Lucidity".

"We lost contact with the island at 02:00 this morning, Sir."

Admiral Forsythe looked up at the clock; it was just past five thirty in the evening. He then pointed to the television perched atop a set of filing cabinets in the corner of the room. The Weather Channel was on (with the volume muted for sounder sleeping) showing a large Category 5 hurricane off the coast of the Carolinas.

"It's not unusual to lose contact during a storm of this magnitude," the Admiral pointed out.

"Yes, Sir," Lieutenant Briggs voice trembled. "But the storm didn't hit the island until approximately 06:00 this morning," she explained, "and I know an update from the staff is not due for two more days, but…" the lieutenant paused.

"Go on."

"Well, Sir," she said, "the helicopter that transported Dr. Black never returned this morning."

"The storm could have caused it to take a detour," the Admiral stated flatly. "Or it could have landed somewhere else. Check with the FAA."

"I already did, Sir," the lieutenant cut in, "and there's no sign of them anywhere. I even contacted the Coast Guard. They said they had tracked a small aircraft on radar heading to the approximate location of the island but it never returned."

"Thank you, Lieutenant Briggs. Keep me informed of any new information."

"Yes, Sir." Lieutenant Briggs turned on her heels and retreated to the door.

Admiral Forsythe pulled open the top drawer of the desk and retrieved a small black remote control. He pointed it toward the television and pressed the mute button. The sound instantly filled the office. *"...like nothing I've seen in my twenty years of reporting the weather. This storm has far surpassed a category 5 with winds of more than three hundred miles an hour."* The man, who was attempting to remain standing upright on the beach, pointed out across the ocean towards the horizon. *"Currently positioned approximately one hundred and twenty five miles east of Myrtle Beach, Hurricane Miranda is shaping up to be a disastrous storm. Unless something miraculous happens soon, the devastation and loss of life will be enormous."*

The scene cut from the reporter on the beach to man in a well-cut suit sitting at a desk. "This is turning out to be the most intense hurricane on record and the mysterious circumstances surrounding the formation of this massive storm assure its place in the record books. Now to Beth for a recap..." The camera cut to a bubbly blonde with short curly hair wearing a tight red sweater and a plaid mini-skirt. "Without warning, just before six am this morning, this massive storm appeared out of nowhere." She clicked the button on her small hand-held remote and the screen behind her showed an image of the storm as it was forming. "Here you see the storm at five forty-five this morning. As you can see, it was barely a tropical depression..." She clicked the button once more. "Here it is at five fifty, now a category 1 hurricane." Click. "...and at five fifty-five, a strong category 4." She clicked once more to show a current image of the storm. Admiral Forsythe couldn't help but notice the eye was positioned over the exact location of the island. By now, he had seen and heard all he needed to know. He clicked off the television, sat back in the plush leather chair, and closed his eyes. Instantly the images from the dream filled his head. The same dream he had been having as long as he could remember. The darkness, always the darkness, consuming him, controlling him. And the voice... he never saw what it was that spoke to him, but he knew it was not human. It was this dream that had inspired him in his life long pursuit of the unknown. Oh, the things he had seen in his forty odd years of service. The things he knew were real but must deny at all costs. Including, he would soon discover, the events unfolding on the island. It was he who had signed the order to have Thomas Hunter transferred from the VA hospital to the NeuroTech facility. He was even aware of a patient by the name of Derek Philips who claimed to have some of the powers that Hunter possessed, though nowhere near as disciplined. Even still, Derek's powers were far greater than any of the remote viewers the Admiral had ever overseen. And as for Thomas Hunter, he was another story entirely.

There had been rumors circulating the upper ranks of a young cadet who was able to see things before the radar could even pick them up. The Admiral took it upon himself to look into the validity of these rumors. As it turned out, Thomas Hunter had far surpassed his expectations. He blew any verified psychic clean out of the water. Hunter saw things and knew things, things he couldn't *possibly* know. Admiral Forsythe had hoped to ignite a spark by introducing the two of them, Thomas and Derek, into the same environment. But could that really be the case? Could the two of them in the same location have something to do with the events occurring on the island? And what exactly *was* going on there? Admiral Robert Forsythe continued to lean back in his chair as he contemplated these questions and at least a dozen more.

(II)

Lieutenant Amanda Briggs sat at her desk in the cramped office pecking away at the keys on her laptop. Of all of her duties, writing reports was the one that she loathed the most. Unfortunately, it was also the duty required of her the most. At least this was an easy report to write. In her three years working for the Admiral, approximately eighty percent of the time she had no idea what she was writing about. He would dictate, she would transcribe. Sure, she picked up on things after a while, enough to know that the Admiral dealt with only the most *bizarre* situations, but most of the time she was left in the dark. At times it could be frustrating, not knowing exactly what it was that was going on around her, but the Admiral was a good man and, for the most part, Amanda enjoyed her job. She had her older brother to thank for her career choice. Captain Charlie Briggs, two years her senior, joined the U.S. Navy fresh out of high school. "*I was never the intellectual type like you, Sis,*" he was fond of saying, most likely referring to her graduation with honors from Smith University. He had even tried to discourage Amanda from joining the Navy, at first, anyway. But he soon came around and realized that it was what *she* wanted. Maybe he was even a little flattered that his little sister wanted so badly to follow in his footsteps. "I need to get my mind back on this report," Amanda said out loud, though there was no one to hear her in the empty office. Her thoughts shifted back to the task at hand and once more her fingers skipped across the keyboard. At 19:00 hours, just as Amanda was finishing up the report, the phone rang.

"Lieutenant Briggs." It was Admiral Forsythe.

"Yes, Sir?"

"Operation Wake-Up-Call is a go." The line went dead.

(III)

"Things started changing a little bit at a time. Not enough to notice at first. Besides, after so many sessions, it was hard to tell dream from reality." Derek hung his head as he spoke, looking down into the gravel and sand at his feet. The fire cast an eerie glow off the top of his bald skull adding to the ominous mood. "It wasn't long after you left, Dr. Black, that we started to notice the game programs overlapping with the dream programs; at first they thought it was just a glitch in the system, but they didn't tell us that, at least not then."

"What do you mean, overlapping?" Gillian cut in.

"Take this place for instance," Derek motioned to the landscape around him. "Somehow this canyon ended up connected to the maze."

"This shouldn't be here?" asked Lisa.

"No," said Derek.

"So let me make sure I'm getting all of this." Bruce held up his hands. "All of this..." he motioned around him, "is just a *computer program*?" Bruce looked down at the doctor and the nut-job sitting sideby-side at the fire. "Are you buying any of this?" Bruce whispered, leaning in close to Lisa's ear.

"Well," she said in an undertone, "it sure would explain an awful lot."

"You're right," conceded Bruce covertly to Lisa. "So what do we do?" he asked the group in a normal volume.

"I vote we stay here for a while, let things calm down a bit," said Derek. "Then, when it's safe, I'm going back to my room." He leaned his head back and stretched out his arms, placing them behind his head as he lay back in the dirt. "Now, if only I had a smoke," he grumbled.

"You're in luck!" Gillian retrieved the pack from her coat pocket. She passed one to Derek then put a second to her lips. Derek fished a lighter from his pants pocket and fumbled to light his cigarette, sucking in hard. "I shoulda' asked for a cigar," he said as he exhaled.

40

Lisa looked back at the fire as she wandered away with her uncle. It cast a thousand dancing shadows throughout the canyon. The only other light came from the stars in the sky. Out here, away from the fire, Lisa had a great view of the giant cluster of stars that is our galaxy. Lisa had grown up in a small town in upstate New York. She remembered the stars from her childhood, back when you could actually see them, not like now with all of the ambient light from the ground interfering with the celestial view above. Here, tonight, she once again saw the beauty in the heavens above her.

"Shouldn't there still be daylight?" Lisa asked Bruce. He seemed to not hear the question as he stared hard at the ground around his feet. They couldn't have been here that long, there should have been at least a couple more hours of sunlight, but then again, there was the storm. Lisa decided to let it go. "So, do you have a plan?"

Bruce, still looking down at his boots, kicked a rock away. "Not really, you?"

A sudden gust of wind ripped through the canyon, carrying with it a cloud of red dust along the ground.

Lisa looked up at the storm clouds coming in from the southeast, slowly obscuring the clear sky above. *Thump*. Lisa heard a noise off to her right, *thump*, and another to her left. Suddenly the noise was all around her; something was falling from the sky!

One landed just a few feet away from her. Lisa got down on one knee and searched in the darkness until her palm touched something wet. She cupped her hands and scooped it up. It made a noise and Lisa screamed and dropped it. Bruce ran to her side. "Well, what is it," he asked.

"It's a fetus, and it's *alive*!"

Bruce reached down and plucked the screaming child from the sand. He held up his open hand to the light. The child was only partially developed, and no larger than Bruce's palm. Its small limbs flailed wildly as it rocked back and forth in Bruce's hand. More tiny beings began falling from the sky, their bodies thudding on the rocks of the canyon floor, one striking Lisa's shoulder. "That's *it*!" Lisa screamed. "This is just *gross*." Lisa ran back to the fire, where Derek and Gillian were now standing. The doctor held her lab coat up over her head. "Follow me," Derek yelled above the cacophony of screaming and crying infants. Derek led them to a small hole in the ground to the east of the fire. He held his flashlight between his teeth and climbed inside.

"And da thildren thall fall fron da thky"

"What the hell is he babbling about now?" Bruce called out from the rear.

Derek pulled the flashlight from his mouth, holding it in his hand as he crawled on.

"And the children shall fall from the sky," he repeated.

"What's that from?" Lisa asked.

"The Canyon program has its own history, it's own religion," Derek explained. "It's a quote from one of the ancient scriptures."

"That was disgusting," said Lisa. "Who would come up with such a thing?"

"One of the programmers," Gillian stated the obvious. "He must have stayed up for a week straight writing that thing, high on caffeine, nicotine, and chocolate. What was his name, Mark or Mike? No, Mitch... Mitch Cooper." Gillian nodded her head to prove she was indeed correct.

"The story goes..." Derek continued, "...that one day a messiah would rise, giving birth to millions in search of the one child that bears the gift. You never really know what the gift is; I guess his point was for you to fill in the blanks. Anyway, the messiah tossed all of the children out of the heavens that did not bear the mark. It rained children for seven days and seven nights... Ah, we're just about there." Derek stopped, switched off the flashlight, and placed it in his pocket. Lisa turned to check on her uncle and, when she turned back around, Derek was gone. Lisa stopped crawling and looked up. A large hole had been cut from the rock, revealing a rectangular metal frame.

Lisa climbed from the opening, stood up, and looked around. She saw three beds side by side. Racks of monitoring equipment were stacked neatly at the foot of each bed and several cameras were set up around the room.

"Is this where they did it?" Lisa asked.

"Yup," said Derek. "Ole' number two, my own little Aurora Chair."

"Huh?" Lisa looked at him blankly as she climbed out of the vent.

"We need to go before she finds us," Derek said. He led them out into the hallway and stopped, turning on his heel repeatedly as if deciding on which way to go. He chose left. Gillian and Bruce followed closely behind as Lisa tailed Derek through the twisting hallways. The walls were white concrete, same as in the lab. The passageway turned to the left, revealing a row of six doors spaced closely together.

Derek stopped after the fifth door. "Five or six, five or six, five or six, six or five?"

"Well, which is it?" Bruce reached for the handle of the fifth door.

"*No!*" screamed Derek. "You don't want to open *that* door."

"What's on the other side?" Bruce asked.

"Believe me, you're better off not knowing." Derek turned the knob on the sixth door and pushed it open. Bruce stood for a time with his hand on the door, ready to turn the knob on door number five and open it. Something in his gut told him not to. Bruce let go of the handle and followed Gillian through the sixth door.

They stood in some sort of recording room. Several rows of monitors were lined up along one wall in front of a table. A small mixing board sat next to a computer that was hooked up to a large rack of electronics. Bruce saw the lab they had just left on one of the monitors, as well as two others that were nearly identical. Derek was on his knees in the corner of the room, fishing something out of his pants pocket. He pulled out a screwdriver and started removing a vent cover. Lisa looked around the room and spotted a shelf stacked with CDs. "Derek, that laptop back in your room, does it have a CD drive?"

"Yeah, I'm pretty sure it does," he answered.

Lisa pulled several of the discs down off the shelf. Each was dated and marked which lab and which camera. Some had patient names. Lisa placed the disks down and searched for something to carry them in. There was a briefcase on the table next to the computer, but it looked too bulky. Something shiny underneath the table caught Lisa's eye. It was a small cooler pack with a long strap on it, easy to carry. Lisa unzipped the pouch and removed the contents. There was a peanut butter and jelly and mold sandwich in a zip-loc bag. Lisa dropped it on the floor. There was some chips that were most likely stale, a plastic spoon and a small can of pears. Lisa left them in the cooler. She stuffed all the discs she could fit into the bag and zipped it shut, then placed the strap over her shoulder. Derek had the cover off of the vent and was placing it down on the floor.

"Where does this go?" Lisa asked.

"It leads to the rest of the labs," Derek said as he crawled into the shaft. "But it also branches off and leads to a well in the forest outside of the electrical room."

Derek pulled the flashlight from his pocket and flicked it on. "I just hope none of them *things* are around. I've killed a couple of them but let me tell you, they don't go easy… or quiet. It's not a pretty sight."

(IV)

There was enough room in the vent for Lisa to crawl easily on her hands and knees, though she could not see much. The light from the flashlight was blocked by Derek's large body as he crawled ahead of her. It happened instantly. One second Lisa was crawling on metal, the next it was hard packed dirt, cold and wet, soaking through the knees of her jeans, and sticking in clumps to her hands as she clawed through the tunnel. She looked around and saw nothing but black, with no sign of Derek *or* his flashlight. Lisa's head filled with a blinding white light, and an equal amount of pain, as she crawled face first into Derek's knee. The man shined the flashlight down into her eyes. "Watch where you're going," he said. "We go up from here." Derek handed the flashlight down to Lisa. "Hold this and wait for the others." He pulled his feet up into the shaft and started to climb. Lisa held her hand up into the light. Her fingers were stained red. She held the flashlight close to the wall of the tunnel. Lisa saw chunks of flesh and fingernails embedded into the earth. It looked as though the tunnel had been dug by hand. Lisa shined the flashlight up the shaft and saw that Derek had maneuvered a good distance already. Gillian and Bruce had finally caught up with them. "We go up from here," Lisa repeated as she stood up into the shaft. She looked at the walls around her; they were made of smoothly carved stone with large indentations good for hand and footholds. Lisa shoved the flashlight into her back pocket and began to climb. Lisa suddenly found herself standing on a long wooden pier, looking out at the ocean surrounding her. The waters were calm and warm with the glow of the setting sun. Lisa turned and looked down the jetty towards the beach. It took a second for her to realize where she was. It was the beach from this morning's dream. Once again Lisa found herself trying to figure how much time had elapsed since arriving on the island. The sky around her grew dark and the seas began to churn. Lisa knew what was coming next. "Bring it on," she screamed at the howling wind. Lightning flashed all around and it began to rain, the wind growing increasingly fierce, whipping Lisa's hair back. She stood her ground, holding onto the railing as the lightning crashed all around her. The waves were now tall enough to splash up over the pier, soaking Lisa to the bone. "Is that all you've got?" she screamed. The wind became even more ferocious. It was getting hard for her to stand, even with the added support of the railing. The boards under her feet began to creak and moan, threatening to give way at any moment.

It was getting hard to remember this was just another waking dream. She'd had plenty of them in the past but something was different about this one. Lisa had felt this way the first time she had the dream as well. Normally, she had a certain amount of control over her dreams and visions, but something else

44

was in control now. Not having control of your own mind was bad enough, but what was happening to her here, on this island, it was like nothing she had ever experienced. The dreams had haunted her throughout her life, making things difficult for her in school, hard to hold onto a job, a boyfriend, any kind of a normal life. The doctors, and Lisa had seen *many*, all said the dreams were a result of Lisa's subconscious mind assuming blame for her mother's death.

Everything went black. The wind stopped and all sound was gone. Lisa instantly felt a presence, as if someone were standing close by, watching her in the darkness. She strained to see, but there was no light, nothing to give her a clue as to who the voyeur was. Lisa stood perfectly still and held her breath, hoping to catch the sound of a creaking board, *anything* to tell her the location of her stalker. Then he spoke. "I've been waiting for you," he said.

Lisa tried to tell which direction the voice was coming from. It seemed to come from around her all at once. "Who are you?" Lisa called out.

"I am everyone and everything. I am **God** here!"

"Where is here?" Lisa asked.

"**Boo!**" The voice came from directly behind Lisa, scaring the crap out of her. She turned and stood face to face with the man. He wore a jumpsuit, just like Derek, but his head was not shaved. There was a peaceful look on his face.

"This is my… world," the man said.

"Your dream world," Lisa added. He seemed surprised at her answer.

"Yes." The man stepped back along the pier, never taking his eyes off Lisa.

"This was my special place." He motioned around him and Lisa was suddenly aware that she could see the beach once more. She saw the waves splashing up over the sand, the long wooden pier on which she stood, and the man who spoke to her. He had dull brown eyes and a pleasantly chiseled face. He looked to be in his early thirties. Lisa watched him as he spoke. "Wrightsville Beach, North Carolina actually," he said. "I used to come here as a child. I used to pray a storm would come and carry me away." The man's face changed from calm to angry. "I soon found myself becoming the storm, cleansing the land as I came ashore." He stopped and took a deep breath. More calmly, he said, "I dreamed of you last night. I was the storm, raging out at sea, tearing apart ship after ship. And then I saw you... Standing on the deck, you looked so sad when the girl was swept over."

"Lisa…"

Lisa could no longer see anything. That voice, was it her uncle?

"Lisa…"

"Bruce," she called out. Lisa snapped out of her vision and looked up. She saw a ring of light, which, as her eyes adjusted, became a ring of black sky filled with stars. Lisa pulled herself up out of the well, falling to her knees, and then onto her back. Bruce followed Lisa out of the well, collapsing in the grass next to her. There were so many stars. "Beautiful, isn't it?" Lisa asked.

"Too bad it's not real," Derek said. "The stars in the courtyard, *those* were real. C'mon, we need to get moving." Derek reached out and grabbed hold of Gillian's arm to haul her up until she stood on the lip of the well. Her lab coat was covered in mud, or at least that's what it looked like in the present light. "Now, follow me." Derek led the way across the field towards the trees, Gillian following closely behind. Lisa and Bruce hung back a few yards to speak privately. "Some vacation, huh Unc?" Lisa said, almost sounding excited. She looked at Bruce and smiled until they both broke out into roaring laughter. "Shh, quiet back there. They'll hear you." Derek stood with his finger pressed to his lips. "The path is just ahead," he whispered.

Lisa recognized the path. It was not too far from this very place that she had arrived after enduring the wormy tree; it was the field, and Lisa began to wonder if the creatures would show themselves again.

Lisa tightened her grip on Bruce's hand and pulled him toward the path. The trees were quiet this time, though they still had an eerie blue glow. "You were having one back there, weren't you?" Bruce asked. "Yeah," Lisa said sheepishly. "It was the beach again, the same as on the boat. At least *that* time I was still asleep." Lisa hung her head and said nothing more.

"Hurry up, back there," Derek prompted from ahead.

Bruce stood speechless in front of the doorway that stood in the middle of the path, *right there,* in the middle of the woods. He saw a room inside, concrete walls, breaker boxes and piping. Bruce walked around to the other side and saw a mirror image of the room inside the open doorway. Lisa stood in front of a large desk sorting through the contents of the cooler pack. "I only took the most recent ones," she said to Bruce as he entered the room. Lisa lifted up the laptop and shook off the papers and wrappers that lay on the keyboard. She placed it back down on the table and opened the disc tray. There was a loud thud and the power went out.

"Don't worry," said Derek. "It's been doing that off and on for a few days now. At least I think it's been that long." He flicked on his flashlight and set it on the table with the beam pointed up towards the ceiling.

"So how are we going to get out of here?" Gillian asked. "They're bound to send someone out looking for Harry when he doesn't show up."

"As soon as the storm blows over we'll head up," Bruce said. "Maybe my boat's still in one piece."

"You have a boat?" Gillian squealed excitedly.

"Like I said, if it's still in one piece, and if there's enough fuel," Bruce responded cautiously.

"There's plenty of gas here for the generator," Derek said.

"Then all we have to do," added Gillian, "is wait out the storm and were home free."

Lisa closed the laptop. "How many are out there?" she asked Derek. He looked at her blankly. "People, *things*… on the island?"

"Oh, aside from us?" Derek paused and twisted his face as he thought for a moment. "Let's see, there's the Madam and that thing inside her. I guess you can only count her as one. Then there's Hunter, you *don't* want to meet him. There's Crazy Pete, but he's chained to a wall."

"Yeah," Bruce said, "I think I met him."

"There's Carlton," Derek continued. "And lately, there's been this young girl."

"Carlton," said Gillian, "Ran into him twice already. Maybe we can learn something from him. Derek, what do you think?"

"Never talked to him much myself, he's not too easy on the eyes, if you know what I mean, but he seems harmless enough."

"Good," Gillian said. "Where can we find him?"

"I'm not going back out *there* any time soon," Derek said. "There are *hundreds* of them things out there, Hunter's little pets."

"Fine," Gillian huffed. "Just tell me where I can find him and how to get there." "Through there." Derek pointed to the open vent on the wall.

"First intersection, go straight. Second go left. Third, straight. Fourth, down."

"How will I find him?" Gillian asked.

"He'll find you."

"Straight, left, straight, down," Gillian repeated as she grabbed Bruce by the arm. "You're coming with me," she said as she pulled him toward the wall.

"Have fun you two," Lisa called out. "Oh, and Doctor, have him back no later than midnight."

Bruce cocked his head and smirked. "Very funny, I'm dying here."

"Be careful what you say," Derek said. "Especially out there."

Part 2: Beyond the gates

CHAPTER SIX

The Mille Umbra

(I)

The lights clicked on and off incessantly, rarely staying on for any length of time. Lisa sat in the darkness running her fingers over the smooth plastic cases of the discs in the bag. She looked at the charger plugged into the wall and saw the green light flicker to life. She had tried to turn the computer on but the battery was dead, so she waited until there was less time between the blackouts before she opened the laptop and pushed the power button. She looked up at Derek who was pacing the room.

"When did things start to change?" Lisa queried.

"What's the date?" Derek asked.

"The twenty fifth."

"Let's see," said Derek. "Christ, it's only been a week; seems much longer."

"So that would make it the eighteenth." Lisa pulled several discs out of the bag and placed them on the table. She flipped through them. Deciding on one, she opened the case and removed the CD. The tray opened with a whine; Lisa placed the disc in and waited for the program to load. Several options popped up on the screen simultaneously. Rooms: labs A through D, dates: August eleventh to August eighteenth, along with a list of patient names. Derek's was among them.

"Do you mind?" Lisa asked as she pointed to the screen.

Derek leaned over Lisa's shoulder to get a look at what she was doing. "No, go ahead," he said, and went back to pacing the room. Lisa clicked on his name and saw more options. She clicked on the eighteenth, sessions 1 through 6. Lisa moved her finger across the small touch pad and clicked on

Session 6. The screen went black for a moment and the video started.

The computer monitor was split in four even sections, each a different camera angle of the same thing, Derek lying on a stretcher in the center of the room. There was a woman in a light green uniform,

49

a nurse, adjusting the electrodes on Derek's temples. She looked up at the camera, nodded, and walked off screen. Lisa clicked the volume icon and turned the sound up.

"In five, four, three, two, one…" A new window opened in the center of the screen, overlapping the other four images.

Derek stood in a dark hallway; one by one the lights came on. Lisa recognized the hallway as the one at the bottom of the stairs, the place she had been first separated from Gillian, Bruce, and Doug.

"We're in," the voice crackled from out of nowhere. "How you feeling, D?"

The lights were now on over Derek's head and Lisa saw him talking on the center screen. "I'm ready," he said, and began walking down the hallway. The nurse came back into view on each of the four screens underneath. She stood by the monitoring equipment making selections on a touchscreen while Derek continued to lay motionless from all four angles. On the center screen Derek had reached a door.

He turned the knob and the heavy steel door opened.

(II)

Derek stood in an almost cavernous entrance hall. It was oval in shape, with two marble staircases that wound up the walls on each side of the room, coming together on the second floor, then branching off again and joining back up again on the third floor. Intricate carvings adorned the wood railings that straddled the staircase and a large chandelier hung from the ceiling suspended just above the second floor by a network of chains. The chandelier was made of large crystals that appeared to glow while casting arcs of light and rainbows around the room. "Where am I?" Derek called out from the laptop's speakers. He turned and tried to open the door leading back to the hallway but found it locked.

"Hello? Anyone there?"

"Yeah, D. we're here," the disembodied voice cut in.

"Where am I?" Derek asked nervously.

"Well, we're not sure."

"What do you *mean* you're not sure?" Derek was getting agitated and began pacing the floor of the large entranceway.

"Well," the voice answered. "Your wave pattern's simply not here, it's not in the system."

"Then where the hell *is* it?" Derek screamed.

"Oh, this is a good one, turn it up." Derek stood behind Lisa as she watched the images on the monitor. Lisa leaned in to turn the volume up. On the small screen Derek stood motionless, looking up into the darkness. Lisa heard the distinct sound of someone laughing.

"Hello?" Derek called out. "Did you hear that? Who's up there, show yourself!"

"Hear what?" the technicians voice asked.

"Never mind, just get me out of here."

"We're working on it D, hang in there."

Derek crossed the room to the nearest staircase and called out, "Hello?" He started up the stairs, slowly at first, pausing every few steps to listen. Derek reached the first landing and stopped. "I hear you up there," he called out and continued up the stairs to the second floor. Derek stopped on the landing and looked down the hall. He saw a long dark hallway with several large oak doors with polished brass knobs that gleamed in the light from the chandelier. Derek turned and looked up the steps to the third floor. "Show yourself!" he shouted.

"Do you wish to see?" A deep voice boomed from the darkness above.

Derek mumbled under his breath, "I'm not so sure."

Squish, squish. The sound came from the third floor landing, like footsteps across a wet carpet. *Squish, squish.* Derek peered through the darkness but saw nothing. *Squish, squish.* The phantom footfalls continued down the stairs. Derek turned and raced down the stairs to the first floor. He stopped in the middle of the large hall and slowly turned in a circle so he could keep an eye on both sets of stairs at the same time. The sound stopped on the first floor landing.

"We see you, Derek," the voice said softly, almost a whisper. The footsteps resumed, slowly, one step at a time. *Squish...* Derek held his breath and waited. *Squish...* Then he saw it. A dark footprint appeared on the stairs… *squish...* another the next step down. *Squish...* They were footprints of blood!

"Get me out of here guys... *NOW!*" Derek screamed.

Lisa watched the Derek on the monitor. The man sprinted across the marble floor to the doorway. He knew better than to try the knob so he slammed his shoulder into the door with all the force he could muster. The door didn't even budge. Derek backed up and rammed the door once more; still, it would not give. Lisa watched the phantom footprints continue across the hall and stop a few yards away from Derek. Lisa heard the laughter once more, closer now.

The laughter came from the second floor landing. The chandelier dimmed and Derek looked up the darkening stairs. Something moved within the shadows. At first it looked like a large man, but the shadow seemed to shift and swirl, twisting in on itself, and then spreading out to fill the entire landing. The shadow glided down the stairs, hovering inches above each marble step as it descended. Derek saw the creature more clearly as it reached the bottom of the staircase and stopped. The *thing* was many men, dark silhouettes of at least a dozen humanoid forms that intertwined within the beast, howling and screaming as the creature laughed another dark, menacing laugh and slowly moved forward. Derek returned his focus to the door, ramming it frantically. There was a loud crack. Derek backed up to get more leverage for his next assault, when, out of the corner of his eye, he saw the shadow moving across the entranceway.

Lisa watched the monitor in horror as the creature's mass shifted. The heads of the shadowy figures joined, their bodies trailing off behind the creature in all directions, looking like a phantom jellyfish. The heads slowly merged into a contorted, screaming collection, the individual faces blurring as each feature twisted and tore to become one. Eyes fell back into empty sockets as they stretched and merged with other features. Noses melted from shadow faces and mouths expanded until the flesh tore, leaving one, gaping hole. The creature now had two distinct eye sockets that looked like black holes swirling within the shadow skin of its new face. Its gaping mouth narrowed to a slit and formed a smile. ***"You have the same look in your eyes that your sister had when we came to take her."*** Derek could not tell if the creature actually spoke, or if the voice was in his head. Two of the shadow figures disentangled and stretched forward like a tentacle. It had no hands, just three long hook-like appendages protruding from the end.

"This is not how I die, this is not how I die." Derek stood completely still with his eyes closed. "This is not how I die. This is *not* how I die."

"Oh, but it is," the shadow hissed. "Would you like to see her again, your sister?"

Before Derek could reply, the hooks on the phantom limb were in the soft meat of his belly.

The center screen disappeared, leaving only the four way split screen of Derek sitting up screaming, clutching his stomach. Lisa saw the blood pouring through his fingers and down the white sheets that covered him. The images on the monitor flickered and went out, the four screens turning black.

"What the hell *was* that thing?" Lisa turned to face Derek. He unzipped his jumpsuit to the waist and worked his way out of the sleeves. Derek was wearing a white T-shirt underneath which he pulled up to reveal his wound.

"I have no idea what it was," Derek said, "but it left a nice calling card, eh." He began to laugh hysterically.

"Derek!" Lisa yelled. "Stay *with* me. What did you mean when you said *this is not how I die?*" Derek stopped laughing and looked straight at Lisa.

"*This* is where I die." Derek held his hands up and turned, gesturing towards the room around him. Then he began to laugh again.

"Derek!" Lisa yelled. "I know you're not as crazy as you want everyone to believe, so tell me, is the thing that attacked you lurking around out there?"

Derek stopped laughing and turned, lunging at Lisa. He stopped a foot away from her face. "Yes," he said. "It's everywhere, lurking, always lurking in the shadows."

"What did it mean about your sister?" Lisa asked. She backed up to the wall and slid down, sitting on the floor.

"There are certain reasons I'm out here on this island," Derek said as he stood, towering above Lisa. "I dream things that sometimes come true. Kind of like visions of things that haven't happened yet." Lisa looked up at him. "Like seeing the future?" she asked.

"You could call it that and you can be *damn* sure there are a hell of a lot of people out there who are interested in a talent like *that*."

Lisa could relate to what he was saying. Her own dreams were a mystery to her as well. "How do you know that your dreams don't *cause* these things to happen?" she asked. Derek laughed and sat down on the floor across from Lisa.

"Believe me," he said. "I've spent years pondering that question."

Derek reached over and pulled out a desk drawer to retrieve a pack of cigarettes and some wooden matches. "Do you mind?"

"No, go ahead" Lisa said. Derek held out the pack. "Want one?" he asked.

"No thanks."

Derek leaned back with his smoke in his mouth and slid the match across the box. The flame burned bright against his skin as he drew it to the tip of the cigarette and sucked in a lungfull of smoke. He tilted his head back and blew the smoke up into the air above their heads.

"Sometimes," Derek leaned closer to Lisa and lowered his voice, almost to a whisper, "I see people dying in my dreams, people I've met only once, and some I've never met at all. I was seventeen when I realized one of those people I saw die was me." Derek sucked in another lungful of smoke. "You can imagine my surprise when I stumbled on this room. I wouldn't come in it at first but I eventually came to the conclusion that I'd rather die in here than out there."

"So *this* is where you die," Lisa asked. "How does it happen?"

"That's the funny thing about dreams; they tell you just enough, but leave out some of the more important details. I'm stabbed, here," Derek placed his hand on his stomach, "in this room. I look up, but I never get to see the face of the person who does it."

(II)

Gillian pushed off the ledge and fell down into the vent shaft. Her heart raced as she descended; she seemed to be falling faster and faster when, suddenly, she began to slow. Gillian stopped and stood in the darkness, not sure if there was a floor under her feet. She saw a light ahead of her and turned tentatively calling out, "Bruce?" There was no reply. "Shit!" Gillian returned her attention to the light. It was a doorway. She saw nothing of what lay on the other side, only a brilliant white light. Gillian's eyes, which were now used to the darkness, hurt as she strained to see what was on the other side of the door. Slowly, as things became clear she saw shapes and shadows, and her eyes no longer hurt from the light.

Bright florescent lights flooded the room on the other side of the doorway reflecting off of the white tiles that covered the room. Gillian saw rows of showerheads lining the walls and the black circles of drains on the floor. A row of sinks and a single door lined one wall; above them was a large mirror. Gillian stepped into the shower room. "Hello?" her call echoed. The lights went out and the showers turned on. Gillian felt the warm water soaking through her blouse. Her nipples rose as the water covered the front of her shirt. "God, this feels so good," she moaned.

Gillian turned around and tilted her head back under the water. Something was wrong. Why was the water so… *thick*, and why was she doing this in the first place? The lights flickered twice and came back on. Gillian turned to the mirrors and saw that she was covered in blood. The showers turned off and

54

the room went silent, the only sound a plop from the occasional droplet of blood dripping from the showerheads and hitting the floor. At once, all of the showers turned back on, spraying a brilliant red across the slick white tiles of the floor, along with the soft white fabric of Gillian's blouse. The drains in the floor were clogged which caused the blood to pool quickly around the room. Gillian reached down and pulled out whatever it was that plugged the nearest drain. It squished in her hand as she held it up to look at it. The blood oozed through her fingers like Jell-O. It was clotting, plugging up the drains, filling the room quickly. Gillian began to leave, but slipped several times, each footstep threatening to send her splashing down, but somehow she kept her balance and made her way to the door. Gillian's bloody hands could not grip the knob. She looked desperately to find a dry spot on her clothes to wipe them and found one on the inside of her shirt. Gillian pushed the door open and fell out onto the floor. *"What the…"*

Gillian felt twigs and leaves under her palms and smelled the earth as her fingernails dug into the ground. She looked up. There were huge trees all around her, their canopies so thick she could not tell if it was day or night. Gillian stood and turned around. She was in the middle of a narrow path in what could only be described as a jungle. Strangely, there were no sounds that she expected to hear in a jungle, no wildlife, no birdcalls, just… nothing. Gillian strained and finally heard the soft crackling of the torches that lit the path. Gillian began to walk forward, the desire she had felt in the shower room gone, replaced with a strange calm and an ever-growing feeling of dread. Gillian got a good look at her clothes and hands as she walked past the dancing flames of the torch. Dirt had caked in with the blood making it look black. "I must look awful," she said to herself.

"Frightening," said a voice from behind her that she recognized.

"Shit!" Gillian yelled. "Will you stop *doing* that? My heart jumped so far up my throat I almost spit it out. Wouldn't I look just *grand* walking around with my heart hanging out of my mouth?" Gillian slowly pulled herself up to her feet, turned, and once again stood face to face with Dr. Alan Carlton. His mostly skinless face gleamed in the torchlight with the duel lenses of the glasses he used to wear now fused to his skull, each reflecting a tiny flame. Gillian slowly raised her hands and placed them on Dr. Carlton's chest. "That's the *third* time you've done that to me; knock it off, Alan!" Gillian pushed him away as hard as she could. Dr. Carlton stumbled backwards and began to laugh. "Hey, I know I look like shit and I didn't mean to scare you but, well... I wasn't even sure it was you. If you haven't noticed, things got pretty fucked up around here while you were gone."

"No," Gillian said sarcastically, "*everything* looks just like it did when I left. Well, except for you; you've actually gotten a little better looking. It's a good look for you Al; you should go with it." "Bitch," he replied with a lipless smile. "It's a beautiful night; let's go for a walk."

"So what's with all the cussing?" Gillian asked. "I don't think I've ever heard one foul word come from your lips before now."

"Well, seeing as how I no longer *have* lips..." Dr. Carlton paused to chuckle. "Actually I think it has something to do with... Oh, I don't know, the fact that I'm fucking *dead*! And now my sorry ass is stuck here with the rest of you."

"So you really *are* dead?"

"Sure as shit," Carlton replied. "C'mon, let's walk."

Gillian listened as Dr. Carlton told her his version of the past week's events, most of which she had already learned from Derek. "It was Hunter's *things* that did this to me," Carlton said.

"Yeah, I had a run in with them already, even spoke to Thomas for a minute or two, but I didn't hang around very long."

"You're shittin' me," said Carlton. "And you're still breathing? He must like you. That or he needs you alive for some other purpose."

"I'd rather not think about that right at this moment, thank you."

"This is far enough," Carlton said as he stopped. Gillian saw a large bonfire ahead in the distance. Several of Hunter's creatures sat around the flames chewing on large chunks of flesh. When Gillian's eyes adjusted to the glow of the fire she could see what lay beyond it. It was a small church. Vines covered the building like a serpent squeezing its prey. From what Gillian could see through the growth, the structure's paint was peeling and the stained glass windows were mostly broken.

"This way," Carlton took Gillian's hand and led her off the path and deeper into the jungle.

(III)

Lisa sat in the darkness of the small room. Derek had turned the lights out and the only illumination came from the laptop on the desk. For the past hour she had been watching various sessions, most of them Derek's, who was presently laying on the floor in the corner of the room snoring.

Lisa had to admit, she'd seen some pretty strange shit… that *creature* from the mess hall and the woman who'd created it... Lisa had witnessed several sessions by different patients that revolved around this program, which seemed to be some sort of survival-horror game. Lisa had watched bits and pieces of Derek and the other patients playing the game; she had even learned some of the story line. The game took place in the early nineteen hundreds. The patients played as a detective sent from Boston to a small town in western Massachusetts to investigate the disappearances and grizzly murders of several townsfolk. The investigation leads the player to a local brothel and the Madam. Throughout the game, the player witnesses the woman sewing together her "creation" one corpse at a time. The player then faces this creature in the final "boss" battle. If they lost, they won the prize of being added to the creature's collection. Just like Doug. On one occasion (Saunders, Peter. Session 4, August 19), things went horribly wrong. At the end of the game he'd faced a choice placed before him by the woman, join her, or die at the hands of her creation. For some reason, Lisa had decided to watch for a while as the woman did her little tramp thing, pawing and groping Pete Saunders. "Unzip my dress," the woman whispered. Peter had reached around the woman's waist and slid the zipper down the back of her dress. One of his hands worked its way under the material, while the other roved the woman's bare skin. Lisa watched as two small bumps formed on the woman's lower back. Peter's hand slid across the woman's flesh, almost touching one of the lumps as it grew larger. He slid his hand around to the front of the woman's dress, caressing her breasts beneath the silky fabric. What had started out as two small bumps just above the woman's waist had now turned into two large appendages that continued to grow straight out of the woman's back. This went unseen by Pete, of course, who was too busy sucking face with the woman to notice. Once the appendages had reached four feet in length, both growths were sucked back into the woman. Unfortunately for Mr. Saunders, whatever was inside the woman came out the front of her and into his abdomen. The woman turned her body and Lisa saw two long blades, side by side, protruding out of Peter Saunders' back just above his waist. One quickly moved left, the other right, slicing the man in half. The woman pushed Peter away and his torso fell to the floor with a splat. Normally, the death of the player signifies the end of the game, *normally*. Lisa watched as the center screen went black and disappeared, leaving the remaining four images of Peter Saunders lying on the stretcher screaming, "I can't move, I can't move!" A nurse in a green uniform rushed to his side, trying to help him sit up. What happened next was cause for Lisa to turn off the laptop. Peter Saunders' severed torso fell to the floor his innards spilling out all over the place; he was dead.

Once Lisa's stomach settled, she turned the computer on again. She selected a patient named Danielle Harris, strangely, the only female listed. The now familiar split screen popped up on the monitor and Lisa watched as the young woman was strapped down to the bed. "You ready?" came a voice from somewhere off screen. Danielle nodded. The center screen popped up, overlapping the previous images but for some reason it stayed black. "Dani… are you there?"

"I'm here," she answered back.

"We're having a little trouble finding you. Bear with us for just a moment and…" The voice was cut off by a shrieking scream. Lisa saw something going on in the images underneath. She clicked on the background, bringing the images forward. Danielle Harris lay on the bed screaming. Her back was arched up into the air and she was pulling at the straps holding her down. The sheet covering her had fallen to the floor and Lisa saw that the woman lay nude on the bed. Lisa watched the impressions of some invisible force pushing down on Danielle, her legs spread wide as she was raped. Lisa watched in amazement and disgust for several minutes until she thought it was over. The movement stopped, and the woman's body relaxed, aside from the shaking that accompanied her sobs. The nurse at her side unbuckled Danielle's straps. She stepped back and gasped as her patient's stomach stretched and rose. Danielle Harris was pregnant. Suddenly, the screen went black, and an image appeared that Lisa recognized. It was an image of a beach and a pier.

(IV)

Bruce stood in a small elevator made of old steel and rusted chain link fencing. *How the hell did I get here?* he thought to himself as the lift descended into the blackness. Bruce heard the clanking and whirring of the elevator's mechanical parts but saw nothing through the fencing, just darkness. "Hello?" he called out, silently relieved when there was no reply. The elevator continued its descent and he waited. Now, Bruce Spencer was not a terribly happy man when made to wait. A short fuse, a bad attitude, call it what you will, waiting just plain pissed him off. "Son of a *bitch*," he moaned. "Is this gonna take all fu..." There it was, just a brief flash, but Bruce saw it crystal clear, as if the image were somehow burned into his retina. He saw a dimly lit hallway, papers strewn across the floor, a broken chair lying against the wall. Bruce saw all of this even though he never took his eyes off the woman. Her milky white eyes locked onto Bruce's, never once blinking, her head lowering to keep eye contact as the elevator passed her on its way down. The woman was nude and covered in scars and fresh cuts. She looked dead. The elevator stopped violently, jerking to a halt, then slowly began to rise until Bruce saw the light from the hallway once more. He stood up on his toes and peered over the ledge. The woman was no longer standing near the elevator; she now stood at the other end of the hallway. Bruce's chin was barely above the floor when the lift stopped. A glint of light caught his eye; it was a key on a ring attached to something small and flat that looked like an ID tag. Bruce squeezed his arm through the bars of the criss-crossed wrought iron door, stretching as far is it would go. *Almost there*, he thought, just another inch and his fingers would be on it. Bruce looked down the hallway and saw the woman was gone. His fingertips found the key and he gently pulled it across the tiled floor until it was close enough to grab. The elevator made a loud creaking sound and dropped an inch. Bruce balled the key up in his fist and began to work his arm back through the iron door. The woman abruptly appeared out of nowhere. The lift squealed and dropped another inch; if it dropped again, Bruce feared he would lose his arm. The woman reached down and grabbed Bruce's arm with both of her ice-cold hands. The lift creaked again and Bruce closed his eyes, expecting the worse. The woman was strong, even if she *was* dead. The elevator gave a shudder but did not drop. Bruce saw the woman's face right up against the bars, and she opened her mouth saying, "Help me." The woman let go of Bruce's arm and he fell back onto the hard metal floor. The sound of a cable snapping ripped through the air overhead and the elevator plummeted. It only lasted a few seconds, but never the less, Bruce's life flashed before his eyes in the moments before the hydraulic brake kicked in. The lift squealed as it came to a halt, bouncing several times before stopping completely. The door opened to the right like an iron accordion and Bruce stood up and stepped out. He felt a cool breeze blowing against his face and the distinct smell of salt water filled his nose. Bruce heard a sound carried with the wind; was someone calling his name?

(V)

Lisa watched the figure on the monitor as he slowly walked towards the pier. Waves splashed all around, sending a mist into the air that distorted the man's features. He wasn't wearing the dull gray jumpsuit like the rest of the patients. His hair blew in the breeze as he crossed the sandy white beach and at once, Lisa recognized him. "Bruce?" she said. The power went out.

CHAPTER SEVEN

The Calling

(I)

Derek sat on the floor in the corner of the electrical room. He opened his eyes, and for a brief moment he thought he was awake until he heard a sound, a loud splintering crash like lightning striking a tree. The vision always started with this sound and Derek knew what would come next. The room looked the same as it did the very first time he had this dream, the cold gray electrical boxes, the lights above his head flickering on and off. Derek heard footsteps but could not turn his head to see who was approaching. Someone whispered his name. Derek felt the sharp pain of the knife sliding into his gut. This is where the vision always ended, but not today. Derek looked at the hand clenching the knife; it was a woman's. His eyes followed the arm up to the shoulder, the neck, the face… Lisa Spencer's face!

(II)

Gillian sat on a petrified tree stump in the middle of a makeshift encampment. Half rotted pallets and tree limbs made up a small shelter and a fire burned in the middle of the clearing. Dr. Alan Carlton leaned against a tree puffing on one of Gillian's cigarettes. "I thought you quit," Gillian said. "Hey, I'm already dead," Carlton replied. "What do I have to worry about?" He smiled and inhaled another lungful of smoke.

"Oh, I don't know," Gillian said. "Around here, you could end up as one giant walking tumor." "Hey, that might be an improvement over this." Dr. Carlton motioned to his face with the lit end of his cigarette. "Thanks for the smoke by the way. That reminds me, I have something for you." Carlton ducked inside the shelter momentarily and reemerged with a purple and green knapsack that had seen better days. Carrying the bag by the straps, he walked over to Gillian and placed it on the ground at her feet. Carlton stuck his arm inside and pulled out a handful of CD's. "His creatures removed all of the disks, but I was able to retrieve some of them, the most recent ones anyway." Gillian took the stack of disks and placed them on her lap, there were six in all, each labeled Thomas Hunter.

"Is all this…" Gillian looked up at the trees above her head as she spoke. "I mean, everything that's going on around here… is it because of him?"

"It would seem so," Carlton answered.

"How is all this possible?" Gillian was asking herself this question more than Dr. Carlton. "How can this all be… *real*?"

"Sorry, I don't have any more answers than you do." Dr. Carlton sat down in the dirt next to Gillian. "I know two things," he said. "One, I'm dead. Two, I'm sitting here talking to you. That's real enough for me. As for what's going on out there… I'm at a loss. Two brilliant minds such as our own, I'm sure if we put them together we could come up with some answers." Gillian smiled and took Dr. Carlton's hand.

(III)

"Bruce," the voice called out. He followed the sound in the darkness until he stood at the end of a long wooden pier. Bruce Spencer stared out into the ocean. Is this what had summoned him? Bruce had spent most of his life out at sea. When he was a boy, his father took him and his older brother Andrew out during summer vacation. They spent days on the water. Bruce's first date with Lori was a candle lit dinner on the deck of the boat somewhere off the coast of Cape Cod. Bruce's thoughts shifted, focusing solely on his wife. "I miss you…" The words left his lips as no more than a whisper. He had been wrong; it wasn't the ocean calling him. Bruce tried to block out the voice calling to him, the voice that he should not be hearing, the voice of his dead wife. "Bruce…" The phantom voice called from behind him, somewhere down the beach. Bruce turned and walked slowly down the pier. He stepped out onto the soft white sand and began to walk. *"Help me…"* another voice called out. *"Daddy… Daddy, help me…"* It was his daughter… it was Ashley. It was hard to tell which direction the voices were coming from. Bruce scanned the beach in all directions looking for some sign of life. *"Ashley,"* he cried out. The wind died down at just the right moment for Bruce to hear the reply. *"Daddy… Over here."* He saw her now, lying on the beach near the water off in the distance. Bruce ran down the beach toward the figure sprawled out on the shore. His heart raced. Ashley's clothes were tattered and torn, her skin a deep blue. Bruce fell to his daughter's side and pulled her into his arms. "I'm here baby, I'm here," he sobbed. She was so cold. It was like cradling a block of ice. Bruce placed her back down into the sand and lowered his ear to her lips. She didn't seem to be breathing. He felt her chest, checked her pulse. Nothing. Bruce closed his eyes and stood up. There was a memory trying to work its way to the surface of his consciousness. Bruce couldn't think straight. The island, the dreams… That's it! "You couldn't have washed up on this shore. This isn't real." Bruce looked down at his daughter; she was moving! No… the sand *around* her was moving. Fingers wiggled their way free and quickly became hands. There were dozens of them and they grabbed onto Ashley and began to pull her down into the earth. Just as her head was about to go under her arms shot straight up into the air, reaching for her father. She opened her eyes. "Daddy… Help me!" she screamed. Her head went under, leaving only her arms above the sand. Bruce grabbed hold of his daughter and pulled. Her arms were cold and damp, and he was losing his grip. Ashley's hands clamped around her father's wrists like a vice and she pulled. In one quick motion,

Bruce disappeared into the sand with his daughter.

(IV)

Lisa shut down the laptop and tried to wake up Derek. It was no use. Whatever dream he was having required his presence there, not here. *Screw it,* she thought. *I'm going out by myself.* On her hands and knees, Lisa crawled into the vent and disappeared. She decided to leave it up to fate or intuition, either one would be just fine with her. At each intersection she let her gut tell her which direction to take. Lisa came to another intersection and stopped. Instinct told her to go left. As she crawled, she noticed something; either the shaft was getting bigger or she was shrinking. Lisa didn't spend too much time thinking about it; in this place, both were possible. Before long, Lisa was able to stand and walk, her footfalls echoing within the aluminum walls of the vent shaft. Every so often there were slits cut into the walls allowing a bright orange light to illuminate her path. The shaft creaked and groaned with every step she took, making it hard to hear much else. Several yards later and Lisa found herself standing in front of what appeared to be a door, but there was no knob, no visible hinges. She wasn't even sure it *was* a door. "Great… What now?" Lisa said aloud.

The door creaked open all by itself. A great light flooded the shaft, making it impossible to see. Lisa stepped through the doorway and stood in the long hallway of an apartment building. Both ends of the hall were engulfed in flames. The smoke filled her lungs, burning her throat on the way down. Lisa coughed and placed her hand to her face, covering her mouth and nose to keep out the soot. Rows of doors lined the hall on either side. Lisa tried the door closest to her; it was locked. She made her way down the hall trying each door as she passed until one finally opened. Lisa looked up at the number on the door. 13. "Isn't *that* just great," Lisa mumbled as she pushed the door open and entered the room.

A sweet scent filled Lisa's nose when she opened the door. There were thousands of candles burning covering every available inch of the apartment. In the center of the room was a small, two-foot wide patch of floor that led to another room in the back. Lisa carefully made her way through the field of flames as the glowing tongues licked her ankles. She stopped just shy of entering the room. Another smell drifted out through the open doorway that was much stronger than the candles. The smell of death was overpowering as Lisa entered the room. There were fewer candles here, some on the dresser, a few more on the nightstand. The soft glow of the flickering flames cast shadows across the crimson walls. At first it looked like wet paint until Lisa's eyes grew accustom to the dim light. She saw the source of the stench… and the blood.

62

The body of a woman lay sprawled out on the bed. Her hands and feet were bound to the posts with what looked like fishing line. Lisa saw deep cuts on the dead girl's wrists and ankles, no doubt from her struggles as she drew her final breath. The woman had fiery red hair and a fairly pretty face.

Her torso was sliced open from neck to groin and her large breasts hung to the side of the open wound. The woman's organs had been removed and arranged around her lifeless body. Her dead eyes stared up at the ceiling as if in longing. "Longing for what?" Lisa wondered aloud. An end to her tortures no doubt. Lisa walked past the bed, avoiding a random pile of entrails on the floor and opened the room's single window. She leaned out and drew in a deep breath of not so fresh air. *Smells like New Jersey*, she thought. As she turned, her foot struck something, sending the object under the bed. Lisa got down on her hands and knees and lifted up the sheet. Carefully, she stretched out her arm until her fingers found what she was searching for. She pulled it out and carried it over to the window. In her hand, Lisa held a blood soaked black leather wallet. She opened it, and in the pouch where you would normally find money were several obituaries cut out from various newspapers, all about young women. The only other thing in the wallet was a New York state drivers license. The name on it read Thomas R. Hunter. Lisa stared hard at the photo of the man. She had seen him before. She had spoken to him in her vision on the pier.

(V)

The call came just before eight o'clock. Jason "Wit" Whitney was sitting down for his nightly dose of bachelor chow when the phone rang. He stared down at the microwave dinner and frowned. Even though it wasn't much better than the rations he was forced to eat while in the field, it was still dinner, and Whitney was starving after the fourteen-hour flight home. Reluctantly, he pushed the meal towards the center of the table, stood, and went in search of the phone. He found it under a pile of laundry that still lay in wait for the washing machine, beneath the suit he had worn to his mother's funeral. Had he been gone that long? Wit pressed the answer button and placed the receiver to his ear.

"Hello?" He was answered by a stern female voice. "Captain Whitney, this is Lieutenant Briggs. Operation Wake-Up-Call has been put into effect. You are to catch a flight at twenty-one hundred hours to Norfolk. Admiral Forsythe will be awaiting your arrival." Wit was about to respond when he realized the line was dead; the Lieutenant had already hung up. "*Fuck!*" Whitney screamed. He held up the phone and dialed Karen's number. It only rang once. Wit pulled the phone away from his ear just in time, he had learned his lesson the last time he was deployed indefinitely. It had taken three days to get the hearing back in his ear.

"*Ahhh!*" the voice squealed over the receiver. "You're home!"

63

Wit placed the phone back to his ear. "Damn baby," he said. "You got the dogs howling across the lake.

Listen, I just got called back out…"

"But you just got home!" Karen complained.

Wit pulled the phone away from his ear for a moment. *I'm going to pay for that one,* he thought. "I'm sorry, baby, but this is one of those calls I thought would never come. I've got no choice."

"When will you be back?" she asked.

"I don't know," Wit sighed. "I don't know."

"Fine!" Karen hissed angrily. Whitney began to say 'I love you' but the line was already dead. "What is it with women hanging up on me?" Wit screamed. He threw the receiver across the room; it hit the wall and landed in the same pile of laundry that the phone had called home for the past four months.

Wit had seen some pretty strange shit in his ten years under the Admiral. He had seen enough to not ask questions and to take things as they came. As a boy, Jason Whitney had had a *wonderful* imagination. He spent days at a time staring out the window of his small bedroom, imagining a whole other world on the other side of the thin pane of glass, a world he could see but never touch. Jason grew older and that world began to fade, as all things do, eroded by time and corrupted by memory. Though some memories fade, others stay sharp and clear in our minds, some forced there by trauma while others are held in place by love. It was Wit's love of numbers that drove him. He excelled at mathematics and language, be it human or binary and, by the time he was seventeen, Wit had already graduated from high school and was just one year shy of obtaining his Masters at Harvard. There wasn't a computer on this planet that Wit couldn't hack, given enough time and the right software. The software was the easy part, as Wit wrote all the programs himself, spending weeks at a time looking at nothing but lines of code. Uncle Sam was lucky that Wit had decided to use his powers for good. At the age of twenty-five, Wit quit his job as a software developer, moved from Silicon Valley to San Diego, and joined the Navy. SEAL training was tough, but Wit had always kept himself in shape, the result of too many schoolyard beatings as a child. He breezed through training and quickly climbed the ranks, eventually commanding his own team.

It was the summer of 1999 when Wit took his team into the hills of Afghanistan, hot on the heels of a rouge Marine said to be trading information with the Taliban. What they found was far from what they had been looking for. Wit's team trailed their mark to a system of caves deep in the mountians.

They followed the Marine, silently trailing the man for three hours, until the cave opened up into a large cavern. Wit's team had split up, individually taking separate routes into the small encampment, a suicide mission. Wit himself had trailed the Marine to a large tent guarded by two heavily armed men. Two more men stood outside talking next to a Jeep, both with pistols tucked into belts on their robes. The two men guarding the tent spoke to the Marine, but Wit only caught snatches of the conversation. Wit was positioned close to the Jeep, and the two men stationed there argued in Arabic, drowning out what the

Marine had said to the guards. The traitor entered the tent and Wit waited. He listened to the men by the Jeep continue their argument, one speaking in a Saudi dialect, the other Turkish. They were arguing about the price of some eggs in a crate in the back of the Jeep and that's when things got a little fuzzy. No matter how hard Wit tried, he could not remember the events that took place that fateful night. All he could remember was hearing a terrifying scream from somewhere in the shadows behind him. Something had lunged at Wit in the darkness, tearing a nearly fatal wound in his throat. Wit ran his fingers over the scar absently as he fought to hold on to the memory. Even now, everything went black at that point. Wit remembered hearing gunfire and the Saudi screaming, "Ghala!" over and over again, and then… nothing. Wit had woken up three days later aboard a carrier somewhere in the Persian Gulf. He was told that he was the only member of his team to have made it out of the caves alive, that he had been found by a young boy on the outskirts of a small town, about thirty-five miles north of the entrance to the cavern. Wit could remember nothing more of what had happened that night, only what had followed.

Captain Jason Whitney received the transfer orders when he returned to San Diego; the Admiral was kind enough to hand them to Wit personally. The Admiral told Wit that he was not the only one to lose men that night. Admiral Robert Forsythe then laid the foundation for all that Jason Whitney would come to know in the years ahead. Whitney's eyes were reopened when he joined the Admiral's team. Wit quickly learned that the imaginary world outside the window of his childhood really existed and he *could* touch it. Wit had seen things that would make a grown man piss his pants. Hell, though he might not admit it, Wit had done it *himself* a time or two. You see, all of our worst nightmares, the monsters of myth and lore, all of them are *real*! And Jason Whitney had seen them with his own eyes. The Admiral called them demons, said they take the form of our worst nightmares because that is all they know. They live in the places of our dreams, Heaven and Hell both within our minds. Whitney had his own theories, but they made no more sense than the Admiral's, and besides, Wit had seen enough to validate some of what the

Admiral had told him. And if he was right, if we all have the ability to touch Heaven and Hell within our dreams, then maybe the Admiral's pet project *did* succeed. Project Lucidity *must* have been a success, or Captain Jason Whitney would not have been given the orders. Who knew what was happening on the island at that very moment, what new terrors the dreaming minds had unleashed? After that fateful night in the summer of 1999, Wit was always prepared for anything, never turning his back, never dropping his guard. As a Commander, Jason Whitney had seen firsthand what could happen if you relaxed too much, took too much for granted. It had happened to his commanding officer not long after Wit had joined the Admiral's team. Wit would have to be smarter than that, would have to remember to think like the dreaming mind, and not question what he saw, just act. Jason Whitney tossed his microwave dinner into the garbage and began repacking his bags.

CHAPTER EIGHT

The Children

(I)

"Excuse me, miss… Could you give me a hand with this?" Lisa turned to find the corpse on the bed no longer staring at the ceiling. It was looking directly at her, and it was talking! "My guts, I mean, would you mind helping me put them back in? I'd do it myself, but as you can see, I'm kinda' tied up right now." The corpse laughed as she said this. Lisa just stood there, a look of surprise and horror on her face. "No?" the corpse continued speaking. "Over there, the top drawer of the dresser. There's a pair of scissors; would you at least cut me loose?" Lisa stood frozen in her spot. "C'mon, honey, I won't bite. Besides, it looks to me like you've got some questions that need answering, am I right? My name's Cherry. You want to know about Thomas Hunter, don't you?" Lisa nodded. "Top drawer, darling." Cherry motioned towards the dresser with her chin. Lisa crossed the room, opened the drawer and rummaged through the contents until she found the scissors. She walked carefully back to the bed so as not to step on Cherry's lower intestine. Leaning over, Lisa cut the fishing line that bound the woman's feet. She then moved on to the woman's wrists, trying not to gag from the stench as she leaned in close.

"Thank you, dear," Cherry said as she sat up in the bed.

"Lisa… My name is Lisa."

"Thank you, Lisa." Cherry extended her hand. "Who knows how long I'd have been stuck in here if you hadn't come along."

"Don't you find this just a little bit weird?" Lisa said as she shook the woman's ice-cold hand. "I mean, look at you, how can you be up and moving around, and *talking*?"

Cherry just smiled. "In my line of work, honey, you get used to weird."

Lisa found herself wondering what line of work that might be. One look at the woman's trashy clothes heaped on the floor gave her the answer. "So, tell me about Thomas Hunter." Lisa said, sitting down next to Cherry on the blood soaked bed. "Is he the one who did this to you?"

"Me and at least twenty five other women," Cherry replied casually.

"The obituaries." Lisa pulled them out of the wallet and placed them on the bed. "There are only sixteen here."

"Some were never found," Cherry said. "Some weren't even missed."

"What about you?" Lisa asked.

"Me? Oh, I was found, but never identified."

"Huh?"

"The fire…" Cherry extended her arm, pointing past the room of candles towards the front door. "He took care of that before he left."

"Where is he now?" Lisa asked.

"Look out the window."

Lisa collected the scraps of paper and returned them to the wallet, which she slipped into her back pocket. She rose from the bed and crossed the floor to the open window. Lisa heard a slurping sound and turned to find Cherry pulling up handfuls of her innards and placing them back in the empty chest cavity. *Yuck,* Lisa thought to herself as she leaned out the window.

(II)

Bruce stood up and looked around; he was alone. "Ashley!" he called out. "Ash, where are you?" Bruce listened to his echo as he began to walk. The passageway was about four feet wide by seven-feet tall, with arched ceilings that were lined with electrical conduit. Every so often, Bruce saw small barred openings next to the wall, rising up from the floor. Drains no doubt. Lighting was sparse in the tunnels as he made his way through the semi-darkness. Bruce heard noises coming from the drains, the scuttling and squeaking of rats, when something at the far end of the passageway caught his eye. Before he could get a good look at it, it had disappeared. "That must have been one big ass rat," Bruce told himself. When he reached the end of the hall, Bruce noticed something on the floor, prints of some type. He got down on one knee to examine the wet prints, they hade been left by a small dog. The tracks led Bruce down several darkened corridors, past doors filled with humming, chugging machinery. Bruce made a mental note to return here later to get gas for the boat. Every so often, Bruce caught glimpses of the creature he was pursuing. Was it leading him somewhere? Bruce froze as he turned the corner. At the end of the hallway stood the animal he'd been chasing; it was his daughter Ashley's schnauzer, Frank!

Bruce and Lori had taken their daughter for a walk to get an ice cream cone on her sixth birthday. Ashley screamed as she watched the small black puppy cross the road. Bruce remembered how his daughter's scream had mixed with the sound of the car's brakes squealing as it tried to stop, creating a sound that made Bruce want to grab the nearest sharp object and stab himself in the ears. Ashley sobbed as she knelt down next to the blood soaked puppy on the side of the road. Lori had stayed by Ashley's side as Bruce ran home to get the car. They drove the dog to the nearest veterinarian and waited, Ashley curled up on her mother's lap, sobbing. The puppy wore no collar and, after several surgeries, several attempts to find the schnauzer's owner, along with several thousand dollars, Bruce finally gave into his daughter's pleas to keep the animal. Due to the amount of stitches holding the wounded puppy together, Ashley had jokingly called him Frankenschnauzer and somehow, the name had stuck.

Frank stood before Bruce in the doorway, water dripping from his furnishings onto the tiled floor of the hall beyond. Bruce looked around at the papers strewn across the floor, the splinters of wood from the broken chair leaning against the wall, and he suddenly realized where he was. It was the hallway he had seen from the elevator. The dog walked slowly down the hallway and stopped before a metal and glass portal in the wall. The sign above the door read: AIRLOCK. Next to the portal was a small keypad and a round lock. Remembering the key he'd retrieved, Bruce reached into his pocket and pulled it out. He held the ring up to the nearest light and read the tag. Bingo! AIRLOCK. He placed the key into the slot and turned. The keypad lit up and a voice from a tiny speaker chimed. "Please enter your passcode." Bruce removed the key and placed it back into his pocket. He reached down to pet Frank. The schnauzer pushed his head into Bruce's hand as he scratched the dog's ear. Bruce lifted the dog into his arms and held onto him tight. A cold wet nose roamed his face, a soft pink tongue licked his cheek, and from behind him there was a voice. "You're lucky."

Bruce turned and saw the woman standing in the hallway behind him. It was the same woman he had seen from the elevator, her naked body covered in scars. She pointed at Frank. "He's been wandering around here for a few days now, never lets me get near him. Is he yours?"

"My daughter's," Bruce answered. "Would you like to pet him?"

The woman slowly moved closer and Frank began to growl.

"It's all right boy, she's not going to hurt you." Frank stopped growling as the woman reached out and stroked the dog's fur, tears filling her eyes.

"Are you ok, Miss…?"

"My name's Danielle. Danielle Harris." The woman dried the tears from her eyes with the back of her wounded hands, smearing blood across her cheeks and forehead. Bruce listened as Danielle recounted the past week's events from her perspective. How things had changed. How others, and then herself, had died. Bruce, in return, told his story leading up to their current conversation.

"When I saw you before you wanted my help. What can I do?" Bruce asked when the woman had finished speaking.

"I need to find my baby." Danielle hung her head and sobbed once more.

"You're baby? Do you know where it is?" Bruce asked.

"Hunter has her," Danielle said in a terrified voice. "Is your Daughter's name Ashley?" she asked slowly.

"Yes!" Bruce shouted, not able to contain the excitement in his voice. "Have you seen her?" The woman said nothing for a moment, then reached out and took Bruce's hand. "You need to know something,

Bruce. Like me and most everyone else around here, even Frank …" she paused to stroke the dog's ears.

"She's dead."

"I don't care. All I know is that she needs me and I have to find her. Whatever it takes. Do you know where she is?" Bruce demanded.

"Hunter has her as well." A look of anger came over Bruce's face. "Who is this Hunter, and where can I find the son-of-a-bitch?" Danielle told Bruce everything she knew about Thomas Hunter, which wasn't much, mostly things she had learned from the programmers. Danielle herself had never spoken to him. Patients were not allowed to enter each other's programs, and with Hunter being in a coma, that was the only way to speak to him, she explained.

"Here…" Bruce handed Frank to Danielle when she was finished speaking. "Hold on to him for a few minutes, I need to go back to the generator room. I'll come back for you when I'm done."

"And then what?" Danielle asked.

"Then…" Bruce said. "We go and get our children back!"

(III)

Blam… Blam… The sound of gunfire rose from the street below. Lisa watched as a blood soaked Thomas Hunter hid behind a dark blue Monte Carlo while several police officers opened fire on him. He reached his arm up over the hood and took several shots without looking, hitting one officer in the arm. Another fell to the pavement as a bullet entered his eye socket and exited through the back of the man's skull. "How did the cops find him?" Lisa asked Cherry as she watched the scene unfold.

"I was able to get a few screams in before he knocked me out and tied me up," the prostitute explained.

"I'm guessing one of the neighbors heard me and called the cops."

Hunter squatted down behind the car as the firing continued, he removed the clip from his gun. Hunter stood up from his cover and leveled the pistol at the officers. "You can't kill *me*, you motherfuckers!" he screamed as the cops opened fire.

Thomas Hunter was struck several times, but it was the headshot that took him down, putting him in the gutter with his discarded clip and the rest of the garbage. Lisa pulled herself back through the open window and watched as Cherry continued to stuff her organs back in. She didn't seem to be having too much luck. As soon as she put a heap in, one oozed back out.

"So when did all of this happen?" Lisa asked.

"Shit…" Cherry seemed to be getting frustrated as her innards fell back out onto the bed. "Let's see… Close to two years ago." Cherry got up from the bed and walked over to the window. "It's time for you to go, dear. He's looking for you."

"Who?" Lisa asked.

"Him…" Lisa's eyes followed Cherry's bloody finger as her arm extended out toward the window pointing to the body of Thomas Hunter. Lisa watched an ambulance screeched to a halt in the street. The doors opened and two EMT's exited with a stretcher. When Lisa turned around, the room was empty and Cherry was gone. Lisa walked through the field of candles to the front entrance, turning once to scan the room, and then opened the door. The flames had engulfed most of the hallway. There was no place to go. Lisa stared into the flames. She felt disoriented, her stomach turned and her head spun, and she closed her eyes. The heat from the flames scorched Lisa's skin as she contemplated what to do. When she opened her eyes, she discovered she was no longer in the hallway, but now stood before a raging bonfire.

Dozens of vile looking creatures sat around the fire feasting on the remains of two small children. Lisa screamed. A thousand thoughts filled her head. *Is this how I die?* Lisa suddenly found herself wishing for the knowledge that Derek possessed. It wouldn't be so bad, at least she'd know when to fight and when to just give up, but *could* she just give up? Could there be a way to change the outcome? So many thoughts… *Focus.* The church… *What if what's in there is worse then what's out here? What if it's locked?* Lisa noticed the torches illuminating a path to her right. *Sure beats running through the woods in the dark,* she thought. *Fuck it, RUN!* Lisa ran as if her life depended on it because, well, it did. Lisa could hear the creatures behind her and she chanced a look over her shoulder as she approached a turn in the path; they were catching up quickly. The creature's screams filled Lisa's ears, the crunching of the leaves under the monster's feet sounding like static. Lisa was about to turn her head and re-focus her attention on the path when she hit something hard. Everything went black as her body came crashing down into the dirt. Lisa felt something pulling on her arm, dragging her into the woods. She felt a hand over her mouth, ice cold, the stench appalling. Thousands of colors swam before Lisa's eyes as she tried desperately to hang on to consciousness. Her limp body was lifted from the ground and slung over a strong shoulder. The last thing Lisa heard before the blackness took her was the sound of the creatures pursuing her.

(IV)

Bruce retraced his way back to the boiler room. The hinges squealed as the door opened and Bruce stepped through. The room was huge, much larger than the island. Hundreds of furnaces threw off heat and noise while blinding yellow-orange flames burned brightly inside of their large slotted-iron doors. On the far side of the room, Bruce found several fifty-five gallon drums sitting on the edge of a large concrete hole filled with stagnant water that smelled like a New York City sewer. Bruce found two drums filled with gasoline and, after rummaging through the nearby storage rooms, he emerged with two large gas cans and a hand pump. He placed them down on the ground next to the barrels and loosened the cap on one of the drums. Bruce slid the long shaft of the pump down into the hole, connected the hose to the first gas can, and began to wind the crank. When the can was full, Bruce removed the hose and tightened the cap. He reached for the second container and heard a loud splash in the pool of muck to his left. Bruce turned and watched the sludgy surface of the water ripple. A loud squeal filled the air and another splash soaked the front of Bruce's shirt as something fell from above, then another, and yet another. Something moved across the surface of the water, reached the concrete ledge, climbed out and scurried away. "Only a rat," Bruce said as he recognized the creature. Just as he returned his attention the gas can, another rat fell from the ceiling, splashing muck up onto the concrete floor near Bruce's feet. Then, as if the sky had opened up, the rats fell in dozens, hundreds, perhaps. The furry black waterfall continued to flow, screams and squeals echoing throughout the room. Bruce slipped the hose into the second gas can and started pumping. The creatures no longer scurried away into the darkness of the room, clinging together as they fell and landed, forming a pile within the reservoir. Bruce watched the pile grow. The rats that didn't land in just the right place scampered about until finding the correct position. They were building something… Bruce pumped faster, until gasoline spilled out of the nozzle. He replaced the cap on the can and set it down next to the first. The rat pile was growing, taking shape, and Bruce began to make out some of the details. Arms were beginning to form, protruding from the large torso of the beast. Rats scurried down its limbs to form hands and fingers. Bruce pushed the barrel of fuel over, adjusting the drum so its contents poured into the reservoir. A rainbow of colors spread across the surface of the water surrounding the creature. A head was beginning to form as the features of its face squirmed and writhed. Bruce uncapped the second drum of gasoline and pushed it over next to the first. "I hope it's enough," he said as he picked up the two smaller gas cans and began to slowly back away. The creature tilted its head back and opened its large mouth to scream. The sound of a thousand rats screeching echoed throughout the cavernous room. Just then, as if someone had turned off a valve, the flow of rats trickled to a halt. The creature leaned forward and looked right at Bruce.

"I hope you're hungry!" Bruce yelled as he reached behind him and pulled out the flare gun that was tucked into the back of his jeans. *Last flare,* he thought. *Better make it count.* The creature opened its maw and lunged at Bruce. "Eat this." Bruce fired the flare into the water around the beast. The creature let out an ear-shattering scream as the flames engulfed the fur of the rats. The monster thrashed, splashing more gasoline up onto its body, spreading the flames more rapidly. Bruce threw the empty gun into the pool, grabbed the two cans of gas, and headed for the door. He paused to smile as the creature's screams died out and stopped, then opened the door and took the hallway leading back to the airlock where he had discovered Frank and Danielle. They were gone. It figured… *damn it!*

CHAPTER NINE

The Hunter

(I)

Consciousness came back slowly. Lisa tried to sit up, but the spinning was too much, her head hurt like the demons of hell were hammering her brains out. She closed her eyes to ride out the nausea. She heard voices, but had no idea how many people were talking, and in her current state she could hardly even make out what was being said. As the minutes passed, the spinning subsided, and Lisa began to understand some of what the voices were discussing. She heard a woman's voice that sounded vaguely familiar, and a man was speaking as well, but there was something not quite right with his voice. Lisa opened her eyes and discovered that her vision had returned, but quickly wished it hadn't, for standing over her was the man. Most of the skin on his face was missing and his huge, once gray but now extremely bloodshot eyes stared at her through glasses that were somehow fused to his skull.

"Shhh…" The man put a finger to where his lips should be. "They're still out looking for you." Confused, Lisa sat up and looked around. She was under a makeshift shelter in a small clearing. In the middle of the clearing, Lisa saw a fire and, next to it sat a woman whom Lisa recognized right away.

"Where's Bruce?" Lisa asked Dr. Black.

"We were separated," Gillian said as she stood up and made her way to Lisa's side.

"We need to find him, I…I think he's in trouble."

"As soon as those *things* return to the church we can leave. Until then, we stay right here." The man spoke now. Lisa noticed the ID card pinned to the right side of his lab coat: Dr. Alan Carlton.

"Ok…" Lisa said, "then tell me about Thomas Hunter."

Gillian looked at Carlton then back at Lisa. "That's funny, we were just talking about him."

"How much do you know about him?" Lisa asked.

"He was our first patient," Gillian said. "He came into our care about a year ago."

"He was a donation from our military backers," Carlton added. "Comatose for several months, the perfect subject for our tests."

"Did they tell you what happened to him?" Lisa asked.

"Gunshot wound to the head," Gillian said. "He has no living relatives and, since he's a vet, he wound up in a military hospital for a while. Hunter was part of the terms of our funding…" Before she could finish, Lisa interrupted. "They didn't tell you how he got shot, did they?"

"No," Gillian replied, "we never asked. Why?"

Lisa reached into her back pocket, pulled out the bloodstained wallet, and handed it to Gillian. "Open it," Lisa said.

"What's this?" Gillian asked. She opened the wallet and several small pieces of paper fell out onto the ground. Gillian bent down to pick them up and stopped as her eyes lit on the photo on the license. She scooped up the scraps of paper and handed the wallet to Dr. Carlton. "What *are* these?" she asked.

"Some of his victims," Lisa said flatly.

"His *what*?" Gillian sounded confused.

"Just read them."

"Where did you get this?" Carlton asked as he handed the wallet back to Lisa.

"I met Hunter's final victim, then I saw him get shot by the police," Lisa said nervously.

"Wait a minute," said Carlton. "You're not making any sense."

"Have you noticed any places that just shouldn't be here?" Lisa asked. "I mean places that weren't part of your program?"

"Come to think of it," said Carlton, "yeah."

"I saw my uncle on the beach while I was looking over some of the sessions," Lisa continued. "When I tried to go look for him, I ended up in an apartment building somewhere. New Jersey, I think. Anyway, I met a dead woman named Cherry. She said she was Hunter's last victim."

"I don't recall anyone named Cherry around here," Carlton said.

"That's the thing…" Lisa added. "I don't think I was *here* anymore."

"Then where were you?" Gillian asked.

"I don't know," Lisa said. "Something just felt different about that place."

"How do you mean?" Inquired Carlton.

"I can't say. It was just a feeling."

"You said you saw Hunter get shot?" Gillian asked.

"Yes, I watched it happen from Cherry's apartment window. He murdered her, and then set the building on fire. Someone called the cops while he was busy carving her up. They were waiting for him when he left."

"And you saw all of this?" Carlton asked skeptically.

Lisa nodded as Gillian handed the scraps of paper to Dr. Carlton.

"He killed all of these women?" Gillian asked.

"And then some," Lisa stated. "Cherry said there were at least twenty five women."

"That's just great!" Gillian complained. "They give us a psychopath without telling us? If I get out of here alive I'm taking *this* one to the board!"

Carlton chuckled. Lisa waited for some sort of comeback but Dr. Black said nothing. Neither did Dr. Carlton; both of them just stood there as if frozen in time.

Gillian had a sly look on her face, the remnants of her last words still on her lips. Carlton stood arched back, his head in the air, his laughter stopped… everything had stopped! Even the fire, though somehow, Lisa still felt the heat from its frozen flames. And she felt something else… "You astound me," said a voice from behind her, Lisa didn't need to turn to know who it was.

"And you, Thomas R. Hunter, *disgust* me," Lisa hissed, keeping her back to the voice.

"Ah, but you respect me."

"Like hell I do!" Lisa shot back.

"Because I can do what you long to do," Hunter continued. "Understand your dreams. *I* understand *mine* Lisa, and understanding is the first step to controlling."

Lisa turned, ready to lunge at Hunter, but stopped cold when she saw what he was holding. It was a baby. "More like controlling others," Lisa said calmly. "Is that what you really want? Do you like playing God that much?"

Hunter laughed. "It amuses me."

"Oh, I bet it does… Just like butchering all of those women?"

"That?" Hunter waved off the question. "That was just a phase. Lets say I was… looking for God."

"And now you've become one," Lisa pointed out.

"I *do* love the irony," Hunter chuckled. "Come, there are things you must see."

Lisa noticed the scenery around her began to grow fuzzy. Suddenly, everything started spinning. Lisa reached out for something, *anything,* to steady her balance. She felt Hunter's strong grip as he grabbed her arm with his free hand.

"Close your eyes," he said. "It'll pass."

(II)

Lisa opened her eyes to find she was no longer in the woods with Gillian and Carlton. She stood in the cavernous entranceway of what could only be described as a mansion. It took her a few seconds to realize that she had seen this place before. The beautifully tiled floor, the carved wooden railings leading up the duel winding staircases, the giant chandelier hanging above her head that squeaked as it gently drifted back and forth. "I've seen this place," Lisa said in awe.

"Have you?" Hunter asked as he started for the stairs.

"What about that… that creature," Lisa asked nervously.

"That, my dear, is who we are here to see." Hunter cradled the infant as he slowly ascended the stairs.

"Whose child is that?" Lisa asked.

"I think you already know the answer to that question," Hunter remarked.

"Danielle Harris," Lisa said under her breath. "It was you who raped her, wasn't it?"

Hunter laughed. "Now *that* I can not take credit for; all I do is collect its children."

"Collect?" Lisa inquired.

"In time, my dear, all of your questions will be answered." Hunter said nothing more as they climbed the beautiful staircase that led to a monster. Lisa had a million questions to ask but remained silent.

Something told her that she didn't need to speak, that in *this* place, all her thoughts were known… to Hunter… or to something else. Lisa had noticed this other presence in the first dream, the one she'd had on the beach. It had been there, as well, as if the world around her were *alive*!

Lisa looked down through the shining crystals of the chandelier from the balcony of the third floor. The baby began to cry. "This way," Hunter said as he headed down the hallway in the dark. Lisa followed reluctantly. Hunter stopped at a door about halfway down the hall, fished a large key ring from his pocket, and flipped through the many keys until he came upon the one he needed. Lisa followed closely behind as Hunter entered the room. She saw a fire burning in a large stone fireplace that encompassed one entire wall. On the floor in the center of the room was a blanket where Hunter gingerly placed the infant. Hunter motioned Lisa towards two large chairs. Thrones actually, with intricately carved designs and symbols adorning them, plush velvet cushions that were soft and felt soothing to Lisa's aching body. "You're correct, by the way," Hunter said as he took his seat. The baby had stopped crying and now lay on the floor watching the shadows dance around the room. Lisa glanced around; although the fire burned bright, the corners of the room were in complete darkness, and she couldn't even *see* the walls in places. "About what?" Lisa finally asked.

"About many things," Hunter answered. "Not having to speak, the world being alive. We're not so different, you and I. I understand how you're dreams make you feel, what they can do to your life, to your mind. There's something special about you, Lisa. The others, I know where they are and what they're thinking, but you… I can only get in *your* mind when you have one of your visions, and even then my access is limited." There was a sudden noise from the darkened corner on the far end of the room. "Ah, He's here," Hunter said with a smile.

Lisa watched as the shadows began to form shapes, human shapes. She watched its limbs twist in upon themselves, only to bring forth new growth, new limbs. The creature spread across the floor like a fog towards the baby. Hunter grabbed Lisa's arm to keep her from moving. She struggled, but his grip was too strong, and Lisa could do nothing but watch as the creature spread across the floor to the middle of the room where it hovered over the infant, as if trying to inhale the child. The creature looked up at Lisa and stared at her with its empty sockets and smiled. Razor sharp teeth that seemed to grow out of the shadows within the beast's mouth gleamed in the firelight. The creature lunged and tore into the soft flesh of the infant's skull. The child bawled and wailed as the monster dragged her back into the corner, back into the darkness. The baby stopped screaming but her limbs were still moving. Lisa knew they wouldn't be for long. Hunter's grip relaxed and he let go of her arm.

"There, that wasn't so bad now, was it?" he said.

"You asshole!" Lisa spat as she stared at the empty blanket on the floor.

"If it means anything to you, the child was his," Hunter said as he sat back in the chair. Lisa cringed as the image flooded her mind, Danielle strapped to the bed, the creature raping her. Some of the pieces were beginning to take shape in her mind, but there was still too much that made no sense at all.

"Let me start at the beginning," Hunter said as he shifted in his chair. "I grew up here, in this house," he explained. "My fondest childhood memories are of this house." Hunter closed his eyes and smiled. "Why don't I show you?" As the words left his lips, the room filled with a blinding white light.

Lisa saw nothing, but heard voices, muffled at first, but they soon became clear.

"You rotten little bastard, I told you *never* to come down here!"

Shadows formed in the white light. Lisa saw the shape of a large man.

"Get over here, you little *prick*!"

Slowly the image sharpened until Lisa saw the man who was speaking. He was in his mid fifties, maybe, and must have weighed at least two hundred and seventy-five pounds. He wore a pair of dark blue overalls and a white t-shirt, had thinning gray hair cropped close to his skull, and wore a pair of large thick black-framed glasses. The man sat at an old wooden desk that had seen better days. On the desk were a lamp, a typewriter and a large stack of papers. The floor was dirt with several small throw rugs had been scattered around. Pipes lined the low ceiling and, somewhere in the darkness, Lisa could hear the humming of an old oil furnace.

"I said get the fuck *over* here!" the man screamed again.

Lisa heard the sobs of a child from somewhere in the room and the soft padding of footsteps. Out of the darkness stepped a child of no more than six or seven. He walked towards the man sitting at the desk with his head hung low. The fat man jumped up from his chair and lunged at the child. "I said get over here you little *fuck*!" the man yelled as he grabbed the young boy by his short dirty blonde hair and dragged him across the room towards a small wooden door. The fat man pushed the door open and shoved the child into the darkened room. "It's Daddy time, Hunter," the man chuckled as he unbuttoned the straps to his overalls. He slammed the door shut and the child began to scream.

"Enough!" Hunter growled angrily. The room went black. Lisa was transported next to a large oak tree at the end of a path leading through the middle of a flower garden behind the house. Lisa had not seen the outside of the home until now, and it was *huge*, looking more like a castle than a place occupied by a modern family. Hanging from a branch high in the tree next to her was a rope swing; sitting on the swing was the boy from the basement. Hunter knelt down next to the base of the tree and ran his hand across a small carving. The tree limb high above her head creaked as the swing slowly rocked back and forth. "How…" Lisa struggled for the words to express her sympathy for the young boy… the young Thomas Hunter. "You poor thing," was all she could say as she watched the child cling to the swing, sobbing his heart out, when it came to her. "Why did you show me this?" she asked. "I didn't." Hunter pointed back to the house. "*He* did. You know, I saw the old man hanging from this very tree." Hunter smiled as the memory came rushing back.

The creaking of the rope changed. Lisa looked up and saw that the boy on the swing was gone. The seat of the swing, a plastic, sand filled barbell with a rope through the center knotted on both sides, lay on the ground next to the tree. Lisa looked up. It was the fat man, Hunter's stepfather, swinging from the rest of the rope that had been cut high above the ground. Lisa looked down the path and saw the boy, a young Hunter, before he had turned into the monster he was today. Lisa looked around, but the murdering bastard was nowhere to be found. "Hunter?" She called out but got no reply. "Stop *fucking* with me Hunter!" The child showed no signs of hearing Lisa's cries as he slowly walked down the path towards her, his eyes on the old man swinging from the tree. Lisa leaned against the tree where the body hung and watched young Hunter dig down into the soil with his fingers and pull out a handful of earth. He let the dirt sift through his fingers leaving four small rocks. One by one, the child threw the rocks at the body hanging in the branches above. Lisa heard a soft *thunk* each time a rock hit the fat man. In a flash of light, the image disappeared, returning Lisa to the present. She stood beside Thomas Hunter, the boy again sitting on the swing, sobbing. "What the hell was that?" Lisa asked.

"What was what?" Hunter asked suspiciously.

She thought about what she'd seen. *Hunter must not know what I saw, where was I?* Lisa asked herself. The only answer that made sense made no real sense at all. It had been *his* vision. Lisa did not know how this was true; she only knew that it was. "The symbols," Lisa lied, pointing to the markings at the base of the tree, "What do they mean?"

"The symbols are all over the house," Hunter explained. "As a boy, I often asked mamma what the symbols carved so elegantly into the woodwork meant. She said she didn't know, but she *did* tell me that the house had been built by my great grandfather, Thomas Rothery who, upon completion of the house, had hung himself from the oak tree in the back yard. Ironic, isn't it? Come with me." Hunter led Lisa back down the path to the house.

"How long did it go on?" Lisa asked.

"Huh? Oh. About four years, though *that* was the last time."

"What happened?" Lisa asked.

"My wish came true."

They had reached the tree line on the east side of the house. Sunlight trickled through the thick branches casting long shadows across the yard. Hunter stared up at the house as if he could see through its walls. "I thought he was just a figment of my imagination for the longest time," he said. "I dreamed about him most every night. Of course, I was afraid at first, but I soon learned he would *never* harm me. He showed me things in my dreams, such *wonderful* things! Sometimes, when I awoke, I swear I heard him calling my name."

"Where does he come from?" Lisa asked.

"From the place of darkness," he answered. Hunter's cryptic reply puzzled Lisa. He seemed to be losing his focus, still staring up at the house. "Does it, the creature I mean, have a name?" she asked.

"If you so wish, you may call it Mille Umbra."

"A thousand shadows," Lisa whispered, saying the words without even thinking.

The words *Mille Umbra* were permanently imbedded in her mind. Lisa had been hearing them as far back as she could remember. It had been a while now, two months or so before taking off on this little *Birthday Cruise,* as her uncle had called it. Two months of not hearing that name, *Mille Umbra,* over and over, night after night. In most of Lisa's reoccurring dreams there was always some small thing that changed. The color of a cup, the position of a chair, the changes were noticeable after having had the same dream so many times. But *one* dream, this one *never* changed. In that dream she saw nothing. Her eyes were wide open, but there was nothing there, just an empty black void. The place of darkness as Hunter had called it. Lisa now knew they were one and the same. In her dream she heard things moving in the darkness around her, their hands on her, caressing every inch of her body, probing every opening. They were even in the air she breathed, in her lungs, and in her blood. They held her immobile and entered her in every way imaginable, while the whole time she heard two words whispered into her ear by some phantom spirit… *Mille Umbra.*

(III)

"This place is like the friggin' Energizer Bunny," Bruce muttered as he turned the corner, only to find another hallway, exactly the same as the one he had just emerged from. No doors, no nothing, just plain battleship gray paint covering every inch. He moved slowly down the dimly lit hallway wondering why he could even see at all. There were no light fixtures, at least, none that he could see. Bruce had long since given up on his search for Danielle and Frank. Bruce had walked, and walked, until he had finally had enough. He turned around and headed back in the direction he had come from. He should have been out of this hellhole long ago, but it just kept going…and going… Bruce stopped as he came to another corner in the twisting maze of hallways. Finally, something familiar, a place he recognized.

Bruce stood in front of the row of doorways wondering which was number one and which was number six. When he had been there with Lisa, the Doc, and the crazy guy, they had not come down the hallway he had been traversing for the past God knows how long, so Bruce assumed he would be standing in front of door number six. But for some reason he just stood there, not sure what to do, thinking about Ashley, thinking about Lori. He finally came to the conclusion that if it was his time to go, it was his time to go, and there wasn't anything he could do to change it. Bruce looked down at the knob on door number five. "Better not push it," he said aloud as he reached for door number six…

"Bruce." Someone called his name. Not just someone, for Bruce knew *exactly* who was calling him. *"Bruce… Over here…"* He knew that voice like a redneck knows the lyrics to "Freebird." It was his wife, Lori! Now, this presented Bruce with two problems. One: the obvious fact that Lori had been dead for four years; two: the voice was coming from behind door number five. And there was something else, more voices, screams of excitement, and music. It sounded like a carnival…

Bruce opened the door and the hallway flooded with bright sunlight. There she was, his Lori, waving to him from across the midway through a crowd of people. He turned and looked at the poorly painted blue door that shut behind him; it had a small sign that read MEN. Instantly, Bruce knew where he was, *when* he was. He turned back to look for Lori but she was gone. Bruce got up on his toes to try and see over the crowd but it was no use. He pushed his way through the throng of bodies to the other side and she was still nowhere in sight. Bruce closed his eyes, remembering that day. It was summer, two weeks after his high school graduation. Bruce had driven out to Agawam to visit a couple of pals.

They'd decided to get drunk and spend the day at a local amusement park. It was there that he had met Lori. Bruce and his friends had been standing in line for The Cyclone, a roller coaster, for quite a while. Bruce noticed her looking up at him several times, then looking away when she saw he was watching her. She had been so beautiful then. She was *always* beautiful, even in her final years, when her body slowly shut down, when she was constantly sick and rail thin. She was *still* beautiful! Bruce's mind returned to that hot summer day. He'd finally worked up the nerve to talk to Lori but couldn't decide what to say. He'd just stood in line, watching her, trying to think of something that wouldn't sound stupid. *What would a woman like that have in common with a guy like me?* he'd thought to himself? So, he waited, and as luck would have it, the carts only fit two people. Bret and Donnie, his high school buds, took a car. Bruce turned to Lori and asked if she was alone, and it had been Bruce's lucky day. He'd climbed on that roller coaster with a stranger and left with the love of his life. "The coaster," he said aloud. The memory faded and the outside world forced its way back inside Bruce's mind; he realized it had grown dark and the midway was empty, only a passing memory.

(IV)

Four nude bodies hung from two exposed beams in the ceiling of the small room, their ankles nailed to the wood with large rusted spikes that resembled railroad ties. All four victims were female, all disemboweled, torn from breast to groin, entrails hanging from gaping chest cavities and spilling out onto the floor. He heard a noise behind him and turned quickly, his heel slipping on the blood soaked floor, sending him crashing down onto the sticky, wet rug. He heard a laugh and sat up. A man stood next to one of the corpses, reeling in her small intestine like fishing line. "It's been a while," the man said. "Hunter," he mumbled.

"It's good to be remembered." Thomas Hunter smiled. He had found the end of the woman's intestine and held it up. Hunter placed the tip of the woman's entrails into her vagina and pushed in with his fingers. He reached his free hand up into the corpse's open stomach and pulled on her intestine, feeding several yards through. Hunter got down on one knee and wrapped the woman's entails around her neck several times before stuffing the remaining length into the victim's mouth. Hunter stood and appraised his handiwork with a sly grin, then turned and continued speaking, "Give my regards to the Admiral," he said. "And, Wit… it's time to wake up."

Wit sat up in his bunk, wiping the sweat from his forehead with the back of a tightly clenched fist. He swung his legs off the cot and sat in the darkness as a rush of images and memories flooded his mind.

Wit had been leading the Admiral's SEAL team for just over a year when he had first been introduced to Hunter. Admiral Forsythe assured Captain Whitney that, although Thomas Hunter lacked the training and discipline of a true Navy SEAL, he would be a valuable asset to the team. And he had been… for a while. Until Hunter's ambition for power and violence (not necessarily in that order) had consumed him, causing Hunter to strike out on his own search for the truth. A search that would take Thomas Hunter to the edge of sanity and beyond, leaving a trail of corpses in his wake that would make the most successful of mass murderers envious. Hunter had slipped through the Admiral's fingers several times before making a mistake. He had always remained one step ahead, until fate, karma, or just plain bad luck, had caught up to him in the form of a bullet in the brain. But Thomas Hunter was too evil to die. Comatose, but still alive, Hunter had been transferred to the Admiral's pet project named "Lucidity". The object of the project was to manipulate a person's dreams, make them see and feel what the operator wanted them to, the perfect weapon. Or so it had seemed. That "perfect weapon" had come back to bite the Admiral on his ass. Wit had seen enough wonders and atrocities in the past decade to know that all that he had seen and learned so far was insignificant in the grand design. There was something out there, something larger and more complex than our species could ever hope to comprehend, and Wit had seen fragments of it right before his very eyes. He'd seen reality distorted out of all recognition, he'd seen Angels and Demons and monsters of myth and lore. Wit had even stepped foot in another reality, several in fact, and on each occasion he had learned a little bit more about himself. Contact with others in the project had been forbidden, but there had been no harm in simply "checking in" on one's self, his choice for a career in an alternate reality, and sometimes, on *very* rare occasions, the result of a choice from Wit's past made flesh. Thomas Hunter was a part of that past, a part that Wit would just as soon forget, but a still a part, nevertheless. The dream from which he had recently awoken reminded Wit of just how powerful Hunter had become. The hum of the vessel's engines died, signifying their arrival at the NeuroTech compound, but Wit already knew they were there, and so did Hunter. Yes, Wit had seen many strange and terrible things in his life, and he knew without a doubt that the Admiral's "perfect weapon" had always been Thomas Hunter.

CHAPTER TEN

The Arrival

(I)

A sheet of time had been spread over the amusement park and it had not been kind. Metals were rusted, the ground covered in dirt, leaves, and paper, the walls of buildings covered with blood. All of the rides were running, all of the concession stands and game booths were open, but there was no sign of human life. Music blared from tarnished speakers atop corroded poles, streetlamps flickered on and off, occasionally exploding in a fantastic display of sparks and light. Bruce began walking in the direction of the Cyclone and listening to the distorted carnival music booming over the sound system. Bruce crossed the tarmac towards a half rotted wooden sign that read TRANCE and entered. He walked through the darkened wooden tunnels that led beneath the roller coaster until he came to set of rusty steel steps that wound to the top of the ride. Halfway up, Bruce began to feel his age. "I sure as hell better have lost some weight next time I step on a scale, *if* I live to see one again," Bruce muttered. He was getting close to the top, just two more levels to go. A loud clicking sound ensued from above as chains pulled the carts into position. Bruce forced himself up the last flight of stairs and the noise stopped. He looked up into the night sky, the glowing edges of clouds passed overhead, all but obscuring a full moon. Bruce walked down the long wooden platform hearing the sound of the boards creaking beneath his feet as he moved along.

The carts sat on the track with the safety bars up; all were empty but the last. A large television sat upside down and at a slight angle, its molded wooden legs sticking up into the air. The power cord hung over the back seat and disappeared down into the tracks. Bruce walked up to the television and reached for the knob, but before his fingers found purchase, the set came to life. Bruce jumped as the speakers blared white noise. He grabbed the small knob and turned down the volume. "Startled so easily?" said a voice from behind him… *Lori's* voice! Bruce turned to find his late wife standing on the far end of the platform by the stairs. She wore an almost see through white gown that fell to mid thigh, her long, tanned legs leading down to a pair of white high heels. Lori's jet-black hair fell to her shoulders waving lightly in the breeze. Bruce moved down the platform toward Lori until there was a loud crack beneath his feet. Bruce felt the flooring give way, leaving him no choice but to step back and watch as the platform collapsed, leaving a ten-foot wide gap between him and his wife. "Almost seems like *someone* wants to keep us apart," she said in a sultry voice. "What, you're not going to talk to me?" Lori pleaded as she walked seductively towards the edge of the hole in the platform, her hips swaying to the rhythm of her heals clicking on the wood. "Do you like what you see?" she asked.

"I always loved to look at you… even at the end," Bruce answered in a sad voice.

"Yes, I never understood that. Why *did* you stay with me?"

"Because I *loved* you!" Bruce just about screamed. Lori leaned back against a steel pole, her hands caressing her thighs. Bruce watched as her fingertips caught the thin material and pulled it up, slowly exposing her shaven pubis. Lori had always said that if a man likes a woman shaved, all he really wants is to fantasize about a twelve year old. Sure, Bruce thought it was sort of sexy, but he didn't complain, Lori kept hers neatly trimmed, so soft to the touch… Bruce needed to clear his mind; he couldn't have this *thing* turning him on. "Why did you bring me here?" he shouted.

"I wanted to see you one last time," Lori sighed.

Bruce wasn't fooled; he could always tell when his wife was putting on a show. "Why?" he asked.

"Do I need a *reason*?" Lori was starting to get defensive; this could get fun.

"Well," Bruce said with a smile, "normally when a dead person comes back to one of their loved ones it's with a message or something. Is this some sort of warning, like an impending apocalypse? Or how 'bout this, you're here to warn me, here to tell me to get off of this island, which, by the way, I'm working on." Lori just stared at Bruce as he rambled on (she'd always hated when he'd done that). She stood there with a smile on her face, a fake one at that. Why wasn't she getting mad?

"No silly, I just wanted to see you," she giggled. Lori'd had the cutest little laugh.

"Well, here I am," Bruce said. "What now?"

"I was hoping to be able to hold you, but…" Lori looked down at the hole in the platform, then up into the sky. "…but I guess *He* doesn't want me to."

"Who is *He*?" Bruce asked. Lori just stood there smiling.

Click, Click, Click… The cart began to move up the track. Bruce turned in time to see the television fall backwards off of the last cart and slam down onto the tracks. He turned his gaze back to Lori, only to discover that she'd removed her nightgown and now stood in nothing but her heels.

"Don't you wish you could touch me?" she practically moaned. Lori ran her hands slowly up her thighs across her navel and continued up to her breasts. She left one hand there and let the other travel down, her fingers finding the moistness of her sex. "Is this what you'd like to do?" she purred.

Bruce heard the coaster tearing up and down the tracks behind him, its loud *clacking* briefly taking his mind off of what he was watching. Lori now used both of her hands to fondle her sex, rubbing, caressing, slowly trailing her fingers up and pulling her sex open for him to see.

"Would you like to lick my pussy?" she moaned. "*He* likes to like my pussy."

"Who *is* he?" Bruce screamed. Lori slowly pulled one of her hands away from her groin and pointed behind him. Bruce turned to find the television screen no longer filled with white static. Bruce saw an image there, a man going down on a woman, and the woman was Lori.

"Who is he?" Bruce demanded.

"Hunter," she sighed. Bruce turned to look at Lori, then back at the screen. The man stopped what he was doing, lifted his head and stared into the camera. "Hi-ya, Bruce." The man smiled and went back to his labors.

The screen flickered and something was different. It took Bruce to a moment to notice what it was. The woman on the screen… it was no longer his wife… it was Ashley!

The coaster was nearing the platform but it didn't seem to be slowing. Bruce stepped back as it

plowed into the television, shattering it into a thousand pieces.

"Why the *fuck* did you show me that?" Bruce screamed. He turned to face Lori, who somehow now stood on the same side of the platform as Bruce. Bruce lunged at her grabbing her by the shoulders. She easily shoved him off, pushing him back towards the tracks, and throwing him down onto the wooden platform. Bruce's head slammed hard against the metal rail of the tracks and he momentarily lost consciousness. He heard the coaster chugging over a hill somewhere close by, somewhere *very* close, and realized that Lori was holding him down by the throat, his neck over the track.

"Time to say goodbye, lover!" Lori hissed. Just about out of options, Bruce rammed his knee up into her groin as hard as he could, but she just smiled and said, "Thank you sir, may I have another?" Out of the corner of his eye, Bruce saw the coaster coming over the last hill towards the loading platform and beginning to pick up speed. Not knowing what else to do, and hoping like hell it would at least startle her enough to get loose, Bruce reached down between her legs and jammed as many fingers as he could up inside of her.

"Oh, yes!" Lori screamed, "Now we're talking." Lori loosened her grip, just a little, but it was enough for Bruce to push the bitch to the right and roll her over onto her back. Bruce pulled himself up as the wheels passed where his head had just lain. He watched as Lori's body was dragged several yards before it came to rest against a far wall.

(II)

"He showed himself to me that night." Hunter explained. "After the police left, after the hearse left and whisked the body away. I was sitting in the attic when he first spoke to me."

"What did he say?" Lisa asked.

"He told me I was special, that he needed my help." Hunter walked up the front steps to the large wooden double doors. He pushed them open and entered the house, Lisa following closely behind. "He taught me how to use my gift."

"What exactly *is* your gift?" Lisa pondered aloud.

"At first it was just the dreams, seeing things that were yet to happen. But he soon taught me to leave my body at will."

"You can do that?" Lisa inquired.

"So can you, as you will soon find out." Hunter looked Lisa up and down, appraising her. "I know it's you," he continued, "I know you're the one. It seems like I've been searching forever, and now you're finally here. *He* will see it too." Lisa followed Hunter as they ascended the stairs to the third floor. He wasn't making any sense. Lisa tried to piece together what he was talking about, but she was still in the dark… always in the dark. The third floor landing led to a dimly lit hallway. Hunter stopped at the first door and once again retrieved his key ring. When he opened the door Lisa saw another staircase. She followed closely behind Hunter as they climbed, and when he stopped for a moment, their hands touched on the railing, sending Lisa's mind reeling in the blackness. When the spinning subsided, arcs of light began to swim before her eyes and the world grew brighter…

…Lisa stood in a field watching the sun slowly set over a large mountain range off in the distance; nothing looked familiar. She spied a narrow dirt road through a thicket of tall grass and began to walk. Closer to the road, Lisa saw a young man, no more than sixteen or seventeen, kicking rocks as he walked down the road ahead of her. The boy cradled something under his arm, though Lisa could not tell what it was from such a distance. She called out, but her cry went unanswered. When Lisa reached the road, she

88

saw that it stretched out for miles in both directions, leaving her with only one option: follow the boy. There was something familiar about the boy that Lisa just couldn't put her finger on yet, but she felt connected to him in some way. His sobs carried on the breeze, and as soon as she heard them, Lisa realized who the youth was.

"Hunter," Lisa called out. There was no reply, not even an acknowledgement of her presence. Lisa recalled the vision of young Thomas Hunter finding his father's corpse, how it seemed as though she had been invisible to him then, as well. "Ok," Lisa said aloud, "I'll go with it."

Eventually, the narrow dirt road widened into a clearing, a cul-de-sac of sorts, with a single gravel driveway leading into a thick canopy of trees. Lisa stopped when she noticed something out of the corner of her eye, something hidden behind a mass of overgrown shrubs. Lisa pulled back the branches to reveal an old wooden sign. In faded and peeling green paint she could barely make out the words "St. Mary's Sisters Of The Fields." There was more writing, but it was too faded to read. Lisa let go of the branches and continued up the drive to find Hunter nervously staring up at an old farmhouse. He stood in front of the large structure looking up at the second story balcony. The teen was still crying as he removed the burden from beneath his arm and held it firmly out in front of him in his right hand, pointing the object at one of the second story windows. Lisa now saw Hunter's bundle clearly and she knew what it was. Hunter just stood there, watching the house as the sky above began to rapidly grow dark, and before long, it was pitch black outside. Slowly, Hunter lowered the hatchet to his side, walked up the old wooden steps, and opened the front door. There was no one to greet the boy, but he seemed to know exactly where he was going. Hunter climbed the stairs to the second floor, took a left down a darkened hallway, and stopped in front of the first door. He put his ear to the door then carefully opened it and stepped inside. *Whack... Whack... Whack...*

Even though there were no screams, Lisa did not need to enter the room to know what he was doing. He soon emerged from the room, his axe, his face, his chest, all covered in blood. Still the boy sobbed as he continued to the next room. *Whack... Whack... Whack...*

Then the next, *Whack...* and the next, *Whack... Whack...* Twelve rooms in all, until young Thomas

Hunter finally stood outside the last remaining door.

Hunter reached the final door and stopped. Hearing a noise, he turned and slowly made his way to the end of the hall. Behind the door a toilet had been flushed. Hunter waited... The door opened with a creak and a scream... *Whack...* "Why God, why?" Hunter yelled as he thrust the hatchet into the sister who was still trying to pull down her gown, chopping at her over and over again. "How can you let me *do* this?" he screamed. *Whack... Whack... Whack...* Hunter stopped swinging and stepped back until he was leaning against the wall, then slowly slid down into a sitting position. He dropped the bloody hatchet on the floor and put his hands to his face. "Why… why didn't you… stop me?" he sobbed.

Lisa's vision went black. Images began to flicker before her eyes like a reel of film, slowly at first, then speeding up until the scenes took on movement. The first was a woman in a field, no… a cemetery. She held onto a small child's hand, Hunter's hand. It was his mother. Lisa had not seen her before but she knew this, just as she knew who else was hidden somewhere in the frame, whispering to the woman from the shadows. The image changed to Hunter's mother washing dishes. Lisa caught glimpses of the Mille Umbra's forms hidden within the shadows of the curtains covering the window overlooking the flower garden. The Umbra whispered in the woman's ear, though this time Lisa heard what he was saying. *"You knew,"* the creature hissed. *"You knew and you did nothing! You could have stopped it all before it was too late. He didn't have to die…"* The woman began to weep. *"Your husband's death was* your *fault,"* the creature continued. Lisa watched as the Umbra leaned in close to the woman's ear. *"See…"* the creature hissed. *"See what the future holds for Hunter…"* The woman shrieked, thrusting her hands to her eyes to block out the visions. "Stop," she screamed, "stop showing me!" The image changed, replaced with the flower garden outside. Hunter's mother was on her hands and knees weeding the bed, the Mille Umbra hidden somewhere beneath the stalks and stems, close to the coolness of the earth and out of the bright morning sun. Still he whispered…. still she sobbed…. Thousands of images flooded Lisa's mind, years of torture at the hands of the abomination that hid in the shadows. The final image shown was of the woman hunched in the corner of a dimly lit room. Her hair was a tangled black mess, her eyes puffy and red (had Hunter's mother stopped crying at all during her years of abuse?). She wore a plain white gown that was covered in tearstains and small streaks of blood. The Mille Umbra was nowhere in sight. His job complete, he left the broken woman alone with her madness.

Lisa snapped out of the vision and returned to the hallway of the convent in the woods. The teenage Hunter still sat on the floor, leaning against the wall, sobbing. He stood, wiping his tears on the shoulder and sleeve of his blood-soaked shirt. Hunter retrieved the hatchet from the floor and returned to the staircase, he paused momentarily at the bottom, as if trying to remember where something was. Hunter turned and headed in the direction of a darkened hallway beyond the reception desk and stopped in front of a door. Finding the door locked, the youth smashed in a small pane of glass with the butt of his weapon's handle. Reaching in, he unlocked the door and entered another passageway. Hunter seemed to be counting doors as he slowly made his way, dragging his feet as though fighting the urge to walk. Finding the door he was searching for he reached for the handle and turned the knob.

The door clicked, then creaked open. "Mama?" Hunter called out. There she was, the woman in Lisa's vision. She sat curled up in the corner of the room, sobbing. Hunter walked slowly towards her, hiding the small axe behind his back as he approached. "Mama," he said again. The woman continued to cry, louder with each footfall. "I'm here for you, Mama."

"I know," the woman sobbed. Hunter's mother pulled her frail body up off the floor with some difficulty. Her knees shook as she hobbled to the bed and sat down. "Come, sit next to me, son," she said and smiled.

"No, Mama, I can't," Hunter replied as he stood at the foot of the bed.

"Please, son," the woman pleaded, "just for a moment, then you can do what you came to do."

Hunter slowly moved around the mattress. He placed his bloody hatchet down on the sheet at the foot of the bed and sat down next to his mother. "You were always such a good boy," the woman said as she pulled a tissue from a box on the nightstand next to her bed and raised it to Hunter's face. Hunter cringed and turned his head to avoid her touch. "Come now, son, all I wanna' do is clean up your face so as to get one last good look at you." Hunter closed his eyes tightly as his mother cleaned the blood from his cheeks. "That's better," she said, managing a brief smile. "I always knew you were a special child, from the first time I held you." She once again began to cry. "There are so many things I should have done differently. I should have left that bastard, left that house, taken you away and hidden you. Hidden you from that *thing…*" she hissed with a sour look on her face. "But I realize now there was no where to go, because *It* would have found you eventually, I know that now."

"Don't you *dare* talk about him like that!" Hunter screamed as he rose from the bed knocking the hatchet to the floor. "He's the *only* friend I ever had!" Hunter reached down and retrieved the weapon. "He was more of a parent to me than you and that fucking husband of yours could *ever* dream of being!" "*You* watch your language in the Lord's house!" Hunter's mother dictated in a stern tone.

"Fuck, Fuck, Fuck!" Hunter stood and screamed. "Who's gonna hear me, Mama? I've already killed all of the fucking nuns." With both hands, Hunter brought the hatchet up over his head. "I'm sorry, Mama," he said, "but now it's *your* turn." As the blade arced through the air, Hunter's mother looked him straight in the eyes, smiled, and said: "Thank you."

(III)

In a flash, the image before Lisa disappeared, only to be replaced with more. Like a movie running at high speed, the scenes played out before her eyes. Visions of terror and carnage filled Lisa's mind as

she watched Hunter grow older, the killing moving on to new locations, none of which she recognized…
until now. A woman with red hair lay on a bed with her arms and legs bound to the posts as Hunter carved
her like a Thanksgiving turkey, slicing her belly open and pulling out her insides. As Hunter labored over
the corpse, Cherry opened her eyes.

"Lisa, so good to see you again," she said in a surprisingly chipper voice considering the situation.

"Don't worry, he can't hear us." Cherry motioned with her chin towards Hunter. "And the best
part," Cherry said with a smile, "is that he doesn't even know you're here."

"Where *is* here?" Lisa asked as she stepped forward.

"You're in his mind, these are *his* memories," Cherry explained.

"But… how is this possible?" Lisa asked.

"What do I look like, a rocket scientist? Well, actually, my specialty *is* rockets if you know what
I mean." Cherry burst into carnal laughter that Lisa couldn't help but join in. "Seriously," Cherry said,
"you have the ability to travel through Hunter's thoughts and memories without him knowing. You don't
have much time and you need to learn how to choose your destination."

"How do I do that?" Lisa asked.

"Your mind is somehow *tuned* into Hunter's. That's the best word I can find to describe the bond
you share with him. Only it's a one-way street. That's why Hunter can't find you unless you're having
one of your visions," Cherry explained.

"But what is *this*?" Lisa asked, motioning around her. "I was talking to Hunter at the house then I
found myself skipping through moments in his life. What is it, a vision within a vision?" Lisa sat down
on a small wooden chair in the corner of the room next to a large oak dresser. Hunter was still busy with
his knife, pulling out Cherry's small intestine and cutting it into two-foot strips, then dropping them on
the floor in small piles.

"A vision within a vision," Cherry repeated. "That pretty much sums it up, only in the original
vision, time no longer moves forward. When you return, Hunter will not even know you were gone. You
need to keep this from him at all costs. He must not know where you've been and what you know."

"That's the thing," Lisa said. "I really don't know shit. I'm still trying to piece together what the hell's going on around here. I mean, why me? What does he want from me?" Lisa stood up and walked to the edge of the bed.

"Search his mind," Cherry said. "You'll find the answers that you need." "But I don't know how," Lisa said, exasperated.

"Concentrate," said Cherry. "Focus on the moments you want to see."

"But I don't even know *what* I want to see, what I *need* to see." Lisa was almost in tears. "How do I find what I'm looking for if I don't know what that is?"

"You'll get the hang of it," Cherry said. "For now, search Hunter's mind for Cooper. He holds the answers to many of your questions."

"Cooper?" *I know that name*, Lisa thought. Did Gillian mention him? "Wouldn't it be easier to just go out and find him? I mean, even if he's dead, he's probably still around here somewhere, right?" Lisa looked down to find that Hunter had been piling up Cherry's intestine on the floor where she was standing and her right shoe was covered with the dead prostitute's viscera.

"It's not that easy," Cherry said. "Even though Hunter can't read *your* mind, anyone else you talk to, he can. Unless you're here, in his head."

Lisa kicked the entrails from her shoe sending them against the wall with a splat.

"Close your eyes," Cherry said, "and concentrate on Cooper."

Lisa closed her eyes and watched the film reel containing Thomas Hunter's life spin in her head. *Cooper…* she thought to herself, *focus on Cooper.* Millions of images flashed before Lisa's eyes, and as she tried in vain to focus on her query, she realized she could *hear* as well. Muffled sounds at first that soon grew louder, conversations, names, but still no Cooper. Just as Lisa was about to give up, a thought came to her. *What did Gillian say his first name was?* It took a moment, but the name came to her; it was Mitch. As soon as the name formed in her mind, a jolt shook Lisa's body. She opened her eyes to find herself standing at the foot of the Statue Of Liberty.

Thomas Hunter sat on the steps leading up to the monument, a short, geeky looking young man with messy brown hair and large wire framed glasses, sat next to him.

"Mitch Cooper?" Lisa called to him. He looked up with a questioning gaze.

"Do I know you?" he asked as he stood.

"My name's Lisa. I'm ah… a friend of Gillian's," she lied. "I brought you something, but you have to answer some questions for me first." At that moment, Mitch looked back at Hunter who was still sitting on the steps talking. He seemed to be carrying on the conversation even though Mitch no longer sat next to him. Cooper returned his gaze to Lisa.

"No, you're going to answer some questions for *me* first. How did you get in here and what have you done to my program?"

Lisa's mind raced to find an explanation that this man might actually buy.

If I only had… Lisa suddenly felt something in the front pocket of her jeans. She reached her hand in and pulled out a small flat, credit card shaped piece of lightweight plastic. On its face were three small flashing transparent buttons. *…some weird looking gadget or something.* Lisa finished her thought. "This is what I brought for you." Lisa held the object out for Cooper to see, still not sure herself where it had come from. "I'll tell you what it does, then you answer my questions."

Mitch looked back at Hunter once more. "Fine, what is it?" He asked sarcastically. Lisa stalled, trying to piece together her fabrications into a tidy story.

"Gillian brought me in to upgrade your systems…" Lisa began.

"Bullshit!" Mitch cut in. "She would never…" Lisa cut *him* off this time.

"Say you want to leave this program and load another, what would you have to do?" For some reason, Lisa knew the answer to this question. She had never been told, but somehow she still knew. "Well?" "I have to end the session, jack out, set the new destination, and jack back in to load." Cooper reluctantly explained. "There's no other way, nothing that wouldn't fry your brain anyway. Now tell me, what have you done to my program?" Lisa ignored his question and continued her ruse. "You know what? Why don't I just show you?" Lisa pressed one of the buttons on the small controller in her hand and thought of the first vision she'd had of this place, the lone apple tree on an ocean of sand. Mitch's eyes grew wide as the landscape around him began to change, the statue shrinking down to became the tree. Everything else just sort of faded out into white sand. "Anywhere in particular you'd like to go?" Lisa asked. Mitch just stood there, amazed. Lisa pressed the button once more, this time thinking of the pier. The image once more changed, the tree stretching out to become the pier, the sand dissolving into water.

"What's this," Mitch said as he looked around. "I've never seen this program."

"This is one of mine," Lisa lied and pressed the button once more. She did not focus in on one place but let it all flow through her mind. Images of places flashed by, barely coming together enough to form a reality before being snatched up and ripped away to become something new. Lisa was used to this by now, but Mitch was not. His face began to turn white and he put his hand to his mouth. "Stop this thing before I hurl," Cooper demanded from behind his hand.

Lisa thought of the monument and the image quickly took shape, molding the world around them into the interior of the statues head, light streaming in through the windows cut into Lady Liberty's crown. Lisa climbed over the railing and looked out the window. Hunter could still be seen sitting on the steps below, carrying on his conversation with an imaginary Cooper. Lisa leaned out the window and let a stream of spit fall from her lips. It seemed to take forever to hit its mark, *Splat,* right on top of Hunter's head.

"When do *I* get to try it?" Cooper asked anxiously.

Lisa laughed. "Oh, the remote," she said. "As soon as you answer my questions." "What do you want to know?" Cooper asked anxiously. "And try not to get too personal."

Lisa pressed down on the button and thought of the canyon. Instantly, they were there.

"I've *got* to have that thing," Cooper whispered.

Lisa looked around, wondering if she was actually in the program. It looked so *real*! Was all of this from memory? "Tell me about this place. And the fire, why is it always burning?"

"Well, the canyon was Hunter's idea, the fire, too. He never told me *where* he got the ideas. If you want an answer to *that* question you'll have to ask *him*. I wrote the program as a favor; he's really not such a bad guy, you know?"

"If you like serial killers," Lisa mumbled. "Tell me about the religion."

"Now *that* I can tell you about."

Cooper sat down on the ground next to the fire and began his sermon. He spoke of a single consciousness being born causing the explosion that created the universe. This consciousness, known as Angere, watched for billions of years as the universe formed, spending decades at a time listening to a solitary sound emanating from somewhere deep within the cosmos. Then, rather unpredictably, Angere witnessed another birth, Life. He watched as Life spread across the universe, taking hold in every nook and cranny. And he watched Life evolve, witnessing the very first thoughts, incoherent babblings that soon led to logic and reason. There were now an infinite number of thoughts in Angere's head. He listened to the thoughts of every civilization, every species, spread across the vast cosmos. Some of these thoughts pleased Angere, thoughts of hatred and jealousy, lust, greed, and violence. These attributes gave Angere hope that mankind would provide an endless source of amusement, something to pass the time in his long, long life. But then there were the thoughts of kindness, faith, and love… these thoughts *angered* Angere, and he vowed to one day destroy the universe his birth had created. As the ages passed, Angere began to wonder if it were possible for *him* to go out into the universe. Instead of destroying it, he would change it, and make slaves of these vile creatures impertinent enough to taunt him with their contemptible thoughts of love and hope.

Centuries passed as Angere pondered what to do about the insolent creatures he found weak. He watched, he listened, and he began to hear *new* thoughts, thoughts more like his. It was then that Angere truly began to listen, and in time he learned that there were others out there like him, other universes outside of his own… a *multiverse*! Angere vowed to find a way to bring these like-minded beings together, and together they would find a way to enter the multiverse and escape the darkness that bound them to an eternity of watching, listening, and waiting for some unknown moment to arrive. Angere put his mind to the task of finding a means of communication with the others. It did not take him long, only a hundred years or so, to make contact with the first of his kind. Through trial and error, anger and frustration, Angere struggled to open the ponticulus that would allow him access to the minds of his brethren. In all, there were nine hundred and ninety-eight others like him, and once Angere had made contact with one, the others quickly followed. He saw and felt everything each one had done throughout its lifetime. With each joining of the minds, Angere felt his power growing, along with his strength and knowledge, all flowing through him in abundance. He sensed that the others felt it, too, a power that bound them, drawing them closer together. Angere had also sensed something else, something that would turn his stomach if he had one. Through the thoughts of the others (for he knew they were not his own) Angere felt compassion and kindness towards the wretched creatures of the multiverse. He vowed to find the source of this degradation and remove those impure thoughts. The traitors were sorted out, seven in all, and punishment was handed down. For the crimes of compassion towards the species of the multiverse, the seven were murdered.

Cooper continued his story but Lisa could no longer make sense of his words. Her mind reeled back through the canyon, back to the statue. She was pulled past Hunter sitting on the bench (talking to himself) then traveled back further still, once more passing Hunter on the stairway, and again as he leaned against the tree in the flower garden of his childhood home (still talking to himself), through the forest to the clearing where Gillian and Dr. Carlton stood motionless, Carlton's laughter still echoing through the trees. Lisa lost consciousness and fell to the ground.

(IV)

We are the sum of our experiences… Randal's father had told him this on several occasions throughout his lifetime. So much so that it happened to be the first sentence young Randal ever spoke. It took a long time for him to realize what his father meant, but when the time came, Commander Randal Smith understood this phrase completely. It was his very first assignment with SEAL team Zero. That zero stood for Zero Hour, which was rapidly approaching. It was four years ago today that Smith's father had died and four years since the Admiral had first contacted him about a clandestine SEAL team. Randal's father had been an Admiral himself, a long time friend of Admiral Robert Forsythe. The Admiral had told Randal after the death of his father that he was being transferred from SEAL team six to a new, classified team. He hadn't known what to think initially, but after that first mission, everything changed. Smith let his thoughts drift as he sat at the large oval table waiting for the rest of his team to join him. He stared at a large picture on the wall, the remnants of the team's prior briefing. It was a large photograph of the NeuroTech compound taken by satellite when the eye of the storm had passed over the island and the compound was in ruins. The conference room was warm, like the waters of the Atlantic outside of the sub that sat 100 miles east of Nags Head, North Carolina, his home state. It was easier to think this close to home, to think about his childhood and his father, and the events throughout his career that had molded him into the man he was today. The door opened and Randal turned his thoughts back to the present. Lieutenant Turner closed the door behind him and took a seat across the table from Smith.

"What do you think happened?" Turner asked as he slid into the chair.

"The shit's hit the fan," Smith replied, "and as usual, we're here to clean things up."

The door opened and Captain Whitney entered. He circled around the table and took the chair next to Smith. "Where's Vasquez?" Wit asked.

"Late as usual," Smith casually twanged with his thick southern accent.

The door opened and Lieutenant Gabriel Vasquez entered the room and took the chair next to Turner. "I see the gang's all here," Vasquez did his dead best Porto Rican accent even though he didn't really speak with one. His mother was Caucasian; she'd raised him with a stepfather in the suburbs of Holyoke, Massachusetts. He didn't know much about his father, other than the fact that he'd knocked his mom up and walked out when he'd found out she was pregnant.

97

The door opened and Admiral Robert Forsythe entered the room followed closely behind by Lieutenant Amanda Briggs. The young Lieutenant stood by the door while the Admiral stepped forward and spoke. "You've all been briefed on Project Lucidity and the status of the Island. Remember, Pandora's box may have opened, so be prepared for anything. In thirty minutes, my friends, we get to see what lies inside."

Part 3: Into the abyss

CHAPTER ELEVEN

The Offer

(I)

Without warning, she was gone. Hunter had only turned away for a brief moment and, when he looked back, she had vanished. No matter, soon enough Lisa Spencer would be part of his world. Maybe his master would even take pity on him and let him have his way with her when the Umbra were through. Oh, the things he would do to that body, the love he would show her with both cock and knife… Hunter continued up the narrow staircase until he came to the trap door at the top. As he lifted the door with his shoulders, sand began to pour in through the cracks, cascading down the steps into the darkness. The door rose into a vast sea of white in all directions, the wind carrying phantom shadows of sand particles, which in some places were thick enough to block out the sunshine entirely. Hunter surveyed the landscape before him, chose a direction, and began to walk. *I must know more about this woman*, he thought to himself. What was her secret, and could she really be the one he'd been searching for all this time? If only he could enter her mind just once, pry the secrets from her flesh, poke around in her brain. Hunter knew he would have his answers soon enough and, even though the Umbra would not let him harm Lisa Spencer, Thomas Hunter had other means to his end. "Soon enough …" he said out loud. "Soon enough."

As Hunter walked, his mind drifted to the past. *'We are the sum of our experiences'*, he had once been told though, try as he might, he could not remember whose lips had spoken these words of wisdom. He wondered what secrets in Lisa's past had made her the woman she was today… and the *God* she would become tomorrow! These questions tormented Hunter as he walked the faceless desert. His mind was soon transfixed by his *own* past, his *own* experiences. Hunter's earliest childhood memory was of torture and rape. At the time, the pathetic child had had no clue as to the nature of his existence, all he'd known was pain. He did, however, know that the one he called 'Papa' was not his true father. And Papa had made that clear to him on every available occasion. At least he had his dreams… his God would show him such wonderful things! All of humanity suffering in the bowels of Hell for it's crime of ignorance. Hunter dreamed of ruling by his God's side, punishing mankind for eternity. He soon learned this was not to be the case, his hopes and dreams shattered into a million tiny fragments, once he'd learned his true purpose. A month after the suicide of his so-called-father, Hunter's dreams came crashing down around him.

Hunter remembered setting eyes on the child for the very first time sitting alone in its stroller next to the park bench. He'd known from the moment he'd looked at the baby that he was going to kill it. He watched as the mother ran to the aid of a screaming child who had fallen off the slide and broken his leg. Hunter had just strolled on over and snatched the baby in the stroller up. He'd ran into the woods until his chest felt like it was bursting, stopping only once to look behind him to make sure no one had seen him take the child. He'd stopped in a mossy clearing in the underbrush, laid the baby down and choked the infant until its face turned blue and its limbs stopped flailing. Hunter had left the baby in the woods and gone home for dinner. That single action had changed his life forever. It wasn't the killing, though. Hell, Hunter enjoyed killing immensely, it was better than *any* dream he had ever had. Of course, as Hunter had grown older, his fondness for that particular memory had soured, in no small part due to the punishment father had handed down to him. Hunter was told that he was not ready, that murder must be practiced over and over again before one was ready to go out and do the Lord's work. Hunter's punishment had been to bring his *real* Father one infant a week until the Umbra had tired of the innocent flesh, and Hunter's other punishment had been the *truth*. Father told Hunter what he was meant to be and what he would *never* be!

Father was one of seven, seven Umbra thought to be dead, but only cast out into a place called the Nexus. Hunter's true father had suffered an eternity of darkness in a cold, dead emptiness, a universe where no life had taken hold. Then one day, Father had heard his name. Someone or something, some*where*, was calling to him. Father learned of the Mille Umbra and was soon united with his brethren, only to have everything ripped away. It was the other six who had deserved to die: Animus, Invidia, Ira, Edax, Salax, and Edacitas. Desideo had not belonged with the likes of *those* creatures.

Pride, Envy, Wrath, Greed, Lust, and Gluttony, what did he have in common with these vile entities?

Unjustly punished, he said he was, and further more, should Sloth even be considered a sin? Why should Father be punished for existing the only way that he knew how? Centuries had passed as Father suffered for his so called crimes of compassion (sure he'd had those feelings, but in a dead universe, how could he act on them?) until, by chance, he'd stumbled across a means of escape. Everything passes through the Nexus: all thought, all life, all matter. You see, the Nexus is a gateway between Heaven, Hell, and the multiverse. Of course, the realities of Heaven were strictly off limits to the likes of the Umbra, and having been banished and left for dead by his brethren, Hell was also out of the question. That left the multiverse. And since all matter passes through the Nexus on its way to the cosmos, Desideo devised a plan. It took time to find the right candidate, one who would easily succumb to the Umbra's temptations, a soul that would allow Desideo to be born into the multiverse as a Human.

On the twenty-second of November, 1913, Thomas Rothery was born in a small cabin in the Berkshire Mountains of eastern Massachusetts. His parents didn't have much, but what they lacked in wealth and possessions, they more than made up for in kindness and love. Desideo suffered in silence for five long years as he devised a plan to one day return to Hell. Day in, day out, young Thomas Rothery was showered with love and affection, to the point of nearly driving the Umbra within him insane. Desideo knew that time was running short, and that he must act while the child's mind was still young and vulnerable. Desideo decided to put his revenge on hold and wage war with Thomas's mind, not that it was much of a battle, as he had chosen this soul for a reason. So, at the age of five, Thomas Rothery murdered his parents and struck out on his own. Desideo later learned that when the bodies were found nearly two decades later by a group of teenagers from a nearby town, that he, Thomas Rothery the second, had become a legend of sorts. It was plain to the authorities investigating the bizarre discovery that a child had lived in the small cabin with the deceased couple, but the body of a child had never been found. Some said there never *was* a child, that the family lived alone in the forest too long and lost their grip on reality, while others claimed that the child still haunted the woods of the Berkshires, awaiting the discovery of his bones.

(II)

In 1942, Thomas Rothery returned home to dispel the myths and rumors of his disappearance. Desideo had fabricated such wonderful lies during his travels around the globe that, when he had appeared out of nowhere in a town that had lost most of its population to disease, desertion, or the war, and offered to fully fund the town's restoration, well, how could they refuse? He asked for only one thing in return, to build a house on the spot where the cabin had once stood. It took Thomas Rothery four years to build the house, an incredible achievement considering the scale and complexity of the dwelling, and the dearth of materials due to the war. The three story wooden structure had four massive turrets that climbed up into the sky, far higher than the rest of the house. Thomas Rothery had taken great care to choose only the finest fieldstones to construct the turrets, aligning the four towers with the points of the compass; a crossroads of sorts, allowing the house to be used as a conduit, a means for Desideo to one day rejoin his brethren. This, of course, did not quite work out as planned. It seemed the house was a means of *communication* with Hell, but did not serve as a means of entry. Still, Desideo begged Angere's forgiveness by sharing the secrets he had learned, that only an Umbra in the physical universe could bear a child that would *unmake* everything! Angere had promised Desideo nothing in return for this knowledge. Nevertheless, Desideo had been given the task of siring this special child and had failed, miserably. Although Hunter *did* display immense power, he did *not* bear the mark. It seemed the son of a God would not do; the Cruor must be female. Desideo had pleaded with Angere for another chance, but the conduit to Hell had been sealed and, for his failure, Desideo had been separated from the body of Thomas Rothery and imprisoned within the house in the woods.

In the subsequent month following Hunter's murder of the infant in the woods, four more children went missing. With each passing week, it had become increasingly more difficult for Hunter to find victims for Father. The neighboring towns also grew suspicious of anyone who dared go near a child. The few carriages that were pushed around town had been avoided like a plague for fear of suspicion being cast one's way. It was even difficult for a young boy to approach an infant without arousing curiosity and being forced to disclose his intentions. Hunter did not dare to go home empty handed, so when he saw the young girl walking down the street, he snuck up behind her and hit her over the head with a rock. Needless to say, Father had *not* been pleased. ***"You are not ready to kill anything larger than an infant!"*** Father had raged. Hunter's punishment for this act was the loss of Mama, driven mad and sent to live in the hills with the nuns. Worst of all, Father no longer spoke to him, but

Hunter still had his dreams. After Mama had been taken away, Hunter had been placed in the custody of Social Services and shuffled from foster home to foster home, which Thomas really didn't mind, because it allowed him to kill throughout his teenage years, careful to never leave a trail as he moved from town to town. As Hunter grew older, he learned to hone his powers, his gift of foresight aiding him in his evasion of the law. Sure, he'd almost been caught in the act a couple of times, but luck always seemed to be on his side when it came to murder.

His victims were mostly female. Thomas had a deep hatred for the species, and being told he was of no use to Father because he was not born a girl didn't help. On Hunter's eighteenth birthday, he'd been released from the custody of the State and had hitchhiked home with two things on his mind: murder and arson. Hunter had snuck into the convent that night and killed all of the nuns. Then it was Mama's turn. She didn't put up a fight like he thought she would, she'd just said thank you. That bugged Thomas for a long time. Maybe it even had something to do with his change of heart about burning the house down. He'd stood for hours out in the garden under the moonlight with the can of gas trying to force his legs to move. Maybe it *was* a change of heart, but as the years went by, Thomas began to suspect it was more the Umbra's will. He felt Father watching from the house that night, felt Father's icy stare as he dropped the gas can and headed toward the road. It was then he'd taken the name Hunter, for it was what he did best, it was all he knew. Surely Father would understand. After all, had the Umbra not been persecuted by his brethren for the very same thing? Young Thomas Rothery the third became Thomas Hunter the night he killed Mama. He caught a bus out of town, not concerning himself with a destination, any place was better than there. Six months and over seven thousand miles later, Hunter had wound his way across the country to the west coast, leaving a trail of bodies in his wake. He had forgotten how much he missed the ocean.

Two weeks before his nineteenth birthday, Thomas Hunter had arrived in San Diego and joined the U.S. Navy. Upon completion of his training, Hunter was shipped off to join the crew of the Nimitz class carrier, the USS John C. Stennis. Thomas had spent the first few months as a grunt in the NAV department slowly working his way up to OPS in the Combat Direction Center. The higher ups took notice of his uncanny abilities to distinguish friend from foe on the radar and Hunter was soon transferred to the USS Ronald Reagan where he worked the ship's "island" for the next year. For the first time in Hunter's life, he was actually happy leading a normal life, out on the sea, away from the bullshit and filth of life on the mainland. His urge to kill seemed to subside. Hunter still thought about murder almost nightly, but for now, his dreams were enough. On his twentieth birthday, he'd received a visit from his executive officer who'd informed Hunter that he had been promoted to Lieutenant Junior Grade and was to report to his new CO in "pri-fly". He even began to make friends with his "Air Boss", CDR Richard Thornton. He was a good man, who trusted Hunter's abilities, and trust was *not* something

Thomas R. Hunter was used to. It was around that time when another of his superior officers had noticed Hunter's "abilities", a man named Admiral Robert Forsythe. Hunter knew little about the man, but soon grew to despise him. By orders of Admiral Forsythe, Hunter had been pulled from duty and transferred to an Oliver Perry-Class frigate where he'd spent the next two months undergoing psychiatric evaluations and tests. The Admiral seemed to be pleased with Hunter's progress, and before he knew it, Thomas had been sent off for "accelerated training" and assigned to a team of SEALs.

Hunter didn't like to think about that part of his life much and was glad to see that his journey across the sea of white sand had come to an end. Hunter stood behind Ashley Spencer who had been buried up to her neck. The young girl's wet hair looked like a blanket wrapped around her tiny head.

"Who's there?" Ashley cried out. "I hear you."

Hunter slowly walked around so that she could see him.

"Oh, it's *you*! I already *told* you everything I know," Ashley hissed.

"You've told me nothing, " Hunter calmly replied. "It's time to be honest with me, young lady, unless of course you want to see something bad happen to your father?"

At that moment Ashley's head filled with visions of her father dying in every gruesome way imaginable. Torn apart limb by limb, skinned slowly while still alive… it was too much for her to take. She closed her eyes tightly but the images just came faster and more brutal. "Tell me about your aunt," Hunter said calmly. "Tell me about Lisa."

"I've told you everything I know," Ashley sobbed.

"NO!" Hunter screamed. "You've told me *nothing*. Now open your eyes!"

Suddenly the visions in her head ceased and Ashley opened her eyes. The man standing above her looked down with a smile on his face but he said nothing more. Then Ashley noticed something off in the distance. Was it just a figment of her imagination? Were her eyes playing tricks on her? It almost looked like the desert was shrinking! The edge of the desert and the horizon seemed to be getting closer.

Ashley darted her eyes back and forth, looking in every direction her limited movement would allow. The desert *was* shrinking… in all directions, the sand seemed to fall away into nothingness, pouring down into a deep dark chasm.

"Tell me…" Hunter asked as he squatted down close to Ashley's face, looking deep into her eyes.

"What makes her special?"

"I… don't know… what… you mean," Ashley sobbed. "I don't know…" Her voice trailed off into tears as Hunter stood, taking several steps back. Ashley's tears turned to screams as the sand grew closer, now falling away beneath Hunter's feet. He seemed to float on the air as he turned and walked away across the see of nothingness. Ashley's screams intensified as her body plummeted into the abyss with the last remaining grains of sand from Hunter's sea.

(III)

Bruce Spencer pushed open the turnstile and exited the gates of the amusement park. The parking lot was more of the same, empty cars with trash strewn about blowing in the warm summer wind. "Hello?" Bruce called out. The sky was still dark and cloudy and most of the streetlamps were out. The ones that were working would flicker and dim as Bruce searched the lot for an unlocked car. He found an early eighties Ford Tempo that was as easy to hotwire as it was to pop open the door with the antenna off an old Toyota. Bruce pulled out his pocketknife and pried off the bottom half of the steering column to expose the wires. He examined the cable carefully and began to cut the wires. The car started with a chug and the whine of the power steering belt. Bruce pulled out of the parking lot and began heading for the New York boarder. He drove as fast as the car would go as the streets and houses looked as deserted as the amusement park. He had to swerve to avoid the random abandoned car here and there, but the drive was quick and, before he knew it, Bruce Spencer was pulling into his brother Andrew's driveway.

It had been Andrew who had inherited the family home when Bruce up and moved to the Carolina's. He said he was tired of the long cold winters and needed a change of pace. Lori didn't seem to mind; she liked the hot summers and mild winters further down the East coast and quickly grew accustomed to the slower pace. Things were much more relaxed in the south and that's exactly what Bruce had been looking for. He opened the door and got out of the car, walked up to the front door, and pushed the buzzer. He turned the knob and the door opened with a creak. "Hello? Andrew? Lisa? Anybody?" Bruce's call echoed throughout the empty house. "What now?" he asked himself. Bruce had chosen this destination because it was where Ashley would have come. She always loved to spend the summers with her aunt Lisa and she simply *adored* the old house with its large fieldstone turret. "What now?" He repeated.

"Now we make a trade." A voice spoke from behind him. Bruce turned to find the patient, Thomas Hunter, standing in the doorway in his dark gray jumpsuit. "Your daughter Ashley for your niece." Bruce lunged at the man but he simply vanished into thin air. "We can do this all day or you can accept my offer and get things over with much more quickly." The voice was behind him again, in the kitchen this time. Bruce turned and faced Hunter, contemplating what to do. There was no way he was handing Lisa over to this creep after what had happened to Ashley. Bruce relived the moment that he had watched as his baby girl had been swept over the railing and dragged down into the sea. But did she drown? Was there a chance that she had survived and washed up on this island in the storm? Bruce *had* to know. "Where is she?" Bruce demanded.

"She's safe," Hunter said. "For now."

"What does that mean? And what do you want with Lisa?"

"Ah…" Hunter sighed. "My dearest Lisa. I simply *must* know more about her."

"I'll tell you two things buddy: Jack and Shit. Take your pick!"

"Oh, don't you worry, *Uncle* Bruce; you'll soon be telling me *everything* you know." Hunter's creatures made their presence known then. They were all over the house, hidden in the shadows of the darkened corners of the rooms. Bruce's mind raced. *What now?* Hunter appeared out of nowhere directly in front of Bruce. He placed his hand around Bruce's throat and picked up the two hundred plus pound man as if it were nothing. "Now you tell me about Lisa Spencer."

(IV)

Lisa fell to the ground with a terrible thump. Gillian rushed to her aid quickly, checking to see if she was still breathing. Lisa was alive but unconscious. Gillian stood. "What now?" she asked Dr. Carlton. He shrugged. "Where do you want to go?" he asked. Gillian thought about this. Her mind could barely grasp what was going on around her, how the dream programs and the game programs had taken over the island, and that somehow Thomas Hunter was in control of it all. "I don't know," Gillian said.

"Should I go back to the electrical room? Do you know where that is?"

"That's where patient seven spends most of his time," Carlton answered.

"Derek Philips," Gillian corrected. "They *have* names you know."

"My dear Gillian, " Carlton frowned. "Why must you let your *emotions* get the best of you?" "Because I'm human! At least I still look like one and not like some deformed horror movie psycho sideshow freak!"

"Ouch, Gillian, that one hurts."

"Good," she pushed. "Why did you have to go and die on me anyway? We were just getting started on this project! What the hell went wrong?"

"Patients six and seven," Dr. Carlton said coldly. "*Sorry*, Thomas Hunter and Derek Philips. You want to talk about sideshow freaks? *They* were the real deal. *That's* what went wrong. It was *their* sessions that started all of this."

"What do you mean by *real deal*?"

"Gifted, psychic, call it what you will. *They* knew what was going to happen in the program before the computer did."

"Well," Gillian said. "Sleeping Beauty over there went through patient seven's sessions. You say that these discs have Thomas Hunter's sessions?" Gillian held up a knapsack containing discs. "Have you looked through them? Is there anything we can use to get out of here?"

106

"No, I haven't looked at them, but I was there! I saw what happened when the two of them were linked into the system."

"So, the laptop is in the electrical room… How do I get there from here?

"We need to find Bruce," Lisa moaned as she sat up. "Is all that true? Is all this because of *him*?"

"I trust Doctor Carlton," Gillian said, "and, after what I've seen, I'm inclined to agree with him." "Why, thank you for the compliment, Dr. Black. So nice after the character crashing tongue lashing you just handed out."

"Yeah, sorry about that, but you're just so damn ugly," Gillian teased.

"Do you know where he is?" Dr. Carlton asked Lisa.

"Yeah," she answered, "and I think I know how to get there."

(V)

Bruce gasped for breath. The psycho was strong, holding him up in the air like Bruce weighed nothing. He punched and he kicked, hell, Dr. Bruce Spencer even tried to bite Thomas Hunter's finger off, but the freak was too strong. It was as if he felt no pain at all. Bruce, on the other hand, was in quite a bit of pain. His head ached and his mind reeled as Thomas Hunter fought for its control. Bruce could feel the bastard inside his head, searching through his memories. Thomas was looking for any memory of Lisa, from the phone call on the day of her birth, to the day of her high school graduation. Hunter sifted through them all until he got to the good stuff, the things that Bruce had encouraged Lisa to seek her father's counsel regarding. Lisa's visions and waking dreams, Lisa's father Andrew Spencer, *those* things now held Hunter's avid interest. Bruce and Andrew had been very close growing up. He knew his brother well and, even though he refused to acknowledge it, there was a darkness there, hidden deep within Andrew Spencer. Thomas Hunter now saw this darkness and embraced it for it was, a darkness he knew well. He had seen this same darkness in father and, in that moment, Thomas Hunter knew it was true. He knew that Lisa Spencer was the one that father had been searching for all these years. The one to bring about the end of humanity and reality as we know it. Hunter felt a little bit of jealousy just then, as it was supposed to have been *him* that started it all. It was what he had been bred to do. But he was a failure. He was not a *she*, for it takes a woman fathered by an Umbra to bring about the end times, a woman with a womb, to carry the child who could unmake existence. Yes, Thomas Hunter knew he had The One, and he knew father would be pleased, if he could only get his hands on her. She was much more powerful than Hunter, and he knew that, but he also knew that Lisa Spencer had no idea what kind of power she wielded.

He would have to be careful. Hunter released Bruce Spencer and he fell to the floor coughing and gagging as he struggled for air. "Think about my offer very carefully," Hunter said. "I doubt father will be so kind." Hunter turned and began to walk away as darkness overtook Bruce and he passed out.

(VI)

"Take my hand," Lisa said as she held out her arms for Gillian and Carlton.

"What?" Gillian questioned.

"Just do it," Carlton directed. "I think I might know where she's going with this."

"Whatever," Gillian moaned sarcastically as she slung the child's knapsack over her shoulder and stepped forward and held out her hand. The contrast of Gillian's warm hand and Carlton's ice cold appendage felt strange at first. Lisa closed her eyes and tried to focus in on Bruce. She simply pictured him within her mind's eye, his smile, his laugh, and soon she could almost feel the warmth of him standing next to her. The sensation quickly changed and Lisa's head spun.

"What the hell just happened?" Gillian asked nervously as she looked around at her new surroundings. "Amazing!" Dr. Carlton cried out. "A third psychic on the island; no wonder things are still changing!" They stood in a large room, a library to be precise, surrounded by psychology books and medical journals. "Where are we?" Dr. Carlton asked. "This isn't part of any of the programs."

"It's my father's house," Lisa said with confusion in her voice. "Bruce?" she called out. "Uncle Bruce!"

Lisa left the doctors behind and began to search the house.

"What the hell just happened?" Jillian asked.

"It would seem our new friend has the ability to travel between programs at will. Simply amazing," Carlton repeated. "Only Hunter has been able to do this as far as I know."

"Derek, I understand. I've seen some of the things he can do with my own eyes, but why her?"

"I don't know. Perhaps you should ask her."

"Bruce!" Lisa called out from somewhere in the house. "Dr. Black, Dr. Carlton, in here." Gillian headed off in the general direction Lisa had disappeared with Carlton in tow. "Where are you?" Gillian called out.

"In here."

Gillian entered the doorway into the kitchen and saw Lisa's uncle lying on the floor, his niece at his side. She could tell right away that he was still breathing and saw no blood, which was a good thing. Dr.

Gillian Black had decided hours ago that she had seen enough blood to last the rest of her lifetime.

"Can you do that thing again and get us back to the electrical room?" Gillian asked.

"I think so." Lisa held onto her uncle tightly and placed her free hand up for Gillian to hold.

"I can't come with you," Dr. Carlton declared.

"Why not?" Gillian pleaded.

"It's the room; somehow it's shielded from everything that's going on around the island."

"I'll find you again," Gillian fervently promised him.

"I know you will." Dr. Carlton smiled.

Lisa focused on Derek this time and the feelings he evoked within Lisa when he was present, his psychological aura, of sorts. Lisa had always been able to know what people were feeling inside. It was just another one of her curses, to feel someone else's sorrows and fears, and it was no wonder Lisa had spent a great deal of her lifetime depressed. It wasn't depression that Lisa honed in on as she searched for Derek, it was dread. He had told her that he knew he was going to die soon and he truly believed it. Lisa held onto this feeling as she tried to recall his features in detail, her head once again spinning as realities shifted.

"What the *fuck*? Derek leapt from the chair and backed into the corner of the room. "Where the hell did *you* come from?" He watched as Dr. Black cleared the surface of the desk. She placed the laptop on the floor with the knapsack strung over her shoulder and simply wiped the rest of the surface clean, scattering papers, candy wrappers, and various other detritus onto the floor.

"Help us, Mr. Philips," Gillian pleaded.

Derek moved in to help lift Bruce from the floor to the desk. He stepped back once more and stared at Lisa wondering what to do. He now knew that his death would be at the hands of this woman but he could still hardly believe it. Why would she want him dead? He'd never done anything to harm her, so what motive could she possibly have? But then again, how in the hell did the three of them simply appear out of nowhere? Derek's mind shuttered with the possibilities.

(VII)

Captain Whitney stood in the airlock of the submarine in full scuba gear. He would be the first one out. Due to the storm raging above, the plan was to enter the facility through an airlock on the bottom floor beneath the island. He would wait for the rest of his team to exit the sub and then swim the remaining hundred yards to the NeuroTech facility. They had enough guns and C4 to supply a small army and that was the way Wit liked it. You simply never knew what you were going to come up against when you were sent on a mission from the Admiral. It took almost twenty minutes for the compartment to fill with water, exit the airlock and wait for the next person to be sent out, so Jason

Whitney floated motionless in the water lost in thought. He thought about the mission mostly and the prime objective of securing the island and rescue any survivors. If there were none, or if the island was not stable, then they were to set the charges and hightail it out of there, blow the whole island and be on their way home. It all sounded routine, but Wit knew that when it came to his team's missions, *nothing* was ever as easy as it appeared to be. Vasquez was next out of the airlock. Wit watched him haul out his portion of the supplies and then float motionless in wait of the others. Wit's mind returned to wandering until it settled on the team's previous mission. That one was supposed to have been quick in and out as well, but as previously noted, things never went as planned. The Admiral's men had tracked the target to a remote outpost in Antarctica. Seal Team Zero's job had been to go in and find out who or what the subject was and if it could be retrieved safely. Turned out that the subject was a demon that had recently escaped from Hell and was searching for a city hidden within the mountains of the continent. Wit had almost lost Vasquez on that mission. Hell, it was a miracle that any of them had made it out alive. The creature had been huge, and strong, and it had taken a lot of bullets to take it down. Wit noticed Smith emerging from the airlock with his supplies in tow. The door closed and the wait for Turner was on. The minutes ticked by and Wit let his mind drift some more. He wondered what Smith and Vasquez were thinking about, and Turner in the airlock. What did *they* think about before a mission? Wit liked to pray. He wasn't quite sure who or what he was praying to, but he knew there was something more, some higher power that influences our every move. He called it the God of choice, for that's all there really is in life,

110

a series of choices. Wit prayed that, when the time came, he would make the right ones. You had to trust your gut, your heart, and your head all at the same time. The airlock door opened with a rush of bubbles and Turner appeared, hauling out his gear. Wit focused on the task at hand and began gathering up his own gear and preparing for the swim to the NeuroTech facility. The team moved swiftly and proficiently and soon they were at the airlock. Wit opened the panel and began typing in the code on a small keypad. The door opened with a hiss and one by one SEAL team Zero entered the labs.

CHAPTER TWELVE

The Plan

(I)

Bruce Spencer opened his eyes. Lisa, Dr. Black, and the patient from the island stood over him. He sat up on the desk. "The airlock," he said. "It's the only way out and I have the key."

"And I have the access code," Gillian added.

"It's not going to be easy," Derek cut in. "Outside of these walls Thomas Hunter knows everything that we're going to do. I can hide from him for a little while but he always seems to find me."

"So, we'll need a distraction," Bruce said.

Lisa took Bruce's hand and spoke. "It has to be me," she said. "He seems to think we have some sort of connection. I can distract him long enough for you to get to the airlock and get out."

"There's no way I'm leaving you behind, Lisa. Christ, that bastard Thomas Hunter told me to hand you over and he would let me have Ashley back."

"She's alive?" Lisa asked excitedly.

"No, not really. Somehow Hunter has trapped her here and he won't let her go until I give you to him."

"All the more reason for me to do this," Lisa said and smiled. "I can find her! Bruce, let me do this." "She *can* do it," Gillian agreed. "Lisa can get us to the labs to get the equipment we need to link her into the system. The labs are just down the hall from the airlock and we can all get out of here."

"Then it's settled," Lisa said. "We hook me up to the program and I distract that bastard so we can get out of here."

"I don't know about this, Lisa," Bruce cut in. "Think about what you're doing."

"I *have* Uncle Bruce. These dreams and visions I've had all my life are building up to something and I need to know what. I need to *know* that I'm not insane! Let me do this Bruce! I can find Ashley and set her free and I *can* get us out of here."

"All right," Bruce reluctantly agreed. "But I'm staying with you no matter what; we all leave here together."

"Deal." Lisa gave Bruce a hug and then turned to Gillian. "I need to know as much about Thomas Hunter as possible."

Dr. Black held up the knapsack. "His sessions are in here," she said. "I haven't seen them, but Doctor Carlton seemed to think they were important."

Lisa picked up the laptop from the floor and set it on the corner of the desk. "Let me have them," she said. Gillian handed the sack over and Lisa retrieved the stack of discs from within. She looked at the dates on the jewel cases and selected the earliest one. Lisa placed the disc in the tray and pushed it in.

(II)

Four screens popped up on the monitor, four images of a comatose Thomas Hunter laying on a bed, a nurse placing electrodes around his bald head. A fifth screen popped up, overlapping the others. Thomas Hunter stood in a long hallway; he looked disoriented as he stumbled down the hall toward the door. He pushed the door open and light flooded the passageway. Hunter stepped out of the doorway and looked up at the Statue of Liberty. A young man sat on a bench nearby.

"Thomas Hunter?" the man on the bench called out.

"How did I get here?" Hunter demanded.

"You're in a coma, Mr. Hunter. You're hooked up to a computer in a lab. The Navy donated your body for our research."

"Good 'ole Admiral Forsythe." Thomas Hunter smiled. "*Still* thinks he can control me."

"Come," the young man beckoned, "sit with me. I'll explain everything."

Lisa had witnessed this scene before. In fact, she had interrupted the moment to have her little chat with the programmer named Cooper. She watched the Cooper on the screen as he explained to Hunter that they were inside of a program and that he, Mitchell Cooper, was written into the code and not physically there. Thomas Hunter stood from the bench and looked around.

"Then none of this is real?" he asked.

"No, this is just a re-creation of Liberty Island."

"I don't like it here," Hunter snarled. The sky grew dark and the wind began to howl. Cooper looked up and saw that the statue was no longer there; it had been replaced with a view of the black clouds that filled the sky. Lightning crashed and thunder rolled. Cooper watched as the grass at his feet turned to sand and a long pier stretched out over the ocean. "Much better." Hunter grinned.

"Where… where are we?" Cooper asked nervously.

"We're meeting on my terms now. Go on, Mr. Cooper, continue telling me about this research of yours." Lisa listened as Cooper explained the goals of Project Lucidity and how it was more than just computer generated dream control. Hunter listened intently, scrutinizing every word, looking for a way to exploit the situation and take control of the program. He got his wish when Cooper said, "In theory, one should be able to alter the program simply by realizing it is only a dream." Hunter decided that he would let Cooper live; after all, he had already provided some very useful information and no doubt he would provide more. Hunter suddenly stopped and stood perfectly still. Slowly, he turned to face the camera and spoke.

"Lisa, my dear, it's so *good* to see you taking an interest in me."

Lisa sat up straight and looked around. Everyone was frozen in place, just like every time she had one of her visions. "Come now, Lisa, don't be shy."

"What do you want from me?"

"I want to get to know you better, that's all. Come out into the facility and talk to me. All I want to do is talk to you."

"And I should believe you, why?" Lisa hissed.

"Believe what you like, but you have to come out of there sooner or later."

"I choose later. Right now, *I* want to get to know *you*, so buzz off and let me do my research."

Lisa ejected the disc and placed in the next. She watched as the program loaded and selected a new file.

Wit hauled his gear out of the airlock and placed it on the floor next to two large gas cans. He tapped one of the containers with his hand and found them full. He stripped out of his scuba gear and unzipped the large sack of weapons and supplies. Wit pulled on his combat fatigues and boots then inspected his weapons. He pulled out his pistol and walked slowly down the hallway toward what looked like an elevator. There were no such features on the blueprints to the island compound; Wit had scoured the schematics until he thought his eyes would bleed. He saw a cable behind the iron gate, which indicated that somehow the elevator was below him, even though Wit *knew* he was on the bottom floor of the NeuroTech facility. Wit returned to the airlock and he saw something strange on the floor. Footprints. The wet footprints of a small dog, leading off down the hallway to the left. The airlock door opened and Vasquez climbed out.

"Definitely something weird going on down here," Wit said.

"All in a day's work," Vasquez smarted back as he struggled out of his wetsuit. Wit followed the footprints down the hall a little way and saw that they ended in front of a closed door. He opened the door and entered the monitoring room. "Vasquez, get in here," Wit called out.

"Yeah, right behind you," Vasquez said as he entered the room. "Holy shit!"

Sitting in the corner of the room on the floor was a naked woman clutching a small dog. The woman looked dead, her skin snow white and covered in cuts and dark bruises. She softly petted the dog's wet fur, scratching the Schnauzer behind its ears. The animal leaned into the woman's hand and demanded to be scratched harder. Vasquez turned and retrieved a blanket from his supply bag and offered it to the woman. She reached out to grab it and Wit saw the deep gashes in her wrists and forearms. The blood oozing out of the wounds was black and partially coagulated. The woman covered herself and the dog with the blanket and spoke. "Thank you," she said. "My name's Danielle."

"Angel," Vasquez said with a smile. Bride of Frankenstein or not, this broad was still kind of hot.

"Is that your dog?" Wit asked.

"No, it belongs to the little girl. Her father's here too."

"What's going on in here?" Turner asked as he entered the room. "Oh, we have survivors."

"It would seem so," Wit said. "As soon as Smith gets in here, we split up and go in search of others. Let's check our communication devices and load up. Wit pulled his headset out and placed it around his right ear. "Testing," he said, standing in the doorway waiting on the rest of his squad. Vasquez and Turner nodded. The airlock door opened and Smith exited, hauling in his gear. "What did I miss?" he asked. "Your momma's good looks," Vasquez, teased. "I'd tap that, hell yeah!"

"You could fuck a mouse in the ass your dick's so small," Smith shot back. "Suit up and get your gear," Wit cut in. "We move out in five minutes."

(IV)

Lisa placed the next disc in and selected a file. She watched Hunter play some of the game programs, excelling at some, particularly the ones that required the player to inflict pain on others. Thomas Hunter was an extremely smart man, and good looking, too. It was a shame he used his power for evil. *He's right,* Lisa thought, *we do seem to have some sort of connection.* It was obvious that Thomas Hunter could glimpse the future. You could tell by the way he played the games; he was always one step ahead, within the program, as well as in real life. Lisa had this gift as well, the gift of foresight, the ability to see future events before they happened. Lisa ejected the disc and placed in the final CD Rom. She selected the very last file on the disc and pressed play. It was the house this time, the home in which Thomas Hunter had grown up. Lisa immersed herself into the video to the extent that she could actually feel what Thomas Hunter felt. For the first time in years, he was going home.

The Hunter on the video climbed the stairs to the third floor and slowly walked down the hallway toward the attic stairs. He unlatched the door and began his ascent. Lisa heard a voice cut in over the video. "Where are you, Tom? This isn't part of our program." Lisa recognized the voice; it was the programmer, Cooper.

"Leave me alone," Hunter said.

"Hunter? Where did you go?" The tech sounded nervous. "Your signal's gone. Tom, where are you?" Hunter reached the top of the stairs and stopped, staring into the shadows as if looking for something.

"I'm home, father," Hunter called out.

"Yes, my son," the creature answered from the shadows. "It is time to fulfill your destiny."

"I lost the book," Hunter said as if ashamed. "But I have it memorized; I know what to do."

"Good, my son. She will be here soon and you must bring her directly to me."

116

"How will I know when I have found her?" Hunter asked.

"You will feel it my son. You will know."

"Thank you father," Hunter said. "I will not fail you this time."

"I know, my son."

"And thank *you*, Lisa," Hunter said as he looked up at the camera. "Thank you for making it so easy to find you. Strange how these things happen, isn't it? I have been searching for you for my entire life only to have you simply fall into my lap. How wonderfully ironic."

"You want me you bastard?" Lisa taunted. "Fine, I'll tell you everything you want to know. Oh, and the deal stands: I come with you and you set Ashley free." "Oh, it's a deal all right." Hunter purred.

(V)

Turner stayed behind with the woman while Smith and Vasquez took the hallway to the right. This left Jason Whitney alone as he traversed the remaining passageway. He liked it this way. Wit was always willing to be a team player but he was still enchanted by the thrill of being on the hunt alone. It made him feel so alive, aware of everything around him, as if Wit and his environment were one. The hallway was long, much too long to be within the confines of the facility. There were doors here and there, labs mostly, but no sign of any survivors. The hall turned sharply and Wit stopped. The corridor suddenly ended and there was nothing before him but blackness. Wit reached his arm out into the murky darkness and it seemed to simply disappear. "What the hell," he said bravely, "I've walked into worse."

Wit stepped into the blackness and was instantly somewhere else.

Wit surveyed his surroundings. He stood on a path in the woods. There were torches illuminating the trail ahead of him so he began to walk. The forest around him was silent, with not a single bird or insect to be heard. Wit heard a commotion in the distance, grunts and snarls, echoing through the trees of the forest. He followed the path cautiously until he spotted a light up ahead. Wit stopped and squinted into the night at the scene in front of him. The creatures sat around a fire, several fighting over the remnants of something charred beyond recognition. They looked half human and half animal, standing upright, but walking half hunched over. They had long, razor sharp claws and teeth, and big dark eyes on heads that resembled pit bulls. Wit looked around and saw a church just beyond the bonfire. There were dozens more of the creatures surrounding the church as if guarding something sacred. Now was *not* the time to be playing the hero; Wit knew he would need help on this one. He needed his team with him to see what was

117

inside of that church. Jason Whitney turned around and headed back down the path he'd come in on. He walked until the torches ended and where he had originally entered the forest through the blackness. Wit pulled his modified shotgun from his shoulder and switched on the flashlight mounted to the weapon. He aimed the beam ahead of him as he silently crept down the path. Nothing happened. He was not transported back to the hallway but simply found himself walking down a dark path in the woods. "Looks like it was a one way trip," Wit mumbled to himself as he walked. The path widened and soon became a huge clearing with a circle of large stones in the center. The five massive monoliths must have weighed thousands of pounds each and were arranged upright in a tight circle. Wit approached the structure and examined the symbols engraved into the stone; they were like no language he had ever seen, with far too many symbols representing any known dialect to him. Wit ran his hand over one of the stones. It was warm to the touch and sent a soft vibration through his palm that traveled halfway up his arm. Wit's fingers tingled for a moment after he pulled his hand away. He noticed that there was just enough room for a person to slide between the stones and more than ample room for one to stand at the center of the monuments. Wit slithered inside the structure and the stones began to glow a soft blue. Wit placed his hand to the stone once more and for a moment nothing happened.

The light emanating from the stone that Wit had placed his palm on turned green and a sudden shock coursed through his fingers. He let go. One by one the remaining stones turned green and the world outside the monoliths began to spin. Wit closed his eyes for a moment and when he opened them the spinning had stopped. One by one the stones returned to a soft blue glow and Wit stepped out from between the slabs. He stood in a field that stretched as far as the eye could see, the monolith the only structure in sight. Wit shielded his eyes with his hand and scanned the horizon. The sun was low in the sky and darkness was slowly setting in. Wit made one final scan of his surroundings and that's when he saw it, something shining in the distance, the light from the setting sun reflecting off the surface of some unknown object. Wit pulled his knapsack on and shouldered his rifle and shotgun before setting off in the direction of the shining object.

(VI)

Smith and Vasquez opened the five doors one at a time and stood back, peering inside. Two of the doors had rooms on the other side. There was nothing but blackness beyond one door and the remaining two contained other worlds. One held a forest with large twisted trees and behind the other was a snow-covered mountain. "Hmm… dark and creepy or cold and windy… I'll flip you for it." Vasquez reached into his pocket and pulled out a coin. "You're on, homey, but I'm warning you, this is my lucky quarter." Vasquez tossed the quarter into the air. "I call heads." He reached out and pulled the spinning coin from the air, slapped it on the back of his other hand, and looked down. "Hot damn!" Vasquez gloated. "I choose dark and creepy; have fun freezing your ass off!" Vasquez laughed as he stepped through the doorway and into the forest beyond.

(VII)

Smith stepped through the doorway. The snow was almost up to his knees making it extremely difficult to walk. He scanned the mountain above him and spotted a cave with smoke billowing out. "At least I know there's a warm fire at the end of this," Smith mumbled as he trudged through the snowdrifts. The wind on the mountain was brutal, stinging his face as he pushed onward. He had covered half the distance in approximately twenty minutes but fatigue was beginning to set in and it would take nearly twice that to make it the rest of the way. Smith stopped and hunched down in the snow and out of the wind. He rubbed his hands together to warm them up and rested for a moment. "C'mon Randal, get your ass moving." Smith stood up after giving himself a pep talk and began climbing the mountain once more. The snowdrifts were so deep in places that Smith sometimes lost sight of the cave altogether. He had to rely on his instincts and trust his own judgment if he wanted to make it out alive. He could see the entrance clearly now, soft flickers of flames bouncing around the walls of the cave. Smith pulled himself up to get a good look at the interior of the cave.

There was a large cauldron hanging above the fire. Smith moved closer to investigate, his eyes on the shadows of the cave as he advanced. Inside the cauldron were the dismembered remains of a man, stewing in the boiling water. Smith saw something out of the corner of his eye, something moving within the shadows of the cave. He quickly removed the shotgun slung over his shoulder.

"That's right," Smith taunted, "I got eight, high powered incendiary rounds with your name on them, now come on, come get some." The creature moved swiftly, but so did Randal; he aimed and fired twice. The beast slowed down a little so Smith fired two more rounds. The creature dropped to its knees and fell forward. Randal pulled out his pistol and placed it against the beast's forehead. He looked the creature over; it was tall, standing almost eight feet. Its anatomy was mostly human, all but the long thin arms and legs with razor sharp claws on all four appendages, and the head. The creature's head was shaped like a shield, with elongated features that came to a point on each side of its face with a third, higher point on the top of its head. It had four sets of eyes, two large and two small, located on each side of its face. Two slits for a nose were placed just below the eyes and the rest of the creature's face was mouth and teeth. Smith pulled the trigger. Blood and brain matter splattered across the walls of the cave and the creature fell dead to the ground.

119

Smith began searching the cave. A wristwatch with blood smeared on the face, a cordless power drill, a set of dentures, and endless amounts of clothing were heaped in piles in the darkened corners of the room. Smith found a heavy winter jacket that looked like it would fit him in this Godforsaken cold.

He placed his weapons on the ground and wiggled his way into the coat. He retrieved his weapons, slung his rifle and shotgun over his shoulder, and holstered his pistol. Smith reached into the pockets of the coat and his hand wrapped around something round and hard. He pulled it out and opened his hand to find a compass. He opened the lid and saw that the needle was pointing not north but southeast. "What the hell? Looks like it's all downhill from here." Smith placed the compass back in his pocket and began his decent down the mountain.

CHAPTER THIRTEEN

The Vessel

(I)

Gillian placed the disc containing the final sessions of Thomas R. Hunter in the tray of the computer and clicked play. The disc contained six sessions dated August eighteenth. Gillian clicked on the first file and waited for the program to load. Four images of a comatose Thomas Hunter appeared on the screen. A fifth window opened overlapping the previous screen. Thomas Hunter stood in the hallway of the load program. He walked down the hall and stopped in front of the door.

"Sorry guys, but I'm going to need a little privacy on this one," he said before opening the door. Thomas Hunter stepped through the doorway and the screen went black. The video feed was gone but the audio remained. There were screams that sent shivers down Gillian's spine. Cries of torture and suffering. All the while, Thomas Hunter whistled a sweet melody that contrasted with the sounds in the background in such a way that Gillian had to fight to continue listening to the session. The whistling and the screams stopped suddenly and Thomas Hunter spoke, "I'm here, father." He was answered with not one voice but many. ***"She will be here soon, my son. You need to be ready."***

"I *am* ready, father. My powers have grown since we've last met and here, in this program, I am ready to take complete control."

"Good, my son." the Mille Umbra answered back. "Remember how special she is; nothing shall harm her, Thomas, nothing!"

"I will keep her safe."

"She is stronger than you know, my son. The only thing working in our favor is that she does not know this. Find a way to lead her to me and I will do the rest."

"Yes, father."

The session ended and the screen disappeared, leaving the four images of Thomas Hunter lying in a bed wired up to the machine.

(II)

They're talking about me, Lisa thought to herself. She watched the doctor select another session on the disk and, when everyone was sufficiently distracted, Lisa climbed into the ductwork and out into the facility in search of Thomas Hunter. She wanted Ashley back and she wanted answers. Who was she? Why was Lisa Spencer so important? These questions and more would be answered one way or another; Lisa was going to make damn sure of that! She let her gut tell her which way to go as she climbed through the network of ducts that led throughout the facility. She eventually exited through a grate into a vast room with five large stone pillars in the center. Lisa walked around the monoliths that towered above her and slipped in between them. The stones began to glow and the room outside began to spin and, when it stopped, Lisa's surroundings had changed to a clearing in a dark forest. She stepped out from between the stones and began walking down a torch-lined path.

Lisa approached the clearing and froze. She was back at the old dilapidated church with the bonfire raging outside. Hunter's pets crowded around the fire fighting over the last remnants of a meal. She remembered Thomas Hunter saying that he would protect her and decided to put it to the test. Lisa stepped out from the tree line and approached the raging beasts. The creatures howled and hissed but none of them even attempted to move toward Lisa. They even parted as she walked between them to reach the door of the church. She opened the door and stepped inside. In the middle of the room was a hospital bed containing the comatose body of Thomas Hunter.

"I wanted to die," said a voice from behind her. Lisa turned to face another Thomas Hunter, but this one's head was not shaved like the Hunter on the bed. "I was tired of looking for answers and never living up to father's expectations." He said in a calm voice. "I was tired of looking for *you*."

"What makes *me* so damned important?" Lisa demanded.

"In time, the Umbra will enlighten you. Be honored he has requested to see you. It is a rare privilege." Thomas Hunter circled around Lisa. "Wow, it really *is* you. I can feel the darkness."

"Answer my question!" Lisa yelled.

"It starts with your father," Hunter explained. "I never met him but I *did* meet his murderer. Met him in a psyche ward in Raleigh, North Carolina. Marcus was a nice guy though. He had a connection to the Umbra, as well, although nowhere near as special as your own."

"What do the Mille Umbra and I have in common?" Lisa pleaded. "How am I connected to them?"

"I will let father answer that question. Come," Thomas Hunter reached out his hand and Lisa took it. They were instantly transported to a new location. They stood near a well, just off the path leading to the electrical room. "He will meet you in the darkness, out beyond the fields." Hunter pointed down the path in the direction Lisa was to follow. "I cannot go with you, but I *will* see you soon." Hunter smiled and disappeared.

(III)

Wit walked across the field for what seemed like hours before reaching his destination. As he approached the object shining in the distance, Wit had thought he'd figured out what it was several times before realizing it was the sunset's reflection off of a statue of a woman standing on a pedestal leaning on a rather odd looking sword. As Wit approached the statue it moved, pulling back on the sword that was embedded into the pedestal, pointing it at him. The statue was gray and there was a plaque with strange symbols carved into the pedestal. The statue spoke, "Stand your ground, warrior." When she spoke it was with two distinct voices, both female, one a pleasant tone and the other a dark, angry voice.

"Who are you?" Wit asked the woman.

"I am two, born of both darkness and light."

"Do you have a name?"

"I have no one to name me," the statue answered.

"How 'bout I give you a name? Wit suggested.

"Would you do that for me?" the statue asked excitedly.

"How about October; your color reminds me of a cloudy fall day."

"October," the statue repeated the name, sounding pleased.

"You can call me Wit. Now, what can you tell me about what in the hell is going on around here?"

"It's Thomas Hunter," the statue explained, "and the girl."

"I know about Hunter. *What* girl?"

"She is very powerful, more powerful than Hunter."

"What makes her so powerful?"

"It's her bloodline. She is born of darkness, yet she walks in the light. She has the power to give life and the power to take it away. Not just *your* life but *all* life! Protect the daughter of darkness at all

123

costs, for she is the key to unlocking this maze." The woman drove the sword back into the pedestal and leaned on the weapon, taking the pose of the statue once more.

"How do I find her?" Wit hastily asked the woman. The statue stood still and did not reply. "Great!" Wit exclaimed, "Where to from here?" It was then he noticed the metal doors in the hillside partially covered in grass and weeds. Wit uncovered the doors and pried one side open. There was a set of stairs beyond.

Wit stepped through the doorway and descended into the darkness.

(IV)

"Where's Lisa?" Bruce asked as he swiftly walked around the room. "Did anybody see her leave? We've got to find her, she's in danger out there."

"Calm down" Gillian said as she stood. "We'll all go look for her. Derek, you know this place better than any of us, so you're up front, Bruce, you follow behind me."

"Gladly," Bruce teased, "It's a hell of a view from back here."

"Dr. Spencer, is this your way of flirting with me?"

"Nope, just stating a factual observation."

"Come on," Gillian motioned, "and try to keep your mind out of the gutter and your eyes off of my ass."

Bruce followed Gillian into the ductwork where they caught up with Derek at an intersection.

"Where to?" Derek asked.

"The caves," Gillian suggested. "I ran into Thomas Hunter there for the first time in a cavern with a pool of blood."

"I know precisely where you're talking about," Derek said with a smile. "It's this way." Derek took the shaft to the left, as Gillian and Bruce followed closely behind. The metal ductwork slowly changed to a soft red stone before ending as a dimly lit earthen passageway. Bruce and Gillian wiped the dirt from their clothing as best they could while Derek wandered up ahead with the only flashlight. "This way," Derek called back to them, the sound echoed around the walls of the cave. Bruce and Gillian quickly caught up with Derek and the three quietly proceeded down the passageway, no one saying a word.

The cave suddenly opened up into a cavernous room with the familiar pool of blood along the far wall. Gillian looked up at the intricate carvings scattered throughout the roof and walls of the cave. She looked hard at the pool of blood as they slowly crossed the large room. She saw the tubes dangling from the darkness above the pool but there was no Thomas Hunter. "His body's been moved," Gillian pointed out. "Then he won't mind if we take a look around," Bruce declared. Gillian, of course, was already doing some investigating of her own. Last time she was here there were creatures hidden in the darkness calling her name. Gillian's head was quiet this time. Hunter's pets seemed to have followed him to whatever hole he was hiding in now. Gillian rejoined the group by the pool.

"I've seen some of these symbols before," Bruce pointed out. "Written on the walls of the room of the man who killed my brother Andrew, Lisa's father. Thomas Hunter was a patient there just before this happened. What's the connection?" Bruce stood with a puzzled look on his face as he tried desperately to make sense of things. It was then that he noticed the droplets of blood on the floor and the footprints. The prints were mostly human, aside from a few claw marks smeared in blood. Bruce followed the trail to another cave. "This way," he called out. Gillian and Derek hastened to catch up and the three exited the cave at the same time. Bruce looked down at the forest below, listening to screams that echoed up the hillside. "The trail goes this way." Bruce started down the small path that descended into the dark forest.

(V)

Vasquez made his way through the thick underbrush as quietly as he could, which was not easy considering the dense vegetation in the forest. The screams bothered him at first but he blocked them out and concentrated solely on the mission. This was turning out to be one of the weird ones. It went without saying that every mission SEAL teem Zero deployed had their share of the bizarre, but this one was *definitely* in the top ten. Vasquez stopped when he came to a clearing. Looking out through the bushes, Angel Vasquez examined the cabin, outbuilding and the surrounding area. He saw no movement and heard no sounds other than the screams from the forest. Vasquez advanced to the front door of the cabin and pushed it open, entering with his weapon of choice drawn, an M16 that had been handed down to him from his father. Angel loved his gun. He stripped it and cleaned it every day, and his weapon was in such fine shape that it looked to have been bought recently, and bore no resemblance to the twenty year old gun it was. It shot fast and never jammed. Angel had named the gun Virginia, after the girl who had given him his first blowjob. The gun's name had been Scarlet before that, back when his father owned it. But she was Angel's now and they'd been through a lot together, killed a lot of really strange things, and seen a lot of extremely bizarre places, like this cabin in the woods, with its blood soaked walls and piles of half eaten animal carcasses. Some of the animals looked vaguely familiar while others were like nothing Angel Vasquez had ever seen in his life. One was half dog and half spider, while another looked like a cross

125

between a deer and a wolf. Vasquez made his way around the piles of dead things as he searched the cabin. He found it empty until he returned to the front room where there were now a dozen or so humanoid creatures with long sharp claws and fangs standing outside the open doorway of the cabin. Vasquez reached for the door swiftly and pushed it shut. He found the lock and slid the bar into the hole, then backed away from the door, his gun at the ready. The creatures just stood there, not trying to gain access to the cabin, they just stood there and slobbered. One of them screamed, then another. The noises were answered with cries from deep within the woods. Vasquez listened as hundreds of screams answered the call and the forest filled with the sound of movement through the trees all around the cabin. Vasquez glanced out the window and saw that there were at least a hundred of the creatures in the front yard and no idea how many surrounded the house from the other directions. Angel heard the sound of a window shattering from one of the back rooms. The creatures were in the house! Something slammed hard against the front door and more glass shattered from somewhere within the cabin. Angel's eyes landed on a trapdoor in the floor and he sprinted across the room. He pulled the door open and climbed down into the cellar of the small cabin.

"There'd better be another way out of this place," Vasquez mumbled to himself as he searched the basement. He pulled out a small bright flashlight and checked every corner of the room until satisfied he was alone. The basement was nothing more than a square hole dug beneath the cabin with large support beams here and there to support the structure. Angel sat down on a wooden crate and pulled out a cigar. He retrieved a box of matches from a zippered pocket and lit the end, inhaling deeply. The room filled with the smell of sulfur followed by the sweet aroma of the tobacco. Angel only had a moment to enjoy the smoke before catching movement out of the corner of his eye. He turned around and aimed his flashlight into a darkened corner of the room. They were everywhere, as if they had simply climbed through the walls. The creatures all attacked at once. Vasquez tightened his finger around the trigger and sprayed the weapon in all directions. Dozens of creatures lay dead but more just kept coming. Vasquez pulled out his knife and began swiping the blade at the creatures that made it past the gunfire. He was putting up one hell of a fight, but there were just too many of them. Two more bursts of gunfire sounded out then stopped as the creatures swarmed over the body of Angel Vasquez and began to eat him alive.

(VI)

Bruce heard the gunfire and picked up his pace. He had to slow down every now and then to allow Derek and Gillian to catch up. Part of him wanted to just sprint down the path in the direction of the shots, but Bruce was a quick learner: if he didn't want to get separated from his fellow travelers he had better keep them in sight. The path eventually opened up into a clearing where there was a cabin. Bruce stopped and motioned for Gillian and Derek to be quiet. A lot of *something* was rushing through the forest but thankfully, whatever it was, was moving away from the cabin. Bruce motioned for the two to follow and began his cautious approach toward the building. He climbed the steps to find the front door had been torn from its hinges. The inside was a mess, with furniture toppled over and scattered about, and the floor and walls covered with thousands of bloody footprints amidst the animal carcasses.

Bruce stepped inside and walked across the floor to the trap door. He tried to lift it but it was jammed.

Bruce scanned the room until he noticed a long thick rod by the fireplace. "Hand me that poker." Derek, who was already standing next to the fireplace, was lost in his own little world. He looked around nervously, muttering to himself. Gillian walked over and grabbed the poker before joining Bruce by the trap door. She handed the rod to Bruce who wedged the tip under the wood and began to pry. It took some effort, but the wood finally gave with a loud crack, and then it swung open.

Bruce grabbed the flashlight from Derek and descended the stairs to the basement. Gillian followed closely behind. "Derek?" she called out.

"Huh?" Derek looked up and saw the doctor's head sticking up out of the floor.

"Come on," Gillian said. "We stick together."

"Oh, ok." Derek reluctantly left his place by the mantel and joined Dr. Black at the stairs.

"I'm not so sure you guys want to come down here," Bruce called out from below.

Gillian knelt down on the steps and got a good look at the basement. "He's military," Gillian said. Bruce hunched over what was left of the body and examined the clothing. There were patches with insignias sewn into the jacket. "Looks like Navy, name of Vasquez," Bruce said as he pried the M16 from the corpse's hand. He noticed a handgun in the bloody mess and picked it up, tucking it into the back of his pants. Bruce rolled the body over and removed the shotgun and backpack the man had been wearing before he met his demise. Bruce rummaged through the sack and took a quick inventory of the ammo and explosives and, against his better judgment, he handed the backpack to Derek. It was that or the shotgun and Bruce would rather see the attractive doctor Gillian Black wielding the weapon. It's strange what can turn a man on these days. Chicks with guns, *hell yeah*, Bruce decided he liked the idea. "Here, the safety's off. All you have to do is point and shoot; it reloads automatically." Bruce handed Gillian the shotgun.

"It's really disgusting down here and I need a cigarette," she said as she took the weapon and slung it over her shoulder. Gillian reached into her pocket and pulled out her lighter and pack of smokes. She slid one out of the box and lit it while climbing the stairs.

"Mind if I get one of those from you?"

Gillian looked up and saw Dr. Allen Carlton standing in the doorway to the cabin.

"Damn, Carlton, is it possible for you to get uglier each time we meet?

"Ha ha," Carlton said sarcastically, "Now shut up and give me a smoke."

Gillian pulled out a cigarette and handed it to the doctor. "I suppose you're going to ask me for a light now, too." She held the lighter up and lit the cigarette for Dr. Carlton.

"Thanks," he said. "Who was down there?"

"A Navy SEAL, one of Forsythe's, I think. There will be others and we need to find them."

"Who are you talking to?" Bruce asked as his head popped up from the stairway in the floor. "Oh, Carlton, is it? Nice to see you again. Oh who am I kidding? I could live the rest of my life without seeing that face and die a happy man."

"This guy's been hanging around *you* for far too long," Carlton said to Gillian.

"What can I say," Gillian teased. "I kind of like having him around." Gillian's eyes caught the expression on Bruce's face when she said this and she blushed and quickly changed the subject. "So,

Carlton, you seen any other SEALs around?"

"Nope, but I'll let you know as soon as I find them."

"Bummer, I was kind if hoping you'd stick around for a little while."

"Why, Dr. Black, you even sounded sincere. Don't worry, I can stick around and dig for information at the same time. Remember, I'm part of this place now, I have my ways. Besides, I have some information for Dr. Spencer over there. It would seem that your niece has a meeting with the Umbra that's running things around here."

"Then we need to find her. *Now!*" Bruce turned and ducked his head down into the basement. "Derek, get your ass up here; we're leaving."

"Right," Derek agreed. "We need to leave here."

Bruce and Derek climbed the stairs and joined Dr. Black and Dr. Carlton who were reminiscing outside the cabin. Carlton stopped talking and turned to face Bruce. "We follow this path," he said as he pointed to a barely noticeable opening in the thick underbrush beneath the canopy of trees. Carlton began walking towards the path. Bruce, Gillian, and Derek fell into line and followed him into the darkness of the forest.

(VII)

Wit traversed the passageway that seemed to go on forever. The walls were made of large carved stones mortared together and the ceiling was exposed wood. Large cross braces were staggered about every five feet and water pipes were attached to the beams with clamps. Some of the lines were leaking, leaving the earthen floor muddy in patches. Wit navigated around the puddles in the dim lighting of the tunnel that consisted of four foot florescent fixtures placed every twenty feet or so. Some had only one bulb that worked while others had faulty ballasts and continuously flickered off and on. Wit let out a sigh of relief when he finally saw a door ahead of him. He tried the handle but it was locked. Jason Whitney leaned his AK-47 against the wall and retrieved a lock-pick set from his backpack, opening the door in less than fifteen seconds. Wit retrieved his gun and entered the room that lay beyond. He flicked on the light switch and instantly found himself in Heaven. The room was filled to the brim with computer equipment. Wit took a seat in front of a large wide screen monitor and pulled the keyboard across the table. He rested his weapon on his lap and began hacking into the system.

It took Wit less than two minutes to gain access to the mainframe. He had access to the cameras, microphones, and motion detectors, as well as all the data on every patient and every session involving Project Lucidity. Wit scanned through the files until he found the name Thomas Hunter. He clicked on the sessions and began to watch until he had gained all of the knowledge possible from the videos. He turned his attention to the cameras next, discovering that the system stored up to two weeks of data from each camera. Wit pulled up the files from the day contact had been lost with the NeuroTech facility and began watching the events that had taken place on the island. A thousand thoughts filled Wit's head as he watched. It would seem that Thomas Hunter had somehow opened a doorway to Hell and unleashed a vile terror on the unsuspecting staff of the facility. He had somehow unleashed a Mille Umbra. Wit had never seen one but he had heard stories. They could take on any shape they desire but tended to lean toward the dramatic and bizarre when it came to showing themselves. Some, like this particular creature, were composed of the souls it had devoured. There could be dozens or there could be thousands of shadowy figures that made up the creature's mass. Other Umbra preferred to take the form of a person's darkest nightmares, like monsters with hundreds of tentacles and thousands of eyes. Wit needed more information, but he had gained all of the knowledge contained within the mainframe of the facility, and it was time to move on. The coms weren't working and Wit needed to make contact with his team. He searched the room only to find a single exit other than the door he had entered. On the rear wall of the room was a vent shaft, with the grate already removed, indicating that the shaft had been recently utilized, so it must lead somewhere. Wit slung his rifle over his shoulder and pulled out his handgun, then tied his knapsack to his right foot and slipped inside the narrow shaft. The ductwork ended when it intersected with a tunnel dug into the earth. Wit climbed out of the shaft and crawled on his hands and knees until he reached the bottom of a well shaft. He placed his backpack over his shoulders followed by his rifle and shotgun and began to climb.

(VIII)

Lisa Spencer came out of the woods and entered the field beyond. She walked until the ground gave way to nothingness and stopped on the edge where the grass just simply vanished. "Show yourself," she called out. "I'm not afraid of you, now tell me what you want!"

"You," boomed a voice from the blackness. ***"We want you, Lisa Spencer."***

"Why me? Why am I so important?"

"You are the vessel that can carry the destroyer."

"Vessel… destroyer? What in the *hell* are you talking about?" The creature moved in closer so that Lisa could get a good look at it. Its shadows writhed and screamed as they twisted and turned within the confines of the Umbra's body. "I'm tired of this bullshit," Lisa called out. "I want answers."

"Then we shall start with your father."

"What does Andrew Spencer have to do with any of this?"

"Not Andrew, you fool! He was simply a vessel much like yourself. I'm speaking of your true father, the Mille Umbra called Animus."

"Animus? Make some sense, beast, or I'm waking."

"Your true father was one of seven, cast out of Hell and trapped within the Nexus. Animus made a deal with a soul about to be reborn into the multiverse, a deal that stripped him of most of his power, but also allowed him to live out his life among man instead of trapped inside the Nexus and unable to do nothing but watch."

"But you made it out, and you didn't have to lose any of your power in the process."

"Yes, the bridge that opened within the house where young Thomas Hunter grew up allowed me to enter this world, but it did not allow me to keep all of my power. I have Hunter to thank for most of what is happening on this island. He's strong, but not like you. Yes, you, the daughter of an Umbra.

With my help, you will give birth to a child that can unmake reality."

"Um, not likely," Lisa said in a disgusted tone. The Umbra just laughed. "Tell me about my true father," she demanded. "Tell me about this Animus."

"Your father was one of seven…"

"Yeah, yeah," Lisa cut the Umbra off. "One of the seven deadly sins."

"Pride," the Umbra added. "I wonder if he would have been proud of what he had done, if he had known the power you hold. It was I who figured it out. Only the daughter of a daughter of a Mille Umbra could change reality as they see fit. With the right guidance this child would be unstoppable! I plan on fathering this child and together we will watch the species of the multiverse fall to their knees and pray for us to save them. Oh, how sweet it will be!"

"What is your name, Umbra?" Lisa asked.

"Desideo," The creature answered.

"Well, Desideo, you can keep living in your fantasy world and you can go *fuck* yourself! I know you have no power here, or you'd have already done to me whatever it is you have planned, so I hold the cards here. Now tell me, how did my father die?"

"Andrew Spencer was killed by one of my brethren, an Umbra by the name of Ira, wrath!"

"You say *Andrew* was killed, what of the Umbra Animus?"

"Animus lived on, eventually entering the consciousness of your father's supposed murderer, Marcus Quincy, allowing your father to join your mother in heaven. The fool even sacrificed himself to save Marcus, allowing him to destroy Ira."

"So, your kind *can* be destroyed."

"There are ways, but they are not easy, and it's highly unlikely a human can figure out how to do it."

"Marcus Quincy did," Lisa reminded the Umbra.

"Only with the help of Animus, only with the help of an Umbra."

"But still, it *can* be done, and I *will* find a way, I promise you that!"

"There is only one ending to this story, Lisa Spencer. You will become mine."

"I write my own story!" Lisa burst into a rage. "And neither you or Thomas Hunter are going to do a damn thing about it! Now tell me, where is Ashley Spencer?"

"Hunter has the child, and I doubt he will be able to stop you from taking her. You may not fear me here, Lisa Spencer, but we will meet again under different circumstances in the very near future and

I will not be as tolerant of your insolence."

"Then I guess this conversation has come to an end. Goodbye, Desideo." Lisa turned her back on the creature and began walking across the field toward the forest.

CHAPTER FOURTEEN

The Gathering

(I)

The needle on the compass suddenly reversed direction and Smith stopped. He turned around and inched his way backward until the compass began to move. Randall got down on his hands and knees and began brushing away and digging out the hard compacted snow. He felt something metallic underneath and began digging until he found an edge of something hard. Smith cleared the rest of the snow out from around a grate before digging through his backpack for a small pry bar. The metal gave easily and Smith removed the cover. He dropped his backpack down into the vent shaft and listened for a thump but there was none. "What the hell," Smith said with a grin and then dropped into the hole.

The vent shaft curved, slowing Smith's descent. He coasted for a moment before coming to a complete stop. Unfortunately, he'd stopped directly over another opening in the floor of the shaft, and poor Randal began to plummet once more. The fall was short but still hurt like hell. Randall rolled over and retrieved his backpack from the ground next to him and stood. He placed the pack over his shoulders and began to search the room. He was in one of the labs. Smith saw the bed in the center of the room, the racks of equipment, and the cameras scattered about. "Whitney? Vasquez? Turner? Ya'll there?" There was no reply; the coms were still dead. Smith searched the room for anything useful but found nothing of interest but the door. Smith opened the door and stepped out into the hallway. He looked around, but nothing looked familiar, and Smith had spent *days* studying the facility's blueprints and building plans. He chose to go right and walked down the hall with his M4A1 at the ready. The hallway ended with a door that led into a cemetery. Smith had been in a multitude of weird ass situations as a spec op SEAL, so he figured he'd just go with it. He walked among the gravestones until he heard noises ahead of him. They sounded animal like, grunts, growls, and high pitched chirps, but they were *definitely* carrying on a conversation. Smith stepped out from behind a mausoleum and saw the creatures that had been making the sounds he'd been hearing. They each held a shovel and were filling in a hole in the ground. The creatures saw Randall and let out an ear-piercing scream. They dropped their shovels and began to charge towards him. Two short bursts of gunfire later and both creatures lay dead with half of each of their heads missing. Smith looked the things over as he passed them by on his way to the hole in the ground that the creatures had been filling in. The grave marker read "Mess Hall". Smith grabbed a shovel and began to dig until he reached another grate that covered yet another vent shaft. He pried it loose and dropped down into the darkness.

There were bodies everywhere and the amount of blood was startling. Smith noticed the smears in the carnage and recognized them for what they were. Someone had been through here recently. Smith followed the trail into the kitchen where he found several bloody footprints on a countertop beside the skillet and fryer. Whoever it was that had been there before him had climbed up into the exhaust vent above the stove. Smith removed his backpack and shotgun and threw them up into the shaft before climbing up onto the countertop and pulling himself up into the exhaust vent. He had to crawl on his stomach for a while, but the shaft eventually widened enough that Smith could crawl on his hands and knees. The shaft suddenly went from metal to dirt and once again began to widen. Smith stopped when he came to a hole in the ceiling; it was the bottom of a well. He stood up and surveyed his surroundings. "Piece of cake," he said to himself. Smith wiggled into his backpack then slung his shotgun and rifle over his shoulder and began to climb.

(II)

"Things are coming together perfectly, father. They are all gathering together."

"You're doing an excellent job, my son." The Umbra paused for a moment while lost in thought. "You may not be the one, Thomas Rothery, but you have brought her to me…"

"Hunter! My name is Thomas *Hunter*!" he exploded into a rage.

"Let it out, my son," The Umbra almost sounded sincere. "What matters is that the chosen one is here and within our grasp."

"She's powerful,"

"More powerful than you can imagine. You must be careful, my son."

"I'm ready. The SEALs will try to regroup and assess their situation. "Witless" and that redneck Smith will soon learn of Vasquez's death and will go in search of Turner. We will be ready for them. We'll dispose of them first and then go and drag Lisa Spencer out of her hiding place by her long beautiful hair if we have to. I will not fail you this time, father."

"I know you won't," the Umbra sighed. "Now go, Thomas Hunter, go and bring me the Daughter of Darkness."

"As you wish," Hunter lowered his head and opened his eyes. He was back in the church, left staring at his comatose body lying in a hospital bed. His pets tried to amuse him, but Hunter had other things on his mind. "Not now," he ordered and the beasts settled down. "It's time to watch and wait."

Hunter sat down on the floor and closed his eyes, concentrating solely on Dr. Gillian Black.

(III)

"Gillian," the voice echoed through her head. "Hunter," Gillian mumbled. "Leave me the hell alone." Dr. Black stopped and shook her head. "Bruce," she called out.

"Right here," he answered from somewhere nearby. It was dark and all she could see were silhouettes. Gillian caught up to Bruce who placed his finger to his lips. "Quiet," he whispered, "I think I hear someone climbing up the well."

"I'm going back to my room now," Derek stated. "I suggest you do the same." Derek turned and headed off down the dark path that led to his electrical room.

Gillian raised her shotgun and aimed at the mouth of the well. Bruce positioned himself on the other side, his automatic rifle locked and loaded. He had his trigger finger ready to squeeze at a moment's notice, but his whole body relaxed when Bruce realized that the hand clutching the stone at the top of the well was human.

"Climb out of there nice and slow," Bruce ordered with his weapon drawn. "Now, down on the ground!" Wit did as instructed and lay face down on the ground. "Those are Lieutenant Vasquez's weapons. What have you done with him?"

"The only thing we did to the poor guy was strip his corpse of his weapons. We found him dead in a cabin in the woods. It was too late for him by the time we arrived. I swear there was nothing we could have done to help him." Bruce lowered his weapon and held out his hand. Wit took it and stood. "Who are you people? And what in the hell is *that*?" Wit pointed to Dr. Carlton.

"He's okay," Gillian cut in, " it's Dr. Allen Carlton. He was my colleague and above all else he was a friend, regardless of what he is now."

"You know, I'm standing right here, Gillian, do you need to keep referring to me in the past tense?"

"Well, you *are* technically dead," Gillian said.

"You're right, which means I can't leave here. But I *can* help *you* to get out."

Gillian lowered her weapon and extended her hand. "Dr…"

"Gillian Black," Wit cut in. "I've read your file, but you," he pointed at Bruce with his weapon, "you don't work here. Who is he Dr. Black?"

"He's a doctor from Raleigh, a family physician. His boat got caught in the storm. He's here with his niece, Lisa, who we're trying to find when you climbed out of that well."

"I'm Captain Jason Whitney, U.S. Navy. So, what the hell happened here?" Wit could contain the question no longer. After everything he had seen and experienced he simply had to know.

"Now *that's* the question of the day," Smith huffed as he pulled himself up out of the well and dropped to the ground by his commanding officer's feet. "Where are Turner and Vasquez?"

"As far as I know, Turner is still back in the room by the airlock with the woman. My coms gave out as soon as we separated, so I don't know for sure."

"And Vasquez?" Smith asked.

"Vasquez is dead," Wit stated flatly, "which means we need to regroup and formulate a new plan."

"We stick to our original plan," a voice called out from the shadows of the forest. "It's the only way." Lisa stepped out of the darkened tree line. "It's me he wants. I'm the only one who can distract him long enough for the rest of you to get out of here."

"And what about you?" Bruce demanded furiously. "How do *you* get out?"

"I'm still working on that one," Lisa answered honestly. "Don't worry Unc. I'll find a way."

"I'm not leaving without you, Lisa."

"Okay, Uncle Bruce," Lisa chuckled. "We'll work on the plan together."

"So," Wit cut in, "Thomas Hunter is running the show around here?

"Yes, he is," Gillian stated coldly. "How much do *you* know about Thomas Hunter?"

"Now is not the time," Lisa cut in "He can hear every word you're saying out here. We need to follow Derek back to the electrical room and then we can talk."

"We need to regroup with Turner." Wit said to Smith.

"Come with us," Lisa pleaded. "Tell Derek where your friend is and he can tell you how to get there." Wit and Smith looked at each other and both shrugged. "Let's go then," Wit said as he shouldered his gear and weapon. "We need to learn as much about what's going on around here as we can and these people seem to know a whole lot more than we do."

"Agreed," Smith said as he fell in line with his commanding officer.

"This way," Lisa motioned for the group to follow before turning on her heel and walking into the darkness of the tree lined path. Gillian, who'd already started back toward the electrical room, was standing just outside the doorway talking to Carlton, while Bruce had already entered the facility and was raiding the vending machines.

"I have to go now," Carlton said sadly. "I'll meet you at the well when you're ready."

Gillian smiled and hugged Carlton.

"Now that there is some twisted shit," Smith remarked as he stepped through the open doorway in the middle of the path that led to a room on the other side.

(IV)

Turner watched the woman as she slept, the small dog cuddled up close to the blanket which had slid down her body, exposing her naked skin to the waist. Turner couldn't help but stare at the woman's carved up body. He couldn't look away, and the more he looked, the more he saw. Like the fact that she wasn't breathing. Turner stumbled to the woman's side and felt for any vital signs but found none. He was about to perform CPR when the woman moved. She reached down for the blanket and pulled it up to her chin, then rolled on her side and began scratching the schnauzer behind the ears.

Turner took his seat and kept watching the woman.

"Ain't that some shit," Turner grumbled. "I get stuck here babysitting a corpse." He looked around the room for something to draw his attention away from the woman but found nothing. Shelving containing spare parts and electronics to keep the lab up and running was mounted along three of the room's walls and on the fourth wall was a metal grate leading into the facility's ductwork. Next to the vent was a desk with a wide screen monitor, keyboard, and wireless mouse sitting on top. Turner saw the tower on the floor beneath the desk and noticed that the power light was on. He stood and walked over to the keyboard and pressed enter. The monitor lit up to reveal a screen saver depicting the NeuroTech logo. Turner fumbled as best he could through the systems files, as computers were Commander Whitney's specialty, not his. Still, Turner was able to navigate through the inventory files until he stumbled upon the backup files for the labs. Turner was just about to click the button on the mouse when the screen went black for a moment and then an image appeared. It was Captain Whitney and Commander Smith; they were walking down a dark path in a dark forest. Turner's senior officers were following a small group of survivors through a doorway in the middle of the path. As soon as they all stepped inside the screen returned to black. "Whitney, Smith, do you copy?" Turner fumbled with his Navy issue headset until he heard a low stream of static. "Whitney, Smith, Vasquez, come in, over." For a moment there was no reply, only static, and then came the voice. "Hello, Turner." It wasn't a member of the team who replied but another more than familiar voice. An ex member of the team. "Thomas Hunter," Turner said.

"You sound surprised," Hunter replied.

"Well, to be honest, the last time I saw you, they were loading your comatose body onto a helicopter.

That was one hell of a head shot you took; even the Admiral was amazed you'd survived."

"Yet here I am," Hunter boasted. "Back from the dead and more powerful than ever. You'd be surprised how much time you have to think while in a coma of two years. It helped me reconnect with my inner power… and my father." Hunter paused for a moment and Turner's eyes went to the woman; she was still wrapped up in a blanket and fast asleep. "Rather fetching, don't you think?" Hunter asked furtively. "You should have seen her with her long dark hair and perfect skin, that is, before father had his way with her." Hunter chuckled and resumed talking. "I saw the way you were looking at her when the blanket had fallen down. There was such lust in your eyes, I'm almost proud of you, Turner."

"Go to hell!" Turner snapped back.

"We're closer to Hell than you could ever know," Hunter said sardonically. "You look bored, Turner. How 'bout I send out my welcoming committee to greet you and properly introduce you to the depths of my depravity?" Hunter snickered to himself. "Get ready, Turner." The com suddenly went dead and Turner heard a loud crash, followed by the sound of metal grinding and warping as the door slowly began to expand inward. In a sudden burst of energy, the door became convex and blew out large chunks of steel into the hallway. The noise startled the woman who had woken from her slumber and screamed. "What the hell was that?" she asked woozily.

"Stay put," Turner said as he readied his rifle and moved to the door. "And here," Turner tossed a small metal pry bar at the woman's feet. "Open that vent shaft." The woman's eyes followed Turner's hand as he pointed to the grate in the wall. "Why?" she asked.

"That may be our only way out of here." Turner poked his head out of the doorway and quickly scanned left and right. He saw nothing but he heard a noise that was getting closer. Hundreds of voices, more animal than human, snarled, growled, and screamed from every direction. "Hurry up back there," Turner said to the woman.

"I'm trying," she grunted. "It's my hands; they're so cold."

Turner could hear the sound of sharp claws digging into the floor, walls, and ceiling as the creatures advanced down the hallway. He even saw movement in the darkness as the beasts drew closer to his location. "Almost there," the woman called out. Turner raced across the room and pulled the pry bar from the woman's hands. One swift twist and the grate fell to the floor. "Get in," Turner ordered.

The woman wrapped herself up in the blanket, pulled the schnauzer into her arms, and entered the vent shaft. The creatures were just outside the doorway. Turner saw their deformed features and razor sharp claws and teeth as they howled in unison before climbing through the doorway from all angles. Turner backed away from the door, hunkered down, hunched over, and backed into the opening leading to the ductwork. He stopped about twenty feet in and braced himself. The creatures slowly advanced into the shaft. Turner waited until they had covered half the distance separating him from them before he began to fire his weapon. The bodies piled up quickly as the creatures fought to capture their prey. Soon the vent shaft was so clogged with bodies that the creatures could no longer move forward. Turner could hear the living pulling the dead out of the shaft one by one. "Let's move," he said to the woman. "We don't have much time."

"Where are we going?" she asked.

"Anywhere is better than here; just keep moving!" The woman did as instructed and began crawling ahead with the puppy still cradled in her arms. Turner looked back once more and pulled the shotgun from his shoulder. He aimed at the pile of bodies blocking the shaft and fired. The incendiary round struck the pile and burst into white-hot flames. "That should buy us some time," Turner said as he slung the weapon over his shoulder and caught up with the woman who was sitting at an intersection in the ductwork wondering which direction to go. "Just pick one and go," Turner grumbled. The woman chose the passage to the left.

(V)

Lisa listened as Bruce and Gillian did most of the talking, explaining what little they knew about what was happening at NeuroTech . The two SEALs just stood there and absorbed the information, asking no questions and offering up no alternate explanations for the events unfolding at the facility, as if the solders actually *believed* that what they were being told was the truth. With the end of the story came the reactions, the first one from Gillian. "Now that *that's* out of the way," she said. "You two are going to tell me everything you know about Thomas Hunter and why we were given a psychopath for a patient."

"His brain should be toast, man," Smith argued. "Christ, he shouldn't even be alive!"

"But he is!" Gillian ground out. "And he's running things around here, so I'll ask you one more time, *what do you know about Thomas Hunter?*"

Smith was about to speak when Captain Whitney raised his hand to silence his comrade. "Several years ago Thomas Hunter was part of our team. He was Admiral Forsythe's pet project, so to speak. Some of the things we saw him do were pretty amazing; it was like he always knew what was going to happen next. His pre-cognitive powers are unmatched by any so called psychic or seer, living or dead." "And you let a man with *that* kind of power over his mind be subject to neural testing and dream control?" Gillian shouted.

"We had nothing to do with the decision, ma'am. Hell, we were glad to get rid of him when he ran off and went on his little psychotic rampage. Of course, we were sent out to clean up the mess and find him. He's not an easy man to track. We were close only once. Found him hiding out in psych ward in Raleigh, North Carolina, but before we could have him transported…"

"He escaped killing five staff members in the process," Lisa cut in.

"How did you know that?" Wit demanded.

"My father died in that very hospital just days after the incident you're talking about. When I last spoke to Hunter, he told me that he had met my father's killer…"

"Hold on a minute," Wit cut in this time. "You are *in contact* with Thomas Hunter?"

"He speaks to me, tells me that I'm special, and that his father needs me." Lisa laughed for a moment before continuing. "Shit, I even met Hunter's so-called father. Now *there's* a nightmare you don't want to have creeping its way into your head at night."

"You've talked to an Umbra?" Smith blurted out before realizing his error.

"Yes, Miss Spencer, we are well aware of the existence of the Mille Umbra," Wit reluctantly explained upon seeing the confusion on Lisa's face. "But what do they want with *you*?"

"The Umbra told me that my father, Andrew, was just a vessel for the shadow named Animus"

"A vessel?" Smith questioned.

"A means to enter our world and walk among the living," Lisa explained.

"So, what is it that *this* Umbra wants from you?" Wit asked Lisa. "What makes *you* special?"

"You say your boy Thomas Hunter has power." Bruce cut in, "Well, he's not alone, let me tell you! I've seen some of the things Lisa can do and I have to admit that sometimes she scares the living shit out of me."

"Thanks, Bruce," Lisa said, taken aback.

"I didn't mean it that way," he tried to backtrack. "All I'm saying is that Thomas Hunter is not the only one with power here. You, too, seem to have some sort of control over the nightmares that have taken over the island."

"Is this true?" Wit focused his attention solely on Lisa and began prying for information. "So, what *exactly* can you do? What power do you have that will help us find and contain Thomas Hunter and return things back to normal around here?"

"He can't read my mind, well, unless I'm having a vision or a waking dream, but that's another story entirely. Anyway, I can move around out there without his knowledge, unlike the rest of you, excluding Derek, of course."

"But I can only stay hidden for short periods of time," Derek spoke up. "Eventually he finds me." "Not if we play our cards right," Lisa interjected. "I know where his body is hidden and, if we can get to it, we can take him out for good, severing the link between the Umbra and the island."

"Sounds like a doable plan," Wit approved. "So where is he?"

"His body is being guarded by his creatures. He's in an old run down church in the middle of the woods. All we have to do is hook me up to the program and I can distract him long enough for you to get to church and dispose of his physical body."

"All right," Wit agreed, "but we need to find Turner first. Derek, tell us how to get to the airlock from here."

Derek walked over to the vent shaft and poked his head inside. "Second right, first left, then down."

"Sounds simple enough," Smith chimed in.

"It may sound simple to you, young man, but let me assure you, there are far worse things than Thomas Hunter lurking around out there. You'd best watch your backs."

"Okay," Wit turned to the crowd and spoke. "Smith and I are going to find our friend and, when we get back here, we begin with Miss Spencer's plan. Are we all in agreement?" None of them sounded too enthused, but they all answered yes. "Then it's settled. You all stay put until we get back."

"And what if you *don't* come back?" Gillian blurted out. "You'd better come back; I am *not* dying on this God-forsaken island."

"We'll be back, Dr. Black," and with those final words Captain Whitney and Commander Smith entered the vent shaft and disappeared into the blackness.

Part 4: From darkness comes life

CHAPTER FIFTEEN

The Mission

(I)

Admiral Robert Forsythe stood looking out over the ocean. The tight eye of the hurricane was stationary above the island leaving the waters calm and tranquil while nearby the storm raged all around them. The Admiral had ordered the sub to surface so he could assess the situation. He held a pair of binoculars in one hand, which were presently pressed to his eyes as he scanned the wreckage of the NeuroTech compound. Behind the Admiral's back in his other hand he held a book. This book had once belonged to Thomas R. Hunter, and was his most prized possession, a simple hardbound copy of the New Testament. The Admiral had seen Thomas Hunter writing notes in the book throughout the years, but when he finally obtained the book, he'd found no writing whatsoever on any of the pages of print. The only writing was on the inside of the front cover, a short note from Hunter's mother. This made no sense to the Admiral, as he had no doubt that the book in his possession was authentic; the writing should be there. Soon after coming into possession of the book, the Admiral had paid a visit to the source of this new acquisition, Marcus Quincy. Mr. Quincy had told the Admiral he needed to read the book in the dark, so he'd tried, only to be disappointed. Was there a special skill the Admiral lacked that would allow him to gain access to this information? Or maybe even after all that the Admiral had seen throughout his career his eyes were still not truly open. Either way, something was about to change; the Admiral could feel it in his bones. He would have access to this knowledge soon enough and, if luck was on his side, he would once more possess Thomas R. Hunter.

(II)

Lisa sat on the floor, her back propped up against the door leading out to the forest. She felt her anxiety and panic rising as the outside world seemed to simply melt away only to be replaced with a new reality, a waking dream. At least it was a familiar dream; it was the morning her father had died. It was four am and something had startled her awake. Lisa had gotten up and began to wander around her apartment examining various items as if it were the very first time she had seen them. The vision came next, the vision of her father dying at the hands of a psychopath. No, that wasn't entirely true. Lisa never really got to see what happened, as if time sped up and the moment passed her by in a blur of blood and screams. She was in the examining room with her father and the patient just like every other time she had this dream. She stood up and walked over to her father who sat in a large, comfortable looking chair, while the patient was chained to the floor in a folding metal chair. The patient stood and froze for a moment. Now, that was the point where the dream accelerated and time sped by, but not this time. Lisa watched as another Marcus Quincy stepped out of the first, then a woman stepped out of this doppelganger and up onto the table separating doctor from patient. The woman was nude and had skin as black as the darkest night. She opened her mouth wide and spit out a mist of black that soon took form; Lisa recognized it as the distorted features of the shadow face of the Mille Umbra. The creature lunged at Lisa's father and took a bite out of the poor man's face. It turned and said something to Mr. Quincy before taking one last bite and discarding her father's corpse on the floor. "Interesting," a voice sounded from somewhere behind Lisa. She turned to find herself back at the apartment she had rented when this incident had taken place. Sitting on the couch was Thomas Hunter.

"It is forbidden to harm a piece of oneself," Hunter explained. "The others felt the loss of Animus and then that of Ira, but now *you* have arrived. I'm envious of you Lisa Spencer, born to be what I was intended for, yet could never be. At least I have my role to play, as do we all. You, my darling, will give birth to the chosen one, the child who can wipe out all of existence. And *I* will be there to raise the child and teach her the ways of the Umbra.

"No!" Lisa protested. "You keep your hands off of my child, she will become what *I* choose for her, not you! She doesn't have to destroy and you know that, she can also create, perhaps even the perfect world where there is no need for sin and that will make the Mille Umbra obsolete!"

"There will always be a use for evil," Hunter sighed. "Good cannot survive without it. There must always be opposites, Lisa, there must always be two."

"Yeah, well, that two does *not* have to include us," Lisa taunted as she felt the power within her rise. "Catch me if you can, *Hunter*." In a flash Lisa disappeared. Thomas Hunter concentrated, focusing all of his power on finding the woman but it was no use. She was gone! But there was something else…

(III)

Wit dropped down from the vent in the ceiling a short distance away from the airlock. Smith was soon to follow. They immediately saw the door to the storage room ripped from its hinges and the dead bodies of dozens of creatures scattered about the hallway and room. Wit saw the charred remains of the creatures in the vent shaft. "Looks like they went that way."

"Lets dig in," Smith twanged and began hauling the corpses of the creatures out of the ductwork until the shaft was exposed. Wit climbed in first, stopping at the first intersection to listen. He heard nothing.

Once his commanding officer had decided on a direction Smith climbed in and followed. Smith trusted Captain Whitney's decisions. Shit, he'd placed his life in Whitney's hands too many times to count and he always made the right decisions. The kid, younger than him by several years was smart, real smart, and Smith respected that by never doubting his commanding officer's decisions. But still, he had to ask,

"Why did you lie to them about Hunter?"

"They don't need to know he's coming with us until it's time to leave," Wit instructed. "Until then we follow the plan we made with the survivors."

The passage ended abruptly at a slotted cast iron door. Wit pulled out his knife and slid it between one of the slots, pushed up on the handle, and released the latch holding the door in place. Wit climbed out of the furnace and into a dark basement. Smith emerged next and joined Captain

Whitney as they began their sweep of the basement. The floor was dirt, covered over with rugs of all shapes and sizes, leaving a musty odor lingering in the air. A typewriter sat on an old rickety desk in one corner of the room, crumpled up papers littered the desk and the floor around it. There were two rooms off to the side and a staircase in the middle. One room was a large pantry filled with mason jars containing various fruit and vegetable combinations, with the second room containing a door that Wit pushed open slowly with the barrel of his rifle. The room was almost completely empty except for a single rug in the center of the room placed before a small wooden bench. Whitney and Smith headed for the staircase leading to the first floor of the house. The stairs led to a huge kitchen with a large window overlooking a flower garden. There were two doors leading from the kitchen.

"You take the double doors behind you," Wit said. "I'll check out this hallway."

Smith opened the heavy oak doors to reveal a stunningly large dining room with a table that could accommodate at least twenty. The west wall was lined with half a dozen windows while the east wall housed a massive stone fireplace surrounded by tapestries of Scottish origin. Smith crossed the great hall and opened another oak door leading to a spacious sitting room complete with its own enormous fireplace. Past the sitting room was a library filled with books from all cultures dating back to the fifteenth century and all were on the same subject: the occult. There were books on witchcraft, folklore, how to resurrect the dead, and how to raise a demon. Smith studied the titles for a while before moving on to the formal living room of the huge house. "More of the same," Smith grumbled to himself as he opened the door leading to the entry hall. "Maybe not." Smith was stunned by the beauty of the intricate carvings adorning the walls and banisters of the duel staircases that wound their way like a double helix to the third floor of the house. Randal's eyes fixed on the figure standing on the second floor balcony. "Welcome, Mr. Smith. It's so good to see you again."

Two words came from Randal's lips, "Thomas Hunter."

Wit followed the hallway to a huge room containing a large oak pool table covered with red felt. The table was set for a game of nine ball. The next room was another sitting room with its own small library. Wit noted the titles of the books. It would seem that all of the great minds from Plato and Aristotle to Einstein and Hawking were there. The last door led to the grand entranceway to the house.

Wit heard the voice and instantly knew who it was. He stopped at the doorway and listened.

"What's it been, Randall," Thomas Hunter pondered for a moment. "Five years?"

"Almost six. Not long enough if you ask me," Smith smarted off.

"Come now, Randall, if my memory serves me correctly, the last time we saw each other I was the one saving your ass."

"Yeah, and said ass wouldn't have been on the line in the first place if you'd have done your job and warned us about the attack. But no, you had to sneak off in the middle of the chaos and go on your little killing spree. You have no idea how often we came close to catching you…"

"I know *exactly* how close you came," Hunter cut in, "and each time it was because *I* allowed it to happen! You only caught me because *I* allowed it to happen. You see, Randall, it has all been leading up to this moment. My entire life, which you, Randall Smith, and even you, Captain Whitney, for I know you're down there listening, even *you* are a part of this historical moment."

"What's so special about this moment?" Wit asked as he stepped through the doorway and into the great hall where he joined Commander Smith. "Why have you done this? To show off, to brag about how strong your powers have grown?"

"My power is infinite here!" Hunter hissed.

"But this isn't about you is it, Hunter? No, this is about the girl."

"What do *you* know about her? You know *nothing*!"

"I know she's more powerful than you and more important to the Umbra. Your usefulness to the Mille Umbra is coming to an end, Hunter. What do you think they'll do to you when you no longer have anything to offer? Do you think your "*father*" will show you pity? Ha!" Wit laughed out loud. "You're nothing more than a puppet to them and they'll throw you away with the rest of the trash when you've served your purpose."

"Enough!" Hunter screamed. "We'll see who's right in the end, but for now, I have someone I want you to meet. Whitney, Smith, meet the Madam."

The woman stepped out of the darkness and began walking a circle around the two solders. "It's been a while since I've done two at once," she said in a sultry voice. She stopped walking and reached behind her back to unzip the tight red dress she wore. At the same time, the woman reached up and pulled two long needles from the jet black hair piled on top of her head.

(IV)

Lisa stood and spoke, "I need to go out there," she said. "I know it sounds crazy, but I need to get into Thomas Hunter's mind and I can only do that without him knowing if I'm out there."

"Then I'm going with you," Bruce told Lisa in a stern voice.

"You can't, you know what I'm going to do, and as soon as you step outside, Hunter will know what I'm doing too. Right now he doesn't know I can do this and I'd like to keep it that way. I won't go far, Bruce. I'll be right outside the door. You can even stand in the doorway if you want but do *not* step over the threshold. Trust me, Bruce, I know what I'm doing."

"If I didn't know you so well I'd cry bullshit on this one but I can tell you're serious. I've seen that look in your eyes before, Lisa. It's the same one your father would get when he knew he was right about something but couldn't prove it. He wouldn't have given up and neither will you."

"Thank you, Bruce." Lisa opened the door leading to the forest and stepped out onto the path. She took two steps, stopped, and sat down among the dirt and leaves. She closed her eyes and concentrated on Hunter as Cherry the dead prostitute had instructed her to do. It only took a moment to find him; he was entertaining himself with the SEALs, Whitney and Smith. He had unleashed the madam and her creation on the poor unsuspecting solders.

Lisa could feel Hunter's hatred toward the SEALs; he wanted to watch them die. She dug through Hunter's memories of his time with the SEALs searching for the root of his hatred. The others never truly considered Hunter to be part of the team and even openly complained about him in front of Hunter, but they were never really mean to him. The SEALs respected Hunter's abilities and knew he was an asset and, given time, they eventually would have accepted him. None of that had mattered to Thomas Hunter. He was just biding his time for opportunity to present itself and, when it did, Thomas Hunter would be free of the Admiral and free of the fools who blindly followed him. Thomas Hunter had no idea how far the Admiral was willing to go to keep Hunter as part of his collection, but the problem was, Thomas Hunter already belonged to the Mille Umbra and *nothing*, not even the Admiral and his team of SEALs, was going to stop the Umbra from getting what they wanted. Lisa returned to the present and watched from above like some phantom camera as the woman grew into the creature stitched together with razor wire. The SEALs held their ground and fired at the monstrosity before it was even complete. It was soon apparent to the SEALs that bullets were having no effect whatsoever on the monster. They switched to their shotguns, which were loaded with explosive rounds. Whitney fired off a round that took out half of poor Doug's face and that was all it took. Lisa appeared on the second floor balcony on the opposite side of the room as Thomas Hunter. "Stop this now!" she screamed out. To her surprise, the scene playing out on the floor below froze. "What a pleasant surprise!" Thomas Hunter said excitedly.

It was now or never. She had done it in the past without really knowing what she was doing, as if it were instinct, now it was time to do it again. Lisa probed Hunter's mind for the name of the fourth SEAL, Turner. She took Hunter's memories and used them against him. She used them to find the location of Lieutenant Michael Turner. He was still with the patient Danielle Harris and Ashley's schnauzer Frank. They were walking across a field not too far from this house. Lisa reached out mentally to the pet whose ears perked up. The dog leapt from the woman's arms and ran off ahead. The woman pursued the dog and Lieutenant Turner followed closely behind. With this task complete, Lisa began probing Hunter's mind even further. The more she searched Thomas Hunter's memories, the more she felt pity for the man. It wasn't long after the suicide of Thomas Rothery that the Umbra Desideo had raped his widow. She gave birth to a girl. Desideo waited for the child to come of age, all the while slowly driving his offspring's mother insane. On her eighteenth birthday, Barbara Rothery watched her mother shoot herself in the head before noon and was raped by Desideo before midnight. She gave birth to a boy. The Umbra was furious, it wanted the child dead, but at the time it could not bring itself to murder its own offspring. So Desideo punished Thomas Hunter, physically by means of Hunter's stepfather, emotionally by constantly being reminded that as a boy he was useless to the Umbra. Thomas Hunter hated women with a passion; the only time he felt even a hint of love for a woman was the moment he murdered her.

"You tricked me!" Hunter snarled. He snapped his fingers and the scene on the first floor resumed playing out. The front door burst open and Turner entered with his shotgun drawn. The onslaught of the three SEALs on the creature was paying off, as the beast was down on one knee and struggling to get up. "This is far from over, Lisa Spencer," Thomas Hunter said as he and the creature below disintegrated into a black mist and disappeared.

"Are you guy's all right?" Lisa called down to the men below.

Captain Whitney was about to answer when the floor beneath their feet began to crumble and fall away. The three men looked up at Lisa with panic in their eyes as the floor gave way and the trio began to plummet into darkness.

(V)

Lisa stood and entered the doorway to the electrical room. "Hunter has the SEALs," she said as loud as she could without shouting. "We need them if we're going to pull this off."

"And Hunter's just going to hand them over?" Gillian sarcastically asked.

"He's toying with them, he wants to watch them suffer. They're out there somewhere in this facility and we can find them. Gillian, you can ask for Dr. Carlton's help, he might be able to locate the SEALs and make our job a whole lot easier. They're putting their lives on the line for us, the least we can do is return the favor, especially if it increases our odds of getting off this island alive."

"I agree," Bruce added.

"Fine," Gillian moaned.

"Not me," Derek said defensively. "I'm staying right here and staying alive."

"Fine, Derek," Lisa conceded. "We'll come back for you when we're ready to leave."

"Where do we find Carlton?" Bruce asked Gillian. "He said he'd meet me at the well, so I suppose we should start there."

"The well it is," Lisa said as she stepped out into the forest once more and began walking down the path toward the well. Bruce grabbed the weapons and followed Lisa out the door. Gillian stopped and turned to Derek. "You sure you want to stay here?"

"Sure as shit, darling," Derek replied.

"Have it your way," Gillian turned and left. She quickly caught up with Lisa and Bruce and it wasn't long before they were all standing around the well looking at one another.

"What now?" Bruce asked Gillian.

"I'm here," Dr Carlton said as he appeared out of nowhere.

"Well? Can you help us find the SEALs?" Gillian asked.

"They're in the maze," Carlton answered.

"Can you get us there?" Bruce asked.

"Not in time, but she can." Dr. Carlton pointed to Lisa.

"But I don't remember how to get there," Lisa disputed.

"I can show you." Dr. Carlton stepped forward. "Take my hands, Lisa, and look into my eyes." Lisa did as instructed. As grotesque as he was to look at, Lisa stared him right in his bulging, hemorrhaging eyes. In an instant, Lisa's mind was flooded with images of people and places.

"Think about the maze," Dr. Carlton instructed.

Lisa saw it instantly, a glimpse of a memory from the doctor. She held on to it. "Everybody join hands." Carlton, Bruce, Gillian, and Lisa formed a circle and held hands. Lisa concentrated on the entrance to the maze. The world around them began to spin and when it came to a sudden stop the four were standing in a cavern before the entrance to the labyrinth.

CHAPTER SIXTEEN

The Maze

(I)

Wit fell through the darkness, waiting for the impact that never came; he just kept falling. He called out for the others through the rush of air from his descent, but got no reply, nothing he could hear anyway. Wit suddenly stopped. There was no impact; he simply ceased falling. He could feel cold dirt beneath him as he lay on the ground. A torch on the wall ignited in a great ball of fire and left a flame bright enough to light the room around Captain Whitney. He stood and looked around. There was only one way out, a long hallway carved into the stone. Great slabs of rock made up the walls of the hallway, and Wit shined his flashlight up but saw no ceiling, only that the walls just kept going up. Wit reached into his backpack and pulled out a can of black spray paint. He marked an arrow to the right and set off in that direction in search of his team. It didn't take long for Wit to figure out he was in a maze; he just needed to learn its purpose. What was the ultimate goal, the final destination? He thought about his team as well. Poor Vasquez. He was a good solder and good man; it was going to be hard to find a replacement for him. Every now and then Wit tried his coms, but they still weren't working. Hunter's doing, no doubt. He was playing with them. Wit was willing to play along; he simply kept marking arrows at intersections and moving forward through the maze. Every now and then Wit stopped to place an explosive charge on one of the larger slabs of stone that made up the passageways. Wit wondered to himself why there were none of Hunter's little "creatures" or God knew what else. Hunter must have something bigger in store for Wit and his team. They would be ready. Wit knew his orders were to bring Hunter back alive but, by the looks of things, that seemed increasingly unlikely. Wit was not going to jeopardize the safety of his team or the survivors just so the Admiral could have his little pet back. If it came down to killing Thomas Hunter then Wit would gladly do it.

"Now that's the spirit," said a voice from behind him. Wit turned to find himself face to face with

Thomas Hunter. "Self preservation. We're not so different, you and I." "I beg to differ. For starters, I'm not a psychopath," Wit pointed out. "Sanity is a matter of perception, Captain Whitney. Who are we to judge what should be considered sane? Even *you*, Wit, in our time together, I witnessed you doing some pretty crazy shit."

"When the situation called for it," Wit replied. He knew it was useless to try and attack Hunter here, after all this was not Thomas Hunter's physical body.

"So, what do you want from me?" Wit asked as he continued his navigation of the maze, making Hunter follow him if he wanted to keep talking. "What's the point of all this?"

"Oh, you'll see soon enough." Hunter taunted. "I don't want to spoil the ending, but things don't look good for you and your team."

"We'll see about that," Wit pushed back.

"Indeed, we will. I don't mean to be rude, Captain Whitney, but I have preparations for your demise to deal with. Hope you don't mind."

"Not at all," Wit replied. "You go come up with some elaborate plan to exact some sort of sick revenge on my team, and I'll keep dreaming how sweet it would be to put another bullet hole in your head." "You always did make me laugh, Mr. Whitney. *You* won't be laughing for long!" Thomas Hunter disappeared and Wit laughed.

(II)

After that fucked up free fall Smith found himself laying face down in the dirt of a circular room. There was only one exit so Smith gathered up his gear and struck out in search of his team. The door led to a cliff overlooking a massive maze with walls the height of skyscrapers. Ascending into the darkness from the center of the maze was a ladder. Smith took it all in, trying to memorize the layout by building a map in his mind. He kept his eyes on the maze as he traversed the rocky staircase that led down to the labyrinth. Smith pushed open the iron gate and entered a long hallway. He needed to follow this hallway until it ended and take a left. Smith ignored all of the passageways until he reached the end of the hall and turned the corner. Smith stopped and raised his rifle. Blocking the path was a creature the size of two elephants. It reminded Smith of a manatee though it lacked any sort of flippers. It stood on long thick legs in the front, taller than a man, but the back legs were short and stubby, reminding Smith of a turtle. Its head was covered with clumps of eyes, with no visible sign of a nose or mouth, just eyes, and all staring straight at Commander Randall Smith. The beast moved remarkably fast as it charged Smith. Randal jumped back around the corner just as the thing's head smashed into the wall. Smith took this opportunity to open fire on the beast, aiming for the cluster of eyes on the side of its massive head. The creature shook off the pain and wedged its body around the corner, ready to charge Smith again. He kept firing into the head of the creature as he backed down the hallway, ready to turn and run at any moment. The monster took about two steps and fell to the ground a few yards away from Smith. The soldier stepped forward and kept firing into its head until he was sure the thing was dead. Next problem, how in the hell was Smith going to get around the thing? It took up damn near the whole hallway, and it was either find a way over the top, or cut his way through. Either would suit Smith just fine. He approached the creature and began to examine his options. The thing had skin like leather but it hung loosely, allowing Smith to grab a handful of flesh and climb up and over the beast. Once on the other side, Smith resumed his navigation of the maze. He stopped to examine a tunnel carved into the rock that wasn't part of the maze. On the wall opposite the entrance to this hallway was an arrow pointing forward. The paint was red, *that would make it Turner,* he thought to himself. Smith moved doubletime and followed the red arrow at the next intersection. "Turner," he called out and waited for a reply but heard nothing. Smith continued on to the next intersection where he again followed the arrow left by his teammate. A burst of gunfire sounded nearby. Smith began running down the corridor looking for the next red arrow. Another burst of gunfire. Smith could have sworn it was coming from one of the hallways he passed by; he was even tempted to go investigate. What if it was Captain Whitney that was firing off those rounds? Smith decided to stick to the plan. He almost missed the next arrow as he ran down the hallway. It was painted on the wall of a passageway to his left. A few hundred feet and Smith turned left again. There was another round of gunfire; it was close. "Turner," Smith called out. Smith rounded the corner and there it was, another of the creatures with the eyes, and it apparently had Lieutenant Turner cornered.

Smith started firing into the beast's head as he advanced, concentrating on the spot that had brought the other creature down. It paid off too; this one went down much quicker. Turner climbed out from his hiding place and patted Smith on the back. "Thanks, buddy, I owe you one."

"Three," Smith said. "You owe me *three*."

"Yeah, I'll get right on that. Wait a minute, you're actually countin'?"

"Yup," Smith said with a smile. "Now come on, we need to find Whitney." Smith climbed over the creature while Turner reluctantly followed.

(III)

Lisa was the first to enter the labyrinth. "Do you know where they are? Where they're going?" she asked Dr. Carlton. "Sorry, no, not for certain," he answered. "But my guess would be to head for the ladder in the center of the maze because that leads to the canyon on the surface."

"You think we'll find them in the canyon?" Gillian asked. "Why would Hunter lead them there?" "Hunter's memory of his childhood home isn't the only place the Mille Umbra has power," Carlton explained. "Its influence is also extremely strong on the surface of the island, but we don't know why. Since Hunter had them at the house before dropping them into the maze, the only *logical* place for them to go next would be the courtyard on the surface of the island. Now we just need to find it. Of course, with Hunter consuming the program, logic may be insignificant."

"Don't worry," Lisa said. "I remember the way to the ladder from here. Follow me." Lisa started down the passageway until she came to an intersection and stopped.

"I thought you knew where you were going," Gillian said sarcastically.

"I do, and it looks like somebody *else* is on the right trail, too." Lisa pointed to the wall on the right and they all saw the black spray painted arrow. "Come on." Lisa entered the hallway. The SEAL they were tracking was making correct choices, which gave Lisa hope that they would find him alive. "You know, it would be a whole lot easier to find the ladder if we could actually *see* it," Gillian complained. "But no, these frigging walls just *have* to be two hundred feet high." "I think that's the point, you educated idiot," Carlton teased, "to make it harder to find."

"Ha, fucking ha," Gillian snidely answered back.

"All right beauty and the beast…" Bruce smiled at Dr. Black, "…less talkin' and more walkin'."

"Why, thank you, Dr. Spencer," Carlton smarted off. "I didn't know you felt that way about me."

Gillian elbowed Dr. Carlton in the side. "He's talking about me, you prick."

Carlton laughed and put his hand to the ribs where Gillian had hit him. "That might of hurt if I wasn't already dead," he said. "Now, come on, let's catch up to lover boy and his niece."

"Prick!" Gillian pushed Dr. Carlton out of the way and followed Bruce down the passageway.

Lisa heard gunfire and froze. Bruce pulled out a pistol that was tucked into the back of his pants and handed it to Lisa. "Take this," he said as he checked his own weapon and then Dr. Black's shotgun.

"You remember how to use it, right?"

"Yes, Uncle Bruce. It hasn't been that long since I've been to the firing range."

"Good," Bruce said. "Now let's go get us a SEAL." Another burst of gunfire rounds sent the group running in that direction. Bruce was the first to turn the corner and enter the room. A large pack of Hunter's pets had Commander Whitney cornered. Somehow, the SEAL had scaled the walls of the room and was shooting down at the creatures from above. A group of the monsters broke off their attack when they saw Bruce and began slowly lumbering in his direction. When Lisa rounded the corner, the creatures stopped and lowered their heads. They parted to let her through as she walked over to them. "Stop!" she yelled. "Go on, get out of here, go!" she ordered. The beasties scattered and disappeared into cracks and holes in the walls. Wit climbed down from his perch on the wall and reloaded his weapon. "So they listen to you, huh?" he said suspiciously.

"Hunter's ordered them not to harm me," Lisa answered defensively. "As for listening to me, I had no idea that would work."

"Okay," Wit responded, "but you're not here by accident."

"What's that supposed to mean?" Lisa objected.

"It means that *nothing* happens by chance when it comes to the Mille Umbra. It knew Hunter would be here. It knew *you* would be here. Hell, it knows what *all of us* are thinking at this very moment."

"Not all of us," Gillian interrupted. "For some reason, Thomas Hunter and this Mille Umbra can't read Lisa."

"Interesting," Wit said as he stood and shouldered his weapon in preparation to leave. "I need to find the rest of my team."

"This way," Lisa said as she turned and left. Wit followed the four back out into the passageway and began to walk. He stayed about fifteen feet behind the group as they navigated the maze, less distraction, more opportunity to think about things and let them soak in. Wit lost sight of them momentarily as they took a hallway off to the left. When he reached the intersection he followed the passageway in a tight corkscrew until he found the four standing in front of a ladder leading up into the darkness. "What now?" Wit asked.

"Now we wait," Carlton said. "The rest of your team will be here soon."

(IV)

Once Smith got his bearings he resumed his search for the ladder. "We're close," he said.

"Are we there yet, are we there yet?" Turner teased.

"Don't make me put a bullet in your head," Smith joked.

155

"Yeah, I wouldn't want Admiral Forsythe shipping my comatose body off to some island to study *my* brain."

"I don't think you have anything to worry about," Smith assured Turner. "You actually have to *have* a brain in order to study it."

"Bitch," Turner spat back.

"Quiet! Did you hear that?" Smith put up his hand to silence Turner and listened.

"Yeah, sounds like someone talking." Turner answered.

"It's hard to tell with the echo from the cavern but the voices sound human."

"That don't seem to matter much around here," Turner said then indicated with hand signals for Smith to keep silent.

"Roger that." Smith mouthed back then shouldered his rifle and advanced forward slowly without another word. The pair of soldiers entered the next hallway and the voices they'd heard stopped. The two walked cautiously forward until they rounded the last corner of the passage to find four guns in their faces.

"Smith, Turner." Captain Whitney lowered his weapon and the rest of the group did the same.

"Good to see you again, Sir." Turner said. "Where's Vasquez?"

Wit looked at Smith. "You didn't tell him?" he asked.

"Didn't come up," Smith said. "Vasquez is dead. Sorry." Smith clasped Turner's shoulder briefly in commiseration.

"Great, so what now?" Turner asked, all business about completing the mission.

"Now we climb," Lisa said as she took hold of the ladder and began to pull herself up with the others following.

(V)

Lisa climbed out of the hole and sat in the dirt to rest as she waited for everyone else to arrive. Bruce was the next to climb out followed by Gillian. "You know, I did have a pretty nice view from back here." Gillian giggled.

"Oh sure, I say it, and *I'm* being a pig. You say it and it's funny? I swear I'll never understand women. Carlton," Bruce called out when the doctor's head emerged from the hole, "is there a mathematical equation that explains the way a woman's mind works?"

"One could get very rich with that sort of information," Carlton chuckled.

"Don't the two of you start ganging up on me now," Gillian moaned.

"You need to keep it quiet up here," Commander Smith said as he climbed out of the hole.

"Why?" asked Gillian, "Hunter and that Mille Umbra thing already know where we are."

"She's got a point," Turner said as he sat down to rest.

"You guys can stay here," Gillian said. "I'm going to sit by the fire." Gillian turned and began walking toward the large rock and the bonfire. "Wait up," Bruce called out. "I'll come with you."

"Me, too." Lisa stood and followed her uncle across the sand.

"Where they off to?" Whitney asked as he pulled himself off of the top of the ladder.

"Said they were gonna' sit by the fire," Turner replied.

"It's as good a place as any," Wit commented as he adjusted his knapsack and weapons and began walking toward the fire.

Turner stood and wiped the dirt from his uniform. "Well, I s'pose."

"Ya'll go on," Smith said. "I'm gonna' hang here for a while."

"Get your ass up," Turner ordered. "Sir."

"Yeah, yeah, yeah, we gotta' stick together." Smith stood and gathered his gear. "And next time you talk to your superior like that I *will* put that bullet in your head."

Smith and Turner dropped their gear on the ground and joined the group sitting around the fire. "Why don't we just leave?" Gillian pleaded. "Hunter's not here, we're all back together, let's just leave while we can and put Lisa's plan into motion."

"And what plan would that be?" They all looked up at once to see who had spoken. Standing in the middle of the bonfire, his skin all blistered and charred, was Thomas Hunter. Neither the flames nor the fact that his skin was melting off seemed to bother him, as if he did not feel pain at all. Gillian tried to think of something, *anything* other than the plan.

"You want to hook Lisa up to the program," Hunter said. "How wonderful!"

"Shit!" Gillian cursed to herself. "Sorry, guys, I was *trying* to think of something else."

"It's not your fault, Dr. Black." Hunter reassured her soothingly. "Your mind's an open book to me; I know *everything* about you. Like that time you had sex with your college professor so he would give you a better grade. And about all the drugs you've stolen over the years to support your habit." "I kicked that habit on my own, thank you." Gillian stood and yelled at Hunter. "You know, I'm not proud of the things I've done in the past, but at least I don't murder children, torture and rape women, leaving their organs laying about in piles."

Hunter turned to Lisa. "So, you've met Cherry. How much more do you know about me?"

"Enough," Lisa answered. "I know what you did to all of those women, and what you did to the Sisters and your own *mother*, Hunter. She loved you unconditionally yet you killed her so easily," Lisa ended nearly sobbing.

"It was *not* easy! I loved my mother, but what she allowed that husband of hers to do to me was unforgivable!"

"Then what about the Sisters?" Lisa demanded. "What was so horrible about *them*?"

"I was testing the waters, so to speak. Come on, if there were a God, would He have let me kill all of those nuns? Apparently so, which means God doesn't give a shit about you who are supposed to be made in *His* image." Hunter gave Lisa a snide grin and licked his flaming lips.

"But Desideo cared about you, or pretended to, anyway." Lisa tried to stir the pot.

"He's the closest thing I ever had to family," Hunter said dreamily.

"But he *rejected* you," Lisa pointed out. "He made you suffer because you could *never* be what you were meant to be for him. You could never be *me*!"

"If you're trying to anger me, child, it won't work. Besides, I'm not jealous of *you*, only what you're capable of giving birth to. *That* right should have been mine. No matter, I will simply raise her as I would have been raised, and together we can create a new reality where *we* are Gods!"

"Delusions of grandeur," Bruce remarked.

"And you," Hunter pointed at Bruce. "You had a brother who was, in fact, a Mille Umbra, yet you never knew. Your entire family was fooled by this creature; you were all oblivious."

"Animus wasn't like Desideo or the other Umbra," Lisa said. "He just wanted to live, not to murder and destroy like his brethren. He was *nothing* like the monster you call father."

"The world is full of monsters." Hunter declared.

"You would know," Lisa said scathingly.

"You will *all* know," Hunter said proudly. "For Father is here to spread the word." A fireball burst from the bonfire and mushroomed up into the sky. When the fire returned to normal, they saw that Thomas Hunter was gone.

(VI)

Turner was the first to see it, a shadow tentacle reaching out from the darkness of the canyon, trying to surround them. The SEALs were on their feet with weapons drawn. Wit watched the shadow figures of the creature's accumulated souls as they twisted and shifted within the Umbra's mass. The figure had, indeed, surrounded them. "When I say now you need to trust me and do what I say," Lisa whispered to the group.

"How do you plan on getting out of here?" Wit asked quietly.

"If I tell you, the creature will know, so *please* just *trust me*."

"Well, by the looks of things," Wit stated, "I don't think our guns or explosives would do much to that thing out there, not unless you can make it take a solid form."

"Yeah," Smith added, "but then you can only damage the thing. You can never kill an Umbra."

"Yes, you can," Lisa said softly. "I just don't know how yet, so now is not the time to make a stand."

"Agreed," Wit said. "We follow you when you're ready."

Lisa stepped forward. "Desideo," she called out.

"Lisa Spencer," the creature answered. "Are you ready to give yourself to me, or do more people need to die before you realize your destiny.."

"If I give myself to you and have this child," Lisa called out, "when she is born, *everyone* will die. What kind of trade off is that?"

"It is the only offer on the table. Let those you love savor what few years remain of their reality or let them die here and be trapped in Hell forever. The choice is yours."

"I'd choose Hell before handing my niece over to you any day," Bruce called out.

"Ah, Bruce, I mourn the loss of your brother, but don't for one second think that I will show you any mercy, for it is not his human side that I mourn."

"Even his dark side was more human than you," Bruce taunted.

"A choice I cannot begin to fathom."

"Yet you still mourn him?" Lisa pointed out. "Which means you *can* experience compassion."

"I mourn him as you would an arm or a leg, a piece of me that is gone forever, no more, no less." "Are you saying you're unable to show compassion? Something one of your brethren did without hesitation? Desideo, you *are* Sloth aren't you? Maybe you're just too lazy to be compassionate?" Lisa questioned, an attempt to keep the others alive for as long as possible.

"I am not unable, simply unwilling. Continue to try my patience and someone will die this instant."

"It might as well be me," Lisa cried out, "because I will *never* give myself to you willingly."

"You'd be surprised how persuasive I can be."

The mass of tendrils that surrounded the survivors began to move closer until there was only twenty feet between them and the heart of the beast. Several of the shadow figure's heads merged into one face and spoke, ***"Still so eager to die, Lisa Spencer?"*** Desideo said.

"If it means you lose," she answered, "then yes, I would gladly die." Lisa took several steps toward the creature. "There won't be another like me in a thousand years. You know that so you won't kill me." ***"You truly have the knowledge of the Umbra within you. You're right, Lisa Spencer, I won't kill you, but for meddling where you don't belong…"*** A shadow tentacle shot out from the darkness and impaled

Dr. Carlton in the face. His physical body fell to the ground but a shadow figure of Dr. Alan Carlton remained. The Umbra slowly reeled in the tentacle grasping Carlton's shadow.

"…I'll take his soul."

"Noooo!" Gillian screamed. She knelt down at Carlton's side and examined his corpse. Although she knew he'd already been technically dead, and saying there were no signs of life was redundant, Gillian could tell by the deadness of the doctor's bulging eyes that he was truly gone, his soul stripped from him by Desideo.

"Who shall die next, Lisa Spencer?" A tentacle shot out and stopped just inches from Bruce's face. "Shall it be your loving uncle? Or how about the good doctor here?" The tentacle moved from Bruce's face to Gillian's. "Your soul is not completely tainted. Yes, your soul would be sweet."

Another tentacle shot out and stopped just shy of Captain Whitney's face. "And what about you, Captain Jason Whitney? Oh, the plots you and your team have foiled. I will be held in great regard among the other banished Umbra for killing you."

"Now!" Lisa yelled. "Everyone together." Lisa rushed over to complete the circle and the group disappeared in a flash of light. They instantly reappeared in one of the labs. Lisa stepped back and spoke. "You guys get things ready down here, I'm going to get Derek." Lisa closed her eyes and disappeared once more.

CHAPTER SEVENTEEN

The Distraction

(I)

Derek woke up in a cold sweat and looked frantically around the room. He breathed a sigh of relief when he realized he was alone. *So this is it…* he thought. Soon he would be dead. *Not if I kill her first,* was his next thought. He didn't ponder this for very long. Derek was not the kind of man who would take another person's life, even if it meant saving his own. He knew he wouldn't be able to do it. *Nothing to do but wait…* Then there was a knock on the door. Derek's mind raced. "What do I do, what do I do?" he mumbled to himself as he paced the room. Derek stopped in front of the door. "Who's there?" he called out. The deadbolt unlatched itself and the doorknob turned, allowing the door to open several inches. "Who's out there?" Derek demanded. He opened the door and looked out, and immediately wished he hadn't. Derek stumbled backwards to the other side of the room.

"Hello, Derek," Thomas Hunter said with a smile.

"You can't come in here. You can't come in here. You can't…"

"You're right," Hunter conceded, "I can't enter the room. I simply wish to talk."

"There's nothing to talk about; I have nothing to say to you!" Derek yelled.

"Fine," Hunter said as he shrugged his shoulders, "then let Lisa Spencer murder you. Yes, Derek, I know all about your visions of dying and I know that it doesn't have to happen."

"How can I stop it?" Derek demanded. "I've tried to change my future but the wheel always turns and brings me right back to what happens in my visions."

"You may not have control of your destiny, Derek, but *I* do. And I'd be willing to let you live if you do something for me."

"Do what?" Derek asked suspiciously.

"Bring Lisa Spencer to me. Get her out of this room as soon as you see her. If you're not in here she can't kill you. You told me yourself you can't alter your visions, but if you bring her to me, I will make sure she never lays a hand on you. Bring her to the attic of the house. Deliver the woman to Desideo and you *will* get off this island alive."

"I'll think about it," Derek said slowly.

"Good, you do that," Hunter said, "but here's a reminder of what awaits you if you choose to not accept my offer." Hunter pulled a knife out of his pocket and threw it into the room. The blade tumbled through the air, just missing Derek's head and embedded itself into the wall behind him. Derek turned and looked at the knife. "The handle," he said, "it's the same as the knife from my vision." Derek turned and Thomas Hunter was gone. He closed the door and walked over to the knife. "So, this is the knife that kills me," Derek said as he pulled the blade from the wall and turned it over and over in his hands, inspecting every inch. A sudden thud on the door jolted Derek from his analysis. It was soon followed by another and then even more. Derek could hear the creatures snarling and growling outside, Hunter's creatures. "You lied to me!" Derek screamed as the pounding on the door increased. He sat down in the chair behind the desk and held the knife up in the light. "There's another way," Derek mumbled to himself. "Maybe I *can* alter my visions after all." Derek heard a loud crash like thunder as the door cracked and burst open. He heard the creatures entering the room, their claws clicking on the tiled floor. Derek gripped the handle and turned it over so that the blade was facing him, closed his eyes, and thrust the knife into his stomach.

(II)

Lisa appeared in the electrical room and the first thing she noticed was that the door was split in two and hung from the casing. The next thing she saw was Derek leaning back in the chair with a knife sticking out of his stomach. "Derek," Lisa whispered. She reached for the knife to pull it out and as soon as she touched the blade Derek opened his eyes. He looked up at her as she slid the knife from his flesh and he spoke, "It wasn't you after all."

Lisa had no idea what he was talking about. "It's time to go," she said to Derek. "We need to get you to the lab."

"I'm not going anywhere," Derek whispered softly.

"Yes, you are," Lisa said as she began to weep softly. "You're going... home."

Derek smiled and took a breath. There was silence for a moment and then he exhaled his last breath. Derek was dead. Lisa held him in her arms and sobbed. She released Derek's lifeless body and stood, wiping the tears from her eyes, knowing there was nothing more she could do. It was time to set the plan into motion and get the hell off this island.

Lisa closed her eyes and pictured the lab, knowing that this would take her where she wanted to go. Lisa opened her eyes and looked at Gillian. "Derek's dead," she said. "I don't know what happened.

The door was shattered and Derek had a knife in his belly. He died in front of my eyes." Bruce placed his arms around his niece and held her tightly as she sobbed. Lisa pulled herself together and stepped back from her uncle. "I'm fine, now lets get this over with! Which bed do you want me to take?" she forcefully asked Gillian.

"The bed on the far right," Dr. Black answered.

"You're not going to shave my head for this are you?" Lisa asked nervously.

"No, you just have to wear this cap." Gillian held up a plastic and cloth cap with electrodes sewn in various places. "Just hop up on the bed and place the cap on your head."

Lisa did as instructed and sat back until she reclined comfortably in the bed. Gillian began placing wires onto the electrodes on the skullcap, and when finished, she stood up and smiled at Lisa.

"Are you ready?" Gillian asked.

"Don't you have to scan me first?" Lisa asked.

"We don't have time," Gillian explained. "Besides, with your brain I don't think it'll matter."

"Then let's do this." Lisa said with determination.

"I'm going to give you a shot that will put you under, but be warned, it's very fast acting. You'll find yourself in the load program, the long hallway."

"Yes, I remember it," Lisa said.

"Good, then you just open the door and who knows what's going to happen."

"Give me that shot and we'll find out." Lisa felt a prick on the top of her hand and before long her vision went blurry. Everything went black for a moment, then the lights illuminated the hallway. Things were back to normal this time, Lisa walked down the hallway with ease and soon stood in front of a door. She knew exactly where she wanted to go, so Lisa turned the knob and entered the door.

(III)

Wit, Smith, and Turner were in the hallway outside the lab solidifying a plan of action. "We let this girl try and distract Hunter," Wit said, "since she seems to think she can do it. If so, it makes our job easy. All we do is head for the church, grab Hunter's body, make sure he's stabilized, and get him to the airlock. We get out of here double time and then we blow this place which closes the door the Mille Umbra opened…” Wit stopped speaking when the door to the lab opened and closed on its own. He rushed to the door and pushed it open, his weapon at the ready. Wit stopped cold when he saw her. There was a Lisa Spencer laying on the bed jacked into the program and there was *another* Lisa Spencer standing in front of him smiling. “You can put the gun down, Captain Whitney. This is simply my avatar in the program,” she said. “That’s my real body there on the bed. Protect it. I’ll give you directions to the church so you can take care of Hunter’s body in a bit. Meanwhile, I’ll find him, keep him and the Umbra distracted, and then we’ll meet up later on. ” Lisa gave Wit directions to the church, some of which made very little sense, confusing him somewhat. “We’re safe in this room, like in the electrical room, because I’ve shielded it from the program and Hunter. He can’t hear us in here, so go get the rest of your team.” Wit called his teammates into the room and closed the door. “Bruce and Gillian can stay here with my body,” Lisa the avatar continued. “Captain Whitney will do his thing with his team and we’ll all meet at the airlock in one hour. That should be more than enough time to get to the church and back. I seem to have some control over this program, so I’ll help keep Hunter’s pets, that sewn together corpse thing, and God knows what else off of your backs the best I can. Are you ready, Captain Whitney?”

“Yes, ma’am,” he answered.

“Give me five minutes before you leave this room. That will give me time to find Hunter.” Lisa turned to Gillian and her Uncle. “You two take good care of me and we’ll be out of here before you know it.

Oh, and no hanky-panky while I’m gone.”

“There *are* two empty beds in the room,” Gillian said with a Cheshire grin.

“Enough, you’re putting images of my uncle in my brain that should never be there.” Lisa walked over to Bruce and wrapped her arms around him. “I love you, Uncle Bruce.” Lisa stepped back and smiled for a moment before she disappeared into thin air.

(IV)

It only took a moment for Lisa to find Thomas Hunter. He was sitting beneath the tree in the back yard of his childhood home. When Lisa appeared, Hunter looked up at her.

“What a pleasant surprise!” Hunter sounded overjoyed. “Your power is growing; Father will be pleased. Come, sit with me.” Lisa walked over to the tree and sat down next to the murderer. It made her sick to her stomach to be so close to such a vile man but she had to play the game and keep up the ruse.

"What were you thinking about?" Lisa asked.

"Freedom," Hunter answered.

"Freedom from what?"

"From everything. I just want to disappear for a while and soon I will have the power to do it."

"Desideo will always find you," Lisa said.

"I'm no longer running from Father. I've accepted my fate and I plan to make the most of it. It's the outside world that I despise and I'll gladly help Father find a way to bring the human race to its knees." "Okay, just a *few* anger management issues," Lisa said.

"You're damn right I'm angry!" Hunter roared. "Entire governments murder more people than I have, yet the cops don't come knocking on *their* doors and putting bullets in *their* heads! At least my killings had purpose."

"And what purpose could your murders possibly have?" Lisa asked sarcastically.

"My murders are art! They tell a story, a story that's not finished playing out. You're a part of it, Lisa, whether you like it or not."

"Stories can change," Lisa argued.

"Not this one. The child *will* be born and there's nothing you or the Admiral's puppets can do about it."

"Fine," Lisa said. "Let's get this over with, shall we?" She stood and waited for Hunter.

"We shall." Hunter stood and Lisa took his hand. "Take me to him," she said.

Hunter led Lisa down the path between the flower gardens and onto the back porch of the house.

(V)

Wit led his team down the sparsely lit corridor. So far the directions the Spencer girl had given him had been very good, until now. "She didn't say anything about this," Turner griped. "All she said was something about the color purple." The team stood in front of a wall of darkness. Smith shined his flashlight against the surface but the light could not penetrate the void. Wit stuck his arm into the blackness and it simply disappeared. "She said this hall would lead us to the forest," Wit said as he stepped through the wall.

"Uh, you can go next," Turner said nervously to Smith.

"Pussy," Smith said and followed Captain Whitney.

"Fuck!" Turner moaned. "I'm taking to the Admiral about a pay increase after this one," and covered the six of his team. Whitney and Smith were waiting for him on the other side. Turner looked around at their new surroundings. They were in a large cavern and in the distance could see a light emanating from within a stone structure.

"Nice to see you didn't wuss out on me," Smith said razzing Turner.

"What *is* that thing?" Turner asked as he pointed off in the distance at the stone structure.

"I've seen one before," Captain Whitney said. "It's some sort of gateway, a portal to different locations in the program. "Come on, I think I know what she meant when she said purple." Wit started off toward the pillars of stone, Smith and Turner following closely behind. When they reached the monolith,

Captain Whitney slipped between the stone pillars expecting his subordinates to do the same. It was a tight fit with the three of them in the structure, which didn't help Wit figure out how to activate the damn thing. He looked up at the light shining above him as it hung motionless at the tops of the stones. Wit pulled out his pistol and took aim at the light. He fired once and the orb shattered, the light spraying out like a liquid, splashing and covering the stones. The light rapidly moved down the stones until the entire structure glowed white. The colors appeared slowly, with large squares of various colors eventually adorning the inside of the pillars.

Smith was closest to the purple panel. "It's like a game, man, like Twister, ball sack to purple square." "Just shut up and touch the square," Wit ordered.

Smith placed his hand on the purple square and the entire structure lit up, becoming a blinding white light. The light slowly faded and Captain Whitney looked out at the forest between the stone towers. When the light had completely died out, Wit stepped out from between the stones and said, "The church is this way," as he started down a torch-lined path. "It'll be guarded by Hunter's creatures so make sure you go in with full clips. They're too fast for the shotguns so we might as well save that ammo for whatever is sure to come next. We're almost there, so no more taking until all of them bastards are dead. Hoo-Ra!" As they silently approached the churched, they could see the bonfire, along with the creatures surrounding the church, at least a hundred of them. Wit stopped and got down on one knee. He counted down with his fingers, three, two, one, and the team began its assault.

(VI)

Lisa followed Thomas Hunter up the stairs and into the attic. She could feel Desideo nearby, watching them from the shadows of the room. "You know," Lisa said, "as beautiful as this house is, it's still pretty damn creepy." Hunter stopped in front of a door at the far end of the attic and waited for Lisa.

"It will be over quickly, I assure you," Thomas Hunter said. "Take off your clothes and get on the bed. I'll be right outside the door."

"What's the matter," Lisa taunted, "Daddy dearest doesn't like you to watch?"

"Bite your tongue, bitch, or I'll remove it for you," Hunter raged.

"Ouch, touchy subject, huh?" Lisa could tell she was getting to him. He wanted to kill her but was afraid of what Desideo would do to him if he did. "There was this house up the road from the home I grew up in. It sat on top of a hill and no one was sure if someone lived there or not. It was a pretty creepy house too; I bet you'd love to see it. Anyway, when I was nine years old I broke into the house one night with some friends."

"You're stalling," Hunter said.

"You know what? It's better if I show you."

In a flash they were no longer in the attic of Thomas Hunter's childhood home. They now stood on the porch of an old dilapidated house that sat on top of a hill. "How did you…?" Hunter began. "You're in the program, aren't you? Simply amazing. It took me nearly a month to learn how to control the smallest of things. You *are* special, Lisa Spencer. After all, you will soon give birth to the new daughter of darkness."

"Come on," Lisa said. "Let's go inside."

Hunter followed her through the door and into a home that was glorious in its prime, but years of neglect and rot had turned the once magnificent structure into a dark, damp, and cold shell of its former self. "Why did you bring me here?" Hunter asked. "You can stall all you want, but in the end, you *will* belong to Father. There's no avoiding your destiny, Lisa. The scripture foretold of your coming and now here you are. Why must you reject your role in the creation of a new universe? You will give birth to a

168

God, yet you fight this honor with disrespect and ignorance, even more proof that the human race deserves to suffer in torment for what it has become!"

"What *have* we become?" Lisa asked.

"You're nothing more than an insect, an ant who blindly follows a pre-programmed set of rules that you live your life by."

"It's called having a conscience," Lisa sneered.

"Ha," Hunter began to laugh. "You let the government and the media control your lives in much the same way. You're told what to buy and you listen. You're told what to think and you happily oblige.

Just look at what the human race has become. You can help change that, Lisa. Bring me back to Father and we can build a new world."

"Ah, here we are," Lisa said as if she had not been listening to word Thomas Hunter was saying. Lisa opened the door and began to descend a set of stairs. "I always found the basement to be the creepiest." "Is there a meaning to all of this?" Hunter asked.

"Yes, Mr. Hunter, there is, and the meaning is this. You no longer control things around here. Go ahead, try to change something, anything." Lisa watched the determination in Thomas Hunter's face turn to anger as he realized he had no control over his environment. "See, we're playing by my rules now." "What do you want from me?" Hunter asked.

"Let my friends go. Yes, Mr. Hunter, that includes the SEALs. Let them go and I will willingly go to Desideo with you. I know how much it's killing you to have a woman controlling you, but look at it this way, you still get what you want in the end."

"As long as you keep your end of the bargain then they are free to go," Hunter said with a smile. "I must speak with Desideo but I'm sure he will agree to your terms."

"Soon enough," Lisa said with a smile, "but first I want to introduce you to an old friend."

The basement suddenly changed, the features distorting until a new room was formed, a room that Thomas Hunter recognized. He saw the wooden bench on the dirt floor in the middle of the room and the carpets on the ground behind the bench. The carpets his false father would kneel on while raping Thomas Hunter as a child. Lisa began to move away from Hunter, as if the room was being stretched and the two were moving farther apart. A door suddenly slammed shut in front of Lisa, locking Thomas Hunter in the room. "Oh, by the way," Lisa said. "I have another surprise for you."

Thomas Hunter's stepfather stepped out of the darkness. The large man removed his glasses and licked his lips. "It's daddy time, Thomas," he said as he unbuttoned the straps of his overalls.

(VII)

Bruce sat and talked with Gillian, speaking of things he'd sworn he would never even think of again. He tried to fight it, but this woman had a way of extracting the information with her good looks and her charm. Hell, Bruce had seen her scornful side when he first arrived on the island, but at that very moment, he didn't care. "That's enough talking," Gillian said. "Right now I just want to kiss you." Dr. Black moved in closer to Bruce who was no longer trying to resist the beautiful doctor's words. "Baby, I thought you'd never ask." Bruce leaned in and kissed Gillian's lips softly at first but this woman made him feel things he had not felt in years, and he allowed himself to deepen the gesture strongly. Gillian softly moaned as Bruce kissed her passionately as his hands caressed her body. "Yes," Gillian moaned.

"Um, excuse me. Gross, are you doing what I think you're doing?" The voice was coming from one of the monitors. It was Lisa's voice. Bruce jumped up and sat in front of the monitor. He saw Lisa on the center screen; she was in the basement of an old house. "I've got Thomas Hunter contained; now I need to focus on the Umbra. The SEAL team should be at the church by now, so hopefully Mr. Hunter will soon be a distant memory. I just wanted to give you an update before going up against Desideo. You two can carry on now. I think it's kind of sweet, and Lord knows how badly you need to get laid, Uncle Bruce. How long has it been, five or six years?"

Bruce stole a glance at Gillian who smiled when she saw him blush. "Be careful, Lisa. Get back here soon so we can all go home."

"You got it, Unc. Listen, I need to go. I love you, Uncle Bruce. Just stay put and I'll be back before you know it." The center screen on the monitor went black and Lisa was gone again.

(VIII)

There were hundreds of corpses laying on the ground, some in piles, while others were in pieces. Captain Whitney, Commander Smith, and Lieutenant Turner stood in the middle of the carnage, their weapons still smoking from the heat of firing so many rounds. "I think that's all of them," Whitney said. "It's time to go inside." Wit walked up to the door of the church and pulled the lever and handle but the door would not budge. After two powerful kicks the door still would not open, so Captain Whitney aimed at the lock and kept firing until there was nothing left of the latch to keep the door closed. Smith pushed on the door and it slowly creaked open to reveal a cavernous hall of worship that rivaled even the most extravagant Roman Catholic Church. One by one they stepped inside and began to orchestrate a plan. "We split up and meet back here in twenty minutes," Wit ordered.

"Hello? Anyone there?" a voice cut in through the team's headsets. It was the voice of Lisa Spencer. "You have your coms back but only use them if you have to. You have forty minutes left so you'd better get a move on."

"You heard the girl," Wit said. "Smith, you take the right side and Turner the left. Check any doors you see along the way and I'll meet you at the altar."

"Shucks, Captain, I didn't know you felt that way about me."

"Shut up, Smith. Time's running out; let's move!"

Smith made his way to the far right side of the hall and began checking offices and restrooms finding nothing and moving on. He passed several stained glass windows before coming to another door with a sign overhead that read "Employees and Staff Only". Smith opened the door and stepped inside.

The room was huge, easily the size of a football field with forty feet high ceilings and large pillars along the walls, spread throughout the room in rows of nine. The room was cast in a shimmering blue light coming from a large swimming pool on the other end of the room. There was a large amount of people gathered in and around the pool. Smith could hear their laughter and screams and all of the voices sounded female. As Smith drew closer, he began to recognize some of the women, and he had been correct, they *were* all woman, and they were all nude. One of them called out to Commander Smith. "Hey, Randall, remember me?" she yelled. "You bent me over the hood of a 69' Barracuda and fucked me in the ass. Do you want another go?"

"Randy," another girl called out, this one was young, sixteen or seventeen maybe. "Do you want to take my virginity again?"

"How is that even possible?" Smith asked.

"Around here," the girl replied, "*anything* is possible."

"Come on, that was almost twenty years ago; you should be in your thirties by now."

"I told you, anything is possible. We are as you remember us because that is how you wish us to be." "We know what's in your heart," said another woman, this one in her early twenties, "and on your mind. We know what you fantasize about, Randall, and here we are. Come join us darling; we want you. We *all* want to feel you inside of us. Take us, Randall." The women began to touch one another, running their hands across bare flesh. Soon they were kissing. "Come join us," one called out. "Don't make us beg, darling." "Yes, my love. Come join us and we will satisfy you in every way."

There were a lot of thoughts going through Randall Smith's head at that very moment. For instance, he wondered if he should fuck two or three of them before killing them, or just blow them all away now. Smith knew the women weren't real. Hell, Smith knew for sure that at least five of them were already dead. He had even attended the funerals for a few of them. Smith decided it was best to not give these women the opportunity to go all homicidal, or even worse, cannibal. "That's all I need, one of you bitches trying to chow down on my man meat. I don't think so." Randall made sure his weapon was fully loaded and opened fire.

"What's going on in there?" Wit called out over the speaker in Smith's ear.

"Nothing I can't handle. You might want to open the door for me though. It's halfway down the hall between two stained glass windows depicting the crucifixion."

The last of the women fell dead to the ground and the reflection of the water on the room's walls had turned red. Smith walked back in the direction of the door and saw a crack of light as Turner poked his head inside. "Let's get a move on; Whitney thinks he's found Hunter." Smith followed Turner out the door and back into the vast cathedral. Captain Whitney was waiting for them behind the altar. "Follow me, the room is back here." Whitney led his team through a maze of passageways behind the stage and stopped in front of a set of large double doors. Wit had his lock pick set out in record time and in seconds there was a click and the door swung open. In the center of the room was a hospital bed with the comatose body of Thomas Hunter strapped to it. Surrounding the bed and hidden in the darkened corners of the room were more of Hunter's pets. The team reloaded, stepped inside, and began shooting, all the while keeping in mind where the body of Thomas Hunter lie so as not to hit him with a stray bullet. The gunfire lasted less than five minutes and all of the creatures were dead on the floor of the room. Turner and Smith began to prep Thomas Hunter's body for transport while Captain Whitney went over in his mind the directions back to the airlock.

CHAPTER EIGHTEEN

The Umbra Desideo

(I)

Lisa walked up the basement stairs and into the kitchen. She took the servant's stairwell to the third floor where she began searching for the door leading to the attic. Lisa ascended slowly, giving her time to think, and by the time she reached the attic, she had formed a half-assed plan and knew she would simply have to improvise. Lisa retraced the steps she had taken with Thomas Hunter until she stood in front of the door leading to Desideo. She took a deep breath then opened the door.

"She has returned to me, just as foretold." Desideo whispered from the darkness.

Lisa looked around the room but saw nothing but darkness all around. "Tell me about my father," Lisa called out.

"I know little of Andrew Spencer," the Umbra replied.

"I'm not talking about my birth father, I'm talking about my *true* father, Animus."

"You know all you need to know."

"What kind of bullshit answer is that?" Lisa raged.

"You are the daughter of darkness. If you needed to know these things you would know them." "I'm tired of this daughter of darkness shit; I choose the light!" With those words, something odd happened. Lisa looked down in amazement as her skin began to glow, slowly at first, but it continued to grow brighter until her skin shone a brilliant white. The light cast from Lisa's body revealed the Mille Umbra in the darkness. Lisa watched the countless number of souls twist and turn within the mass of the creature. "I said, tell me about my father!"

"As you wish," Desideo conceded. "Animus was a fool! After being banished from Chaos, the five others joined with me to vanquish humanity from the cosmos, but not Animus. He took pity on your wretched species. Instead of destroying your kind he became one; how sickening!"

"What about you? You were banished for being to lazy to care about destroying humanity. Why the sudden change of heart? If you didn't care about the fate of the inhabitants of the universes in Hell then why care now?"

Desideo screamed out in rage over Lisa's questions. His shadows moved faster as they intertwined and broke off to join with a new shadow soul. ***"When we were banished all I could do was watch. I examined every species from every universe! I scrutinized the monotony of the daily lives of every species in every reality in Heaven and what your kind calls the multiverse. But I also got to witness the realities of Chaos, and I began to enjoy the suffering and agony endured by the species unlucky enough to populate the universes in Hell."***

"Then you enjoy what you do?" Lisa asked.

"Immensely!" the Umbra answered smugly.

"Then my father is *not* dead! I see that Pride lives on in *you*! Enjoy it while it lasts, because sooner or later, you'll tire of the fight and lose interest in humanity's demise. It's in your nature. It's who you *are*, Desideo! You're nothing but a lazy piece of shit that wasn't even good enough to rule in Hell!"

The Umbra just laughed. "Much like your father, Lisa Spencer. He was also deemed unworthy by

Animus and banished into the Nexus."

"At least my father did something with his life! Animus even killed one of your brethren. Ira wasn't it, or rather, Wrath? Are you trying to fill his shoes now, too? Pride and Wrath, now *that* would explain your bloodlust for all living things, wouldn't it?"

The Umbra said something but Lisa was distracted. An image flashed in her mind and she saw the SEAL team carrying Thomas Hunter's body through the woods. *What are they doing?* Lisa thought to herself. *They were supposed to kill him!*

"Two can play your game," the Umbra laughed. "It seems you are just as easily distracted."

The light emanating from within Lisa suddenly increased its intensity. She felt a force pulling her away.

She saw Desideo advancing on her, his shadow tentacles only feet away. Before the Umbra could touch her, before she lost consciousness and was pulled from the program, she heard the Umbra speak. He said, ***"It is time to wake up, my son."***

(II)

Wit had no idea where they had come from but the creatures were hot on their heels. There were thousands of them coming from every direction in the woods. The team had almost reached the clearing where the transport device was and, as soon as they were in the open, they would make their stand. Turner was up front with the limp body of Thomas Hunter slung over his shoulder as he ran. The team was halfway across the clearing when Whit chanced a look over his shoulder. The creatures were coming out of the woods by the dozens. "Pick up your pace pricks; that's an order!"

Turner arrived at the stone structure first. He placed the body of Thomas Hunter down on the ground and stepped into the machine to activate it. Captain Whitney and Commander Smith were firing on the creatures to hold them off long enough for Turner to get the transporter fired up. Turner stepped out of the machine and called to his teammates, "Head 'em up and move 'em out; the calvary's here." Commander Whitney turned and saw Turner standing in front of the structure with Thomas Hunter standing up behind him with a large knife. Before Wit could get out a cry of warning, Hunter had the knife to Turner's throat and was sawed through. Hunter used his free hand to grab hold of Turner's hair, pulling while he cut until the head was completely severed. Hunter let the body fall to the ground and held up the head of Lieutenant Turner for Smith and Whitney to see. The SEALs raised their weapons and fired at Hunter who simply vanished into thin air before the first bullet reached him. Wit felt something tug on the shotgun slung over his shoulder. He turned his head and saw that he was face to face with Turner's severed head that had been placed over the barrel of his shotgun. The head spoke in Turner's voice saying, "Hunter said he's sorry that he couldn't stick around, but he had important business to attend to." Whitney heard the creatures advancing on their position and threw the head of his teammate on the ground. He grabbed Smith by the shoulder and pulled him into the machine. Wit pressed the purple square and watched as the outside world morphed into a new location.

(III)

Gillian slipped out of bed and wiggled into her lab coat when she heard the alarm. She raced to Lisa Spencer's side and checked the instrumentation on the machines. "What the hell?"

"What's wrong?" Bruce asked as he slid into his jeans and pulled his shirt over his head.

"She's gone!"

"What do you mean she's gone?" Bruce growled.

"The computers can't find her in the program."

"Then where the hell is she?" Bruce asked angrily.

"Don't get all pissed off at me, I'm trying my best to understand what's going on, just the same as you." "You're right," Bruce said. "I'm sorry. It may be nothing more than a glitch in the system." Bruce carried a blanket over to Gillian and draped it over her shoulders. The doctor continued pushing buttons on various machines and entering commands using a laptop hooked up to the system. Gillian was scanning the hard drive for Lisa's file with no success. All at once, the monitor for the video feed from Lisa's session lit up a brilliant white.

"Uncle Bruce?" It was Lisa's voice.

"I'm here sweetheart."

"Something… has a hold on me. It's pulling me from the program. Help me, Bruce. I can't hold on." "Lisa," Bruce cried out. "I don't know what to do." He turned to Gillian and asked, "Should we unhook her from the program?"

"We can't," Gillian stated. "Without a lock on her signal the computer can't pull her consciousness out." "So she could be lost in this place forever?" Bruce yelled.

"Technically, yes."

"Why the hell didn't you tell me about this earlier?" Bruce shouted.

"I warned you of the dangers, but it was her call, and we *all* agreed in case you don't remember."

"Again," Bruce said with his head hung low, "I'm sorry."

Gillian placed her arms around Bruce and pulled him close. He began to sob as the screen on the monitor returned to static and Lisa's voice was gone. She kissed his neck and whispered, "It will be okay, Bruce. We'll get off this island and, who knows, there are plenty of pharmaceutical companies in Research Triangle Park who'd kill to have me on their staff."

"The only staff you're going to be on is mine, baby." Bruce pulled Gillian's face to his and kissed her softly on the lips. "You're right, we need to…" The door suddenly burst open and two of the Navy SEALs staggered in covered in blood and mud. "What the hell happened?" Bruce demanded.

"Something unanticipated," Captain Whitney replied.

"That's it? That's the best answer you've got? We deserve to know the truth," Bruce raised his rifle at the two SEALs. "I'll ask you again; What. Went. Wrong?"

"Thomas Hunter woke up," Commander Smith answered. "He killed Lieutenant Turner and got away.

Shit, Captain Whitney and I almost didn't make it out of there either."

"I thought you were supposed to kill him," Bruce nearly yelled.

"Yeah, well, Uncle Sam has other plans for him," Whitney cut in. "I'm sorry. We were just following orders."

"Orders that allowed a psychopath to roam around freely and most likely be behind the disappearance of my niece?" Bruce screeched in frustration.

"What are you talking about? She's right there." Commander Smith pointed to the body of Lisa Spencer lying on the bed."

"Not *that* Lisa, you idiot," Gillian chimed in. "The computers can't find her in the program. We heard her voice on the monitor and it sounded like someone was abducting her."

"And you think it was Thomas Hunter?" Captain Whitney asked.

"It would make sense," Bruce argued. "It was shortly after he escaped from you that it happened. So, whether you like it or not, we are going out there to find my niece and *kill* Thomas Hunter once and for all!"

(IV)

Lisa looked down on the city below her, marveling over the beauty of its symmetry. The streets looked like an elaborate crop circle from above. She watched the cars move at incredible speeds through intersections from both directions, timed so perfectly that the vehicles never touched. Lisa was in awe over the sheer size and height of the buildings in the city. Every building looked like it was made out of solid gold and each had a glow from the rising sun. Lisa stood on the rooftop of one such building looking over the edge at the city below. Her skin still shone white but the brightness was fading.

"Amazing!" Lisa said out loud.

"Yes, it is." The voice came from behind her… that voice… it couldn't be, could it? Lisa turned around and saw her father standing in the sunlight. He held the hand of a woman Lisa had never met, but knew almost everything about, a woman Lisa prayed feverishly she would one day meet. Claudia Spencer, her mother! "Mom, Dad?" Lisa dared not hope it was true, as the island was tricky, but Lisa Spencer also had a sneaking suspicion that she was no longer on the island.

"Yes dear," her mother answered, "It's really us."

Lisa ran into her parents embrace. "How is this possible?" she asked, nearly in tears.

"You are in Heaven, my darling," Andrew Spencer said softly. "Your mother and I spent years planning your extraction at this particular moment in time."

"What's so special about it?" Lisa asked, confused.

"You have more than one destiny, my dear," her mother answered. "You have a choice!"

"But you're not going to like the outcome of either," Andrew Spencer added.

Lisa placed her hands on her fathers face. "I'm ready to fulfill my destiny, dad, but I don't know what to do. Help me, please." Lisa pulled her parents closer and began to sob.

"You will know what to do when the time comes, my dear, but be warned: sacrifices will have to be made. Have faith, my darling angel, for it can help you conquer anything!"

"And don't doubt your gut feeling," Claudia Spencer added. "Believe in yourself and you have the power to perform miracles."

"I hope so," Lisa sighed. "After the mess the SEALs have made it's going to take everything I have to get the others off that island alive."

"If anyone can do it, darling," Lisa's mother said, "it is you. I've watched you over the years and I've seen your powers grow. You just need to believe in yourself and know that you are stronger than

Thomas Hunter and Desideo."

"More powerful than an *Umbra*?" Lisa didn't sound convinced.

"The essence of the Mille Umbra flows through you," her father explained. "You have the power and the knowledge to defeat Desideo and you *will* win in the end. You just can't see the big picture yet. No matter, when the time is right, you will see what needs to be done."

"You must go now, my love," Claudia Spencer said in tears. "Hold me one last time until we meet again." Lisa wrapped her arms around her mother. "I love you, mama." Lisa whispered. "I love you too, my sweet girl." Lisa let go of her mother and wrapped her arms tightly around her father.

"And I love you too, you old bastard," Lisa teased.

"Older than you think." Andrew Spencer winked at his daughter and said, "It's time for you to go."

"Will I see you again soon?" Lisa asked.

"Not soon enough," Claudia answered with tears in her eyes. "Remember, you have your own destiny,

Lisa. And when you have fulfilled your destiny then you can come home."

"I love you mom and dad," Lisa repeated tearfully.

"And we love you, too," Andrew said softly, "with all of our hearts.

Lisa's world began to spin and she felt the familiar pulling sensation. Everything around her went from blinding white light to pitch black. Slowly her vision returned and she saw a fire burning. A sudden voice from behind Lisa startled her. She turned to see a man chained to a wall and he was singing a song. "She told me that she loved me, she said she would be true…"

(V)

"Here's the plan," Bruce dictated. "Gillian, you stay here and keep watch over Lisa's body.

Whitney, Smith, and I are going hunting for Hunter. We'll split up and meet back here in one hour, whether we find him or not. Gillian, find a way to retrieve Lisa's consciousness from the system, 'cause at the end of that hour, we're out of here no matter what!"

"I'll do what I can, Bruce, but you know I can't promise anything."

"What happens to Lisa if she gets removed from the system without a lock on her consciousness?" "I don't know," Gillian answered honestly. "She could remain in a coma indefinitely or even wind up a vegetable."

"Let's try to avoid that," Bruce said. "Gillian, if Lisa happens to pop up on the monitor again, tell her to get her ass back here within the hour."

"Be careful, Bruce Spencer," Gillian demanded. "You come back to me!"

"Wouldn't miss it for the world," Bruce said with a smile.

Captain Whitney approached Bruce and handed him a headset. "It was Turner's; I thought it might help us to keep in contact."

"Good idea," Bruce placed the compact earpiece in and adjusted the microphone. "Ready when you are," he said. Bruce followed the SEALs out the door and into the hallway.

"We split up like before," Smith suggested. "There was this row of doorways that led different places. I know where two of them lead now so that leaves three. I'll take Mr. Spencer with me while you follow your previous course until it splits off somewhere new."

"Couldn't have said it any better myself," Whitney said as he patted Smith on the back.

"Let's do this!" Bruce demanded. Captain Whitney turned and headed off down the hallway, while Commander Smith and Bruce Spencer made their way to the hallway of doors.

"If I remember correctly," Bruce recalled, "one of these doors will bring us exactly where we want to go. Check each room, look for a room with another door inside."

"In here," Smith yelled. Bruce followed the sound of his voice until he found the room the Commander had entered. The two stepped through the doorway and turned to see the other five doors.

"This one down here," Smith opened the door on the far left, "has just a single room on the other side, but this one," Smith opened the door next to the one they had arrived through, "this one makes my dick hard. I want to know what's on the other side of that blackness."

"I've been through that door," Bruce explained. "It took me to a carnival I had been to many years ago, when I first met my wife."

"Was she there," Smith asked.

"Yeah, problem is, my wife's dead. Bitch even tried to kill me. The blackness gets into your brain and feeds on your worst fears."

"Then we go in together," Smith said.

Bruce grabbed on to Commander Smith's backpack and the two stepped into the blackness.

(VI)

Hunter inhaled deeply and his lungs hurt. Walking was difficult but he was quickly getting used to controlling his muscles again. The pain was nothing; he had endured much worse, yet here he was alive and well, born again, and able to taste blood in the first fifteen minutes of his resurrection. It was a good day! It had felt wonderful to kill Turner personally. During his time with the SEALs it was Turner he'd hated the most. Always having to have the last word, pushing Hunter's buttons every chance he got… Yeah, the blood of Lieutenant Turner was a sweet awakening. Thomas Hunter looked up the stairwell and winced, knowing it was going to be a long, painful climb to the top, although his strength was returning quickly, along with his power. Hunter walked across the marble floor to a spot near the entrance to the great hall. He closed his eyes and began to levitate. Thomas Hunter rose into the air between the wall and the massive chandelier until he had reached the railing of the third floor balcony. He climbed over the rail and headed down the hall where he stopped and opened a door. Hunter eagerly climbed the stairs to the attic. After so many years he was finally going to be face to face with Father again. He would prove to Desideo that he was worthy of the Umbra's embrace, even if he had to get the girl himself. Yes, that would be the greatest reward, to feel her skin with his real hands. Hunter shuttered as the waves of pleasure moved throughout his body. He stopped in front of the door and paused for a moment to smile. He turned the knob and opened the door.

"Welcome back, my son," The Umbra said proudly.

"Thank you, Father."

"You have done well, my son. Lisa Spencer will soon be ours. Do not let her exit the program. Bring both her avatar and her physical body to me and you will be greatly rewarded."

"I will not fail you, my lord," Hunter said as he got down on one knee. "Her physical body is nothing. I shall have the madam fetch it for me while I distract Lisa Spencer and lure her into your trap."

"Excellent!" The Umbra said. "The child will be yours to raise until her fifth birthday. Only then will she have completed her training and become capable of altering reality. The two of you will rule by my side as humanity crumbles and begs us for extinction!"

181

"Yes, Father. I will go now and set Lisa Spencer's fate into motion." Thomas Hunter turned to exit the door and stopped. "Father?"

"Yes, my son."

"I love you."

"I love you too, my son. Now go, bring me the sacred mother."

Thomas Hunter closed the door and opened his mind. "Where are you?" He still lacked the ability to locate Lisa but there were others out there that he could sense. Her uncle, for instance, would make excellent bait to lure Lisa to him. On the other hand were Whitney and Smith. Hunter decided on a most splendid plan to set into motion. He closed his eyes to concentrated on his task, unable to conceal the smile on his face.

(VII)

The doorway Bruce stepped through took him to his old office in Raleigh, North Carolina, the practice he'd had before Lori died. Bruce entered the empty lobby and hallways. "Hello, is anybody there?" he called out but received no reply. Bruce thought about taking the elevator, but only long enough to remember where he really was and how many bad things could happen if he made the wrong choice, leaving the stairs as his only option. His old office was on the third floor, and once there, he took a left out of the stairwell and walked to the office at the end of the hall. He opened the door to his former practice and found the office empty. Bruce made his way past the lounge and offices to a large oak door with his name on a plaque. He opened the door and there she was, his daughter, Ashley. She was sitting in the chair behind his desk atop the headless body of his wife, Lori, whose arms were wrapped tightly around his daughter. Lori's head was on the table, looking up at Bruce when he entered the door. His wife's body had changed clothing since the last time Bruce had seen her. She was no longer wearing a see-through nightgown but instead was in a charcoal gray pantsuit with a white blouse, the collar and lapels red from the blood still oozing out of her stump.

Ashley squirmed within the arms of the headless corpse.

"Help me, daddy," Ashley cried out. "She's hurting me!"

"Don't worry, darling," Bruce answered. "I'll get you out of here."

"It's about time you showed up," the severed head of Bruce's wife spat from the table. "Stop all that wiggling around back there you bitch or mama's going to show you the meaning of pain!"

182

"Don't listen to her, darling," Bruce said calmly to his daughter. "She's *not* your mother; she's just something Thomas Hunter cooked up from our memories to mess with our heads."

"Messed up heads?" Lori screamed. "You want to talk about messed up heads? Just look at what your father did to me."

"You were trying to kill me for fuck's sake!" Bruce protested.

"Is that any way to speak in front of our child?" the severed head asked.

"You are just a figment of a psychopath's imagination and you are *not* her mother! Now let her go!"

"Oh, I don't think so," Lori's head replied in a sing-song voice.

Bruce removed the rifle from his shoulder and took aim at the severed head of his wife. "Think again!" Bruce pulled the trigger and kept firing until there was nothing left but a bloody mass of pulp and a few bone shards. The body of his wife dropped limp and Ashley leapt from the corpse's lap and into her father's arms.

"Thank you, daddy," Ashley sobbed. "Thank you." Ashley placed her hands on her father's face. "I have to go now, daddy. You've set me free and now I can be with my *real* mother. I'll be watching over you, dad." Bruce sobbed as he held his daughter tight. "And about Gillian," Ashley added. "Mom gives you her blessings, and so do I." Bruce only squeezed tighter. "Goodbye, daddy," Ashley whispered. Bruce felt the fabric of his daughter's clothing getting softer and shrinking, her hair no longer in his face. Bruce looked down at the empty pile of clothes in his arms and saw that his daughter Ashley was gone.

CHAPTER NINETEEN

The Sacrifice

(I)

The man finished his song and lifted up his body, which separated at the waist. Lisa reached down and grabbed hold of one of the chains bound to his leg and pulled. The lower half of the man's body slid across the floor leaving him hanging from the chains attached to his wrists.

"Now why did you have to go and do a thing like that?" the man groaned.

"Shut up and listen," Lisa ordered. "You're going to tell me everything you know about the madam and the creature she created or you'll never see your legs again."

"You can't do that!" the man protested.

"I can and I will," Lisa said smugly and with a single thought the lower half of the man's body disappeared.

"What the hell?" the man looked puzzled and then it came to him. "I get it, you're just like *him*. But a lot nicer, I hope."

"I don't have to be. Just tell me what I want to know and you can have your legs back."

"Can I please have my legs first? Without them my intestines tend to spill out on the floor."

Lisa saw it in her head and it happened. The man's torso rose into the air and his entrails climbed back up inside his stomach. The man's legs appeared beneath his torso in a sitting position. Lisa gently lowered the man's top onto the bottom. "Oh, thank you! I say, that's the kindest thing anyone's ever done for me. See, I knew you were nicer than Hunter."

"Only as long as you live up to your end of the bargain," Lisa said firmly. And so he did, telling Lisa all about the game program and how it had slowly come to life. He named all of the staff members that the madam had used to create her monstrosity. He left out Doug of course, because he had not seen the madam or the creature since she had chained him to the wall. He also told Lisa a very important piece of information; he told her that the creature had a weakness.

"You're going to take me to her," Lisa told Crazy Pete.

"That wasn't part of the deal, nuh uh, and besides, you don't have the key."

184

"I made half of your body disappear, what makes you think I need a key?"

"Good point," Pete conceded. "But if you take all of me, you could put me back together, right?"

"I could but I won't." Lisa lifted Pete's severed torso up in the air.

"What are you doing now, you crazy bitch?" His intestines did not fall out this time; in fact, Pete noticed new skin growing over his severed body.

"If you ever want to be reattached with the rest of your body you'll do what I say. I need someone to carry you." Lisa thought about her uncle and found him in his office in Raleigh. She thought about him being there with her and Bruce appeared out of thin air.

"What the…? Oh, hey there, Lisa. I see you've met Crazy Pete."

"Yup, he's my new best friend," Lisa said sarcastically. "He's taking us to see the madam. Oh, and you get to carry him."

"What am I, your damn pack mule?"

"C'mon, Bruce. I'll even empty out all of his organs to make him lighter."

"You'll do no such thing," Crazy Pete protested but it was too late. The new skin that had grown over the wound tore open and his insides came spilling out, heart, lungs, and all. Lisa mentally removed the chains binding Pete's wrists and he dropped to the floor. Bruce reached down and picked the man up, slung his arms over his shoulders and wore Crazy Pete like a backpack.

"That's a good look for you, Bruce," Lisa teased.

"You better be able to put me back together," Pete grumbled.

"All right you two, let's get moving, I'm not carrying this thing around with me all day."

"Well, Pete," Lisa said. "Lead the way."

(II)

Captain Whitney opened the door and stepped inside. He looked around the bar that he'd been to many times; it was the bar he'd met Karen at. He saw her across the room. She sat at a round table recessed in the wall. She was talking and laughing with three men that Jason Whitney did not recognize. He started to walk over to the table when Karen climbed underneath and began masturbating the men, one in each hand, the third in her mouth. Her lips alternated between men as they laughed and joked amongst themselves. Wit was nearly in a rage by the time he reached the table; he grabbed hold of the thing and turned it over, exposing the whore beneath. Wit was taken aback when he looked down at the woman who was no longer his girlfriend but his mother, who still sucked and stroked feverishly. Wit pulled out his pistol and shot each of the three men in the head. "Tom!" Wit called out. "I know you're watching, you sick son of a bitch!" Thomas Hunter *hated* to be called Tom. "Why don't you come out and show yourself instead of hiding behind some twisted fantasy of yours?" The bar's patrons were still running around in a panic after the gunfire. "That's right, empty this place out so it's just you and me, *Tom.*" Wit waited for a reply but there was none. "Why do you hate women so much, Tom? Is it because you've been rejected once too often? I don't think so, you're not a bad looking guy, Hell, if you were born a girl I might even have fucked you." Apparently *this* struck a nerve.

"Captain Jason Whitney," Hunter's voice boomed from the bar's loudspeakers. "Not all of this was a fantasy. Your girlfriend *is* out blowing three marines at a bar tonight. Do you actually think she's faithful to you when you're never around? You mean *nothing* to her!"

"Yet she keeps coming back, so I must be doing something right. Unlike you, a man so pathetic he has to kill the woman he rapes just so she can't tell anyone what a lousy lay you are."

"You think you're so funny, *Wit*, but you won't be laughing when you see what I have in store for your pal Commander Smith." All of the televisions in the bar suddenly flickered to life and all of them showed the same image, Commander Randal Smith sitting on the bench seat of a subway car.

(III)

It seemed like hours had passed since Randal had first boarded the train. He had nowhere else to go. As soon as he'd stepped through the doorway and into the blackness with Bruce Spencer, Commander Smith found himself alone in a room with no exit. He'd sat on the wooden bench for God knows how long before the train pulled up and the doors opened. Randal boarded the car, the door shut and the train began to move. He'd searched the car only to find both doors locked and little of interest among the blood-soaked seats. After a while one of the doors unlocked and hissed open. Smith sprang from his seat and dashed for the door before it closed tightly behind him. Smith stopped and raised his rifle at the creature blocking the isle. The thing stood about four feet tall and its body looked like a wingless, featherless bird with a long neck, and on that neck sat a human head. The creature lunged at Smith and he opened fire. "That wasn't much of a challenge," he said as the thing fell dead after only a few rounds of ammo. The next door hissed open and Randal found himself in his current location, sitting at a bar drinking a warm beer, and waiting for the next door to open.

"Are you still up for a challenge?" Randal looked up and saw Thomas Hunter standing behind the bar. He wore an apron and was presently wiping a glass dry with a small hand towel. Smith stood and raised his weapon. "That thing is of no use to you right now," Hunter said as he pushed the barrel of the gun out of his face and turned to pour two large shots of whisky. Commander Smith aimed and pulled the trigger. Nothing happened. "I told you, Commander Smith, your weapon is of no use against me. It still works, I assure you, it simply won't work against *me*." Smith pointed the gun straight up and fired. Shards of glass and metal fell all around as the ceiling was sprayed with bullets. "Sit down," Hunter said to Smith as he placed two glasses on the bar, "and have a drink with me." Hunter raised one of the glasses and pushed the other in front of Smith who just looked at it. "Oh, come now, Mr. Smith. Celebrate with me."

"What, exactly, are we celebrating?" Smith asked. The glass in front of Commander Smith slid like being pushed by a phantom hand toward him, almost falling off the table and onto his lap, but he caught it with his free hand just in time.

"Now raise your glass and we'll toast."

"Whatever," Smith said as he lifted his glass.

Hunter tapped the rim of Smith's glass with his own and said, "To my rebirth," before downing the shot in one gulp. Smith pulled his pistol from its holster, placed it against Thomas Hunter's head and pulled the trigger but nothing happened. Hunter just laughed. "You'll never learn, will you?" The exit door directly behind Smith opened. "I'll be seeing you around," Hunter said as Smith's barstool rose into the air and was flung out the door with its occupant still aboard. Smith landed on the hard dirt and rolled. He tried desperately to catch his breath as he tumbled but the fall had knocked the wind out of him. Smith raised his head and looked around at the dozens of creatures closing in on him. He'd seen this particular species once already on his journeys through the NeuroTech compound. It was the shield-faced creature from the cave on the snow covered mountain, only this time there were a shit ton more of them. They were less than ten feet away when Smith collapsed and fell unconscious.

(IV)

"Captain Whitney," Lisa mumbled to herself, "Smith?" more incomprehensible babbling. "What are you talking about up there?" Bruce grabbed Lisa by the arm and forced her to look him in the eyes. "What's going on, Lisa?"

"I need to go, Bruce. Smith and Whitney need my help."

"What about you?"

"You've seen what I can do. I can handle my own out there." Bruce knew she was right. "Besides, you get to carry 'ole Pete around for a while; he'll keep you company. Now, you be a good boy, Pete, if you ever want to be reunited with your insides and your legs."

"Fuck you, *bitch*!" Pete replied.

"Hey now," Bruce purposefully slammed Pete's head against the stone wall of the passage they were currently walking down. "Watch yourself there, partner."

"Thanks, Uncle Bruce. I'll catch up with you as soon as I can. And stop worrying about Gillian. I've been keeping tabs on her and she's doing fine."

"Thanks for meddling in my relationship," Bruce said. Lisa kissed him on the cheek.

"I need to go. Love you, Unc." Lisa's world spun into a brilliant white and when she came to rest she was standing by a set of railroad tracks that ran through the middle of a desert.

As she looked around, Captain Whitney appeared to the left of Lisa. "Where is he?" she asked of Commander Smith. "I'm not sure," Wit answered. "They took him this way." Captain Whitney followed a large group of footprints in the sand that led away from the railroad tracks and into the desert. "We can't be far behind," he said. "If we hurry, we can catch up to them."

"He's fine," Lisa said matter-of-factly. "Hunter's toying with you and he's leading us somewhere but where? He *must* know I'm with you by now." Lisa caught up to Captain Whitney and surprisingly kept pace with the highly trained solder. Either that or he had slowed down for her, but Lisa liked her first thought much better. "Are you afraid of Hunter?" Lisa asked as they walked.

"Of Thomas Hunter? No. It's what he can do that terrifies me."

"Do *I* scare you?" Lisa asked.

"You?" Wit chuckled. "Hell no, I ain't afraid of you."

"Stick around awhile, you just might change your opinion."

When they reached the top of the next dune Whitney was the first to see them. He crouched down with his binoculars and stared off in the distance where the pack of creatures was carrying Commander Smith toward a dark object farther on.

"It's an apple tree," Lisa said.

"How do you know that?" Whitney asked.

"I just do. This must be where Hunter is leading us."

"Why here?" Wit asked.

"It's me that he really wants and that tree will lead me closer to the Mille Umbra."

"What is it that's so important about you?" Whitney asked.

"I can give birth to the antichrist," Lisa said flatly.

"Which you have no intention of doing, *right*?" Wit gently nudged Lisa's shoulder with his own.

"Oh, yeah," Lisa said, distracted. "Right." Lisa stood up and moved down the dune too quickly for Captain Whitney to stop her. He thought, *well shit, there goes the element of surprise*. The creatures would surely have seen them by now. Whitney ran after Lisa who was nearly halfway down the hill and gaining ground on them with ease. "Slow down, Speed Racer," Captain Whitney cautioned.

"What's the matter," Lisa teased, "Big bad Navy boy can't keep up with a woman?"

"Yeah, well, you're no ordinary woman," Wit said as he reached Lisa's side.

"I think I remember saying something like that." Lisa smiled.

The creatures dumped Smith on the ground near the tree and began to take up defensive positions. Whitney checked the magazine on his rifle and slid it back in the slot. "Let's do this!" he commanded. Lisa put her hand in the air, signaling for Captain Whitney to stop. "I've got this, SEAL boy." One of the creatures began to charge Lisa. Whitney's finger tightened around the trigger of his rifle. Lisa raised her hand in the air and made a fist. The creature charging suddenly stopped as its head imploded as if all the air had been sucked from inside. Lisa unclenched her fist and the creature fell dead to the ground. The remaining members of the pack seemed to take the hint and began to scurry off into the desert leaving Commander Smith lying on the ground by the tree. Wit was close enough to see a pile of worms that formed a puddle of muck at the base of the tree and realized that the worms were falling out of the rotting fruit on the tree. He began to see movement in the puddle; *something* was rising out of the muck. It was hard to make out his features through the black oil-like substance that covered the face, but Captain Whitney was sure that *something* was Thomas Hunter.

"Ah, my two favorite members of SEAL Team Zero. Oh, wait, you're the only members *left*." Hunter cackled as he stepped onto the sand. Lisa turned to Captain Whitney and grabbed hold of his face. She placed her forehead against his and whispered. "Take this map," she said. "It will lead you back to the labs."

"What are you doing?" Captain Whitney asked suspiciously.

"I'm gonna' fuck him up!" Lisa screamed as she charged and grabbed hold of Thomas Hunter, dragging him down into the muck until they both disappeared.

(V)

"Will you shut up back there," Bruce grumbled as he walked. 'Ole Crazy Pete had been talking and singing to himself the entire time Bruce had been carrying him. "Aren't you supposed to be giving me directions?" Bruce asked, obviously annoyed.

"Just keep going straight," Pete said and then went back to singing. "If you didn't love me, you wouldn't cut me to pieces. If you didn't need me, you wouldn't be such a tease."

Bruce swung Pete around and forced his severed torso up against the wall in a chokehold. "Now listen up, buddy. I don't need you, I could find the Madam on my own and tell my niece you got killed. Then you'd never get put back together. So what's it going to be? Either you shut the hell up or I leave your ass here to rot." Bruce glared at Crazy Pete with deadly intent.

"Take your next left, it's just up ahead. We're getting close."

"We'd better be," Bruce growled. Bruce took the first corridor to the left and found himself in a long hallway with a single door at the end.

"There she is," Pete said. "You'll find the Madam on the other side of that door. You go on in and leave me here, I'll wait for you."

"Nope, you're coming with me."

"Come on, man!" Pete shouted. "You go through that door and you're as good as dead."

"I'll take my chances, and so will you, now *come on*!" Bruce followed the hallway until it ended with a single door. Bruce looked down at the handle and saw that the key was still in the lock. He turned the knob and slowly opened the door. The room contained a vanity complete with matching metal stool, with one mirrored wall, but to Bruce's surprise, the room on the other side of the mirrored wall was not

190

an exact replica. "Peter, my darling," the Madam purred. "It's so good to see you, and I see you've brought along some company. Tell me about yourself, handsome," the Madam crooned to Bruce.

"What do you want to know?" Bruce asked.

"Your darkest fantasies, of course. Would you treat me like an animal and fuck me from behind, or would you like for me to be on top, in control?"

"How about neither, you disgusting bitch! How about you tell me everything you know about Thomas Hunter instead?"

"Leave him out of this for now," the Madam whispered close to the glass. "*This* moment belongs to you and I. Now, tell me, what is your name, my darling?"

"His name is Bruce, Bruce Spencer," Pete said proudly "Uncle to the woman Hunter seeks."

"Yes, oh yes!" the woman moaned. "You are a pleasant surprise, indeed." The Madam moved closer to the glass. "Would you like to kiss me, Bruce? Would you like to feel my lips on your cock?" she whispered enticingly.

"Slow down there, sweetheart, I mean, we barely know each other."

"All I'm asking for is a kiss." The woman placed her lips to the glass and closed her eyes. "Kiss me," she moaned. It was at that moment Bruce Spencer did something the woman was completely unprepared for. He picked up the metal chair from the vanity and smashed the mirrored wall. The Madam fell back and landed on the floor. Bruce quickly climbed through the mirror to the room on the other side. He hastily scanned the room and spotted a pile of scrap fabric. Bruce gathered several pieces and tied the madam to the chair.

(VI)

Whitney and Smith stood a short distance from the apple tree debating on their next course of action. Their orders were to bring Thomas Hunter back alive, but that was proving to be a very difficult task as Hunter had complete control over their environment. "We're going to have to lure the puke to the airlock," Captain Whitney said.

"First we need to figure out a way to overpower him and get him back to the sub," Smith sighed. "That's where Lisa Spencer fits into the picture," Whitney explained. "Hunter seems to be fixated with the woman for some reason. Maybe we can figure out a way to exploit his preoccupation with her." "So

191

what's it gonna' be Captain? Do we run back to the lab with our dicks tucked between our legs or do we go in after that son of a bitch guns blazin'?"

"Smith," Wit said with a smile, "you're reading my mind."

"We go in together and we don't get separated," Smith said. "Are you ready?"

The men stood side by side and each placed an arm around the other. "Ready," Wit said, and they dove head first into the pool of worms.

Wit felt a force pushing in on him. He could see and hear nothing and barely felt Commander Smith's arm around his shoulder. The worms were trying to climb into his ears and up his nose. It wouldn't be long before they found other orifices to climb into and Captain Whitney didn't even want to think about *that*. He simply kicked his feet and paddled his free arm hoping that Smith was doing the same. Wit felt Smith's arm glide from his shoulder and reached out with his hand to grab hold of his teammate before he slipped away. It was a futile gesture. The forces of the current in whatever substance they were swimming in was just too strong and Wit lost his grasp on Smith altogether. Wit used both hands to swim and soon freed himself from the current. He only had a moment to relax before another force pulled him deeper into the muck and through a network of drainage pipes. The liquid around him felt more like water so Wit chanced opening his eyes. He saw a light up ahead and began swimming with the current until he broke the water's surface. Captain Whitney was thrown up into the air out of what was no more than a puddle of water that had pooled up beside the railroad tracks of an underground train. The lights on the tunnel walls flickered and Wit heard the soft rumble of a train in the distance. Now he just had to figure out which direction it was coming from. Jason Whitney frantically searched his surroundings for a way out but it was no use. He even tried stepping in the puddle but it was now only an inch or two deep. There was no doubt about it, when Captain Jason Whitney saw the light from the train coming down the tracks at incredible speed, he knew that he was going to die.

(VII)

Lisa held on tightly to Thomas Hunter as they descended into the depths of the muck. She knew exactly where she wanted to go and how to get there. It was time to end this, and if that meant sacrificing herself to save the others, then so be it. Lisa was ready to die. She saw her destination and closed her eyes to prepare for the ride. She tightened her grip on the murderer as they were pulled into the network of tunnels and flung in every conceivable direction before being thrown from the fountain in the center of the flower garden behind Thomas Hunter's childhood home. Lisa landed hard in the dirt, momentarily losing her breath. She rolled over to make sure Thomas Hunter hadn't found his footing yet. He lay motionless next to a concrete bench that he had obviously hit his head on but he was still breathing. Lisa willed her muscles to move and slowly stood, forcing her body to work through the pain.

She looked down on Hunter with disgust and then up at the attic widow on the house. She could feel Desideo staring back at her through the blackness of the glass. Lisa raised her hand and Thomas Hunter's body began to levitate. She motioned with her hand and Hunter's body followed her down the path, his feet leaving trails in the dirt as they made their way to the back porch. Lisa entered the kitchen and climbed the stairs to the attic of the house for the second time in the past few hours. Only *this* time,

Lisa had a feeling she wouldn't be coming back.

(VIII)

Commander Smith was thrown from the small puddle of water in the corner of the room. He landed on the concrete hard but raised his head and looked around. "Not this place again," he moaned as he took in his surroundings. He got up from the floor and took a seat on the single wooden bench in the center of the room and waited for the train that would be coming soon. He didn't have to wait long; within moments, Smith heard the familiar sound of grinding metal and squealing brakes. The train slowed to a stop and the door hissed open. Smith stood and entered the car. He didn't waste any time waiting for the doors to unlock; *this* time he used brute force to make his way forward to find out who or what was steering the train. Smith used his rifle on doors he couldn't muscle open and shot at anything in his path. There were more of the birdlike creatures with human heads, but each new car brought a different nightmare. In one, a creature that had the lower half of a hairless kangaroo and head of a worm attacked Smith. Smith made short work of the creature with his shotgun by blowing the thing's head clean off. Another car was full of creatures that looked like miniature gorillas, each no more that two feet tall and void of any fur. They moved so quickly that a few of them even made it past the guns and attacked Smith close up. He kept firing with his rifle and withdrew a knife to fight off the creatures that attacked him from all directions. The car after that was empty but for a door that took more than a rifle and shotgun to open. Smith removed his backpack and rummaged through it for a small block of C4. He attached it to the door complete with a detonating cap and took cover. Smith stood up and saw the gaping hole in the door leading to the control room of the train, but he saw no driver. What he did see, however, was a man on the tracks up ahead that looked an awful lot like Captain Whitney. Smith frantically searched for the brake, pulling every handle and pushing every button, but nothing happened. Smith steadied his rifle and began firing at the controls of the train until all of the lights on the console went out and the brakes kicked in. Smith watched as the horror on Whitney's face turned to relief when he saw his teammate at the controls of the train. Sparks flew in all directions as metal scraped against metal and the train came to grinding halt just inches from

Captain Whitney. Smith shot out the window and held out a hand for his superior officer. Wit took Smith's hand and climbed through the window.

"Are you OK?" Smith asked.

"Just peachy," Wit answered. "It's not every day you narrowly escape dying." "Nope," Smith added. "In our line of work it's every *other* day."

(IX)

Lisa entered the room with an unconscious Thomas Hunter still in tow by her powers. She turned to look at the door and it slammed shut. The body of Thomas Hunter floated across the room and stretched out across the door, his feet still hovering several inches off the ground. "Show yourself!" Lisa demanded.

"I am here," the creature answered.

"I *said* show yourself; I want to see you!"

"As you wish." Desideo moved forward into the dim light. Lisa saw the tangled mass of souls that made up the creature's body. She even saw Dr. Alan Carlton swimming within the confines of the Umbra's profile. ***"You have returned to fulfill your destiny."***

"On one condition," Lisa said boldly. "I give myself to you and the others go free."

"Of course, you have my word."

"Your word means *nothing* to me!" Lisa shouted.

"I will honor your request," Desideo said. "You keep your part of the bargain and I will keep mine."

"Very well," Lisa conceded. "What do I do now?"

"Come closer, my child," the Umbra whispered. Lisa slowly moved forward into the blackness of the room, drawn to the Mille Umbra as if in a trance. ***"Yes, my dear, closer."*** It was almost as though instinct had taken over; somehow Lisa knew what had to be done. She raised her arm and reached out to touch the creature, knowing that by doing so her soul would be stripped from her physical body and become trapped within the creature forever.

194

One of the shadows writhing within the Umbra reached out and took Lisa's hand. She watched in amazement as the blackness of the creature crawled up her arm and spread across her body. She felt her body being pulled inside the creature's mass and encompassed by the hundreds of souls floating within. Each form spoke the same two words over and over again as they raped her one by one. Each soul whispered the words "Mille Umbra" into Lisa's ear as they defiled her in every way imaginable. Before Lisa was lost within the bowels of the creature forever she heard Desideo speak. It was not to her but to Thomas Hunter that the Umbra spoke. It said, ***"Now that she is mine, you may kill the others; they are of no consequence."***

"Yes, my Father," Hunter answered with delight.

Lisa formed one final thought before being consumed by the creature that was raping her. She thought of her Uncle and Gillian as well as the remaining members of the SEAL team. She had to find a way to get them off the island.

CHAPTER TWENTY

The Escape

(I)

Captain Whitney and Commander Smith stood on the tracks and stared out the opening of the tunnel. They had walked for what seemed like miles, following the railroad tracks as they looked for a way out of the tunnel. Wit saw a light up ahead and it soon became apparent that the two SEALs had found an exit from the tunnel. When they stepped out into the murky sunlight both stopped and stared. On both sides of the tracks were millions of glowing green orbs floating in the air. Each was tethered to the ground with a chain approximately four feet long, making the landscape look like a vast field of glowing balls of light. Wit stepped off the tracks and walked into the field to examine the orbs. The outside shell was about the size of a basketball and clear but within was a glowing ball of green light the size of Wit's clenched fist. It took a moment for his eyes to adjust to the brightness and then he saw them, black shadows swimming within the green light.

"They're demon souls," a voice called out from behind Wit.

The SEAL's turned to find Lisa Spencer standing on the tracks.

"I don't have much time so shut up and listen," she said. "You can't fight Hunter on the island, he's too powerful. Get out and fight another day. This leads us to our first problem. You two are no longer *on* the island. You've passed through the gateway to Hell and the only way out is to find a boy named Sirnib." "Where do we find him?" Smith asked.

"You must go to the city of Loo Rin; just keep following the tracks until you reach the city. You'll find him in a bar called The Hell Hole. I must go, so please, do as I say."

Before Wit could say another word the girl had disappeared.

"Why don't we go back to the train and out the other side," Smith offered. "Then we can follow the tracks the other way; we're bound to find one of the loading platforms sooner or later."

"I can see the city from here," Wit said. "Looks like it's about seven miles away. We listen to the girl. She's right; we can't fight Hunter while he controls the program, but maybe this Sirnib will know of a way that we can." Smith, knowing that his commanding officer was right, joined Captain Whitney on the railroad tracks and the two solders began to walk toward the city.

(II)

Gillian almost fell out of her chair. She'd been startled awake by the Spencer girl having a seizure on the table. The doctor stepped back and watched in horror as Lisa's stomach began to expand as she fought the restraints. When the stomach resembled a full term pregnancy the convulsions stopped and the body of Lisa Spencer laid still. Gillian stepped closer and placed her hand on the stomach. She felt a child moving around inside. "It's a girl," a voice spoke from the doorway. Gillian looked up to see Lisa Spencer's avatar. "How do you know?" the doctor asked.

Lisa ignored her question and continued talking. "I'm carrying the antichrist, a child who will be able to change reality in any way they wish. I want you and Bruce to take care of her, Gillian. You need to get my body out of here and hide the child from Hunter and Desideo. Give her a good life; she doesn't have to be evil."

"What will you name her?" Gillian asked.

"Alexondra," Lisa answered.

"It's a pretty name," Gillian said.

"Thank you, and goodbye Gillian Black. Take care of my daughter and my uncle."

Gillian looked up and the avatar was gone. She sat back down and stared at the motionless body on the bed and the stomach that contained a child, a child fathered by the Mille Umbra. Her first instinct was to kill the fetus, but then she remembered Lisa telling her that her own father was a member of the same species as Desideo, and Lisa didn't seem like a bad person. But raising a child? Gillian had never really considered having children. Her work was her life; Project Lucidity had been her child. And then there was Bruce. Sure, she liked him, but could it really work out between them? *He is rather handsome,* Gillian thought to herself, *and he is a doctor, intelligent, funny, even charming in his own way. Yep, I'm hooked. But a child?* Gillian's thoughts raced as she contemplated a future with a man she could quite possibly be in love with and a child who happened to be the antichrist.

(III)

The woman was tied to the chair firmly; she wasn't going anywhere and she knew it. Bruce Spencer clenched his fist and swung at the Madam, landing the punch in the center of her forehead, knocking over the chair. The Madam squirmed and squealed as she fell helplessly to the floor. Bruce lifted her up and straightened out the chair. "That was for Doug," he said as he rubbed his clenched fist and punched her in the jaw again. Bruce reached for the rifle on the table and aimed the barrel at the Madam's face. "Now tell me, how do I stop Thomas Hunter?" The Madam ignored his question and spit a mouthful of blood on the floor. "She can't help you." Bruce instantly recognized the voice. "Lisa?" He turned to find his niece in the doorway. "Hi, Unc," she said with a smile. "You need to get out of here, get back to Gillian, and get my body off this island. Do whatever it takes, Bruce, and don't let Hunter take my body. Dr. Black will explain the rest, now go." Bruce was about to reply but his niece had vanished. "How touching." Another voice that Bruce recognized. He raised the gun and pointed it at

Thomas Hunter. "What have you done with Lisa, you bastard?"

"She has fulfilled her destiny. She is safe now and I assure you that no harm will come to her. You, on the other hand, YOU I am going to enjoy skinning alive!" Hunter pulled a large knife out from a pocket of the jumpsuit he wore. He tossed it from hand to hand as he slowly advanced on Bruce.

Bruce raised the barrel of the AK-47 and pulled the trigger. Hunter disappeared before the first spray of bullets left the clip. He reappeared behind Bruce and grabbed hold of him, knife to Bruce's throat. "Nice try, Doctor. Looks like I'll be operating on *you* today."

Bruce placed his left hand over his clenched right fist and drove his right elbow into Thomas Hunter's chest, causing him to lose his breath and loosen his grip on the doctor. Bruce seized the moment and slammed Thomas Hunter into the wall, clocking him in the head with the butt of the rifle. Bruce Spencer was smart enough to know that his luck would eventually run out and Thomas Hunter would kill him, so he ran. He ran down the hallway as fast as he could as he made his way back to the lab where he knew the comatose body of his niece and Gillian would be waiting for him.

(IV)

The tracks led to an abandoned station just outside the city where they branched off in three

separate directions. Wit chose the set of tracks that led directly into the heart of the city and the two solders continued walking. "So," Smith said. "We're going to a bar in a city in Hell to meet a young boy? This mission is definitely turning out to be one of the most bizarre ones yet."

"It's up there, all right," Wit agreed.

The buildings on the outskirts of the city were no more than shacks with the occasional brick structure. Wit was examining one such structure that was built just off the tracks when it happened. In the blink of an eye, Captain Whitney and Commander Smith were transported somewhere else. They appeared on a crowded city sidewalk amidst a throng of pedestrians large enough to separate the two momentarily until Wit grabbed hold of Smith and pulled him into an ally. Wit spotted an elderly man walking slower than the rest of the crowd and pulled him aside. "Where do we find a bar called The Hell Hole?" he asked.

The old man paused for a moment and said, "I think it's somewhere in…"

It happened again. Wit and Smith were transported somewhere else but this time they were not alone. It would seem that the entire crowd of pedestrians had made the journey with them.

"Where were we?" The elderly gentleman asked. "That's right, The Hell Hole. You'll find it in the district known as the Den." He then turned and made his way down the street as if nothing had ever happened. Wit grabbed the arm of another individual and pulled him aside from the crowd. Wit looked up and noticed that this new person was not quite human. He had leathery gray skin on his hand and webbed fingers. His head was human shaped but his features were more fish than man.

"Where do I find the Den?" Wit asked.

"You must be new in town," the fish man laughed. "Two blocks east, take a right on Crowley Street and just keep following it; it will lead you exactly where you want to go."

"What about these time shifts?" Smith asked.

"The jumps will not deter you from your destination; just keep following Crowley Street." The fish man waved and joined the crowd of pedestrians once more, disappearing from sight in the throng.

Wit and Smith followed Crowley Street until it was evident they had crossed over into the district known as the Den. At first it appeared to be like any other seedy part of town in any number of major cities, but upon closer inspection, the differences were vividly evident. First of all, not all of the prostitutes and drug dealers that roamed the streets were human. One such abnormal prostitute approached Captain Whitney and grabbed his ass. "You're looking pretty fine in that uniform, 'tholdier." The woman spoke with a lisp due to having an abnormal mouth shaped like a vagina with dozens of two-inch long tentacles surrounding the orifice. Commander Smith pushed the woman aside and kept on walking. No one seemed to be paying particularly close attention to them even though they were in uniform and carrying weapons.

"Excuse me, ma'am," Smith asked another of the prostitutes. "How do we get to The Hell Hole?" "I've got the only hole in Hell you'll ever need, sweetheart, right here." The woman lifted up her skirt and Smith got a good look at the hooker's genitalia. She had a hole all right, a hole filled with teeth like thorns that curved inward, assuring that whatever was placed inside went in easily but would never come back out the same. ""Sorry to waste your time, ma'am," Smith said as they continued walking.

"Take your next left," the prostitute called out, "it's two blocks down on the right." "I think she likes you," Captain Whitney teased.

"Did you see that thing?" Smith asked. "Ain't no way *my* peckers goin' in that hole!"

Wit chuckled to himself as they walked. Smith was always a good man to have around when times were tough; he always kept them laughing.

The next time shift landed them across the street from the bar. Wit was expecting much more than a stairway leading down to a pub that wasn't much more than a hole in the wall. Smith was already halfway down the steps before Captain Whitney noticed the neon sign that read "live-nude-female of the species". "I can't wait to see *this*," Smith said with excitement. Wit descended the stairs where Smith was waiting for him at the door. Smith pushed the door open and the two soldiers entered the bar.

Whitney and Smith stood in awe at the size of the place. Wit counted at least a dozen round stages scattered about the floor, each with its own pole rising from the center of the platform. At the far end of the dual bars that ran down each side of the room was a much larger stage, the curtain lowered. Wit glanced at Smith to find his eyes darting from stage to stage, like a kid in a candy store who couldn't decide which delectable treat to choose. Not all of the dancers were human. One of them resembled the fish headed man from the street, while another looked more ape than human. Wit scanned the room twice before he saw the kid. He had short blonde hair and blue eyes. The kid was dirty, like he hadn't bathed in weeks, matching the rags that he wore for clothing. The child was on the other side of the room, standing in front of the large stage. The music suddenly stopped and the room went dark. A spotlight switched on, illuminating the curtain hanging from the rafters of the rear stage. The curtain opened to thunderous applause even though the stage was still empty. Wit saw a shadow move in the background and a form began to take shape. The dancer was somewhat humanoid, though she had six legs equally spaced from one another that circled her torso, forcing her to walk like a crab. She had two arms on each side of her body that swayed with the music. Her face was beautiful; she had luscious red lips that matched her hair and her eyes. She wrapped two of her legs around the pole, grabbed on with two of her arms and she began to spin. The woman flung her body high and low on the pole, making it a sort of dance within a dance. "Have you ever seen anything like it?" Smith asked.

"Can't say that I have," Wit remarked.

"She has fourteen vagina's you know," a small voice yelled out over the music. Wit looked around to find it was the young boy who was speaking.

"What would you do with them all?" Wit asked.

"What *wouldn't* I do?" At the same time the boy spoke these words, Commander Smith said the exact same thing. Both started laughing. "I like the way this guy thinks. Let me guess, you two are new here?"

"We're just visiting," Wit said. "We're looking for someone named Sirnib, is that you?"

"Depends on who's asking," the boy said defiantly.

"Lisa Spencer told us to find him, said that he could help us."

"Spencer…Spencer, why does that name sound… Spencer, as in *Andrew* Spencer's daughter? The daughter of Animus?" the boy almost sounded excited.

"That would be her," Wit answered.

"Of course I'll help you! Come with me!" The boy hastily trotted to a door near the side of the stage and waited for Smith and Whitney to catch up. "What do you need?" the child asked.

"We need to find a way out of here and back to the island, back to Lisa Spencer. She needs us and the island is under the control of Thomas Hunter and an Umbra named Desideo."

"That sounds like some bad news, fella's, but cheer up, I know *just* the thing you need."

"What and where is it?" Captain Whitney asked.

"What it is," the boy explained, "is a Rive, an object of power that can transport you anywhere you want to go, anywhere in Heaven, Hell, and the known universe. If you can imagine it and it exists, the Rive will take you there. Now, you need one to transport at least two people…"

"Six," Captain Whitney interrupted. "We need to move at least six people."

"Now, that narrows our options," the boy said. "Let me think… I got it! There's a Rive that should suit your needs in the private collection of an associate of the late Animus. I can give you directions, but I can't go there myself, 'cause that would raise too much suspicion."

"How do we get there?" Smith asked.

"Just do as I tell you and everything will be fine." Sirnib led the two SEALs down a flight of stairs and into what could only be described as a church, though every inch of the chapel, from the pews that held the worshipers, to the altar that the minister delivered his sermon from, was made from human skulls. "Just relax," Sirnib assured them. "It's just through here." The boy pulled back a curtain and beckoned the two SEALs to enter. "What's on the other side?" Smith asked.

"You'll find out soon enough," the boy said with a smile. "Just remember this: north up the beach to a small shack, you can't miss it." The boy pushed at the soldier's legs, trying to force them into the room beyond the curtain. "C'mon, you don't have much time and you're wasting too much of it here."

"The kid's right," Wit said. "Lisa seemed to think we could trust this kid so let's trust him." Wit stepped into the room and disappeared. "Well," the kid said. "Are you going in or are you more pussy than the Diorian female on stage back there?"

"Fuck you, kid," Smith said and stepped inside.

"That's the spirit!" Sirnib said and pulled the curtain closed.

(V)

Bruce Spencer ran as fast as he could as he retraced his path down the passageway that had led him to the Madam. He could hear the creature's screams growing from within the woman. Thomas Hunter must have let it loose. Bruce reached the first turn just moments before the creature came crashing through the locked door in pursuit of him. He ran even harder to reach the next doorway on his journey back to the lab. Bruce fumbled with Gillian's keys until he found the right one and opened the door. Bruce stepped inside and locked it. He made his way to the vent on the back wall and climbed inside. Bruce heard the creature just outside the door, and he was in luck, because the Madam was passing by the room as she searched for Bruce further down the corridor. He climbed deeper into the vent dragging his guns and backpack behind him. Bruce followed the shaft until it branched off in two directions. He tried desperately to remember which passageway he had emerged from but the memory just wouldn't come. Bruce sat down for a moment to think and looked up. He had been wrong, the passageway split off in three directions, not two, and that third vent shaft was his ticket out of there.

Bruce stood and began to climb up the shaft that led to the laundry room of the facility. Once there, Bruce exited the laundry room and traversed the hallway north until he came to the first intersection. Bruce took a right and the airlock came into view. Just beyond that were the labs. Bruce opened the door to the lab and breathed a sigh of relief. Gillian jumped from her chair and ran into Bruce's arms.

"Bruce!" she squealed. "I'm so glad you're back."

"We need to move," Bruce said sternly. "Hunter's on his way here as we speak. He's got the Madam with him."

"What do they want?" Gillian asked, almost afraid to know the answer.

"They want Lisa," Bruce answered. He paused for a moment when he first saw his niece's swollen stomach. "And what's growing inside of her."

"We are *not* going to let that happen," Gillian said matter-of-factly. "I promised Lisa we would take care of her child and by God that is one promise I intend to keep."

"I'll be there by your side, Gillian. You're not in this alone." Bruce placed his arm around Gillian and held her close as she began to weep. "Are you all right?" Bruce asked.

"Just a little overwhelmed," Gillian smiled and replied. "I'll be fine, Bruce. Really."

"I know you will, you're a strong woman. I like that about you."

"Oh yeah, and just what else do you like about me?" she asked with a sly grin.

"I like the fact that even though a psychopath and some fucked up creature made from human corpses are on their way here to kill us you can still find time to flirt with me."

Gillian laughed. "You're right." She began to unhook the electrodes attached to the skullcap and disconnected Lisa's IV as she prepped the body for transportation. Suddenly the door was ripped from its hinges and the Madam's creature roared just outside the threshold. The beast stepped into the room, and what was left of Doug's face stared intently at the body of Lisa Spencer while the creature's limbs swiped and grabbed at Gillian and Bruce. The pair managed to avoid the creature's grasp, but Lisa was not so lucky. The creature moved swiftly, scooping Lisa up in its arms and fleeing out the doorway and down the hall. Bruce took aim with the gun but he could not get a clear shot without risking the life of his niece. "Fuck!" Bruce yelled as he fired off a burst of rounds simply to blow off steam.

"It's alright, Bruce," Gillian tried to reassure him. "We'll find her and get the hell out of here."

(VI)

Commander Smith plummeted through the darkness until he landed on something hard and then sunk down into a thick syrupy liquid. Dozens of hands pushed down on his head and shoulders making it impossible to reach the surface. This is where Commander Randal Smith's SEAL training came in handy. He knew to stay calm, and he knew that with the amount of air in his lungs, he could hold his breath for about four minutes. Smith let the hands push him down until he had sunk well out of their grasp. Next he had to prepare himself for the kicking legs and feet. Smith let himself sink deeper; he was below the thrashing bodies that were tethered to the surface of the ocean with thick chains. Smith clung to one of these chains as he blindly searched through his backpack for his re-breather and goggles. He found the re-breather first, which was a good thing, as his lungs were starting to burn. Smith exhaled and then took a deep breath from the breathing apparatus. He found his goggles and placed them on his head. He pressed a button on the side and the liquid was slowly drained from the lenses and Smith opened his eyes. He couldn't see very far, so he began to pull himself through the thick liquid using the chains that tethered the bodies above him. Smith vaguely saw a larger structure ahead of him and instantly knew that there was a pier above him. Randal swam up between the beams until he broke the surface under the pier and took in a deep breath of air. Smith saw millions of bodies thrashing about that were barely held above the water by chains attached to collars around their necks. Each soul thrashed about wildly, grasping at anything that came within reach. Smith avoided the clutching limbs as he pulled himself up onto the pier.

"Took you long enough," Captain Whitney said with a straight face.

"Hey, you try landing in an ocean of blood filled with a shitload of people who don't particularly want to be there," Smith spat back. Captain Whitney just laughed.

"C'mon Smith," Wit reached out to help Smith up. "We need to head north, but my compass is all fucked up; the needle just keeps spinning."

Smith stood and stuffed his goggles and re-breather into his pack. Just then he remembered the compass he had found in the cave on the snow-covered mountaintop. He reached into his pocket, pulled it out, and held it up. "That's odd, it seems to work just fine here," Smith mumbled, recalling that when he'd found it, it had only faced in one fixed direction. Whitney and Smith walked down the pier toward a lamppost illuminated bright red from a globe with the skin of a human head stretched over it.

"Dude," Smith exclaimed, "that's just fucked up!" He looked at the compass and turned until the needle pointed north. "This way," he said, and headed north toward the shack.

The kid's directions and instructions had been right; the building was no more than an eight by ten foot shack. Captain Whitney knocked on the door, "Hello? Anyone in there?" he called out. There was no answer. Smith reached for the knob, turned it, and the remaining members of SEAL Team Zero entered the room. "Come out, come out, wherever you are," Smith called out as he closed the door behind him. Both men saw what happened at the same time. In the semi darkness of the room they watched the walls move outward and the ceiling up. The room grew to huge proportions, with piles of miscellaneous parts scattered about on tables set in rows throughout the room. "Hello?" Wit called out once more.

"Come in, come in," a strange voice answered. "Through the door in the back."

Captain Whitney and Commander Smith entered the room and saw the strange being sitting behind a large desk cluttered with various odd objects and papers. The creature was more insect than human and it had a large "finger" of sorts on the top of its head that it used to scratch its face. The being wistfully looked at the compass Smith held. "Does that thing work here?"

"Yeah," Smith answered.

"A kid named Sirnib sent us," Captain Whitney cut in. "We were led to him by a woman named Lisa Spencer; she said you could help us."

"Now *there* is a name I have not heard in a long time," the creature said sadly. "What can I do for you?" "We need to get out of here and back to our reality. We were told you had an object that could do that for us," Wit responded.

"I do," the creature answered, "but it will cost you. What say you trade me that compass for the Rive?" "Sure," Smith said. "It's a deal."

The creature wiggled out from behind his desk and opened up a compartment hidden behind a large painting. He opened the safe and pulled out a small statue carved from a strange black stone that resembled onyx. "The compass," the being requested. Smith relinquished the compass, which was retrieved by one of the insectoid's six arms. Reaching out with another of its hands it passed the onyx object to Commander Smith. "How does it work?" Smith questioned.

"Just tell it where you want to go and it will take you there."

Smith thought about the Island and of Thomas Hunter and Desideo. "You ready?" he asked Captain Whitney. His commanding officer nodded and Smith held up the statue and spoke. "Take us to the NeuroTech laboratory where we left Lisa Spencer," he said. Smith and Whitney both felt a tingling sensation spread throughout their bodies and the world around them went black.

(VII)

Captain Whitney and Commander Smith landed near the airlock. Wit looked down the hall and saw the iron door had been ripped from the entrance to the elevator since they'd last been there. He looked down the hall toward the labs and saw that the door and part of the wall had been ripped from the room Lisa Spencer had been in. Captain Whitney drew his pistol and slowly advanced down the hall. He was stopped in his tracks by a burst of gunfire coming from the lab, the bullets hitting the wall just feet in front of him.

"This is Captain Jason Whitney," he called out. "Stand down!"

Bruce Spencer leaned out into the hall with the rifle still pointed at the SEALs. There was a moment where Wit thought he might be in danger, but the doctor eventually decided that the SEALs were real, and lowered his weapon. "Hunter's regained control of the Island," Bruce explained. "He has Lisa. First the bastard took her consciousness and now he has her body." Captain Whitney entered the wrecked room and saw the overturned bed and no Lisa. "The Madam's creature took her," Bruce continued.

"We're going after her…"

"*You're* leaving," Wit cut in. "You and Dr. Black are going to the airlock and back to the sub. Smith and

I will find your niece and take care of Hunter."

"*Not* going to happen," Bruce said sternly. "I agree that Dr. Black should leave, but Smith can take her. *I'm* going with you to find my niece and to be damn sure Thomas Hunter doesn't make it off this island alive." Bruce waited while the SEAL contemplated the ultimatum.

"Bruce?" A disembodied voice called out. "Bruce, it's Lisa."

Dr. Spencer ran to the monitors but there was no image on the screen.

"I'm here Unc, but I don't have long. Look for my body in the maze. You can't let Thomas Hunter have the child. If it becomes necessary and all is lost, I want you to kill my physical body to kill the child." "Lisa, I don't know if I can…"

"Done," Captain Whitney chimed in. "Are you coming, Dr. Spencer?"

Bruce stared at the monitor for a moment, waiting for Lisa to say more, but she was gone.

"Let's go," Bruce said. He turned to Gillian and placed his hands on her shoulders. You need to go with Commander Smith. I'll take care of things here and see you topside."

"Bruce, I can't just…"

"You're not going to win this argument, Gillian, you're going with Smith and that's the end of it." The expression on Bruce's face brooked no argument. Gillian looked at him with tears in her eyes. "Don't worry," he told her. "I'll come back to you. One way or another I'll find you." Bruce pulled her close and kissed her lips.

"All right you two," Smith interrupted. "We need to go."

"You better come back to me, Bruce Spencer," Gillian said before turning and joining Commander Smith at the airlock. "We'll leave the access card and key here for you. The code is 072946." Gillian pulled a tube of lipstick from her purse and wrote the numbers on the wall. She slid the card through the reader and dropped it on the floor then punched in the code. She turned the key and the door hissed open. Commander Smith wasted no time loading gear into the airlock and then climbing in. "Let's go, Dr. Black," Commander Smith called out. Gillian smiled and waved one last time before entering the airlock and closing the door.

(VIII)

The minutes ticked by like hours as the airlock slowly filled with water. Commander Smith had already helped Gillian into the diving gear that poor Vasquez had used. He instructed Dr. Black on how to operate the equipment and maintain the proper mixture of gasses. Gillian was only half listening, knowing that she would retain any information given while her mind raced off in a thousand directions, a gift she had developed in collage. When the water was up to her neck, she slid the goggles over her head and placed the mouthpiece in before joining Commander Smith who was already submerged and waiting for the airlock door to open. The red light above the door turned green and the outside door opened. Commander Smith grabbed his gear and swam away. Gillian looked out the door and saw the submarine only a few hundred yards away. *Piece of cake*, she thought to herself and swam out into the open water.

(IX)

After having been there twice already, Bruce found his way to the maze with ease. Captain Whitney insisted on being out front so Bruce let him play the bad ass Navy SEAL that he was. Bruce hung back barking orders on when to take a new passageway and when to stay his course. In all actuality, Bruce had no idea where he was going, as his memory wasn't quite what it used to be. He'd gotten confused a few turns back. He thought that he had corrected the error, but he still had a nagging suspicion in the back of his skull that they were going the wrong way. No matter, Bruce was simply retracing his steps to the ladder leading to the courtyard. He knew that there was no promise that he would find her there; after all, Lisa had said her body was in the maze, not on the surface.

"Look," Captain Whitney called back to the doctor. "There it is."

Bruce looked ahead of them and there it was, the Madam's creature, and it still carried the body of his niece. Bruce took off running. The SEAL tried to stop him, but Wit wasn't expecting it and Bruce managed to slip by the younger, more agile Captain. "Hey! Come back here, you bastard!" Bruce shouted as he ran, hoping the creature would slow down or turn back, but it kept going forward as if leading them somewhere. Captain Whitney felt it, too.

"It's leading us into a trap," Captain Whitney shouted as he quickly caught up with Bruce.

"I know," Bruce panted, "but that thing's got Lisa and I'm not letting it out of my sight."

"Fair enough," Captain Whitney conceded. "I just want you to be ready when the time comes. Do what I say and you *will* live to see Dr. Black again." Wit took the lead once more and began firing at the creature. The Captain was a much better shot than Bruce so there was less chance of a stray bullet hitting his niece. Bruce struggled to keep up with the SEAL who'd quickly covered half the distance between him and the creature and continued to gain ground quickly. The SEAL, shooting while running, kept aiming for the creature's legs, slowly damaging the beast until it finally had to come to a complete stop. The monstrosity placed the pregnant body of Lisa Spencer down on the ground and turned to defend its prize. Bruce was confident enough to fire at the beast now that his niece was no longer in its grasp. When he caught up to Captain Whitney, they were mere yards from the obscenity, while Lisa lay unconscious on the ground behind it. The SEAL stopped firing and held up his hand for Bruce to do the same.

"Come out, come out wherever you are," Wit yelled out, knowing that Thomas Hunter was listening.

"C'mon, you pussy, show yourself," Wit taunted.

"You can bully my teenage daughter," Bruce joined in, "but you can't face two grown men?"

"You're a coward, Thomas Hunter!"

"Enough!" The voice echoed throughout the cavernous maze. "I am God here and you will *all* bow to me!" Hunter appeared in front of his creation and raised his hand. Captain Whitney and Doctor Spencer both found themselves frozen in time, unable to move. Thomas Hunter walked up to Captain Whitney and leaned in so his face was only inches from the SEAL. "Do you know why Karen sleeps around on you, Wit? Do you? It's because you can't satisfy her. It's not your fault entirely; she has some serious issues that include fetishes that would make most men vomit. She kept it a secret from you because she actually *believes* that she's in love with you. She didn't want you to know about her secret desires." "Why are you telling me this?" Captain Whitney asked.

"Because I'm not such a bad guy. I just wanted you to know before you die that she truly *does* love you."

"Well, you won't have a better chance than now to kill me, so what's stopping you?"

Hunter grabbed Whitney by the throat and Bruce heard a click. Somehow, Wit had managed to push the button on the detonator. The bombs he had placed throughout the maze on his first journey there were detonating. Time returned to normal and Bruce dropped to his knees.

"Take her body and climb the ladder," Captain Whitney said to Bruce. "Get to the courtyard; you'll want to be outside any buildings when this island goes down." Wit raised his other hand to show Thomas Hunter the Rive he clenched tightly within his fist. "Take me to the airlock," Wit said and both the Captain and Thomas Hunter disappeared. Bruce sprang up and raced to his niece. He lifted her up and carried her over his shoulder as he tried to remember his way through the maze. Bruce heard the creature roar behind him, along with the explosions from the C4 that Captain Whitney had planted, and he began to run like hell. He took a doorway to the right and sprinted through the spiral that led to the ladder. Bruce began to climb, but the weight of his unconscious niece was wearing him down, and he still had a long way to go. He stopped to rest for a moment, but when he heard the creature's shriek, it was even closer, and explosions were going off more quickly, as well. Bruce gathered all of his energy and climbed like his life and that of his precious niece depended on it, which it did. He stayed focused on the opening above that grew closer with every rung. He could see the stars shining down from above, a beautiful sight after the horrific events that Bruce Spencer had witnessed in the past twenty-four hours, and the stars gave him hope. He heard the beast bellowing below him now, no doubt ascending the ladder in pursuit of its master's prize. When Bruce was just a few yards away from the top, he chanced a look below him. He saw the creature and it was gaining on him fast. *Get to the top*, he thought, *deal with it up there*. Bruce rolled his niece from his shoulder as he climbed out of the hole. He quickly picked her up and moved her further away. Bruce stood with his rifle aimed at the hole, waiting for the creature to emerge. He felt the ground beneath him shake as the explosions continued. Bruce saw one of the creature's arms emerge and he began to fire. The beast slowly rose from the opening when a terrible blast shook the entire canyon, cracking the ground. A column of flame burst from the hole, engulfing the creature. Bruce heard its cries of agony as it burned alive. Water began to fill in the canyon, slowly rising, rushing in from some unknown source. Bruce hefted the pregnant body of his niece and began to climb the hillside of the canyon hoping to find higher ground and avoid the rapidly rising waters. It was a futile gesture, however, as the waters rose faster than he could climb. Bruce stopped climbing and let the water do the work for him. The highest peaks were completely submerged and Bruce found himself clutching his niece as he tried to stay afloat in the open water. Bruce looked around the dark ocean frantically until something floating in the distance caught his eye. It was a boat, *his* boat! *Looks like she weathered the storm after all*, Bruce thought as he began to swim toward the boat with the body of Lisa in tow.

(X)

Captain Whitney brought his knee up into Thomas Hunter's right kidney. He shoved the Rive into his pocket and pulled out the syringe before Hunter had a chance to recover. Wit swiped the card and entered the code, turned the key, and waited for the hydraulic hiss as the airlock door. Thomas Hunter had recovered from Wit's assault by then and was back on his feet. Captain Whitney spun around low to the ground with his left leg extended, knocking Thomas Hunter to the ground. Wit was on him fast; he had the needle in Hunter's neck and the plunger depressed before the psychopath had time to react. Hunter stood and wobbled for a moment. "What have you done to me?" he slurred.

"It's just a sedative," Whitney told Hunter. "A rather fast acting one at that. It'll be lights out for you in oh, about five more seconds, and when you wake up you'll be safe and sound in the brig back on the sub." Thomas Hunter dropped to his knees. Whitney took the opportunity to drag Hunter into the airlock. "This isn't how it ends," a barely conscious Thomas Hunter mumbled while Wit climbed into his gear. *Funny*, Wit thought, *he should be out by now*. The entire complex shook as an explosion rocked the facility nearby. Wit watched as pieces of the ceiling collapsed and water began to pour in through the open elevator door at the end of the hall. Although he had no control over his muscles, Thomas Hunter was still awake. He was chanting a single phrase over and over again.

"Nach Tanna Hurakk Tu, Nach Tanna Hurakk Tu, Nach Tanna Hu…" Wit shoved the re-breather in Hunter's mouth and pulled him underwater. The light above the door turned green and Wit purged the airlock. He threw his duffle bag full of gear over his shoulder and grabbed Hunter by the collar of his jumpsuit and started swimming toward the sub. Wit looked back at the facility and saw more explosions as the island began to sink. He focused on the sub and the task at hand, getting Thomas Hunter back into custody. Of course, as Wit would soon discover, that wasn't going to be as easy as it sounded.

Captain Whitney heard a pop from below and the airlock door flew by him at incredible speed, missing his skull by mere inches. The next thing he knew, he was no longer traveling toward the sub. He turned and saw a long black tentacle reaching up and wrapping around the body of Thomas Hunter. Wit pulled out his knife and swam back to cut his prize free. He sliced into the limb and the tentacle was instantly pulled back, dragging Thomas Hunter with it. Wit tried to hold on to Hunter's arm, but the creature was too strong. As Wit lost his grip, he had no choice but to watch Thomas Hunter be pulled below. Wit continued to the sub, entered the airlock, and awaited pressurization. He thought about Doctor Spencer, wondering if he had made it out with Lisa's body and the child that grew within? Even though the capture of Thomas Hunter was a loss, the Admiral would still be *very* pleased with the results of this mission. The child alone would be enough, but Captain Whitney also had the Rive in his pocket. He had overheard the Admiral mention such an object on many occasions and Captain Whitney knew his superior officer would be overjoyed to possess such a thing. *Yes*, Wit thought, *this has definitely turned out to be one of the stranger missions I've been on*. He'd lost two good men who would be difficult to replace, but Wit had faith in Admiral Forsythe; he would find the right men and SEAL team Zero would be back up and running in no time.

EPILOGUE
The Aftermath
(I)

No one saw the dark figure of a man walk out from the ocean and across the beach. He looked up at the night sky and smiled, his bald head dimly reflected in the full moon's glow. A thousand questions raced through his mind. Why had Father saved him and why was he given another chance? Father told him it was not his fault, that the woman, Lisa Spencer, was much more powerful than anticipated. But still, something wasn't right. Something in Father had changed. Was He weaker? If so, Thomas Hunter would take time and learn how to exploit this flaw, and hopefully be free of the Umbra for good. He had reached the parking lot of an ocean view hotel. Hunter waited behind the bushes for a man to reach his car. As soon as the unsuspecting victim slid his key into the lock, Thomas Hunter was on him with a small knife. He went into a rage, stabbing the man repeatedly in the eyes, eventually breaking the blade from missing his victim one too many times. Hunter grabbed the man's keys and wallet before popping the trunk and rifling through his luggage for a set of clothes that fit. Once changed and cleaned up, Thomas Hunter stepped into the vehicle, started the engine, and drove off into the darkness.

(II)

Lisa Spencer listened to the Umbra's thoughts. She knew her uncle had gotten away with her physical body but Thomas Hunter had also escaped. Desideo was completely unaware that Lisa's consciousness had not been detached from her soul. She still had her powers and they were growing day by day. The Umbra was unaware of Lisa's communications with the survivors of the island as they had made their escape. That had been Lisa's first sign that her powers had continued to grow even as she was held captive within Desideo. She would bide her time and wait for opportunity to present itself. This would give her time to learn how to control the Umbra without its knowledge. And when the time was right.

Lisa Spencer would take complete control of the creature that was oblivious to her intentions.

(III)

On the other side of the continent, Admiral Robert Forsythe sat in his plush chair behind his massive oak desk in the office of his San Diego facility. He held Thomas Hunter's bible in one hand and the Rive given to him by Captain Whitney in the other. He thought of all the places he could go with such an object. He could instantly be anywhere in the universe, visit the glories of Heaven and the depths of Hell. The Admiral turned and placed the objects in a safe hidden behind a small panel in the wall. He got up from his chair and walked around the large desk, his eyes still on the safe. He paused for a moment and then turned and headed for the elevator. The Admiral waited patiently for the door to open, his mind obviously occupied by something else. He had made this trip so many times that he didn't have to think about it, he would arrive at the labs by instinct alone, giving the Admiral time to think. What was he going to do with the child? He couldn't bear the thought of the child growing up in a cell in the San Diego facility, but he had to find somewhere that he could control its environment. Care of the child was of no issue, as doctor's Spencer and Black had already offered to raise the child. This was fine with the Admiral, for he knew he could trust the two, and he knew they would not let the child find her way into he clutches of the Mille Umbra. Besides, Dr. Black already had the clearance to work and live at this new complex, and it would only take a matter of days to prepare the paperwork that would allow Dr. Spencer access to low levels of classified information. In his mind, the matter was settled; the child would be raised at the Colorado facility. The elevator door opened and the Admiral exited. He walked down the hall and entered a door marked "Observation Room B". Admiral Forsythe stood just inches from the glass, watching as the surgeons carefully sliced open Lisa Spencer's stomach to get to the womb. Doctor Black sliced open the embryonic sack and cautiously removed the child. "It's a girl," she called out. "Lisa wanted to name her Alexondra."

The Admiral pushed a button on the intercom and spoke, "Alexondra it is, and we welcome you into this world, young lady." Suddenly lights on the equipment started flashing and an alarm went off. Lisa was flatlining. Doctor Spencer climbed on top of his niece and began CPR while the nurse prepped the chest paddles. "Clear," the nurse shouted and Dr. Spencer moved out of the way. The nurse placed the paddles on Lisa's chest and pushed the button, distributing several thousand low amperage volts coursing through Lisa's chest muscles and heart. She came back for a second and then she was lost again. "One more time, clear," the nurse called out, but nothing happened. Bruce continued CPR on his own while

Gillian kept Lisa's lungs filled with oxygen. Several minutes passed by with nothing, no sign of life. Suddenly the lab was filled with the sounds of a child crying and the buzz of the flatline from the machines hooked up to Lisa Spencer. Gillian switched off the machine and took the child into her arms.

"There's no more you can do for her, Bruce," Gillian tried to console him.

"I know, I know…" Bruce stepped behind Gillian and looked down on the child, who was the spitting image of her mother. Soft jet-black hair blanketed her head and in the few moments that she held her eyes open, they saw Lisa's bright blue irises staring back at them. They were all so busy admiring the child that no one noticed the blood dripping out of the electrical outlets and up the wall towards the ceiling…